Advance Praise fo

T0007567

"Daniel Burke's *Red Screen* takes the reader on an enthralling journey into the metaverse, where the forces of might and magic bleed dangerously into the real world of corporate malfeasance, deadly technical anomalies, and family dysfunction. Prepare for a wild virtual ride that will ensnare you in its spell!"
Regina Buttner, author of *Down a Bad Road*

"Following the finest tradition of stories such as *Dot Hack*, *Summer Wars*, and *Belle*, the line between the digital and real worlds becomes blurred, and events on both sides begin to affect them equally; Burke's *Red Screen* takes you into a whirlwind of a thriller, jumping between both worlds to show you the consequences of greed. You won't see online video game grinding, bug seeking and player vs player kills in the same light after reading this book. A must read for fans of thrillers, video games and virtual reality."
Ricardo Victoria, author of the Tempest Blades series

"In this whipsaw of a thriller, author Daniel Burke leapfrogs between the actual world and the realm of virtual reality with the commanding presence of a cyber juggernaut. What is believed to be a mere Metaverse game turns out to be far more. Players are not only dying in the game but in the real world as well. Enter Shea Britton, a techno geek and VR wizard who dominates a game called the Land of Might and Magic, where the Gray Warrior, the suspected killer is believed to be stalking his victims. Can Shea bait the Gray Warrior long enough for FBI profiler Parker Reid to stop him for good or will victims continue to fall? You'll be riveted to the edge of your seat in this high-energy page-turner. Outstanding!"
Lawrence Kelter, bestselling author of the Stephanie Chalice Mystery Series

RED SCREEN

- a novel -

by
Daniel Burke

ISBN: 9781951122720 (paperback) / 9781951122737 (ebook)
LCCN: 2023941376
Copyright © 2023 by Daniel Burke
Cover illustration © 2023 by Alexz Uría

Printed in the United States of America.

Shadow Dragon Press
9 Mockingbird Hill Rd
Tijeras, New Mexico 87059
info@shadowdragonpress.com
www.shadowdragonpress.com

Dedication

For Christopher, Mason, and Uriah, may the Metaverse never become more to you than the Real-Real.

Acknowledgement

The virtual world in *Red Screen* was inspired by a game called British Legends which was the world's first commercial multi-player computer adventure game. Decades before the metaverse and with no computer graphics or sound effects, the programmers who made British Legends created a virtual world where players from all over the planet could join and interact with each other inside a fantasy realm that existed only as text on a screen. Despite the primitive technology, or maybe because of it, players saw, heard, smelled, and felt the world of British Legends in a way that most players of today's technically advanced games do not. British Legends players weren't inside a virtual world, it was inside them, which made it all the more real. As the game's tag line had claimed at the time, "you've never lived until you've died playing British Legends."

Chapter 1
The Anomaly

ANGELA **H**ARDING, **D**IRECTOR OF World Simulation Development for Xperion, Inc., watched the team leads trickle into the conference room with coffee cups and laptops in hand for the Monday morning incident review meeting. The mostly young, scruffy-looking lot, indistinguishable from the college kids streaming into the classrooms of nearby Stanford University, was responsible for keeping the company's wildly popular Metaverse simulations running for its hundreds of millions of customers, a task that often meant long hours and sleepless nights, especially over the weekends when usage peaked. They took their seats, SIM Devs, short for simulation developers, on one side of the table—Angela's side—and simulation operators, the Ops Team, on the other. The Ops Team director's chair was unoccupied. Maxwell Morris, as usual, was running late. They would hold the meeting for him, and as she always did, Angela would hold her tongue.

She was never late, no matter how little sleep she managed after the all-night troubleshooting sessions that had become more frequent with the company's success. Angela was always the first one in the room and even the first one in the office, except for Marcus and Jasmine Day, of course. It was an unwritten rule—no one arrived before the company's founding couple. The lights in their corner office windows, Marcus's on the operations floor and Jasmine's, or Jazz as she was better known, on the development floor, were the first lit before dawn and the last extinguished after sunset. Even on the rare occasions when Angela arrived before them, she would sit in her car and wait for the lights in the founder's windows to signal it was acceptable for her to enter. Arriving before the Days would be like beating them at something, and the Days did not take losing well.

At 8:07, Maxwell Morris stepped through the door and after making his way around the table to acknowledge and exchange greetings with the attendees, he took his seat opposite Angela and flashed his knee-weakening smile. A tall, athletic man with gray-frosted blond hair and skin tanned and weathered from hours navigating his sailboat up and down the coast, Maxwell was as handsome as he was brilliant. He was also a company institution, the first employee not to have the last name of Day.

Angela returned his smile, all irritation with his tardiness gone. The son of a bitch was better looking at forty-five than he had been when she'd first met him ten years ago. It pained her to admit she was still as attracted to him today as she had been when she was a starry-eyed intern. Ridiculous, she thought, still pining for this man after years of nothing more than daydreams and lingering glances—hers, not his. Maxwell preferred men, boys really, and he always sailed with one or two twenty-some-thing, hard-bodied deckhands.

"Okay, I think we have everyone. Let's get started," she announced and waited for all side conversations to stop. When the room was silent, she turned her attention back to Maxwell. "It's all yours, Em."

Maxwell thanked her, then addressed the room. "As every-one is well aware, the IPO is on track." His smile turned into a wide grin. "I am looking at a roomful of soon-to-be millionaires. I expect to hear no more grumbling about working for worth-less stock options." Laughter and the claps from high fives filled the room. "I don't have to tell you how important it is that we have no outages; nothing that can cause bad press before our ticker symbol hits the NASDAQ. I know your teams are all put-ting in long hours, but we must do even more to keep the SIMs online and performing." Maxwell turned to the woman on his right. "Okay, Sangeeta, take us through the list of the weekend's issues." He turned his attention back to the room. "For every item, I want to know the resolution plan and timeline."

Sangeeta tapped on her laptop, and the list of problems, crises, and near-calamities that had occurred with the compa-ny's simulation systems since Friday evening filled the large monitors hanging on the walls above Angela and Maxwell. The review process was routine, and Sangeeta ran quickly through each item, calling on different individuals seated at the table to answer Angela's and Maxwell's questions. Hardware and system configuration issues were addressed by the Ops Team, while software bugs, including a nasty one that caused the new soccer tournament SIM to suffer a full-blown world crash and reset, were handled by Angela's SIM Dev Team. It took Sangeeta forty minutes to go through every item on her list.

"That's all of them," she announced.

"Not too bad," Maxwell said. "Overall, it seems like we had a relatively quiet weekend." He fixed his gaze on a nervous look-ing Asian man. "Except the Soccer World crash. Is your team on top of this, Yen? We're just beginning to see usage growth in this SIM. Hate to interrupt that. Especially now. You know? With all our financial hopes and dreams hanging in the balance."

Yen nodded, his anxious eyes looking at Angela for help.

"We got it, Em," Angela said. "Leave Yen alone. His team will have the issue resolved by the end of the week."

Yen coughed and appeared even more nervous by her promise.

"Good enough for me, Angela." Maxwell winked at Yen. "Anything else, Sangeeta?"

"Yes, sir. We have the *other* thing to discuss. The anomaly."

At that moment, Jasmine Day appeared in the doorway and, like a curious echo, repeated, "The anomaly?" Every head turned to face her as if pulled by the same string.

"Good morning, Jazz," Angela said, feeling her pulse quick-en. Hers would not be the only heart in the room beating faster. A surprise visit from Jasmine sent adrenaline pumping through the veins of all who knew her.

Xperion's cofounder scanned the meeting attendees before acknowledging Angela with a nod. She was a compact woman with dark eyes and long, jet-black hair that flowed down her back like liquid ebony. Age turned some women soft, but not Jazz. At fifty-two, she was as muscular and hard as twenty years ago when she had won the San Francisco marathon. She glided into the room with just the hint of a smile dimpling her high cheek bones and a hungry look in her eyes. Dressed all in gray and circling the table, she reminded Angela of a shark who had come upon a pod of seals in the bay and was looking for the tastiest one for her meal. The analogy was not unwarranted, as Jasmine Day was indeed a predator, though now part of an endangered species.

She and her husband, Marcus, were some of the last of their kind, the Californian Tech Entrepreneur, a species once prolific in the coastal plain nestled between the Santa Cruz and Diablo mountains, now all but extinct, lost to a drought like so much of the California paradise, not one of water, though, but one of something just as precious—venture capital. Like the wildlife that fled the aridification of the Southwest for lusher northern environs, the technical talent that had driven the innovations that created Silicon Valley had mass migrated to the Zhongguancun technology hub in Beijing, where investment money still flowed in torrents. This irony could not be lost on Jazz, whose parents had fled communist China for the opportunities of the American capitalist system, only to see the roles reversed a generation later with Americans now fleeing a stagnant entitlement system for the vibrance of the conquest-driven Chinese model.

"The anomaly," Jazz prompted, coming to a stop behind Angela's chair.

"Yes, ma'am," Sangeeta replied.

"We're talking about a player in the Land of Might and Magic that appears to have hacked the simulation," Maxwell explained.

"The SIM *has* been hacked," the gravelly voice of Jonathan Heinz, the company's head of cybersecurity, responded. "There's no doubt about it. Whoever this person is, they've found a way past our authentication systems and are either exploiting holes in our code or creating new ones."

"I don't see how that's possible," a senior development lead on Angela's team named Rituraj objected. "This mythical hacker would have to get through the SIM security layers, and there's no way to do that without leaving a trace. We'd see something in the logs, and we don't."

"He's doing it," Jonathan assured.

"You have no proof," Rituraj shot back.

"Okay, okay." Angela raised her hands to end the squabble. "What we know is there appears to be a character in the simulation who is bypassing the leveling rules, making himself..."

"Immortal," Maxwell finished her sentence.

"Yes," she said. "And by doing so, he's wreaking havoc with

other players. He's killing everything he encounters."

Jazz folded her arms across her chest and asked, "Why can't we just remove the character?"

"Because we can't see him," Jonathan replied. "He's figured out a way to evade the logging systems. It's crazy." Jonathan glanced around the room. "It's got to be someone inside." His eyes met Angela's. "Someone on the SIM Dev Team."

Rituraj slammed the lid on his laptop. "No way. We would know."

"If we can't see this anomaly, how do we know it exists?" Jazz asked with a hint of irritation in her tone.

Sangeeta tapped on her keyboard and a new list appeared on the monitors. "Customer complaints. Lots of them." She read from the list: "'My level forty character just got trashed by some fucking gray monster. He cut the heads off three of us. All high-level characters. No normal player could do that. We couldn't damage him at all. It's bullshit. We're talking a lot of money to build these characters. Fuck you, LMM. I'm not coming back, and neither are my friends.'"

She read another one just like it and was about to read a third when Maxwell raised his hand to stop her. "We get the idea, Sangeeta. So far this hacker," he looked at Rituraj, "if that is what he is, is just cheating." He turned to Jonathan. "What's your take on the security risk?"

Jonathan grimaced. "Could be huge. If he can get into the main simulation engines, what's stopping him from getting into user profiles? Or financials?"

"Layers and layers of encrypted access controls," Rituraj practically shouted.

Jonathan looked at Maxwell and then at Angela while appearing to avoid Jazz's gaze. "If he figures out a way to shut down the simulation, he could hold us hostage."

"You mean demand a ransom?" Angela asked.

"Yeah, probably a big one."

Jazz made a loud "shush" sound, ending the speculation. She leaned on the table and slowly made eye contact with each of the team members. "LMM is our most popular SIM," she growled. "Over fifty million users."

Their attention upon her rapt, everyone nodded.

"You all understand what would happen to our IPO if

LMM goes off-line, even for just a day, right? The *Wall Street Journal* and The *China Financial Times* would tear us apart." She slapped the table, causing everyone to jump. "We'd list 75 percent lower than we've planned. That's quite a pay cut—one I'm not prepared to accept, and neither should any of you."

No one spoke; no one even breathed. Maxwell raised his eyebrows and smiled at Angela. His unspoken words were clear: *she's your boss, you deal with her.*

Angela swallowed and turned in her chair to face the agitated cofounder. "Finding the anomaly is our top priority."

"I should hope so." Jazz took a deep breath and let it out slow—calming herself or preparing to strike, Angela did not know which. The predatory smile returned. "I'm sure your people are doing everything they can." She glared at Rituraj. "Sometimes, though, we have to find help from those who can do more."

Angela prayed Rituraj would remain silent and closed her eyes when he did not.

"No one knows the LMM simulation better than my people," Rituraj snapped. "We just need time."

Jazz's smile turned dangerous. She had found her seal. "There is no time. I demand results immediately. I won't tolerate complacency or mediocrity." She stabbed her index finger into the table with a thud. "This valley is full of the rotting carcasses of mediocre companies." Thud. "Xperion won't be one of them." Thud. "If the anomaly interferes with the IPO, I will reevaluate my technical leads, starting with you, Rituraj." She spat his name. Then, Jazz turned her wrath on Angela. "I want you in my office in ten minutes," she said and stormed out, leaving all but one seal relieved.

Chapter 2
The Mouse and the Monster

IT WAS EARLY, STILL several hours before dawn. A single lamp above her door filled the narrow brick and stone passage with an unnatural white light. The air was cool, and still, and quiet. The only sounds came from Musuka's pounding heart and the heavy breathing of the giant standing behind him.

Everything had gone as Musuka had planned. He had used the magic to blind the watchers, allowing him and Akandu to enter the tower unnoticed and climb the great stair. Then, with the watchers still blind, they had passed through the halls and found where she slept. All that remained was for Musuka to use magic to unbolt the door to her chambers and Akandu would slay her. But fear had taken hold of Musuka, and he was no longer sure he could go through with it. He closed his eyes and fought to control his urge to flee.

As if sensing his thoughts, Akandu placed one of his enormous gray hands on Musuka's head and squeezed, just a little at first, but enough.

"What is the problem, mouse?" The giant's low, rumbling voice shook Musuka like thunder.

Musuka tried to wiggle free of Akandu's hold, but the giant's grip tightened. It felt as if the powerful gray fingers were about to crush his skull. Musuka shut his eyes against the agonizing pressure that threatened to pop them from their sockets.

"P-p-please s-s-stop," Musuka begged, losing all control over his stutter.

"It hurts?" Akandu rasped. The skin on the back of Musuka's neck tingled from the giant's hot breath.

"Y-y-yes. I-I ka-ka can't take the pa-pa-pain. Please stop."

"Speak like a man or keep your pathetic mouth shut," Akandu growled.

"W-w-why m-m-must we k-k-kill her?" It was just the kind of question a miserable mouse would ask, and Musuka hated himself for asking it. He knew why. The witch sleeping inside the chamber knew his magic, knew how he passed unseen and opened doors that should not open. Killing in the dream world was no longer enough. If he was to become what he had to become, he would have to use the magic to kill in this world, and that meant she had to die. *Sh-sh-she had to.*

"Open the door, mouse, or I will put an end to our alliance." The giant's fingers tightened, emphasizing the manner of termination.

"We m-m-must be ka-ka-careful, or they will ka-ka-catch me."

Akandu laughed a pitiless, menacing laugh. "Why do I care what happens to a mouse?"

The pressure in Musuka's head was unbearable. He would lose consciousness soon. Akandu had done it to him before. Musuka took a deep breath and, summoning all his courage, he said in a clear, stutter-free voice, "Because without me, you're nothing here."

Akandu's grip loosened, as if he was surprised by Musuka's declaration and perhaps the boldness of its delivery. "Is that so?" he said with a rumbling chuckle. Then the fingers squeezed even tighter than before, causing Musuka to cry out. The world went dark, and just as Musuka was certain Akandu intended to kill him, the pressure stopped. The giant had let him go.

Musuka turned and looked up into Akandu's black, empty eyes. He sensed the balance of power had shifted, if only for a moment, and he considered sending the giant away. He hated Akandu almost as much as he hated the queen, but like the giant had said, they had an alliance based on mutual need. Musuka needed Akandu's strength and fearlessness, and Akandu needed Musuka's magic to bring him into this world.

"Suit yourself, mouse," Akandu growled. "I will go back to where I belong." The giant spun and headed back toward the stairway.

Musuka called after him, "P-p-please d-d-don't go."

Akandu stopped and looked over his shoulder. "Open the door and stop wasting my time."

Musuka bent over the chamber's lock and waved the magic

box. The locking mechanism clicked, and the door opened.

The giant pushed Musuka aside and ducked through the doorway, drawing his great sword as he went. Musuka sighed, then followed him in and closed the door.

Chapter 3
Losing the Party

THE PATH ZIGZAGGED UP the steep mountainside, climbing high through the dense coniferous forest toward Jade Mountain's snowpack. The towering trees blocked most of the midday sun and what little light made it through took on a greenish hue as it filtered through the thick canopy of needles. Up ahead, the trees parted and blue sky appeared.

The ranger ran toward the light, wanting to escape the gloomy green twilight, but most of all needing to see what she'd come to see and get back to the party she'd left unguarded. Something scampered through the thick carpet of pine needles off to her right, and she spun to meet the sound, bringing her charged crossbow up in the same motion. A small deer darted between the trees and raced down the hill. Lowering the crossbow, she scanned the area, making sure the deer hadn't been spooked by something other than her.

Many creatures called the primal forest home. Most were animals, and other than the occasional hungry bear, were harmless. The trees did conceal dangers, though. Boarmen and Wargarian raiding parties prowled the forest paths, always on the lookout for defenseless travelers to ambush and slaughter. The ranger was anything but defenseless, as hundreds of Boarmen and Wargarians had learned over the years, but fending off raiders would delay her, and every minute the party was without her put them at risk.

She was the party's guide and leader. The other four members included two would-be fighting men, a useless cleric and an even more useless dwarf, all know-nothing *càiniǎo*, as vulnerable as infants. After agreeing on terms, they had set out from Staghead Gate four treks ago.

As was their agreement, she had led them on a training expedition, which included a few small experience-building skirmishes and fabrication opportunities. She had taught them how to navigate, helped them develop their natural skills, taught them how to spot and appraise adversaries, and showed them how to use their weapons. She'd also taught them how to bury and reclaim their *Shēngmìnglì*; not that that was something she encouraged. They had gotten their coin worth, as did all her customers. In just four treks, they were close to being able to range into the wilds between the gates on their own, far sooner than if they had stumbled around by themselves, as did most cheap *càiniǎo*. All that remained was to get them through the Jade Gate.

The path led to a rock outcropping that jutted from the western face of Jade Mountain like the prow of some enormous ship. The ranger walked to the edge and gazed out upon the valley several thousand feet below. The great pine forest covering the mountain gave way to an even greater forest of giant oak, hickory, and chestnut trees that stretched across the valley like a vast emerald sea until it broke against the distant snow-covered peaks of the White Mountains.

About a mile beyond where the pine trees surrendered to the hardwoods, the Jade River cut a north–south line through the forest. The rushing water formed a border separating the wild hill country from the relative safety of the flat lands. A road ran along the river's opposite bank until it veered west and cut its way through the trees heading toward the Jade Gate and the end of their expedition. All she had to do was get the party across.

Fording the deep and fast-moving river was possible with ropes. She'd watched Boarmen raiders do it, but she had not led the party here to lose them while attempting such a dangerous crossing. Luckily there was no need to try. Just before the road made its westward turn toward the gate, a stone bridge crossed the rapids. It was a short hike from where the party waited to the bridge, then another easy jog to the gate. At least, that's what she thought.

She retrieved her spyglass from her pack. Its polished brass interconnecting tubes gleamed in her hand. It was a remarkable instrument, and one of her favorite possessions. A smith on the other side of the world had fab'd it for her years ago. Moved by the beauty of the piece, the ranger had the smith engrave her name, Darshana, on its outer barrel. She touched the script and imagined she felt the etched lettering. Of all the items she carried, only the glass bore her name. It seemed fitting. After all, Darshana was derived from *darshan*, which meant sight in the ancient language her mother had insisted she learn.

The bridge came into focus. Nothing moved over its narrow span. She aimed the spyglass at the road and followed it west all the way to the gate. It looked deserted as well. *Good.*

At full magnification, the distant gate's massive stone arch filled her view. All the gates in the Land looked similar, differing only by the type and coloring of the stone blocks they were constructed from. The Jade Gate was made of the same gray-blue granite that formed the bones of Jade Mountain. Nothing about the gate's appearance indicated it was anything other than a monument to some vain ruler's triumph. Although, a traveler with any sense might wonder at its placement in the middle of a remote valley forest far away from the nearest city or town.

Darshana refocused the glass on the bridge and followed the road south until it disappeared into the distance. Beyond the spyglass's range, she knew it continued for another ten miles until it reached the trading town of Vaux Hall, and the river went on for several hundred miles beyond that before draining into the Southron Sea. The road appeared empty in both directions. Yep. This was going to be an easy day.

She pulled the glass back to the bridge and trained it on the path that led up the mountain's western face. It was the same path Darshana had followed to the outcropping. The party waited for her about a half-mile below in a small clearing where the path that led down from the Jade Mountain pass met the path to the bridge.

The five of them had spent all morning climbing up to the pass from the east and then descending in route to the bridge. They had fought their way through several Boarmen raiding parties. She had let her charges do most of the fighting, only stepping in to assist when any of them got into trouble. Every engagement was an opportunity to learn techniques and gain experience. They'd thank her for it some day.

Darshana turned the glass toward where the clearing would be hidden by the trees and was alarmed to see a thin line of gray smoke rising into the otherwise flawless blue sky, marking the clearing's exact location. "What in the seven hells?" she muttered under her breath. "Morons!"

Returning the spyglass to her pack, she raced back down the path. She could think of no reason for them to start a fire and about two thousand for them not to. Every raider, treasure hunter, and predator in the area who saw the smoke would head toward its source, and if they got there before Darshana, she would lose her safe passage bonus. "Damn!"

The clearing was still a quarter mile away when she heard the shouts. The voices were familiar, Darian and Xu, the party's wannabe fighting men. Neither of them would last long against an experienced attacker. Darian was strong, but he was clumsy and slow with his sword. Xu was fast and better with his sword, but he was weak and would not withstand many hits. She'd almost lost him during their first skirmish not two miles from the Staghead Gate.

CRACK. A loud thunderclap drowned out the shouts. Ava, the cleric, had one attack spell, Lightning, and it sounded like she must have just used it. Darshana frowned. The spell was difficult to control. Cast by an inexperienced cleric like Ava, it made a lot of noise and light, but did little damage to who or what the party was fighting.

Another sharp thunderclap reverberated through the trees, followed by the metallic ringing of swords striking swords and then a long, high-pitched scream that could have come from Xu or Ava. Then silence. Darshana crept to the clearing's edge and almost gasped.

Xu and Ava's lifeless bodies lay on the ground near a small, smoldering campfire that still emitted the thin wisp of gray smoke that must have attracted their killer. A few paces from them, Darian stood holding his long, heavy sword. Its tip was pointed at the chest of the largest warrior Darshana had ever seen. Darian was tall—over six-three—but the man staring down at him, if it was indeed a man, was at least a foot taller.

The warrior was formidable. He—or it—had gray, almost blue, skin. Its massive chest and muscled abdomen were bare except for a heavy leather mantel that concealed half its brawny chest and covered its shoulders. Spiked armor plates fastened to the mantel protected the warrior's neck and shoulders from a downward blow, although it was difficult to imagine any foe tall enough to deliver such a strike. A chain or cord encircled its neck, and there appeared to be objects dangling from it. They looked like ornaments, but she couldn't make out their shapes or colors.

What appeared to be a heavy steel helmet covered its head. Long, black hair, bound at several points by leather cord, flowed from under it. The helmet's brim cast a shadow, hiding the details of the warrior's face, and a metal strip descended from the helmet's reinforced brow, protecting the warrior's nose and further obscuring its features. The whites of the beast's eyes glowed within hidden sockets.

Its mouth was bent into a cruel smile, revealing fanged teeth that, like its eyes, seemed to glow against the black of its braided beard. It was a monster, and as she leveled her crossbow on its exposed chest, Darshana sensed it was too strong for her. If she got too close, she had little doubt it would kill her. The question was, would the bolt from her crossbow take it down or disable it long enough for her and Darian to escape?

She was about to squeeze the trigger and find out, when, moving faster than should have been possible for something that large, the warrior spun while drawing a longsword from a sheath on its back and cut Darian's head clean off. The head fell to the ground like a rock, followed a second later by Darian's body. The warrior wiped the blood from his sword and returned it to the sheath on his back.

Darshana holstered her crossbow. *So much for the bonus.* Keeping her eyes on the warrior who was busy picking through the party's few belongings, she eased away from the clearing. She turned to make for the bridge and spotted Falin peering out from behind a tree. The dwarf's reddish-brown cloak blended in well with the tree's trunk. He would have been invisible had it not been for his yellow beard. The dwarf was staring at the warrior and did not appear to see her.

Darshana crept toward him. Her feet found the forest floor without snapping a twig or rustling the mat of decaying pine straw. The dwarf only knew she was there when she wrapped her arm around his neck and clasped her hand across his mouth. She pulled him to the ground behind the trunk, out of the warrior's line of sight.

Falin fought her for a moment until he looked up and his

blue eyes widened in recognition. He calmed, and Darshana mouthed the word "quiet."

She removed her hand from his mouth, and he blurted, "Where?"

Clasping his mouth again, firmer this time, she whispered, "*Quiet,*" and fixed him with a stern stare.

He nodded.

Darshana unclasped his mouth, and in a low whisper, the dwarf asked, "Where have you been?"

"Spotting the road."

She unwrapped her arm from his throat, and they both looked around the trunk at the grisly scene below.

"Get your shovel out," she said.

"Why?"

"You need to bury your *Shēngmìnglì.*"

He corrected her pronunciation. "Shun-ming-lee. I want to make it to the gate."

"No way to do that now."

"Aren't you supposed to be the all-powerful ranger? Go down there and kill that thing. That's what we paid you for, isn't it?"

Darshana ignored him and studied the large gray form bent over Ava's and Xu's bodies.

"What is it anyway?" he asked.

"Don't know. Looks like some kind of mixed breed. Maybe part man and part—" she thought for a moment "troll?"

"Troll?" the dwarf scoffed. "I thought they only came out at night."

"Not this one."

"What's it doing?"

Darshana took out her spyglass and trained it on the warrior.

"Cutting off Ava's ears."

"That's awful. Why would it do that?"

She focused the glass on the cord around the warrior's neck. The objects dangling from it that she'd thought were ornaments were in fact ears, and there were dozens of them.

"Looks like he keeps them for trophies."

"Is that even possible?"

Darshana shrugged. "Sure. Why not?"

Something moved behind the gray warrior, and she focused the glass on a giant black stallion with glowing red eyes and fiery red nostrils that looked as if they might actually spout flames. "Big man, big horse," she uttered, not meaning the comment for the dwarf.

"What do you see?" the dwarf asked through excited breaths.

"It's got a horse. A big one. Looks very fast and quite terrifying."

Darshana re-aimed the glass at the warrior. It tucked Ava's ears into a pouch attached to the wide belt wrapped around its waist. It paused like it was thinking or maybe sensing, then it looked straight at her and grinned. *Uh-oh*. She ducked behind the tree, knowing it was too late. Stuffing the glass back in her pack, she turned to the dwarf. "Listen to me. Unless you want this all to have been a waste, you have to bury your *Shēngmìnglì* now."

Darshana started for the path.

"Wait. What about me?"

"Get digging."

"How will you outrun the horse?"

"I won't have to. That man-troll will be too busy cutting your ears off to catch me," she said as she bolted for the bridge path.

Chapter 4
Race for the Gate

DARSHANA BOUNDED DOWN THE bridge path. She paused a few hundred yards from the clearing to see if Falin was following. Her eyes searched for movement in the green gloom of the forest. The dwarf would never be able to keep up. His only hope for preserving his gains was to bury his *Shēngmìnglì*. Otherwise, the gray warrior would do to him what he'd done to the rest of the party, and that would be it for Falin.

No sign of the dwarf. She waited another moment, then resumed her flight. Her long legs carried her down the mountain faster than any friend or enemy she'd encountered in all her ranging. Nothing could catch her when she ran at full speed. Nothing except maybe her pride and the sting of Falin's words. They caught her before she reached the bridge and echoed in her head as she ran. *Aren't you the all-powerful ranger?*

The grade flattened out, and the path widened. After a quarter-mile or so, the forest thinned, and the roar of the Jade River grew in her ears. She glimpsed the bridge through the thinning trees and was only yards away from where the forest yielded to the river bottoms when the shame of the dwarf's words brought her to a stop. She was Darshana, one of the most dangerous and feared rangers in the Land, and here she was running from what? A troll? She didn't run from trolls or troll-men, no matter how big and terrible they were. They and all other manner of evil beasts fled from her. She needed to go back and face that gray warrior, just like Falin had said. *Isn't that what we pay you for?*

Darshana turned back toward the mountain, intending to bring the battle to the warrior. She would not have to go far. The gray beast mounted atop its demonic stallion was barreling down the path toward her. It was still hundreds of yards away, but it was closing fast. *Bring it*, she thought. Then she retrieved her spyglass and aimed it at her pursuer. The brute gripped the fire breathing stallion's reins in its left hand and held high in its right the terrible longsword it had used to remove Darian's head. Affixed to the end of the sword appeared to be a yellow streamer. She brought the flag into focus and gasped. That was no banner flying from the sword. It was Falin's beard, still attached to his head. The warrior had driven the sword through the dwarf's neck and out the top of his skull.

Darshana had been wrong; the beast hadn't taken the time to cut off Falin's ears. It had just taken his head, and now, no doubt, it was coming for hers. To hell with her pride. Fighting this thing was suicide. She stowed her glass and bolted for the bridge.

She could outrun anything on two legs, but a horse had four, and she wouldn't be surprised if the one baring down on her could fly. The gate was another mile beyond the bridge, and Darshana had no doubt the horse would catch her before she made it halfway. Her only chance was to slow it down or, better yet, kill it. She didn't even have time to bury her *Shēngmìnglì*—not that Darshana would ever choose that shameful option.

She reached the bridge and came to a stop a few paces onto its roadbed. The Jade River rapids crashed around its great stone piers. Spray from the surging river breached the ramparts and soaked the roadbed. The roar of the raging water was deafening. Two towering stone pillars rose above either side of the bridge span. On top of each was placed a stone carving of a woodsman wielding a great axe, symbols of the woodcutters who made the valley their home. Two identical pillars bordered the roadbed on the opposite bank. They sported statues of great tusked mountain boars, symbols of the warlike Jade Mountain clans: the people Darshana called Boarmen.

Pausing beneath the woodcutters, she picked through the leather pouch on her belt that contained her spells. Darshana was half-human and half-elf. Her elvish blood allowed her to use magic, but because she was only half-elf, she could not create her own. She had to purchase it from enchanters or other spell weavers.

Purchased magic came in the form of small, glowing, crystal orbs the size of acorns from the great oaks across the river. Her pouch contained about a dozen of them. Each was identified by its color and fine elvish runes printed upon them in blazing fire writing. Using magic had costs beyond the price of the spells, though. Every spell took its toll. They drew life energy from the caster, and the most powerful spells drew so much they required rest after casting.

She avoided the red orbs. These spells could lay waste to a whole group of foes, but after casting one, she would be too weak to repulse any counterattack. They worked well against a party of Boarmen, but who knew what effect they would have on the beast racing toward her. If she cast one, and it did not drop the warrior, her head would be up on that sword, too.

A purple orb caught her attention. *Venectus Arraknus,* read the flaming runes. *Spider webs—strong as steel and as sticky as tar. That might work.* Darshana took the spell ball in her hand and closed her fist tightly around it. She could almost feel its pulsing energy. The elvish invocation words burst from her mouth, "*Inectius Nuvium Su.*" Then she crushed the orb and opened her hand, releasing a cloud of purple dust. The cloud hovered in the air before her. She pointed to each of the pillars and shouted the elvish word "*gi*"—go.

The cloud split into two with each half encircling the pillars. Then, like tiny thunderstorms, the clouds began to flash with lightning and drop rain, but instead of water, thousands of little purple spiders fell. They crawled up the pillars and began casting great silvery webs between them, forming a sticky silver barrier across the bridge entrance. The spiders and the webs had reached midway up the pillars when the warrior and the great horse burst through the trees.

Darshana turned and ran across the bridge and down the gate road into the forest. Now, it was all up to the spiders. If they spun the web higher than the horse could jump and strong enough to resist the slashes from the warrior's sword long enough for her to make it halfway to the gate, she might escape.

The road cut a straight line across the valley. She ran without looking back, sucking in air and willing her long legs to carry her faster. The familiar stone arch that formed the Jade Gate grew nearer with every stride. Erected atop a small hill, its immense bulk rose above the trees. She had passed through every gate in the Land, but none so often as this one. This was her territory. The final destination for all her *càiniǎo* training expeditions. That made her current predicament all the more humiliating. This place was hers.

The gate was close now, less than a quarter-mile, less than a minute to safety. Her legs burned with every stride, and her heart felt as though it might explode in her chest. But she was going to make it. Despite the humiliation, she felt exhilarated. She had beaten the monstrous gray warrior to the gate. She would live to fight again. A sensation telling her a missile was closing on her put an end to her internal celebration. She darted to her left to elude the strike, and an arrow grazed her right shoulder. *Damn.* Her pursuer had a bow, and it was shooting at her from the back of its horse, at full gallop, with accuracy. *What was this thing?*

Zigging and zagging to avoid the arrows whistling past her, she ran as hard as she could for the gate. It loomed above her, a great square, stone edifice with a huge arched opening that was over two hundred feet tall and one hundred feet wide. The road continued beneath the opening and kept going for miles until it reached the White Mountains. Passing through the arch, however, did not always lead to the road beyond. The gate was a portal, and travelers passing under it could reach any other gate that was known to them. Darshana knew every gate in the Land. She could teleport anywhere, but the only place she wanted to go now was out.

A swoosh-thump sound followed by a red flash told her one of the beast's arrows had found its mark. She'd been struck low on her back, a kidney shot, a kill shot. The elvish armor beneath her cloak had failed to deflect the missile. It was difficult to comprehend the power of the bow and the strength of the wielder to launch an arrow capable of penetrating the armor Darshana had believed impenetrable.

A bar graph appeared in her upper right indicating her lifeforce was almost depleted. *Critical.* "Come on, Darshana," she urged herself. "Just a little farther."

Twenty paces from the arch, a window materialized in front of her revealing a menu listing all the places the teleportation gate would take her. She swept her hand over the selections, frantically scrolling through dozens of gate names until she reached the bottom of the list where the word EXIT pulsed in big white block letters.

Another flash of red alerted her she'd been struck again. A loud voice announced, "character death imminent." The thunderous beating of hooves filled her headset, and she braced for the sword's cut. She punched the glowing word, and summoning all that remained of her strength, she leapt through the arch, and the world went black.

Chapter 5
A Special Agent

THE ROOM WAS DARK and cold when the buzzing on his night table woke him. Dr. Parker Reid rolled over on his side and reached out to draw his wife's warm body close, but his arm found only an empty bed. It took him a moment to remember where and when he was. Carrie was gone. Almost three years now. He imagined her lying beside him in her satin nightgown, turning into his embrace, her eyes shining in the darkness, and then he remembered her gasping for her final breaths in his arms. Blood, her blood, mixing with his in the terrible instant before they both died.

Parker lay on his side, staring at the empty pillow beside him. "Why could they resuscitate me, and not you?" he asked, his voice hoarse with grief. He pushed the memory back to the place in his mind where he did not visit, not willingly anyway, and retrieved his phone, then groaned when he read the two-word text message. *CHECK EMAIL.* The message was from Becky Fulbright, Behavioral Analysis Unit Five's senior agent. It was a quarter after three in the morning. A text from Becky at this hour was never good.

He sighed and tossed back the covers. It had taken multiple surgeries and many months of agonizing rehabilitation for him to be able to sit up and get out of bed on his own, though sitting up was the easy part. Standing and walking was a different story.

On the night they died, a .44 caliber hollow point had passed through his left thigh, taking out his femur and nearly severing his femoral artery. The fortunate proximity to a level-1 trauma center and an expertly applied tourniquet had kept him from bleeding out, barely, but the blood loss and bullet damage caused something the doctors called catastrophic, volumetric muscle loss. They had recommended amputation, telling him

22

the leg would never heal, likely waste away, and cause unending pain. He'd refused and set out to prove them wrong. A torturous rehab regimen arrested the muscle degeneration and restored maybe 50 percent of its function. He needed a cane to walk, but he still had his leg. They had been right about the pain, though. It was unceasing, and unlike the memories, he could not will it away.

He hopped into the bathroom, relieved himself, and splashed cold water on his pale, gaunt face. The person in the mirror still seemed like a stranger. Years of immobility had transformed his once athletic six-foot-two frame into the scarred and bony figure staring back at him. He looked more like an emaciated scarecrow than a onetime starting quarterback for Ohio State. He brushed his teeth, then washed down two Oxycodone tablets The painkillers were only to be used when the pain was severe, which seemed to be all the time. Some days he ate them like candy, and his doctor had begun giving Parker a hard time about renewing the prescription.

Retrieving his cane, he made his way down the hall to his office, eased himself into his desk chair, and logged into the Bureau's secure network. Two emails with red subject lines topped his inbox queue. The red meant priority. The color didn't guarantee the messages wouldn't descend into the unread abyss, but these two were fresh, and Becky had woken him to read hers. Perhaps as an internal act of defiance, Parker's eyes settled on the second message first. It was from an agent in the Nashville field office. The subject line read, *Unredacted M.E. Reports, Jyothi Reddy—Collector*. It had come in yesterday evening. Unrelated, he thought, but that would be wrong.

The M.E. report concerned his latest and most disturbing case involving a young computer programmer who, two weeks ago, had been found murdered in her Nashville apartment. The Nashville police had requested FBI assistance due to the manner of death and the obvious ritualistic nature of the killer's M.O.. The case had come to the Critical Incident Response Group and had been assigned to the Violent Crimes Apprehension Program. ViCAP had promptly turned it over to Unit Five for behavioral analysis, and Becky had added it to Parker's already substantial caseload.

He doubted the medical examiner's findings would contain

any new revelations. The crime scene investigator's report had left little doubt as to the cause of death. Jyothi's head had been removed in such a clean manner that it could have only been accomplished with an expertly wielded heavy-edged weapon. The absence of any other obvious wounds and evidence of strong arterial bleeding from her neck indicated her head had not been removed postmortem. The consensus was the murder weapon had been a sword—a sharp one.

The scene had been made even more gruesome by how the killer had displayed the victim's body. He had posed the young woman in a kneeling position with her hands clasping her upturned head which rested face-up on the floor between her knees, as if looking back up from where it had fallen. The killer had also taken trophies. Both Jyothi's ears had been removed and were not found in the apartment. This had led the field agent working the case to dub the killer the Collector. The investigators all agreed to keep the missing ears out of the press as a way to weed out the inevitable false leads and claims that accompany such horrific crimes and to differentiate the perpetrator from any copycats.

Parker would read the report later. He turned his attention to Becky's message. The subject line asked: *What do you think?* He eyed the glowing red text. "I think it's too early for this shit," he growled and clicked on the link. The message in the body was short and to the point. *This came into ViCAP last night— Boss called at 1:00am—got to move on it. Looks like Collector has gone mobile. Call me ASAP!!!*

The email had an image attached. He clicked on it and waited for it to render. What materialized made him shiver as if a cold wind had blown through his office. The photo showed what appeared to be a Black male, though it was hard to be certain from the lighting. The man was kneeling in a mat of coagulated blood, headless. A bloody stump of a neck, rimmed with yellow subcutaneous fat and a white circle of bone denoting the bisected spinal column and thyroid cartilage angled toward the camera. On the floor between the victim's knees, tilted back as if gazing at a point above the stump, was a head with closely cropped black hair missing both ears.

"Shit."

He pulled out his phone.

Becky answered before he heard it ring on his end. "Good morning, Dr. Reid."

"Where?"

"Vegas."

"When?"

"Yesterday. Metro police received a call around 3:00 p.m. their time. The victim, a Charles Tate, was supposed to check out of his hotel before noon. He never did. Housekeeping found him like that. The Vegas Homicide Unit took one look at the scene and called for us. The lieutenant out there, a woman by the name of, I kid you not, Divine Speed, knows the chief. That's why you and I are waking up to this. Our boss's motives notwithstanding, it's good they brought us in early. It sure looks like our Nashville unsub."

Parker stared at the image and sighed. "Let's hope it's him."

"It's him. Look at the photo. The scenes are identical."

"Maybe. You got any more info on the victim?"

"Not much. They were still processing the scene when I spoke to this Lieutenant Speed. All she had was the victim was Black, had a California DL, and was fifty-six."

"I don't like it. The victims appear very different, a young Indian woman living in Tennessee and an older Black man from California killed in Las Vegas. The timing and distances are wrong too. The murders happened within two weeks of each other on opposite sides of the country. Doesn't seem like enough time."

"It's a three-hour flight, Parker. Worst case, six, and only if you have to connect through Atlanta or Dallas. Heck, the killer could drive from Nashville to Vegas and still have plenty of time to gamble and see the sights before killing Mr. Tate."

"I know what's possible. It's what's probable that concerns me now. The Nashville murder was well planned. CSI turned up nothing in the victim's apartment, and the killer managed to avoid being caught on video—not that easy anymore. My guess is this murder will prove to be just as well planned. That kind of planning takes time. Two weeks doesn't give him much."

"So, what are you saying? We have multiple Collectors? Isn't that a lovely fucking thought?"

"I don't know. All I know is there's a lot of symbolism in beheading, and I'm not prepared to commit to a single perpetrator yet."

"The files are full of killers who decapitate their victims," she countered. "I've sat in on your new agent seminars. You cover several of them yourself, showing all those pictures of disembodied heads to the new agent trainees."

"All postmortem, almost all the victims sharing similar traits, and none of them killed with a sword. A sword, Becky. It's not the weapon of choice for your run-of-the-mill psychopath. It smacks of religious or political extremism. Maybe you should turn the cases over to the counterterrorism team."

She laughed. "Nice try, but despite the sword, this screams serial nut job to me. He's your unsub. How do you want to handle it?"

"Need to get the victimology down and see if anything links these two," he paused and studied the image on the screen, "other than the way they died. I guess I'm going to Vegas."

"I already made the travel arrangements," she said. "You're on American out of Reagan at 8:30 a.m."

"First class? You know? 'Cause of the leg."

"No can do," she scoffed. "We're the FBI. Our accountants carry guns."

He sighed and glanced at the time on his computer monitor. "The flight's in four hours. I was hoping to go back to bed."

"You can sleep on the plane."

"What about a hotel and car?"

"Relax. You're in a nice hotel. I'm sending you the details now. As for a car, the Vegas office will have an agent pick you up at the airport and assist."

"I don't need a babysitter."

The phone went silent for a moment. He heard her breathing. "Parker, after what happened in Detroit, I can't send you into the field alone."

Six months ago, he'd gone to Detroit to visit a crime scene and had a seizure while driving back to his hotel. It had not been his first, but it had been the first he'd had on the job, in public. He'd hid the others. The doctors had not determined what caused them, but high on their list of reasons was brain damage from the shooting. Luckily for him and the other motorists on Route 94 that morning, it happened while he was stuck in traffic. The incident had unnerved his superiors, prompting suggestions he retire and take care of himself, but the job was all he had. He would hold on to it as long as he could.

"Pack up, Doc. A car will be there for you by six."

"I don't need a babysitter," he repeated.

"Think of the agent as a chauffeur if that helps."

After the call, Parker worked his way down the stairs to the main floor. During his recovery, he'd had his bedroom moved into the living room. Then, after his mobility had improved, he'd had it returned to the second floor and used a stairlift to reach it. He'd stopped using the lift when he returned to work full-time. Mind over muscle, he'd will the damn leg stronger or break his neck trying. He hobbled toward the kitchen for some tea. Passing through the dining room, he stopped to look at the large, partially complete jigsaw puzzle arrayed on the table.

Carrie had loved puzzles. On those rare nights when both of them were not too exhausted or distracted by their demanding jobs, they would work on one together. Usually, the puzzles were pictures of places they'd planned to travel to one day. This particular one, The Great Pyramids of Giza, had been purchased a week before her death. He picked up a piece and snapped it into place. "Another puzzle to solve, baby."

Chapter 6
Dream Machines

TONY FOLLOWED THE COMMANDS of the navigation system and guided the van into the neighborhood full of multimillion dollar homes. "What do these people do for a living to afford places like this?" he asked, shaking his bald head.

Shea didn't look up from the article on the latest immersion suit tech she was reading. Tony made the same remark every time they did a service call in a wealthy neighborhood, and since the gear sold by InVerse, Inc. could only be afforded by the wealthy, he said it multiple times a week.

"Jeezus, get your nose out of that phone and look at these homes, will you?" He jabbed a thick, calloused index finger at the windshield. "Look at that one. The damn garage is bigger than my entire house. It's got four bays. Who the hell needs a garage with four bays?"

She yawned and glanced over at him. "A rich person with four cars."

"Four cars," he repeated, as if he couldn't believe it. "Probably all electric too; no waiting in line for no $12 gas for these people. Nope, no carbon tags, no oil change surcharge."

"Come on, boss," she replied. "You got an electric car. I've seen it."

He shook his head. "Not mine. It's Marci's. Had to get her one. Couldn't take the chance of her being stranded or stuck in no gas line for hours. Schools won't let her pick up the grandkids in no gas car either. Damned if I won't be paying it off for fifteen years." He stared at her. His bushy gray eyebrows stood out against his dark brown skin. "Fifteen years. There's no way that damn car is going to last fifteen years."

Shea didn't respond. Encouraging him would lead to another lecture on how the working class was being crushed to save the planet while the rich were getting richer from it. She reached over and retrieved the tablet with the day's route schedule from the van's center console. She brought up the stop-list and whistled, then turned and looked into the van's cargo area. "That rig back there is a model ZX."

Tony glanced in the rearview mirror and shrugged. "Jealous?"

"Damn right I'm jealous. That's a top-of-the-line rig. It's got the fastest processors available and twice the memory as the model S."

"Waste of money. Gloves and headgear are all anyone really needs."

She rolled her eyes. "You know that's not true. Gloves and headgear will get you in the Verse, but you need a cybersuit and rig to really experience it."

"Bah," he spat. "I go in all the time, and I don't wear a cybersuit or ride a rig." He grinned at her. "I'm not even sure they make cybersuits in my size."

She laughed. Tony was a big man.

"What is it you metajunkies call people who verse without rigs?"

"Half-ins," she replied, "and we call ourselves junkers. not metajunkies."

"Okay, junker. What's wrong with being a half-in? Saves a lot of money."

"Are you serious?" she asked, knowing he was goading her. "You know you can't play anything competitive without a rig. Half-ins don't feel motion and all their movements are standard and predictable."

"So?"

She scowled at him. "It makes them easy to kill."

He shrugged. "Guess you're right, kid. Rigs are great. Glad we sell so many of them."

The NAV directed Tony to make a turn, and he steered the van deeper into the neighborhood.

She stared at him, expecting a *but*.

"What?" he asked.

"I know you too well, boss. You got something else to say."

"Nah," he said, a big grin spreading across his face. "Rigs are great. They require lots of maintenance, which keeps us employed."

"But?"

His massive shoulders rose and fell in another exaggerated shrug. "Not everyone needs one is all." He nodded toward the back of the van. "Especially one as powerful as that one. Damn thing costs as much as I make in a year. You really think whoever's getting it needs that kind of full motion simulation power in their home?"

Shea poked at the tablet's screen. "Probably not." She dropped the tablet onto the console and leaned back in her seat. "But I do."

"You already have a rig. I helped you build it, remember?"

"I know, and it's a good one." She hooked her thumb toward the cargo area. "Just not as nice as that one."

Tony's eyes gleamed. "Can't beat the price, though. You're the only one I know who's ever built a rig from the shop's junk pile." He chuckled. "Management would have a cow if they ever found out."

"Had to," she said. "I'd go broke if I had to rent rig time at MetaSpots."

He shot her an angry glance. "That's because you spend too much time playing that damn game."

She looked away. *Here we go.* Tony never missed an opportunity to badger her about the time she spent in the Verse. Neither of them said anything for several seconds. When Tony spoke again, his voice took on a softer, fatherly tone. He was going into what Marci called his Papa Bear mode. "Just worried about you, kid. As smart and pretty as you are, you should live life in the real world, beating boys off with a stick, not whacking them with a simulated sword."

Shea scrunched her brow and glared at him. "Who says I don't?"

"When would you ever have time? Don't you think I know you race right home and go into that mighty magic land?"

"Land of Might and Magic," Shea corrected. Her face flushed. Tony had become like a father to her, and like her own father, never tired of giving advice on how she should live her life. It could be annoying.

The navigation system chimed and a soft androgenous voice announced, "Destination approaching on the left."

Thank God.

The NAV led them down a long, tree-lined driveway to a residence of similar size and style as the other homes in the neighborhood. Shea noted this one only had a three-bay garage. Tony parked, and they unloaded several large, white cardboard boxes and stacked them on a handcart. Some boxes were heavy, requiring both of them to lift. All were emblazoned with the blue InVerse logo and the tag line "The Gear that Gets You There" written both in English and Chinese. Tony grabbed the tools and ladders and headed for the front door. Shea followed, pushing the heavy cart.

A dozen precisely placed sprinkler heads sprayed an immaculate emerald lawn, manicured shrubbery, and dazzling flowerbeds without a drop hitting the walkway. Their rhythmic chick-chick beat seemed loud in the quiet suburban paradise. Shea studied the back of Tony's head and imagined she could hear an old-fashioned mechanical adding machine tallying up the costs for the luxurious landscaping and the water to keep it all alive throughout the scorching Atlanta summer.

The door opened before Tony reached the bell. Shea wasn't surprised. Security cameras were everywhere. A fit, blonde woman with an unnaturally smooth, tanned face stood just inside the doorway. She wore a top-of-the-line cybersuit and judging by the bulges in the groin and chest, it was equipped with the arousal-zone stimulator, or the sex pack, as it was known. Shea thought they were gross, but to each her own. The woman was frowning and gave off an annoyed vibe.

"It's about time," she said. "You were supposed to be here first thing this morning."

Shea knew the confirmation email had promised an arrival between eight and ten. It was only half past eight.

"We're sorry, ma'am," Tony said sounding as contrite as if they had actually been late.

Impressive control, boss, Shea thought, not sure she would have been able to resist the urge to correct the customer herself.

The woman stepped back from the door. "Well, come in. I am meeting friends for an excursion at noon, and I want to use the new rig, and it *better* work. The last one was a piece of garbage. It got hung up all the time. I was trapped upside down in it for over a goddamn hour. My husband is a very successful lawyer, and he thinks the mental suffering caused by that malfunction may warrant a settlement." She folded her arms and raised a fine blonde eyebrow. "A big one."

Shea watched her boss, looking for signs the customer-friendly façade was cracking and thinking about what she might say if the volcano behind it erupted. Tony was a softy at heart, but he could get excited, especially when mistreated by the economically privileged, and this rude woman oozed privilege.

Shea held her breath as she listened.

"Yes, ma'am," Tony said, even more politely.

"You can't bring that cart in the house."

"No, ma'am. We will carry it all in."

All eight hundred pounds of it, Shea thought.

The woman made a dismissive gesture. "Follow me," she commanded. "I'll show you where to set it up."

Shea took as many of the cartons as she could carry and followed the woman and Tony into the house. They passed through a richly decorated living room containing furniture Shea knew cost more than she made in six months and made their way down a hallway with both walls filled with framed photos of the woman and a tall, athletic man who Shea assumed was the lawyer-husband. At the end of the hall, they entered a large, empty room.

The morning sun streamed through open slats in the blinds covering a row of large windows overlooking an enormous swimming pool. The slats cast a grid-like shadow on the polished wood floor. The woman strode to the center of the room where a rubber mat had been placed and pointed down as if ordering a dog to sit. "It goes right here," she said.

Shea set down the cartons and studied the space, ticking off the items on the checklist she and Tony went through with every setup. "Ceiling height looks good. Over ten feet. Ample power outlets. No obstructions within a ten-foot radius." She glanced down at the large mat. "Anti-slip sweat mat in place." She nodded at Tony and looked at the woman. "It's a perfect spot for a commercial OmniRig."

The woman wrinkled her brow, and Tony said, "OmniRig is what we call the omnidirectional immersion platform you purchased for full-range movement inside the Metaverse environments."

"I know what an OmniRig is," the woman snapped.

Shea almost asked her if she knew what junkers called them but thought better of it. When you pay over a hundred thousand dollars for an entertainment device, you don't want to hear it referred to as a hamster wheel.

"What did she mean by commercial?" the woman asked Tony.

"It's a high-end unit. We normally don't install these in homes. Most people just go with the headgear and suits and rent rig time."

The woman snorted. "We don't rent."

"Well," Tony smiled, "the room is perfect."

"Of course it is. I already told you. We had one in here. It didn't work. Two people like you came and took it away."

People like you. Tony was going to have a stroke.

"Yes, ma'am. We'll get the new one set up right away and check it out."

"I'll be in the next room." She looked down. "Don't scratch the floors. They are Bocote," she said as she left.

Shea mouthed "bitch" at Tony and smiled.

They retrieved the rest of the boxes, careful not to mar a wall or bump into a piece of the expensive furniture. Shea breathed a sigh of relief when she discovered the screw holes in the floor made for the prior installation aligned with the new unit's base.

"Good thing for you," Tony chuckled. "I was going to send you to tell her if we had to drill new ones," he crossed his arms and mimicked the woman's superior pose, "into the Bocote."

They spent the next two hours assembling the components. The woman returned to the room every ten or fifteen minutes to remind them of her noon deadline. A few times, she hovered in the doorway watching them and repeated her warning not to scratch the floors.

After they'd bolted all the sections in place, Shea stepped down from the ladder and admired the completed machine. Standing nine feet tall with an eight-foot diameter, it dominated the once empty room. Shea had heard people say OmniRigs resembled miniature Ferris wheels, but she didn't think so. Ferris wheels had hubs and spokes. Rigs had neither. Ferris wheels rotated around center axles like the wheels on her motorcycle. Rigs had no center axle. As far as she could tell, the only thing rigs had in common with Ferris wheels was they were round, but they weren't wheels. They were rings, or to be more precise, two-ring systems with one smaller ring nested inside a larger outer ring. Rigs rotated, but they did not spin around a center point; they flipped end over end like a coin.

Shea engaged a manual lock, preventing the ring system from moving, and stepped onto the running track. At their core, rigs were essentially high-tech treadmills, albeit ones capable of rotating their riders 360 degrees on two axes—not something you expect or want to happen while jogging at your neighborhood gym. The running track was mounted on the inner ring and depending on the position of the outer ring, it could rotate to create up or downhill grades of any pitch, and if the safety protocols were disabled, it could do full loops. Also attached to the inner ring were the harness and saddle systems that held the rider in place.

Shea stepped into the harness and checked to make sure the restraining belts and buckles were correctly installed. Then she did a slow jog on the track to make sure the belt felt right on the rollers. The track was the reason junkers called rigs hamster wheels. It was not uncommon to go to a MetaSpot and find rows of rigs with riders whiling away the hours running on the tracks like pet rodents chasing food pellets.

Shea looked up to see the woman staring at her from the doorway.

"Another twenty minutes, ma'am."

The woman gave her an annoyed look and disappeared down the hall.

Shea looked over at Tony, and he mouthed "bitch" again for good measure.

She climbed out of the rig and double-checked all the connections while Tony made one last pass with a wrench, making sure every nut was tightened. After all the hardware system checks were complete, he moved the ladders out of the rig's operating space and powered up the unit. Small LEDs outlining the rings illuminated white, then flashed as the system booted. Shea watched and waited for the lights to turn blue, signaling Tony had paired the rig's systems with the control app on the touch pad in his hand.

"Ready for a test ride?"

Shea smiled. "Always." She retrieved headgear and a pair of cybergloves from a case. She pulled the padded helmet down over her ears and adjusted the cybermask to fit snugly around her eyes. The eyecup displays in the mask lit up in real-world view, allowing her to see her surroundings. Under her coveralls she wore a lightweight cybersuit, one *without* a sex pack. She connected the lead from the cybermask to the lead from her suit, then pulled on the gloves and fastened their wires. A virtual control panel hovered a little to her right.

She stepped inside the rings and strapped herself into the harness, then connected her suit to the rig. The LEDs around the rings glowed green and a genderless voice that sounded like the same one used by the van's nav unit announced, "Welcome." Shea reached up with her right hand and pressed a button labeled ENTER on the control panel. The real world dissolved and was replaced by a giant InVerse logo floating in a white background. A musical tone played in her ears while a spinning blue wheel and the words Biometric Authentication In Progress filled her view.

After a moment, the logo screen disappeared, and Shea was standing in an ornate, golden hall with high vaulted ceilings covered in fantastic murals depicting the Greek god, Apollo. The room was known as the Sun Lobby, and it served as Shea's jumping-off point for the Metaverse. Every verser had their own lobby where they could configure their Metaverse personas and prepare themselves for entering the simulated worlds. Not all lobbies were like this one. Shea had picked the Sun Lobby design from a thousand alternatives. The programmers who created it used an actual place for inspiration. It was a replica of the Galerie d'Apollon of the Louvre Museum in Paris.

Down the center of the hall, resting on the polished parquet floors, were three tall, rectangular glass display cases. Inside each stood what looked like people, but were, in fact, Shea's Metaverse avatars. Most junkers had many of them, but Shea always felt she only needed three, one for work, one for play, and one for dating, though she had had little use for her dating avatar lately.

All three were female. Shea had no interest in Versing as

a man. Inside the case nearest to Shea stood her work avatar. A little over five feet tall and wearing sky blue coveralls, the avatar could have been Shea's identical twin. They were even dressed the same, though the avatar's coveralls hugged her slight curves better.

Shea stepped closer and stared into the case. The avatar stared back, her short, black hair pushed to the side, revealing Shea's youthful brown face with the same geeky "I can fix anything" expression. All the avatar's features matched those of Shea's southern Indian mother, except for the eyes. Those large aqua green orbs were all the product of her northern European father's chromosomes.

Next to each case was a white marble pedestal on which was placed a computer touch panel. The touch panel displayed the figure's name and several buttons. InVerse company policy required Shea to use her employee identification code for her work avatar's name, but Shea just called her Tech.

As Shea reached out to press the button on the touch panel to select Tech for her test session with the customer's rig, a ray of sunlight shone through one of the lobby's windows and landed on the next case over, bathing its occupant in bright light and catching a gleaming exposed portion of the silver armor the personae wore beneath a plain green cloak.

Unlike Tech, this one looked nothing like Shea. Tech was small, nerdy, and boring; the armored avatar was none of those things. She stood just over six feet tall and had a muscular, though still feminine, build. Long, glossy black hair flowed over one shoulder and yellow, catlike eyes peered out from under a curtain of bangs. Her mouth was turned up in a self-assured grin and her light green complexion seemed to glow. Shea smiled back at the avatar and stepped over to the case.

"We'll play later, Darshana. Maybe we'll go back and kick that gray monster's ass."

"Hey, kid," Tony's voice startled her. It sounded like it was coming from public address speakers hidden somewhere among the intricate wood carvings in the ceiling. He was using the control program to tap into the speakers in her headgear. "Stop fooling around in there. The customer is all over me. Do the test ride and get out."

"You got it, boss."

Before returning to Tech's case, Shea glanced over at the third, and long-neglected avatar. Like Tech, this one looked much like her real self, though with long hair, red lipstick, and maybe slightly larger breasts. Dressed in a too-small black evening dress, this was Shea's dating avatar. They shared the same name and the same nonexistent love life. Shea frowned at the pouting face, thinking maybe she should just delete her. Then she stepped back over to Tech's console. "Time to go to work," she said as she pressed the activation button and chose the InVerse test course from a list of Metaverse entry points.

Tech disappeared from the case, and a second later Shea was standing at the entrance of an obstacle course. "Here I go, boss," she called out as she sprinted forward.

Inside the course, Shea ran through a series of physical challenges designed to test the rig's capabilities. She raced up and down ladders, swung from ropes, did backflips off platforms, and ran as fast as she could through zigzagged paths going up and down steep grades. Her virtual motions in the simulated obstacle course caused the running track to vary its speed and resistance while the rings flipped and spun, making her feel every simulated movement.

Once she was sure everything was functioning as expected, she dashed for a door labeled EXIT and popped back into the real world. Her hair was slick with sweat when she removed the headgear. The course may have been simulated, but the workout was real.

"How'd she handle?" Tony asked.

"Like a dream." Shea beamed at him. "Isn't that what we sell, boss? Dream machines?"

"Sure. All you have to be is rich enough to afford one," Tony groused.

Chapter 7
A Dwarf Sends His Regards

SHEA AND TONY MADE three more calls after installing the rig at what they'd come to call the Rich Bitch's house. All the other stops were standard component swaps and tune-ups at MetaSpot businesses, which was good as Tony had been so upset by the audacious display of wealth, Shea worried he'd have a heart attack during one of his rants. Besides, his words sometimes hit a little close to home.

Shea agreed, in principle, with most of Tony's sentiments, but her parents were successful professional people, and unlike Tony, who'd grown up in poverty, she had come from the upper middle class. Her parent's home was nothing like the Rich Bitch's to be sure, but it would be worthy of Tony's ire. Shea treated her comfortable upbringing as something of an embarrassing secret, especially around her boss.

It was a little after five when they pulled into the InVerse service center parking lot. Tony stopped the van in front of her motorcycle.

"Another day, another Metabuck, kid."

"You don't want any help putting the tools away?"

"Nah, I got it. Go get a jump on your weekend."

"Thanks, boss," she said, opening her door.

"Wait. I got something for you." He reached behind his seat and produced a small InVerse component box and handed it to her. "This ought to give that bucket of spare parts you waste all your time in a little more kick."

She took the box and opened it. Inside was a circuit board which she recognized as an OmniRig Central Control Processor card. The circuit board, known to techs by its abbreviation: CCP, matched the movements in the Metaverse to the real movements in the rig and cybersuit. It controlled how physical body movements were mapped to Verse movements and how Verse movements were mapped to physical motion in the rig. It was the heart of the system. Every rig had one, but like the class disparity Tony railed against, not all CCPs were equal. There were basic units that did the job for most users, and then there were more advanced, and expensive, units with faster chipsets and memory that gave their users an edge in high-intensity movements like those needed for competitive sports and fighting. The unit in the box was a next generation ultra-high-end model. It was a twenty thousand dollar part.

"Holy shit, Tony. Where did you get this?"

He grinned. "Don't worry about it."

She stared at him as realization dawned. "You swapped out Rich Bitch's CCP, didn't you?"

He shrugged. "Maybe."

"What did you replace it with?"

"The one from her old rig. Good, but not like that one." He nodded toward the board. "Seems those *Other-people-like-us* reported it was damaged and claimed they dispo'd it." He winked at her.

"Oh my God. This is amazing, but if her old one is damaged, won't it just cause her problems again?"

"Nope. It tested fine. The only thing wrong with her old rig was her."

Shea studied the board, wanting to keep it, but worried about getting Tony in trouble. He needed the job. "I don't know, boss. What if someone finds out?"

"Who's gonna find out? Do you think she needs that kinda power for her *excursions*?" He made air quotes when he said excursions.

Shea tucked the box into her backpack and punched his shoulder. "Catch you Monday," she said as she hopped out of the van.

"Kid?"

"Yeah?"

"Take some time out of your Versing to study. You need to finish your classes or you're going to end up like me… just an old tech fixing rich people's shit."

"Aw, c'mon, boss. I could do a lot worse. I like what we do. In fact, even after I finish school, I'm still going to ride around fixing rich people's shit with you." She shut the door and Tony drove off. She watched the van disappear around the building. Shea didn't have the heart to tell Tony she had earned her degree in biochemistry in May and now had no idea what she was going to do with it. Her parents expected her to go to medical school as they had, but Shea didn't want to be a medical doctor. Healing the sick was a noble profession, but it didn't excite her. She was a hunter, even if all her hunting took place in a simulated world.

* * *

The roads were clogged with thousands of commuters all engaged in the same stop-and-go struggle to get home and put the workweek behind them. She weaved her bike from one open patch of roadway to another, threading through the mass of cars in the same way she zigzagged to avoid obstacles in the InVerse testing course. Lean right, then back over to the left, careful not too far, a little throttle, then some brake; not too much and never while turning; then a twist of throttle and bolt forward through an opening, taking care not to clip a truck's mirror. There was a rhythm to it. Once she was in the groove, she could move through the dense forest of cars like the deer on Jade Mountain raced between the evergreens; at least, as long as there were no cops.

She made it to the old cement block and metal roof industrial shed she called home without being crushed between angry drivers or pulled over. When she'd first offered to rent the boarded up and somewhat dilapidated structure, the owner had told her over its long history the building had been used for everything from a farm equipment repair shop to a church, but Shea was the first to live in it. It had everything she needed, plumbing, electricity, heat, and most importantly, ceilings more than high enough to accommodate an OmniRig. It was also cheap.

The single tall metal bay door retracted as she approached, triggered by her phone when she crossed an invisible GPS fence line. It rattled to a close once she and the bike were inside. The building had four rooms, including the large bay area where she spent most of her time. The bay contained her rig and several metal shelves and workbenches filled with her tools and electronic components in various states of disassembly. She'd carved out a small section for a living room which she'd furnished from a thrift store. Her bedroom was once a small office, and a tiny breakroom served as her kitchen. She'd done a little creative plumbing to allow a bare bones bathroom with a drain in the center of its concrete floor to double as a walk-in shower. It was spartan, some would say to the extreme, but to her it was heaven.

A slender black cat dropped from a shelf as Shea removed her helmet, and the cat padded across the floor toward her, meowing loudly as she came.

"Well, hello there, Trinity. Did you miss me?" Shea cooed as she ran her hand along the excited feline's arching back. "I bet you're hungry."

She scooped up the cat and carried her into the kitchen. "It's going to be a late night tonight, girl," she cooed while spooning cat food into a dish as Trinity watched and purred like a buzz saw. "I can't wait to see what this new CCP can do." Grabbing a bottle of water and a pear, she left Trinity to her dinner and returned to the bay. She took a seat behind the desk she'd fashioned from an old wooden door and sawhorses and logged into her laptop to catch up on her messages.

Shea had several email mailboxes to go through. She had her personal box which she shared only with family and close friends, taking great pains to guard it from the nonstop message pollution everyone was subject to, her work box, her seldom used dating box, and an account for Darshana's off-SIM communication. This is the one she used to conduct Land of Might and Magic business.

Munching on the pear, she scanned through Darshana's emails. A message from Xu caught her attention. He demanded she return the money he and the rest of his party had paid her to guide them through their initial LMM journey. Fat chance. She contemplated telling him to fuck off but tapped out a more civilized response.

She spoke out loud as she typed, "Dear Xu, though I am sorry your team members did not complete the expedition, no promises were made as to the survival of your characters. You received excellent training and experience and now are all well prepared to enter the Land on your own. Of course, I can't claim my safe passage bonus, as you all died because you were morons and lit a fire for no good reason." She took a deep breath and erased the last sentence. "I wish you and the rest of your team all the best and look forward to our next meeting. Safe travels and may the Seven Wizards bless you. Darshana." She winced after typing the corny phrase.

Several other messages asking about her guide services cluttered Darshana's inbox. The questions were almost always the same, and she had keystroke macros that pasted in most of the answers. How much? *Depends on the party size.* Do you train singles? *As long as you pay the fifty-coin minimum.* How long? *Plan on five treks, each taking between two and three hours.* What will we learn? *Everything you need to survive between the Gates.* Do you guarantee completion? *No, and I get a five-coin bonus for each member who makes it from the starting gate to the end.*

Finished with Darshana's emails, she moved on to her personal account. As expected, she found a note from her mother asking again when she was going to send out her med school applications. Shea thought about replying "never" but promised instead to apply when she reviewed her MCAT results, which, unbeknownst to her mother, remained unopen on Shea's dresser since being delivered a month ago. No doubt she'd get into her parent's alma mater. Though, if she desired anything less than going to med school, it was going to med school in Philadelphia. Another message was from a former classmate also inquiring about her application status. *It's a full-on conspiracy*, she thought. Then she came to a message that made her drop the pear core on her keyboard.

"Greetings from a Dwarf!"

"What the fuck?" She said out loud, wiping pear juice from the keys. She never gave her personal email to anyone in LMM.

She opened the message, hearing Falin's Boston accent in her mind as she read. "Greetings, Darshana, or should I call you Shea? This is your old friend, Falin. You know, the Dwarf you left to lose his head on Jade Mountain? No hard feelings. I got my head back, but I did lose all my experience points. Fucker didn't give me enough time to bury my *Shēngmìnglì*. I hate that friggin word, by the way. Xperion should stop using appropriated Chinese and call it lifeforce. Anyway, as you can see, I know who you are, which I bet is driving you nuts. Don't worry. Your secret is safe with me. You remain Clark Kent to the Real, but I know you are the Land's wicked, badass Superman, or, I guess, Superwoman. Let's get together. Meet me at the Hunter's Horn at Staghead Gate tonight, 10:00 p.m., Atlanta time. Cheers."

Trinity jumped onto the desk, startling Shea. She stroked the cat's sleek black fur. "How did that little man, assuming that's what it is, learn who I am? This is bad, Trin. Really bad."

Chapter 8
The Arizonan Hotel

AMERICAN **F**LIGHT **1706** **LANDED** at Harry Reid International Airport in Paradise, Nevada at 11:43 a.m.. Parker Reid, no relation to the former senator, waited for all the passengers to deplane before pushing himself out of his seat and making his way down the jetway, an impatient flight crew trailing closely behind.

"Are you sure you don't need a wheelchair?" the gate agent asked as he hobbled past.

Ignoring her, he limped into the terminal and went in pursuit of his luggage. After a harrowing ride on the airport tram where he almost toppled over when the train came to an abrupt stop, he descended the escalator into the bustling casino-floor-like atmosphere of the baggage claim area and spotted a young, Black man wearing gold rimmed sunglasses, holding a sign with Parker's name printed on it. Appearing to recognize him, the young man tossed the sign in a trash can and approached with an outstretched hand.

"Good morning, Dr. Reid. Welcome to Las Vegas."

Morning, Parker thought, *was ten hours ago*. He took the young man's hand. They were about the same height, but the man had broader shoulders and muscular arms that strained against the sleeves of his summer weight, light blue business suit. He wore a crisp white shirt, no tie, and tan leather loafers, no socks. A firearm in a shoulder harness was visible under his jacket. His grip was firm and confident, a contrast to what Parker knew was his own frail grasp.

"Forgive me, son, but you don't look old enough to get into the clubs here, and you sure don't look old enough to carry whatever it is you have strapped under that coat. You *are* with the Bureau, right?"

As an instructor at Quantico, Parker had grown accus-

44

tomed to being the old man in the room. He grew older with each new class, while the New Agent Trainees, NATs, grew ever younger, but this man seemed too young to be accepted into the academy, let alone be a posted agent.

"Yes, sir. Special Agent Jaden Breaux, Las Vegas Field Office."

Parker raised an eyebrow. "Bro? Like, 'How's it hanging, bro?'"

The young agent smiled politely. "That's funny, sir. Of course, it's not very original. It got old when I was about eight."

Still trying to draw a bead on the man's age, Parker asked, "When did you go through the academy?"

"Over a year ago. I guess you don't remember, but you were one of my instructors. Made me want to be a profiler."

Parker considered Jaden for a moment. He thought he did recall him. "I do remember you, now. You asked all kinds of irrelevant questions."

Jaden laughed and grabbed Parker's bag from the baggage carousel before Parker could attempt to struggle with it.

"Still interested in BAU when you grow up?"

"Not sure, sir. I'm gravitating toward cyber. That's where all the action is these days."

They made their way to the garage and over to a flame-orange electric sportster.

Parker studied the car, contemplating the least painful way to lower his body into the passenger seat, while Jaden placed his bag in the trunk.

"No normal cars, Breaux?"

"It's Vegas. This is a normal car."

Parker half-lowered himself, half-fell into the seat. After stopping to pay the parking fee, they left the cool shade of the garage and zipped out into the fierce Mojave sun.

Cursing himself for forgetting sunglasses, Parker squinted to read the road signs. "Where are you taking me?"

"I was told to bring you back to the office."

"Take me to the crime scene."

Jaden glanced over at him. "I should call my supervisor first."

"Don't be a bitch, Breaux. I flew all the way here to see the scene, not your supervisor."

"Did you just call me a bitch?"

Parker grinned at him. "No. I told you not to be one."

"Should I call Vegas PD, or would that be being a bitch too?"

"Well, you have to call them. It's their case."

Parker stared out the window at the passing hotels while Jaden spoke to a Detective Sergeant, Martin Higgs, with the Metro Las Vegas Homicide Bureau. Higgs said he'd been told to expect a call from an FBI criminal behavioral analysis expert, but he was surprised one had flown out in person and so soon.

When Jaden told Higgs that the FBI prided itself on being responsive, Higgs growled, "Blow me." Then he informed them the crime scene investigators had finished their work early that morning. The room had already been turned back over to the hotel's management. Higgs said, in what Parker thought was the most obnoxious Chicago accent he'd ever heard, he would call the manager to let him know they were on the way, and he would join them as soon as he could.

The Arizonan Hotel was an older, somewhat seedy hotel located in the Fremont District of downtown Vegas. Far away from the crowded mega casinos that lined the stretch of Las Vegas Boulevard known as the Strip, the Arizonan catered to a more budget- and perhaps privacy-conscious clientele. One of its selling points, Parker had learned from the balding, potbellied manager, was the Arizonan was one of the few hotels remaining with no security cameras on the guest floors. Beneficial if you wanted to avoid having a visit from a drug dealer or escort captured on video—less so if one of those visitors happened to cut off your head.

"You do have some security cameras," Parker said to the manager who had come from behind the front desk to escort them to the room where Charles Tate's headless body had been found less than twenty-four hours earlier. Parker pointed his cane at the camera enclosures he spotted around the lobby and the hallway leading to the casino.

"Yes. Of course, this floor and the two casino floors are all monitored."

"What about the elevators?"

"Those too."

"And the stairwells?"

"Yes. I told all this to the police. Our security people will get them all the video files. There's a process for this kind of thing, you know." He leaned in close to Parker. A powerful smell of mint emanated from his breath, like he'd just consumed a handful of Tic Tacs. Parker wondered what it was masking. Halitosis? Booze? Vomit? "This isn't our first time. We've had guests—" he seemed to search for the right words "—die before."

"Murdered?" Jaden asked.

The manager looked around and then at him. "Keep it down, will you? People are spooked enough. Yes. A couple years ago a woman shot a man in 514, and before that a homeless man was knifed in a stairwell."

The manager led them into the elevator. Parker looked for the camera. It was in the ceiling, hidden behind a gold plastic bubble. "All the cameras functioning?"

"As far as I know. Like I said, our security people are on it."

The elevator door slid open, and they followed the manager out and into a long hallway. He stopped in front of a door about midway to the end.

"Here's the room." He gestured toward the door. "We removed all the crime scene tape as soon as Detective Higgs said we could. It was attracting gawkers."

"How much cleanup have you done?" Parker asked.

The manager emitted a nervous laugh. "None. It's not something our housekeeping staff can do, or even would, for that matter. We have to bring in a special team." He rubbed his thumb and fingers together. "It'll cost a fortune. Everything has to be stripped and replaced. This room will be out of commission for weeks." He waved a card key at the lock and pushed the door open. "You'll see."

Parker smelled the rancid metallic stink of blood before he saw the large circular stain on the floor by the side of the bed. It was a scent he knew well, but it still made his stomach churn. He no longer doubted what the manager was covering with the Tic-Tacs. The blood had soaked into the green carpet and had dried into a dark, purplish-brown color. Blood splattered the bed linens and mattress, and little oxidized dots were visible on the ceiling and walls.

Jaden squatted down next to the blood and pointed out what looked like two tracks leading from the large stain toward several smaller oval ones about three feet away. "This is interesting."

Parker pulled the crime scene photo from Becky's email up on his phone. He moved to where he guessed the image had been taken and studied the stain patterns. "The killer must have dragged the victim there to pose him."

"Pose him?" Jaden said.

Parker held out his phone for the squatting agent to see.

Jaden grimaced. "That's nasty."

"I bet they don't see stuff like that in cyber," Parker grinned as he limped over to a medium-sized suitcase sitting open on a chair near the window. He picked through the items inside. "Is this all of Mr. Tate's things?"

The manager, who was staring at the bloodstain, answered without looking. "That's most of it. There are some things hanging in the closet and toiletries in the bathroom."

"What about his wallet and phone?"

"The police have them."

Parker reached into the suitcase and drew out a light-blue bodysuit. It reminded him of a wet suit except it wasn't made of heavy neoprene like those he and Carrie had worn when they went diving in Cozumel. It was made of a lighter mesh fabric and appeared to be covered with crisscrossing cords forming a grid pattern. "I wonder what this is," he said, holding it up.

Jaden shot him a disbelieving stare. "Where have you been for the past five years? It's a cybersuit. You know, for going into the Metaverse."

The young agent walked over and examined the suit. "It's a nice one too. Better than mine."

"You have one of these?"

"Sure. Everyone does. I mean, except you, apparently."

"I don't have one," the manager said behind them.

"Or him," Jaden said as he looked through Tate's belongings. He pulled out a shoebox-sized case and opened it. "Here's the headgear that goes with the suit."

Parker peered into the box. "Okay, I get it. It's that computer game thing, right? Virtual reality?"

Jaden rolled his eyes. "You need to get out more, sir—or, in." He examined the contents of the small case. "This gear is sweet. Mr. Tate must have made the big bucks."

The room door rattled with a hard knock that startled everyone. Jaden dropped the case and moved his hand inside his jacket. Parker touched his arm. "Easy, Breaux."

The manager looked through the peephole.

"It's Detective Higgs."

Martin Higgs was a medium build, olive-skinned, man with bushy black hair and a two-day beard. He was shorter than Parker but taller than the manager, and like Jaden, he was dressed in a light-colored business suit that Parker could not decide whether he thought it was gray or silver. He had a gun and a gold badge clipped to his belt.

Higgs nodded at the manager. "Morning, Bob." He sniffed. "Stinks in here. You should crank up the AC until you can remove the carpet. It'll help with da smell." He took two more steps into the room and stopped. "So, which one of you is da hot shot mind hunter?"

Jaden pointed at Parker, and Parker leaned on his cane. "I guess that's me, though I usually go by the Great Mind Hunter, not Hot Shot."

Higgs laughed. "Fair enough. When you guys are done poking around in here," he sniffed again and frowned, "the Lieutenant would like to meet with you."

Jaden stepped closer to Parker and in a hushed voice said, "Advice, sir. When we meet her, no jokes about her name. She's a little touchy about it."

"Dat she is," Higgs agreed. "I'll wait in the hall." He turned and walked out the door.

Parker spent several more minutes examining the room. He noted the door jamb was intact, and all the furnishings were in place and undamaged. In fact, except for all the blood, nothing about the room hinted at the violence that had taken place there.

Parker limped into the bathroom. On the vanity next to Tate's toothbrush were two pill vials. Each bore a small yellow crime scene investigation sticker with a number printed on it. He picked up the first one. Number 32. Omeprazole. Then he examined the second. Number 33. Jaden appeared in the doorway.

"Anything interesting?"

Parker shook the second vial. "Halcion."

"What's that?"

"Sleeping pills."

"How about the other?"

"Antacid." He set the sleeping pill vial down. "I think we're done here."

"Should we get samples?" Jaden asked.

"Ah, someone was paying attention during evidence collection class." Parker pointed at the yellow labels. "Looks like CSI cataloged and sampled them."

They collected the hotel manager who was still staring at the bloodstain and joined Higgs in the hallway.

"What do ya think, Mind Hunter?"

Parker shrugged. "Definitely murdered."

Higgs scowled. "Dat's genius."

As they were getting into the elevator, the manager scolded a young Hispanic woman for attempting to bring a cleaning cart on with them.

"They are not supposed to use the guest elevators," he explained.

Parker leaned against the metal wall and closed his eyes. The cool stainless steel felt good on his back but did nothing to ease the throbbing in his leg. During examinations, his doctor always asked him to rate his pain between one and ten, with ten being severe. Right now, it was a solid nine.

He opened his eyes. "How do they get between the floors?"

The manager turned and looked at him. "I beg your pardon?"

"The maids. How do they get between floors if they can't ride in these elevators?"

"Oh, there are service elevators. And we don't call them maids. They are housekeeping staff."

The door slid open, and they exited. Parker split off from the group and followed a sign to a restroom. Inside, he retrieved a vial of painkillers from his pocket and popped two in his mouth. He washed them down with water he slurped from his cupped hand and splashed what remained on his paler-than-usual face. He studied his reflection as he dabbed his stubbled cheeks with a paper towel. The weariness he felt on the inside was evident by the bags under his sunken eyes. *Rough.* Would Carrie even recognize him? He grinned. Of course, she would. Her handsome jock was still there, just thinner and paler.

Back in the lobby, he found Jaden standing alone talking on

his phone. The manager had returned to his place behind the front desk, and Detective Higgs was nowhere in sight. Parker hobbled over to the desk and waited for the manager to finish with a guest.

"Is there something more I can do for you?" The manager asked after the guest stepped away.

"Yes. I was wondering. Do the service elevators have cameras?"

The manager stared into space for a moment. "I don't believe so. No. As a matter of fact, I'm sure they don't."

Parker rubbed his still damp chin. "Can guests ride them?"

The manager shook his head. "No. They require an employee keycard."

"Ah. Anything keep track of when they are used?"

The manager eyed him, then shrugged. "The unions don't like it, but yes. The card reader system logs when keys are swiped."

"All card readers?"

"I believe so."

"Guest rooms?"

The manager hesitated before answering as if he was reluctant to admit this privacy infringement. "Yes."

Parker patted the desk counter. "Good to know. Thank you."

Jaden came up behind him and said, "That was my supervisor—the one you told me not to call. She's pretty pissed I ignored her request. The SAC had wanted to meet with you."

The manager asked, "What's a SAC?"

Parker winked at him. "Special asshole in charge." He turned to Jaden. "Where's Higgs?"

"He just left. We're to meet him and Lieutenant Speed at the Metro Detective Bureau in twenty minutes."

Chapter 9
Victimology

THE LAS VEGAS METROPOLITAN Homicide Detective Bureau was located in a sprawling office complex that serves as headquarters for the combined commands of the Clark County Sheriff's Department and Las Vegas Metro Police. As the crow flies, it's a short hop from the Arizonan Hotel; just a couple blocks west then across twelve lanes of freeway, but since Parker and Jaden weren't crows, they had to get back into the orange roadster and navigate the maze of downtown streets. The pills Parker had swallowed at the hotel did little to make sitting in the cramped car less painful.

Higgs was waiting in the main lobby and escorted them through security and up to a conference room. When they entered the room, two women and a man were seated together at the end of a long rectangular table, engaged in a deep discussion about something one of the women was showing on a tablet.

"Gotcha Feebs here," Higgs announced, sounding like a hotdog vendor at a Chicago Cubs game and putting an abrupt end to the conversation.

The woman who had been sitting at the head of the table stood and came to them. She was a tall, slender Black woman with shoulder-length black hair and brown eyes so dark Parker couldn't tell if she had pupils. She was dressed like Higgs in a silvery-gray suit with a gold badge and a gun clipped to her belt, though unlike Higgs, her suit was unwrinkled and looked expensive. Her crisp appearance and the authoritative way she moved to greet them left little doubt she was in charge.

She introduced herself as Divine Speed and offered her hand, first to Parker and then Jaden, her eyes lingering on the young agent. Motioning toward the woman and man still seated at the table, Divine said, "This is Tammy Basker. Tammy's an analyst in our Crime Scene Investigation Section and next to her is Roberto Chavez. He is the detective working the case."

They sat down and Divine continued. "When I called Michael last night, I had no idea we would get such a fast response. Normally these kinds of consultations take weeks to arrange.

Michael was Michael Warner, the assistant director who ran the FBI's National Center for the Analysis of Violent Crime, known within the Bureau as N-See-Vac. All the Behavioral Analysis Units fell under the N-See-Vac organization, including Unit Five where Parker worked. Michael Warner was Parker's boss's boss's boss.

Jaden shot him a nervous glance.

Parker remembered the young agent's warning not to make a wisecrack about the Lieutenant's name and grinned at him. "Well, Assistant Director Warner is certainly capable of moving with Godlike speed with the right prompting."

Jaden cringed and backed away from the table, giving Divine a clear line of sight to Parker, distancing himself from the pun and perhaps the entire FBI.

"Yes. He is," Divine said. "Michael and I go way back. We served in the Navy together, and I am well aware of his ability to be aggressive." She let the comment hang for a moment. "He warned me about you, Dr. Reid."

"Yes, ma'am."

"We won't have any trouble, will we?"

"No, ma'am." Parker smiled.

Divine turned to the CSI analyst. "Tammy, why don't you run us through what you found at the scene."

The analyst looked up from her tablet. She was a small, distinctive-looking young woman who Parker guessed was in her late twenties or early thirties. Her hair was dyed a distracting iridescent red, and it seemed to glow against her white, freckled skin. Magnified green eyes peered out from behind thick glasses with fire hydrant red plastic frames. A silver stud with a blood-red stone was embedded on the right side of her nose. Parker didn't need his doctorate in Behavioral Psychology to conclude she craved attention and liked the color red.

"Good afternoon," she said, and promptly launched into the details of the investigation. "My team and I arrived at the victim's room last evening at 5:42 p.m., and we were there until a little after two this morning. Total time on scene was eight hours and twenty-three minutes. We took 246 photographs and collected 189 samples for further processing and evidence."

She tapped on her tablet and a grid of photos appeared on a large monitor hanging on the far wall. The photos were numbered one through four and showed the hotel room as the crime scene investigators had found it when they first arrived. Except for the headless victim, it looked pretty much the way Parker had just left it.

"As you can see," she said, "the crime took place in a confined space. We measured the room and found it to be approximately 350 square feet, including the bathroom and closet."

"Not much space for a violent sword fight," Divine said.

Tammy nodded. "We don't think there was much of a fight."

She tapped on the tablet some more. A new grid of four photos appeared. These had been taken after the CSI team had placed scene markers near items to be preserved for analysis and evidence. Distributed as they were around the victim's body, the markers looked like little numbered yellow tents pitched by a miniature army after felling a giant. A marker had been placed beside each of the strange oval blood patterns Jaden had pointed out while they were in the room. Using her finger on the tablet, she drew a red circle around them.

"Anyone want to guess what these are?"

"The killer's footprints," Parker offered. "He stepped in the victim's blood."

"That's right," she said. "Very good." Tammy batted her long lashes at him.

"They don't look like footprints to me," Jaden said. "Why are there no tread patterns?"

"The killer wore booties, like the type doctors wear over their shoes in operating rooms," Parker said.

Tammy nodded. "Right again."

"There sure is a lot of blood," Divine said.

"The human body contains almost a gallon and a half of it," Parker said in the tone he used when lecturing at the academy. He glanced around the room. "Mr. Tate's heart would have beat for ten to twenty seconds after his head was removed, pumping almost all of it out of the severed carotid arteries. It would have burst out like champagne from a bottle when the cork is popped."

Higgs grimaced. "Dat's quite an image. Jeezus."

Tammy smiled and batted her eyes some more while she tapped on the tablet bringing up a single close-up image of Charles Tate's body slumped over his head. It was the same photo from Becky's email.

"I've seen this one," Parker said.

She swiped, and another image appeared. This one was similar but taken from a different angle. It showed the victim's hands placed beneath the head lying face up on the floor.

Jaden stroked his chin, deep in thought. "How does the body stay in that kneeling position? Is it supported somehow?"

Tammy shook her head. "Nope. No outside support. It was just balanced on its center of gravity. The killer knew how to arrange the weight so the body remained like that. Then, when rigor set in, it added a good bit of stability." She drew an arrow on the screen running straight down from the victim's neck cavity to where his butt was resting on the back of his legs. "See, the body is not really kneeling. It just looks that way. All the body's weight is centered right here on its calves. It's sitting, not kneeling."

She swiped to the next image, this one showing a close-up of Charles Tate's head lying on a white sheet. She drew a circle over the place where one of his ears should have been. "The killer removed both of them."

"I assume you didn't find them at the scene," Parker said.

Tammy shook her head. "Nope. We looked everywhere."

"We want to keep that detail to ourselves," Parker said.

"Agreed," Divine said.

"Did the killer take anything?"

"You mean besides da victim's ears?" Higgs said.

"Yes. Was Tate robbed?"

Chavez shook his head. "Not that we can tell. His wallet contained a few credit cards and $325 in cash. We won't be sure until his family goes through his things, but we don't think the killer took anything."

"Phone?"

"Got it and a tablet. We hope to get the passwords from his family so we can go through them and his social media accounts."

Parker nodded. "How about prints? What did you get there?"

"We collected dozens of them," Tammy said. "As well as numerous hair, fiber, and other biological materials."

"In this case, that's more of a curse than a blessing," Chavez said. "It's a hotel room. Most of what was obtained will be from hotel staff, the victim, and other guests. Accounting for and excluding all the knowns will take weeks or even months."

"We are fairly certain the killer wore gloves," Tammy said. "After all, he was smart enough to cover his feet, and there's this." She tapped and brought up a close-up image of blood smudges under the victim's arms. "We think these were made by the killer's hands when he manipulated the body." She drew an arrow on the screen pointing to a spot on one of the victim's biceps. "See this wide swoosh shape? We see this when rubber or latex cleaning gloves are used."

Parker turned to Chavez. "Did any of the other guests hear or see anything?"

"Nothing. We talked to all the guests on the floor and those in the rooms below and above. No one heard or saw a thing."

"Do you have the security video files yet?"

"Got them an hour ago. Had to get a warrant first."

"Had no problem getting a judge to sign dat one," Higgs said. "This is how we are going to catch him. Da creep will be on the video in the right time window, and we'll track him down."

"I see," Parker said, considering Higgs for a moment. The detective's exaggerated Chicago accent and tough demeanor was beginning to get on Parker's nerves. It had been hours since he'd eaten. Low blood sugar and the pain in his leg were making it harder for him to hide his irritation. "So how, exactly, will you know him when you see him?"

Higgs snorted. "Dat's easy, Mind Hunter. He'll be the one carrying the sword."

Divine glared at Higgs, and the gruff detective seemed to whither under her intense stare. She looked back at Parker, and for a moment he thought he might wither a little, too.

"Why don't you tell us what you think, Dr. Reid? Michael said there was no one in the Bureau better at reading a crime scene than you. What kind of lunatic are we dealing with?"

In Parker's experience, killers who stalked and executed their victims were not insane—not in the way the law interpreted it, anyway. The courts defined insanity as not knowing right from wrong. Killers like the one who cut off Charles Tate's head knew what they were doing was wrong, otherwise they wouldn't go to such great lengths to avoid being caught. They were psychopaths, for sure; true monsters, but not lunatics.

He looked at Divine, who was still staring at him with her pupilless eyes, and ultimately decided not to correct her. "Our unsub," he began, "is a planner. He's very organized, and this is not the first time he's done this. He's good at it, and unless we catch him, he's going to do it again, and probably get even better at it."

"Now, dat's fricken insightful," Higgs quipped, prompting Divine to redirect her withering stare back at him.

"I get why you say he's a planner," Chavez said. "I mean, he would have to be to kill the way he did, but what makes you say this is not his first time?"

Parker poked at a spot on the carpet with his cane. It looked like a wad of ancient chewing gum.

"Agent?" Divine prompted. "How do you know the killer has done this before?"

Parker looked up and met her eyes. "Oh. Well, like I said, he's good at it, and we are investigating a very similar case in Nashville. Same ritualist M.O.."

"This creep cut someone else's head off in Nashville?" Higgs asked.

"Appears so," Parker said. Despite what he'd said to Becky this morning, he did not believe the murders were committed by multiple unsubs.

"Great," Divine said. "We have a serial killer who beheads his victims. The media is going to love that."

Parker nodded and told them what he knew about how Jyothi Reddy had been killed. When he finished, he shifted in his seat and rubbed his throbbing leg. "Mind if I walk around? I've been sitting all day, and my leg is killing me."

"Please," Divine said.

Parker levered himself out of his chair with his cane and hobbled to the windows that lined the opposite wall. He stared out at the tall tower of the Stratosphere Hotel rising above the northern end of the Strip.

"How else do the cases compare?" Divine asked.

Without turning around, Parker said, "Entry. Just like with Reddy, the killer gained access to the victim's room without forced entry. Which means he was let in or had a keycard. Right now, I'm leaning toward the keycard."

"Why is that?" Divine asked.

"Because I think the victim was sleeping when the killer entered the room."

"Why?" She pressed.

"Mostly because, as Tammy said, there was no fight. There's no evidence of a struggle. No one heard shouting or banging. There was no overturned furniture, no broken lamps. I think he came in and bound the victim without waking him. I think you will find he used duct tape. Then, based on the blood pattern and lack of spray, he positioned the victim so his head was extending over the bed and removed it with one clean, powerful cut." He turned back to face the room and glanced at Higgs. "Probably using a sharp sword or maybe an axe. Death was instant, and luckily for Mr. Tate, likely painless."

Tammy bobbed her unnaturally colored head. "We found evidence of adhesive consistent with duct tape on the victim's wrists, ankles, and face."

"The M.E. report said the same in the Nashville case," Parker said.

"Maybe Tate was drugged," Chavez said.

Parker leaned on his good leg and nodded. "I think he was, but not by the killer."

"By who, den?" Higgs said.

"Himself. There was a container of prescription sleeping pills in the bathroom. My guess is he popped a couple and was dead to the world—no pun intended—when the killer entered."

"Maybe there were two of them, Mind Hunter," Higgs said. "One held a gun on Tate while the other bound him."

Parker shrugged. "Possibly. It's another explanation for the lack of struggle, but I think our killer is on his own."

"Because?" Divine said.

"Mostly the trophy collection and the way the victims were posed. Both victims' bodies were kneeling with their heads in their hands, like they were offering them to the killer. It suggests the killer wanted it to be clear he dominated them. Feels too personal to be a hit."

"Seems like someone sending a fucking message to me," Higgs said. "Like something drug cartel killers would do. Probably took the fricken ears back to Mexico."

Parker shrugged again. "Could be. Though organized crime victims are usually other criminals. The woman in Nashville had no record. What about Tate?"

Chavez shook his head.

Parker turned his attention to Divine. "You wanted to know what I think."

She nodded.

"I don't think you will find this guy on video. I think he is well aware of his surroundings and is not likely to allow himself to be recorded in an elevator carrying a sword. There were security cameras all over the Nashville victim's apartment complex, and nothing unusual was found on the recordings."

"You can't get on or off the victim's floor without being seen by a camera," Chavez said.

"Not true."

"What do you fricken mean, 'not true?'" Higgs erupted.

"The hotel manager told me no cameras are installed in the service elevators. My bet is he used one of those."

Higgs and Chavez exchanged glances.

Parker's gaze returned to the window. "The good news is the manager told me all the keycard transactions are logged."

"We knew that and already have the files," Chavez said.

"Good. If we're lucky, they'll tell us exactly when the killer used the service elevators and when he let himself into Mr. Tate's room." Parker rubbed his thigh and winced. The pain had reached ten. He pulled out his vial of painkillers and popped two into his mouth, dry swallowing. "The logs will be good for nailing down the timeline, but unfortunately, they won't break the case."

"Is dat so? What will, Mind Hunter?"

"Victimology," Parker answered. "We need to know why the killer selected Jyothi Reddy in Nashville and Charles Tate here. On the surface, these two people appear to be totally unrelated. They were different races, genders, and were not close in age. They also lived on different sides of the country. Their selection appears random, but an organized killer like this one rarely chooses victims randomly. I believe they are connected somehow."

"How do you suggest we find that connection?" Divine asked.

"We dig into their lives. What do we already know about Mr. Tate?"

Chavez peered into his tablet. "Charles Nelson Tate," he read, "was a fifty-six-year-old African American male from Irvine, California who had no police record of any kind—not even a traffic ticket. He worked for a company called CyberTek where he was an electrical engineer."

"I've heard of that company," Jaden said. "They make suits and masks for the Metaverse. Explains the expensive gear in Tate's bag."

Chavez tapped on the screen and nodded. "Yeah. Says here they're growing fast." He grinned. "Might buy some of their stock for the retirement account."

Parker turned back to the table. "Am I the only one who doesn't know anything about this meta thing?"

Jaden shook his head and addressed the room. "I know it's hard to believe, but Dr. Reid has never been in the Metaverse."

"Really?" Tammy said, eyeing Parker through her red-rimmed glasses like he was an unusual piece of evidence she just uncovered. "We have one of the largest MetaSpots outside of China right here in Vegas." She turned back to Jaden. "You should take him."

Parker waved his hand to dismiss them and began to pace in front of the window. "Forget about the Metaverse. What else you got on Tate?"

Chavez continued, "He was married. I spoke to his wife this morning, obviously distraught. He had two grown male children, both in their early thirties and four grandchildren. He was here on business, attending a computer and electronics conference—one of the biggies. The conference ended yesterday. Charles should've been home last night."

Parker looked at Higgs. "Doesn't sound like a target for the drug cartels."

Chavez nodded. "Right. All indications are Charles was a good family man with no known enemies or illegal dealings. He was, as we say, a low crime-risk person. That's all I have so far."

Parker paused his pacing behind Chavez and glanced down at the tablet. "You got the medical examiner's report in there?"

Chavez laughed. "You kidding? We won't have that for a while."

"How long?"

Chavez sighed. "They are always backed up. Could take weeks."

Parker looked at Divine. "Any way to get some divine speed on that?"

The room grew still as if everyone had stopped breathing at once. She studied him for a moment, then flashed a bright smile, dissolving the tension. "I will make a call. What else?"

Parker leaned on his cane. "I need to eat and check in to my hotel." He looked down at Chavez. "Something connects these two victims. I know it." Parker retrieved one of his cards from his coat pocket and placed it on the table next to the tablet. "This has my secure email address. I would like to see the M.E. report when it comes in, and anything else you are willing to share from the case file." He smiled at Divine as he spoke.

"Roberto will get you everything," she said and stood. "If there's nothing else, I look forward to our next consultation." She looked over at Higgs. "Come see me after you escort the agents out."

After she left, Higgs said, "Looks like I have an ass whipping in my future. I hope you're wrong about the video, Mind Hunter, and we do see a guy with a sword. I really do."

"I hope you do, too, Higgs. I just wouldn't bet on it."

Chapter 10
The Hunter's Horn

THE SUN WAS SETTING, and the early stars had begun to shine when Darshana stepped through the gate. The road beneath the great arch ran east and west, and like all gate roads, its course was arrow straight, at least for the first quarter mile, or the last, depending on your perspective. She was facing the fire of the dying day. Behind her, the purple edge of night was advancing fast. There would be no moon, but if the sky remained clear, a million stars would hold back the darkness. Remaining to be seen was whether she should welcome the starlight or curse it. One never knew when entering the Land if they would be the hunter or the hunted.

The road west cut through an orchard of ancient bent and gnarled apple trees and ran straight into the safe town of Staghead. No fighting or killing was permitted within Staghead's borders or on the road between it and the gate. There were seven such safe towns in the Land, each under the control of one of the seven great wizards. It was the wizards who enforced the no-killing rule. Some were more diligent than others. Staghead was controlled by a wizard named Em, and Em was exceptionally diligent.

Traffic on the road was heavy tonight. She passed players of just about every race and experience level. Some were headed back toward the gate, but most were making their way to town.

A group of five *càiniǎo* warrior types had encircled a pair of *càiniǎo* elves. A few of the warriors had their swords drawn and appeared ready to pounce. No doubt they were looking to pick up some easy points and whatever valuables they could rob from the over-matched pair. In the wild, the elves wouldn't stand a chance. They would be killed and forced to start over as if they'd never been in the Land before, a process known as respawning.

"Yo. Morons," Darshana called as she approached the group. "You're going to regret it if you kill those elves."

"Mind your business or you'll be next," one of the taller warriors shouted back.

She laughed at the bravado. She was a level fifty ranger. If it wasn't for the no-killing rule and the certainty of death for breaking it, she would put a bolt from her crossbow in between each of their eyes before they realized she'd drawn it from her belt. It would be a nice test of the new CCP Shea had installed in the rig before Darshana came through the gate.

"You're in a safe zone."

"Come a little closer, elf-bitch, and we'll show you just how safe this zone is," another warrior yelled, prompting laughter from the rest.

"Suit yourselves," she said and raised her hands to show she was out of the fight. "Hack away and give my regards to Em when he comes and FODs you."

"What's a FOD?" the tall warrior asked as she passed.

"Look it up, newbie, while you still can."

All wizards had the power to incinerate a player on the spot by just pointing and uttering words known only to them. This power was called the Finger of Death. Players just referred to it as FOD.

Wizards were the Land's equivalent of gods. They could not be killed, and they could do anything to any player, no matter what level that player was. They dealt out summary justice using their FODs and from time to time, they screwed with players just to test them.

Over the years, Darshana had experienced more than her share of twisted wizard humor and testing. She'd been teleported into the midst of battles, deposited in dragon's lairs, and even imprisoned in a dungeon where she had to solve puzzles to win her freedom. If she'd learned anything from her ordeals, it was as Tolkien might say if he'd written *The Hobbit* today, wizards, even virtual reality ones, were subtle and quick to anger. They weren't to be trifled with. Especially not by advanced players who had something to lose.

Death in the Land was nothing for players like those *càiniǎo* warriors on the road. It was part of learning the game.

Darshana herself had died dozens of times at lower levels. T-shirts emblazoned with the game's marketing line summed it up: *You haven't lived until you've died in the Land of Might and Magic.* But, at higher levels, death was more impactful and could be traumatic. The Verse was full of tales of advanced players taking their real lives after losing their LMM characters.

On the other side of the orchard, small mud-brick huts with thatched roofs and brightly colored doors began to appear on either side of the road. Flickering yellow light shone through some of their windows, giving them a warm, homey look, although it was unlikely anything wholesome was going on inside. The huts were not just pleasant computer-generated scenery. Players leased them from Em for privacy and storage. They weren't cheap. Most players couldn't afford them, but the ones who could had a place to satisfy their prurient desires and horde treasure.

Shea could afford a hut, but she never considered leasing one. She didn't come to the Land looking for fantasy sex. She didn't need the storage either. Darshana carried all her belongings on her back, and Shea saw no point in hanging on to treasure. She converted whatever Darshana collected to coin as fast as she could and exchanged that on the outside for dollars. Like her sex, she preferred her money real.

The huts gave way to more substantial buildings. Many had signs advertising everything from weapons to magic spells. A few offered smith services that fabricated things like Darshana's spyglass. Others advertised quest and training guides. These were her competition, and most were disreputable, offering little more than what could be gleaned from the free training SIMs available throughout the Verse.

Darshana shook her head as she passed by one sign that proclaimed: *Level-up in an hour or your money back.* "Scammers."

Beyond the shops stood a large stone and wooden structure with a green placard swaying above its doorway. The sign, illuminated by a pair of lanterns, identified the structure as an inn. It bore no words, just pictures of a beer stein and a fox hunter's bugle painted in gold.

Dozens of players milled about outside. Most were gathered in small groups of two or three. A few single players wandered about and appeared to be avoiding the others. Their uncertain movements and timid behavior betrayed their fear over leaving the inn's grounds. The fear was justified. The Hunter's Horn marked the extreme western boundary of Em's safe passage mandate. One step farther in any direction other than back toward the gate and the novice players were free game. The Land could be brutal.

Falin had said to meet him at ten. She tapped the side of her head and a window opened in the simulation displaying the system clock. She'd come early. The dwarf was up to something, and even though there was no risk of ambush, she wasn't about to walk into a situation without reconnaissance. She tapped away the window and headed for the entrance.

So many players were coming and going that the inn's door had been propped open to ease passage. She made her way through the crowd. Experienced players cleared a path for her. Character levels were easy to discern if you knew what to look for. All characters had a faint aura that appeared around them when they moved, just a barely perceptible shimmer. Darshana's was red. It said, 'Fuck with me, and I will kill you.'

She made her way inside the inn's large common room. Lanterns suspended from rafters cast a yellow glow upon dozens of tables surrounded by players as diverse in level and description as those on the road. They were all hunched close together and talking loudly to be heard over the hum of a hundred competing voices.

Darshana moved between the tables. Conversations would get low when she neared, but the caution was unwarranted. She was not interested in their plans and schemes. She was only interested in finding one obnoxious, yellow-bearded dwarf.

A thorough search of the room yielded no sign of Falin. Darshana found a small niche away from the light where she could watch the door without being noticed and waited for the dwarf to arrive. Twenty minutes later, she saw him moving through the crowd. He looked about the same as the last time she saw him before he lost his head. Some players made changes when they respawned, subscribing to the new life/new look motto. Falin had not.

Just as before, he was taller than most dwarfs. She guessed he stood almost five feet. His unusual height and yellow beard made him easy to spot, which was fortunate because nothing else distinguished him from the other *càiniǎo* dwarfs. They were all dressed and equipped about the same, as if wearing some kind of dwarfish uniform.

Like the other dwarfs, Falin wore a coat of heavy iron-ring mail draped over a green linen tunic and gray wool trousers stuffed into enormous black boots. A wide belt was cinched tightly around his prodigious midsection and hanging from it was a short sword in a leather sheath and a pouch similar to the one Darshana used to hold her magic. As dwarfs did not use magic, there was no telling what he kept in his. Clasped around his neck was a hooded cloak that was the same reddish-brown color as the one he had worn on their last trek. On his back was a large treasure-hunter pack, a small round oak shield, and a double-headed battleax she knew he did not know how to wield.

The dwarf bounded her way, pushing his way through the other players. Just as he was about to stride by, Darshana stuck out her foot and tripped him. He toppled over like a felled tree and hit the floor face-first with a crash. The speed of his fall and the absence of any attempt to prevent it told her much about his cyber-presence, as did the way he popped back up on his feet.

"What happened?" he said to no one in particular.

The crowd by the door laughed and someone shouted, "Did you trip over that pretty yeller beard?" That prompted another roar of laughter.

Darshana stepped out of the shadows and shoved him from behind. "Keep moving, Dwarf."

He spun to face her, fumbling to draw his sword. "Oh. It's you," he said.

She glanced at the weapon. "Put that back where it belongs before you get us both FODed and follow me." Darshana led him to a corner deep within the inn where she'd earlier spotted an empty table for two.

"Why did you trip me?" he said as they sat.

"I wanted to know something."

"What?"

"I wanted to know your setup. Now I do. You're a half-in."

"No, suh," he said, sounding more like the Boston adolescent she was sure he was than a dwarf from some far-off mine.

"You can't tell whether I am in a rig or not just by tripping me."

"It's the way you fell. All simulated. You didn't try to keep your balance or even put out your hands to break your fall."

"Ain't that a pissah. So what?"

"Half-ins can't fight. You need to get in a rig if you want to survive in here."

"You're full of shit. You didn't notice last time."

"Yes, I did, but I wasn't sure then. Now I am." Darshana leaned closer to him. "Why are we here, and how do you know my real name?"

"I have a business proposal."

She thought about her schedule. It was full for the next several weeks. "I got treks planned for months, so I'm not sure when I can fit you in."

The dwarf shook his head. "I'm not talking about training." He removed a rolled-up paper from his pack and handed it to her.

Darshana unfurled enough of it to read the words *Notice of Quest* printed in flowing red script, then glared at him. "You've got to be kidding. You brought me here for a quest? I don't do this stuff anymore." She handed the paper back to him. "This is not a game for me. I'm in here to make money."

Falin unrolled the quest notice and held it up for her to read. "So am I. This is no quest for points or treasure, although I'm counting on there being plenty of both. This is a bounty hunt. Look at the picture. Recognize him?"

In the middle of the notice was a picture of the gray half-man, half-troll that had killed the previous version of Falin and chased Darshana through the Jade Gate. Below the picture were the words: *The player who brings this creature's head to my door will receive 10,000 coin and a resurrection spell.* It was signed with a single glowing red elvish rune.

"Táma," Darshana whispered then ripped the paper out of Falin's hands. She balled it up as she glanced around to see if anyone was watching. The table nearest to them was full of midlevel players who appeared too caught up in their own dealings to take note of the fifty-level ranger and novice dwarf beside them.

Darshana tossed the crumpled paper at him. "If this is real, you are in way over your head."

He smoothed the paper out as best he could and rolled it back up. "Oh, it's real."

"Where did you get it? These things are posted in taverns that don't allow *càiniǎo*." She said the last word with as much contempt as she could.

"I have my ways, Shea."

"Whoa." Darshana grabbed his beard and pulled his head toward her. "Do not use that name in here. And how the hell do you know it anyway?"

"You have your talents, and I have mine."

Releasing him, she said, "Oh crap, you're a goddamn hacker, aren't you?" Darshana stood up. "We're done."

"Wait, wait," he said motioning for her to sit back down. "10,000 coin. Think about it. That's... that's... a million dollars. A million dollars to kill one player, and a wicked fuck of a player at that. You know you want to kill him. I mean, he really embarrassed your ass last time. Now, didn't he?"

The player behind Falin was probably smirking, and his headgear cameras were not picking up the facial expression. No rig, cheap gear, and a criminal. She shouldn't be wasting her time with this noob, but he had a point.

Darshana dropped back into her chair and leaned over the table. "Look, I don't know who you really are, but if you are hacking LMM, they are going to catch you and ban you from the Verse or maybe even put you in jail. The company that owns this," she spread her arms to indicate the surroundings, "doesn't mess around. I know people who've been banned, and I don't want to be one of them. So, if that's what you're up to, I want nothing to do with it. Not even for a million dollars."

This time his gear picked up his grin. "No one is getting banned. I'm wicked good at what I do. Trust me."

"Trust you? I don't know you."

"We'll get to know each other on the quest."

"The quest? Did you notice who signed that bulletin?"

"Yeah. Táma. So what?"

Darshana brought her hand up and covered his mouth. "Shh, moron. You have to be careful with that name."

He pushed her hand away. "Geez. A little paranoid, aren't we? She's just a pretend wizard in a game."

She was surprised he knew Táma was a woman. Most

noobs assumed all wizards were men, but he obviously didn't know her reputation for FODing.

"Says the pretend dwarf who wants to go on a pretend quest."

"Like you, I don't give a shit about the quest. I want the money."

Darshana looked around again to make sure they had not drawn the attention of the players at the nearby table then lowered her voice to a whisper. "Wizards get alerts when their names are used, especially when they are spoken loudly. Just saying their names can get their attention. And you don't want this wizard's attention. Do you even know what her name means?"

The dwarf's yellow beard swayed as he shook his head.

"Darkness. That should tell you all you need to know. She's what puts the evil in the whole 'good versus evil' theme of the Land. She's the one you align with if you chose the dark side in your character profile. I would've thought that gray monster would have been one of hers."

"I guess he pissed her off."

"Well, that's the peculiar thing, ain't it? There's something very wrong with a wizard offering a bounty on a player's head, especially one this substantial. If she wants this player dead, why doesn't she just summon him and FOD him? That's what wizards do." She stood up again. "I'm not interested."

"Come on. Don't be a coward."

Ignoring the taunt, Darshana turned and made her way through the crowd and out of the inn. She had taken a few steps on the road back toward the gate when she realized he was following her.

"Go away. I told you I'm not interested."

Before Falin could respond, a bent figure in a filthy blue robe stepped in front of them. His face was concealed by a hood and pale fingers clutched a gnarled walking stick that may have been hewn from one of the ancient apple trees. When he moved, a slight shimmer of gold rippled through the folds of his robe.

"Good evening, Darshana," the figure croaked. "Leaving so soon?"

She knew him before he dropped his hood, revealing the deep-set blue eyes and long white hair that seemed to glow in contrast to his clean-shaven ashen face. She dropped to one knee and glanced at the dwarf mouthing, "Kneel."

"Em, what a pleasant surprise."

The wizard chuckled. "I bet."

"Who's the old beggar?" Falin asked before he disappeared in a flash of lightning and a deafening thunder clap.

She suppressed a smile as she considered Falin's smoldering remains.

"That one needs to learn some manners," Em rasped.

"Yes. He does."

"I trust you will teach him?"

"I don't intend to see him again."

"Unfortunately for you, Darshana, I think he will be stuck to you like gum on your shoe."

"Why is that?"

The wizard studied her for a moment. "Stand up. I'll accompany you on your walk back to the gate. At least for part of the way." He took her arm, and they strolled past the shops. There were fewer players on the road now, and the ones that were had the good sense to give them a wide berth.

"The dwarf has tripped over something, and I'm not talking about your leg."

Shit. The bastards knew everything. "I told him I wanted nothing to do with the quest."

"Yes, probably a wise move. But here's the thing: I want you to have something to do with it."

Darshana stopped in her tracks, holding the wizard back. "Why?"

Em said nothing for a moment. He was shorter than she was, and she looked down into unblinking, crystalline blue eyes that peered up at her from within the wells of their sockets. They flashed the same golden light that enveloped him when he moved. "We have a problem, my dear, one that is beyond the seven to solve."

His words stunned her. "The Gray Warrior is a problem for the seven?"

"Yes. We don't know how, but he's invisible to us."

"What does that mean?"

"We can't locate him in the Land. As you know, dear, Wizards can track and watch from afar any player in the Land, but not this one."

"How can that be?"

Em shrugged. "He's exploiting some quirk in the simulation."

"Quirk?"

"Bug."

Bug? "Does this mean the Game Ops can't locate him either?" The Game Ops were employees of the company who operated and managed the simulation. No player, at least none Darshana knew, had ever spoken to a Game Op, but everyone knew they were there watching.

Em smiled again. "You presume there's a difference."

Did he just confirm wizards worked for the game company? That very question had been debated in all the gaming forums since LMM went live and it still was. Evidence had been put forth to support both sides of the argument. She had always suspected they did. They were just too powerful to be players. Now, it seemed it was no longer speculation.

"Are you saying the people at Xperion can't locate him in the Land either?"

He smiled, and she took that as a yes.

"Oh, that doesn't sound good."

"No, my dear. It's not. Especially in this case. There's something very wrong about this character."

"Yeah, he appears to be more powerful than you wizards."

Em's eyes flashed again. "I said invisible, not more powerful." He wiggled a gnarled finger. "He can be FODed, just like anyone else."

"Okay. Why haven't you FODed him then?" she asked.

The wizard's smile broadened, revealing gleaming white pointed teeth. He looked like a vampire. "Like I said, we can't find him."

"Ten thousand is a lot of coin. With a bounty like that, it won't take long before someone does."

Em gave a dry chuckle. "Unfortunately, many already have. He's taken out dozens and more than a few level fifties. His actions are becoming quite—umm—disruptive."

"Huh. Is that so?" she mused, pondering her own close call. "What do you want me to do?"

"Track him," Em said.

"Then what? If he's killing other level fifties, what makes you think I'll fare any better?"

Em made the dry chuckle again. "You're Darshana."

"Yeah," she snorted, "and I want to keep being Darshana."

"Just track him," Em repeated. "Once you get close, we'll do the rest."

"The quest notice said the bounty is for killing him. Do I still get the ten thousand if I only track him?"

Em shrugged. "That would be up to Táma."

"Screw that," she quipped before she could catch herself. Emboldened by not being FODed, she asked, "What's in it for me?"

The wizard's vampire-smile softened. "My gratitude, and all the protection that comes with it."

She peered down at the wizard. What choice did she have? Help Em and trust he'd reciprocate, or decline and incur his wrath? *No choice.* She sighed. "How will you know when I find him?"

The wizard winked at her. "I always have my eye on the top players," he said. "But just in case..." He untangled himself from her arm and held out an open hand. A silver spell orb sparkled in his palm. "Use this when you get close to him."

Darshana took the orb and studied it. An unfamiliar gold rune glittered on its surface. "I don't recognize this one."

"*Arcesse*," he said. "It means summon."

"I can summon you with this spell?"

"You can summon anyone with it," he said. Then added, "Except our gray warrior."

"Because you can't see him?" she said.

"Yes. In order to summon a player, you need to know their unique player ID, and we don't know the Gray Warrior's."

"What is yours?"

He smiled. "Em the Magnificent, of course."

"What happens if you're not in the Land when I cast it?"

"I'll know."

Darshana tucked the orb into her spell pouch.

He took a step back from her and raised his stick. "We'll talk again soon." Then he disappeared in a golden flash.

Chapter 11
What a Hacker Knows

SHEA TUGGED AT HER cybermask. Sweat had seeped between the padding and the skin on her forehead and cheeks, forming a vacuum seal. It felt like the mask was holding on to her, almost as if it didn't want to let go. An image of the parasitic face-hugging alien from the old-time science fiction movie she'd watched the night before flashed in her mind. The seal broke, and the mask came free with a suction cup pop. She exhaled a relieved sigh, glad to be free of the creature before it had a chance to plant its eggs.

Trinity meowed somewhere nearby, invisible in the darkness of the bay beyond the feint blue glow of the rig's LEDs. Shea made a psp-psp sound, and the cat dropped from her hiding place, landing with a soft thud. Her motorboat purr announced her approach as she trotted across the floor and leapt into Shea's lap.

"Pretty girl," Shea cooed as she stroked Trinity's fur.

The rig's blue light reflected off the cat's glossy coat like a character aura in the game, and for an instant, Shea thought she might still be in the Land. "Snap out of it," she said to herself as her hands continued to glide over Trinity's back. Maybe Tony was right. Maybe she was spending too much time in the Verse.

Shea unbuckled the harness and carried Trinity and her headgear to the makeshift desk where her open laptop sat. A message from Falin with the subject line WTF was waiting for her in her personal inbox.

She glanced at Trinity. "'WTF,' indeed."

The cat meowed and rubbed itself against the laptop screen.

The body of the message contained three words, *Can we talk?* and a link to a private chat session.

"How did I get myself into this, Trin?" she said as she considered the dwarf's request. It was as Em had said, Falin was like gum on her shoe, and she did not know how to scrape him off.

She clicked on the link and opened the thread. It was just her in the session for a few seconds, then a chime sounded, and a user identified only as Dwarf joined.

Falin? she typed.

What the hell happened in the game? One minute we're standing outside that inn with that old man, and the next I got red-screened.

Red-screen is what players called what they saw when their characters died. It had been over two years since Shea had seen one.

Em FODed you to teach you some manners.

Dick.

She laughed and typed, *It could've been worse.*

How?

He could've FODed me too.

Falin responded with *LOL.* Then he added, *Did he know about the bounty?*

Yes. He said the Gray Warrior is a problem for the wizards. He said they cannot see him.

I know.

The answer caught her off guard, and she banged out a response, *How do you know that?*

He didn't reply. She typed, *How deep are you into the LMM system?*

Still no response. Shea was about to disconnect when Falin's tardy reply popped up, *Pretty deep.*

Shea knew nothing about the person behind the dwarf. Wizards had been known to impersonate lower-level players from time to time when it suited their purpose. Could Falin be a wizard pretending to be a player? She typed, *Are you a wizard?*

The response came back instantly, *Fuck no.*

Then how do you know the wizards can't see him?

This time there was another long pause. *Because I can't see him either.* Then, before she could reply, a new line popped up. *And I can see everybody.*

That rocked her back. *How?*

Just have to know how to ask.

Ask who?

The LMM system. I can access the service programs used to create the game simulation. I haven't mapped all the services yet, but I know the ones that keep track of player positions and profiles. That's how I know who you are.

Trinity meowed and stepped on the laptop's keyboard. Her paws typed out nonsense before Shea could shoo her away.

Falin replied with a long series of question marks.

Sorry, cat, she typed, then added: *Is that how you learned about the bounty?*

No. Got that off a dark web game hack site. You must know about those.

Shea scowled and typed. *Cheaters use them.*

Whatever.

She was still skeptical. *How long have you been hacking the LMM system?*

Why do you want to know?

Because I'm wondering why you don't just make yourself a level fifty and go after the Gray Warrior yourself. Why do you need me?

The cursor pulsed in the message window, ticking off the seconds with no response. She was about to resend the message when the reply came, *I can pull information out of the system. Making changes is harder and riskier. Impossible to do without leaving a trail. I asked around. Besides the wizards, no one knows the Land better than you.*

Shea thought about his response and typed, *If you can't locate him with your hacks, why do I need you?*

He replied with a smiley face emoji and then sent another link.

What's this?

It's why you need me. Click on it.

Clicking on a strange link made her squirm. She held her breath and clicked the link and a browser window opened showing a map of the Land. Green dots covered the image along with a smaller number of red dots. She'd consulted maps like this when planning expeditions and recognized the green dots right away. They marked the 217 known gates. When she moved her mouse over a green dot, a fact card window opened that showed the gate's name, a picture, and basic information that included the terrain, weather, and nearby towns. Most of what displayed was what you'd expect to find at a travel site for real-world locations, but these fact cards also included information about threats from local tribes and known monsters and survival probability percentage by character type and level.

Shea typed. *You can find this map on the LMM gamer's tips web page.*

Look at the red dots, he replied.

The red dots were clustered around many of the green dots. In some cases, the green and red dots overlaid each other and Shea had to zoom into the map to separate them. When she placed her mouse over a red dot, another fact card window popped up. This one contained a single table listing Expire Dates, Player IDs, Character Names, and an empty column titled KEID.

Who are these players?

Select the red dot on Jade Mountain.

Shea did as he directed and brought up a table showing, Xu, Darian, Ava, and Falin. All showed the same Expire Date, the day the Gray Warrior had killed them, and all showed blank KEIDs.

She wrote the dwarf's unique player ID on a piece of scrap paper. She didn't know how to trace it to his real identity, but Tony knew someone who would. It wasn't fair Falin knew her real-world name, and she did not know his. Then she typed, *What is a KEID?*

Falin replied, *Kill Event ID.* Then, an instant later he sent another message, *0x1c4d33e6 is the KEID for when that fuck Em FODed me.*

Every kill in the game has an event ID?

Not just kills. Everything has an event ID. At least everything is supposed to.

Except the Gray Warrior's kills? She asked.

It's wicked FUBAR. The Gray Warrior has no events.

FUBAR?

Fucked Up Beyond All Recognition.

Shea smiled and typed, *LOL.* Then she added, *This must be the bug EM told me about.*

Falin's response came back like an excited shout. *DID HE SAY ANYTHING ELSE?*

She typed, *Not really,* and stared at the screen. *Just they can't see him.* Trinity jumped down into her lap, and she stroked the cat's fur while she considered Falin's data. So many kills. After a moment, she poured Trinity on to the floor and tapped out, *Can you show the times of the kills?*

Five minutes, came the reply.

Trinity meowed and Shea said, "I'm hungry, too." She went to the kitchen and scooped some food into Trinity's bowl. Grabbing a yogurt for herself, she returned to her laptop and found a one-word message waiting for her. *Refresh.*

Shea refreshed her browser and hovered over the red dot marking where she'd lost the party. Falin had added Expire Time to the table. Xu and Ava had both been killed at 15:06, Darian two minutes later, and Falin eight minutes after Darian. Something didn't look right. She typed, *The times are wrong. He attacked our group in the morning, but all the expire times show in the afternoon.*

He replied, *Players from all over the world in the SIM. All the times are set to the same time zone.* Then he sent another message. *GMT. Subtract 5 hours.*

Shea cursed herself for not knowing that and began hovering over other red dots. She noticed kills on weekdays happened at night, many after midnight. Weekend kills showed no pattern. They occurred at every hour. This wasn't much of a surprise. It appeared, like Shea, the Gray Warrior had a day job. It also showed Shea, and the monster tended to be in the Land during the same time periods which was something.

This is all very interesting, but how does it help us find him?

I have my programs set up to alert me when and where he kills.

How do you do that if you can't see him?

I can see that I can't see him. Get it?

Shea thought about it for a moment. *You look for players who've been killed without KEIDS?*

Exactly. The gray fucker has a shadow...

I get it. So, what happens the next time you see his shadow?

I message you, and we go get him.

Shea didn't like the "we" part. Based on her quick survey of the expire times, chances were good she would be in the Land when the next kill occurred. If she were near a gate, she could get to the kill area fast, but not if she had to wait for Falin. Besides, at his level, the dwarf wouldn't be any help in a fight.

Can you have it alert me too?

Once again, Falin's reply took several contemplative seconds. *I want to be there to claim my half of the bounty.*

She smiled. *Don't worry. I will give you your share.*

I want to be there.

The dwarf was definitely stuck to her shoe. She sighed and typed, *We need to get you leveled up, then.*

Chapter 12
Another One

BOOM, BOOM, BOOM. **T**HE shots reverberated off the concrete floors and steel piers like M-80 fire-crackers detonated inside a steel drum. The gun fell from his blood-slick hand with a clang. "Carrie!" Parker screamed as he dragged himself to her crumpled body and pulled her into his lap. She stared up at him. He could see the confusion and pain in her eyes.

"What happened?" she'd asked. Parker would never know if she heard his answer. Those were her last words. Not *I'm hurt*, not *help me*, or *I love you*, but *what happened?*

It had been months since their last date night. They had driven into Alexandria and enjoyed dinner at a seafood place overlooking the river, then they'd gone to the evening show at the small community theater she'd adored. He'd surprised her with tickets, something special to make up for the long gap in their outings. Not entirely his fault—they both had demanding careers—but his had been the greater burden on their marriage. He saw things that took time for him to process, and that made him distant. Not that night, though. She had all his attention that night. They had laughed at dinner and enjoyed each other's company like they hadn't in years. Arm in arm, they had walked from the parking garage elevator toward the car. She had been going on about how wonderful the show was, and he was so captivated by her enthusiasm and the renewed sparkle in her eyes that he'd not seen the man with the gun until it was too late.

Parker had been working with the New Jersey State Police and the Ocean County Sheriff's Department to develop a profile for a killer they'd dubbed the Jersey Shore Devil. The Devil had committed a series of rapes and murders in the seaside communities along the Garden State Parkway from Tom's River all the way down to Cape May. Eight women had been raped and strangled over the course of three years. A reporter with the Atlantic City Fox affiliate had learned about Parker's involvement and ran a series of pieces on the evening news titled: *The FBI's Next Generation Mind Hunter's Search for the Jersey Shore Devil.* The reporter had interviewed Parker twice. The Devil had watched.

Boom. The Devil's first shot had gone low and struck Parker in his left leg. The massive .44 caliber slug had disintegrated his femur, a good portion of his thigh muscle, and shredded his femoral artery. Boom. The second shot had been higher, better aimed. It struck Parker in the chest as he was falling, just missing his heart. It passed through his left lung, destroying a substantial portion of the superior lobe, and after exiting out his back, struck Carrie in her neck. Boom. The third shot had taken out his left kidney, ricocheted off ribs nine and ten, then, like shot two, exited out his back. This one slammed into Carrie's lower abdomen, severed her aorta, and lodged in her spine. It was never clear which one killed her. The M.E. indicated blood loss from the destruction of her external jugular was as likely a cause as the catastrophic aorta bleed.

Instinct, training, anger, fear, all of it came together when Parker hit the pavement. He'd drawn his weapon and brought it up just as the Devil, who would later be identified as Lawrence Bader, an out-of-work engineer, stepped forward to deliver a final kill shot.

Knock, knock, knock. Disoriented, Parker woke from the nightmare of a memory. The room was dark, but bright light seeped in around the drawn blackout curtains. His phone buzzed somewhere. It took him a moment to realize someone was pounding on the hotel room door. A muffled "Doctor Reid, are you okay in there?" came from the hall. He slid off the bed, ignoring the familiar agony in his leg and limped to the door. The peephole showed a fisheye distorted view of Jaden Breaux's face staring back at him.

Parker cracked open the door and squinted into the hallway light. "What?"

"Sorry, sir. Are you okay?"

"Of course, I'm okay. Why wouldn't I be?"

"Ms. Fulbright has been trying to reach you. She thought

you might be having some kind of emergency."

Parker's mouth was drier than drought-depleted Lake Mead. He pulled opened the door and went in search of something to drink. "Come in," he croaked as he struggled to remove the plastic wrap from a paper cup.

Jaden stepped in and flipped on the lights.

Still asleep, the tiny muscles in Parker's pupils reacted too slowly to the brightness, causing an explosion of pain. He took the cup into the bathroom and filled it from the faucet, noting the red plastic sign under the mirror reminding guests water usage was metered and they would be billed a surcharge for usage over the daily limit. Beneath the warning was the line: *We encourage showering together.*

Parker popped two painkillers and brushed his teeth. Jaden stood just outside the bathroom door, looking uncomfortable. The young agent stared at him.

"What are you looking at, Breaux? You never seen another man in boxer shorts before?" Parker knew damn well the agent's stares had nothing to do with his scant attire. The spider webs of purple scars on his back, left thigh, lower abdomen, and chest drew the eyes of all who saw them; even experienced medical personnel gawked.

"I'm sorry, sir." Jaden pointed at the room door. "It looks like everything is okay. I'm leaving now."

"Wait," Parker said. "Did Becky say why she was looking for me?"

Jaden shook his head. "No. She just said she'd tried to call you several times. I tried, too."

Parker limped past the uncomfortable agent and retrieved his phone. It showed the missed calls along with a string of texts from Becky. He scrolled through them. The first few were from yesterday afternoon and were just requests for status. *Did you arrive at Vegas okay? Did the field office send an agent to pick you up? Can I get an update?* Several more had come in that morning. The first was another appeal for status. *Are you alive?* The next was more interesting. *We got another one, call ASAP.* The last two were expressions of frustration. *I'm thinking you're dead,* and *I'm sending an agent to collect your body.*

He selected the call option from the last message. She picked it up on the first ring and wasted no time with hellos.

"Where the hell have you been?"

"Sleeping. Jeezus, Becky. Tell me about this other one."

Jaden went to leave, and Parker motioned for him to stay.

"Clearwater, Florida. Another woman," she said.

"So soon."

"Here's the thing. It happened five weeks ago."

Parker looked around for his cane and pantomimed using it to Jaden. The agent began to search for it.

"Five weeks?"

"Appears to have been a mix-up between the Clearwater police and the Pinellas County sheriff. It just hit ViCAP yesterday. Methods appear to be the same. A twenty-three-year-old White woman named Abby Loveridge was beheaded in her apartment. The killer took her ears."

Parker steadied himself against the wall, taking the weight off his bad leg, and thought about the timeline. "Two weeks," he whispered.

"What did you say," she said.

"Five weeks places her killing approximately two weeks before the Nashville victim."

Jaden handed Parker his cane and mouthed, "Can I go?"

Parker shook his head and used the cane to hobble over to the window. He pushed aside the heavy curtains and stared down on the hotel's swimming pool. From his nineteenth-floor vantage point, the 200,000-gallon artificial lagoon looked like a puddle teaming with insects. Last night he'd paid five dollars extra for ice in his scotch. The hotel probably spent more than his salary each summer replacing the water lost to the desiccated Mojave air.

"Okay. Send me the M.E. reports and crime scene analysis."

"Already in your inbox, Sleeping Beauty."

Parker glanced at Jaden. "I guess that makes Breaux my prince."

Jaden gave him a quizzical expression.

She laughed. "How's the hotel? Nice, right? Told you I'd take care of you."

"Yeah. I'm thinking about going to the pool and showing off my scars. What do you think? Maybe I could charge for closer looks."

"You *should* go take a swim. Fuck the scars."

He frowned. "Later."

"Wait. Parker, what's your plan?"

"Breakfast," he said, and pressed the disconnect button.

He brought up her email and scanned the M.E. report. The woman had died the same as Jyothi and Charles, an edged instrument had separated her head from her body at cervical vertebrae C3. Death was instant. Time of death was listed as sometime between 12:30 a.m. and 1:30 a.m., also consistent with the other attacks. He took a quick glance at the toxicology report and turned from the window to find Jaden staring at him.

"You're starting to creep me out, Breaux."

"I'm sorry, sir. Can I go now?"

"Did you hear from Chavez on the autopsy?"

Jaden nodded. "Yes. They were able to bump it up." He took out his phone and tapped on it. After a few seconds, he said, "Chavez says they are just finishing up now. Preliminary report will be available Monday." He smiled at the screen. "He says they know the cause of death."

"No shit." Parker said. "Ask him about toxicology results."

Jaden tapped and waited. "Toxicology is going to take about two weeks, and that's with the rush." He smiled at the phone again. "Chavez says no guy with a sword on the video."

"No surprise there. What time is it?"

"A little after one."

Parker pushed his fingers through his graying hair. "I need breakfast. Where can we go?"

"We, sir?" The agent looked deflated.

"Stop calling me that. Parker or Reid. Take your pick, and no more doctor either. I am not a physician, and this is not the academy."

"Yes, sir. I mean, okay, Mr. Reid."

"Christ. That's even worse. Give me twenty minutes to get dressed. Think of some place where we can get eggs."

Chapter 13
Scrambled

THE ALL-DAY BREAKFAST restaurant was in a small strip mall in a residential part of Las Vegas that tourists and gamblers probably didn't know existed. Parker and Jaden sat in a booth by a window with a view of the Spring Mountains rising above the sun-faded marquee of a sporting goods store. It was a Saturday afternoon, in the slow hours between lunch and dinner, and other than a bored waitress and a table of four older women who were all wearing golf attire and oversized sun visors, they had the place to themselves.

"Scrambled eggs. That's all you eat?" Jaden asked.

Parker took a sip from his cooling tea and made a face at its bitterness. He dumped in another packet of sugar and stared at the younger man. "Let's just say the changes in my plumbing forced me to narrow my diet choices considerably."

Jaden pushed aside the remains of his salad. "That's got to suck."

Parker nodded at the agent's bowl. "What about you? You don't get muscles like yours by eating lettuce."

"All kinds of plant-based proteins available. And there are always smoothies."

"Plant-based proteins? Smoothies? With that name and Louisiana accent you try so hard to hide, I would have taken you for a crayfish and gumbo man."

A grin split Jaden's face. "It's 'crawfish,' and I do make exceptions when I go back to Mawmaw's."

"You get back down there often?"

"A few times a year. Holidays and occasions."

"LSU Tigers fan?"

"Don't pay much attention."

Parker leaned against the booth cushion and spread his arms across the back rest. "Let me guess, you went to Tulane?"

"I did."

"That explains the disinterest in football."

Jaden laughed. "That's where I went to law school."

"What about your undergrad?"

"Stanford. History and Philosophy."

"Ah. California. That explains the diet."

Jaden laughed again. "What about you?"

"I'm a Buckeye, through and through. I majored in football, but the NFL wasn't interested so I stuck around for a law degree."

"How did you end up with a PhD in psychology?"

"I'm good at analyzing people, figuring out what makes them tick. When I joined Behavioral Analysis, the Bureau sent me to a program at George Mason University. I'd still be making student loan payments if I had done that on my own." He ate a forkful of eggs. "What about you, young man? What led you to the FBI?"

"Daddy's a Deputy Chief of the New Orleans Police and Mama's an assistant DA for Orleans Parish. A career in law enforcement was preordained."

Parker grinned and studied him. "I guess that explains your acceptance into the academy right out of law school."

Jaden's expression flattened for a moment. Then the smile returned. "I spent a year clerking for Armando Ramirez when he sat on the Court of Appeals for the Fifth Circuit, before he became Justice Ramirez. My guess is a Supreme Court Justice's referral may have had some influence along with my perfect grades and charm, of course."

Parker laughed. "Touché, Breaux."

Jaden's expression turned serious. "I overheard some of your conversation with Ms. Fulbright. Is there another victim?"

Parker nodded and pulled up Becky's email on his phone. "A young White woman, Abby Loveridge. Just a kid actually. Lived in Clearwater, Florida. He killed her two weeks before he did Jyothi Reddy in Nashville."

"Two young women and an older man. All three different races and ethnic groups and killed in different cities." Jaden said.

"Very observant, Breaux. Maybe it was more than referrals and good looks that got you in."

Jaden ignored the jab. "You told Vegas PD victimology would be the key to catching this guy. There doesn't seem to be anything tying these three together, though."

"Reddy and Loveridge were both single women who lived by themselves in apartment buildings and worked as computer programmers. That seems like something, doesn't it?"

Jaden shrugged. "Tate wasn't a woman or single, and he wasn't a software developer."

"That's true, but he was alone in an apartment-like setting when he was attacked, and he worked with computers as well. His company makes those masks and suits for the Metaverse."

"CyberTek."

"That's it. There's a pattern forming, Breaux. All the victims were attacked in their sleep by someone who gained access to their apartments without attracting attention, and they were all technology professionals. I looked it up. Technology careers account for about eleven percent of the job market. If his victims were randomly selected from employed adults, we could expect a one in ten chance one of them would work in a technology field. The chances of all three being techies is one in a thousand. Seems very low."

"I agree. Too low to be random. Could it be related to where he hunts? I bet urban, middle-income populations have a higher percentage of technology workers."

"It would account for some increase in the odds," Parker agreed. "But not a hundred percent. I don't think it is where he hunts, but what he hunts."

Jaden took a sip from his water. "Three isn't much of a sample size. Could just be a fluke."

"I like the skepticism, but I'm thinking it's too much of a coincidence. Maybe our killer is hunting what he knows."

"You think he might be a technology worker?"

"Possibly, but like you said, the sample size is too small to infer anything from the data, and we really don't want a larger sample."

Jaden nodded. "True dat."

"Whoa, Breaux. Some of that Cajun just leaked out."

"It's been known to happen. What's the significance of the victims being in apartments instead of single-family homes?"

Parker spread his hands. "Maybe not significant, but unusual. How did he get in? People tend to be more diligent about locking apartment doors, and hotel rooms lock themselves. This guy got in to all the victim's locations without forced entry and without attracting attention. For Tate, I thought we might see something in the hotel access logs, but according to Chavez, they found no evidence of unusual keycard activity. The only card used to enter Tate's room the night he was murdered was his own, and his last entry was 8:27 p.m.. He was killed after midnight. How did the killer get in?"

"Followed him in?"

"Then waited for him to fall asleep before cutting off his head?"

"Maybe he was drugged. Maybe his sleeping pills were tampered with. I figured that's why you had me ask Chavez about the toxicology report."

Parker shook his head. "The M.E. reports for the other victims showed no indication they were drugged."

"Then why the interest in Tate's toxicology results?"

"Adderall."

Jaden's eyes widened. "Adderall?"

"Yeah. There were no sedatives in the women's systems, but both of them had traces of Adderall in their blood."

"Isn't Adderall the drug they give kids for attention deficit disorder?"

"It's a common focus enhancer. More than just kids take it. I'm sure if we went and tested the truck drivers at a truck stop we'd find a large percentage of them would test positive."

"Hmm. I don't remember Adderall being mentioned during the DEA seminars at the academy."

"I doubt it's high on the list for the DEA guys. They have bigger fish to fry than busting truck drivers."

"And technology workers, apparently," Jaden quipped.

"So how did he get in?"

Jaden shook his head. "Maybe Tate's hotel door didn't lock. You know, he didn't pull it shut all the way."

Parker shrugged. "I guess. What about the others?"

"People forget to lock doors all the time," Jaden said. He leaned back and his expression turned thoughtful. "Maybe the killer tampered with their locks ahead of time. Jammed the bolt or something and removed the blockage when he left. That could be what he did to Tate. Maybe taped the locking mechanism to prevent it from engaging."

Parker grunted and pushed his eggs around his plate with his fork. "I think that's a possibility. Might be part of his setup."

Jaden raised one of his eyebrows in a way that reminded Parker of an actor whose name he could not recall. "Setup? You think he stalks his victims before killing them?"

"Without a doubt. He knows they will be alone. Knows their sleeping patterns." Parker thought for a moment. "Maybe even knows they take sleeping pills. Has to know he can handle them before he attacks. Take Mr. Tate. He was an older guy, but he was not a small man. If he'd woken up while he was being bound, he could've given the killer a lot of trouble." Parker ate some more eggs. "The killer definitely gets to know them—or already knows them."

"That's what he must be doing between kills," Jaden said. "Learning how to get past their door locks and if they take sleeping pills."

Parker motioned for the waitress to bring the check. "Yeah, but two weeks is not much time to select and study a victim. Especially ones scattered across the country."

Jaden nodded.

"I think he knows who he is going to kill well in advance, maybe even has a list. The two weeks is the time he gives himself to make final preparations and get into position."

"So, did Higgs have it right? The killer is a hired assassin?"

Parker shook his head. "The victimology doesn't support it."

"So, what's next?"

"Back home tomorrow, but today I want to see that place the criminalist mentioned. Where they use the things Tate's company sells."

"You want me to take you to the MetaSpot?"

"Yeah, Breaux. If it's not too much trouble."

Jaden wiped his mouth with his napkin and frowned. "I can't think of anything I'd rather do on a Saturday."

Chapter 14
Meta Madness

THE LAS VEGAS METASPOT was located in a repurposed Walmart a few miles west of the strip. Parker stood at an observation window overlooking the cavernous interior. No longer brightly lit and filled with endless aisles of groceries and home goods, it was now a dark alien world bathed in ultraviolet-enhanced greens and blues and packed with rows of large circular flipping and rocking machines. With a mix of curiosity and revulsion, he watched the machines' masked occupants dressed like scuba divers, punch, kick, dance, and ungulate. It all seemed to him like some unworldly ballet where bodies and machines moved to music he could not hear.

Jaden had gone to the check-in desk where he waited with about a dozen others who had queued up to access the touch screens overseen by two employees dressed in bright yellow jumpsuits. Most of those in line appeared to be in their mid-twenties, but there were a few younger and some that appeared closer to Parker's age. Almost all of them had backpacks or bags slung over their shoulders that Parker assumed contained cybersuits and headgear like those they had found in Charles Tate's luggage.

Tired of waiting and getting sore from all the standing, Parker had made up his mind to hobble over to the desk and flash his Bureau credentials when Jaden approached with one of the yellow-suited employees in tow. The young person of indeterminate gender had short hair dyed fluorescent green that glowed under the black lights. A name tag on the baggy jumpsuit identified the employee as Chi Chi who preferred to be addressed as They or Them. The employee's uniform reminded Parker of the coveralls worn by the imprisoned serial killers he interviewed as part of his research.

Jaden introduced Chi Chi as the manager.

"Assistant manager," Chi Chi corrected with a nervous smile. Big, dark eyes rimmed with thick, black eyeliner appraised Parker. The eyes settled on Parker's cane. "We can still set you up in a rig if you want to try it."

"Pardon me?"

"The cane," Chi Chi said. "We can set you up so you can move in the rig even if you have a bad leg. We do it all the time for disabled people." Chi Chi pointed out the window at a row of the spinning machines with wheelchairs parked next to them. "See. None of those guests can use their legs in the Real-Real, but they're running and jumping in the Verse."

"Real-Real?"

"Junker slang for the real world," Jaden said.

Chi Chi smiled up at him. "That's right. Jaden here knows all about us junkers."

Parker grinned at Jaden, then eyed the assistant manager. "Chi Chi," he said putting an edge in his voice.

"Yeah?"

"Call me disabled again, and I will beat you with this cane."

Chi Chi put their hand on their chest. "Oh my. I meant nothing by it. Won't happen again. Jaden said you have some questions?"

Parker nodded toward the window. "I'd like to know what goes on in there. In the Verse as you call it."

"Oh, honey. Everything, anything goes on in there."

"Is it all games?"

"Lots of games, but lots of other things too." Chi Chi raised two razor-thin eyebrows, then nodded toward the window. "There's everything from fitness training to world tours going on in there and all kinds of funky stuff in between."

"I play soccer in the Verse," Jaden offered.

"Soccer?"

"Yeah. It's just like the real thing. We have leagues."

"Why not play the real thing then?"

"We're in a desert. It's 110 degrees. Besides, our league has teams from all over the world. It's a lot of fun. You should try it. Maybe you could play football again."

Before Parker could reply, Chi Chi motioned for them to follow. "Come on. We'll go to the Ready-Room where we can watch some of the action." Casting a devilish look back at Parker, Chi Chi said, "Don't worry, honey; we don't show the funky stuff."

They followed Chi Chi to a large room that resembled an airport gate lounge except the furniture appeared more comfortable and there was a bar. About half the seats were occupied by cyber-suited customers who all looked like they were waiting for a flight. Floor-to-ceiling windows lined one wall, but instead of looking out onto a runway, these looked out onto the rows of rigs. Enormous monitors displaying scenes from inside the Metaverse covered the remaining walls.

"This is where our customers wait for available rigs and take breaks from Versing," Chi Chi explained.

Parker shivered. "It's cold in here, and it smells like a locker room."

Chi Chi sniffed. "I guess it does get a little gamey. Our guests tend to work themselves into a sweat. They come in here to cool off."

Parker shook his head and limped toward one of the monitors that displayed a view of a towering, granite rock formation that rose straight up above a forest of tall ponderosa pines. As he neared, he could make out small, colorful dots moving along different routes on the sheer cliff face.

Chi Chi materialized beside him. "El Capitan in Yosemite National Park."

"I recognize it," Parker said.

Chi Chi removed a tablet from their jumpsuit pocket and tapped on its screen. "I can control the display with this."

The view on the monitor zoomed into a group of the colored dots, revealing climbers.

"It looks real," Parker said. "Is that all computer graphics?"

"Sure is, honey."

"Why the gear and ropes when nothing happens when you fall?"

Chi Chi shrugged. "You're right. There's no risk of injury, but some guests want an experience as close to reality as possible. I've never tried it myself, but I'm told it's so close to the Real-Real that it can be used for training. That might be what some of these people are doing. Climb it a few dozen times here without risk, then go do the real thing."

"I spent a few hours in this SIM preparing for a real climb,"

Jaden said.

"You climbed that thing for real?"

Jaden grinned.

"Maybe you're not as smart as I thought you were," Parker said as he moved on to another display.

This one showed a debris-littered city street. The crumbling buildings were windowless and covered with blackened pock marks from artillery and rocket strikes. A sand-colored tank turned onto the street and crept toward Parker, but it never made it to him. A soldier in desert camouflage with a missile launcher on his shoulder stepped from a doorway and fired at the tank, which exploded in a fireball.

"People don't get enough of this shit on the news?" Parker asked.

Chi Chi shrugged. "I guess not. This simulation is called BattleSpace, and it's very popular. If I had to guess, 20 percent of our guests are inside this SIM right now."

"Can you show me what it looks like from their perspective?"

"We can't plug into our guests' view." Chi Chi made air quotes and continued, "Privacy. You'll just have to try it for yourself, honey. I'm told it's a lot of fun."

"I've been shot in real life. There's nothing fun about it," Parker said and limped past several monitors until he came to one overlooking a dirt cart path running through a village of thatched-roof huts on its way to a great stone fortress. Two young men who appeared to be in their late teens, one taller and maybe older than the other were peering into the display.

"What are you guys looking at?" Parker asked.

The two jumped.

"Dude," the taller and older looking one said. "You scared the crap out of me."

"Yeah, dude," the shorter one concurred.

Their eyes were wide and darted from side to side, and the taller boy's lips quivered. They were amped-up on something—caffeine, energy drinks, or maybe, Parker thought, Adderall.

"Sorry about that."

"It's okay," the taller one said and gestured toward the screen. "Some noob just went into that hut."

"So?"

The shorter one stared at Parker as if Parker had said the

stupidest thing the boy had ever heard. "Those huts belong to the Gorn Men." He pointed to where the taller boy had indicated. "They are nasty, and there's probably a bunch of them in there."

Just then the door on one of the larger huts burst open and a man, or what appeared to be a man, with light green skin tumbled out and landed on his back in the dirt. A blood-drenched sword was in his right hand and a round, wooden shield strapped to his left forearm. He raised the shield just in time to catch the blow from an iron pike that had been launched from inside the hut.

Before the green man could get to his feet, two hulking, bearded men with dark complexions and bare chests rushed from the hut and began slashing at him with their own short swords. The green man deflected their blows with his sword and shield, managing to sever one of the bearded men's legs below the knee before the other attacker buried his sword in the green man's chest.

"Game over," the short boy yelled and gave the taller boy a high five.

"I see you found the Land of Might and Magic," Chi Chi said.

Parker ignored Chi Chi and continued to watch the monitor, transfixed by the brutality and realism. The bearded man drew his sword out of the green man's chest and licked blood from the blade. Then, he sheathed his sword and took out a long knife. He bent down and used the knife to remove the ears from the dead green man. "Hmm," Parker said. He turned to the tall boy. "Why'd he take his ears?"

"Trophies, dude. Those Gorn Men are nasty fuckers," the tall boy shouted.

The shorter one giggled in agreement. "Yeah, dude."

Parker nodded toward the screen. "Lot of trophy taking in there?" He asked.

The tall boy grinned like a demon; eyes wild. "You bet. Isn't it awesome?"

"Awesome," Parker mimicked. He glanced at Jaden who seemed just as shocked as he was. "What do you think?"

"Awesome."

Parker turned to Chi Chi. "Are there many games where they kill each other with swords like that?"

"A few, but this is the one everyone plays."

"Yeah, dude. LMM is the best. I'm going to work for Xperion when I finish college," the grinning boy said.

"Xperion? What do they do?" Parker asked.

"Oh sweetie," Chi Chi exclaimed and waved their hand. "Virgins are so cute. Xperion is the best SIM developer on the planet." Chi Chi pointed to the monitor. "LMM is theirs."

Parker turned to the boys. "Is that what you guys want to be? Computer programmers?"

They nodded in unison. The older one said, "I think everyone who plays LMM wants to write SIM programs."

Parker thought about his and Jaden's discussion over breakfast. The victims had all been technology workers. Breaux had argued that may have been related to the urban locations where the victims lived. Parker had dismissed the theory. "Wouldn't account for all being tech workers," he'd said. But what if the where wasn't physical?

"Chi Chi," Parker said. "What percentage of your customers work in technology fields?"

"Oh my. In general, or in this simulation?" Chi Chi nodded at the monitor.

"This one."

"LMM is kind of a geek thing. I would say lots. Way more than half."

A distant memory from what, at the time, Parker had thought was a useless college class came back to him. The owlish face of his Research and Evaluation Methods instructor popped into his head. It was an online class during the pandemic. She was lecturing him and twenty other bored advanced psychology students, on confounding statistical variables. "Sunburns don't make you crave ice cream," the bespectacled white-haired woman had barked as she'd leered into the camera. "People who spend time in the sun often get sunburned, and they often crave ice cream. If you don't account for the heat," the instructor had ended with a raspy chuckle, "you might conclude sun burns lead to ice cream eating."

Parker studied the boys. "Everyone wants to be a programmer?"

They nodded.

Maybe the killer wasn't targeting technology workers.

Maybe he was targeting Metaverse gamers, and they were disproportionately technology workers. *The game was the heat.*

The image on the monitor was replaced by a blank white background with a single text line in red lettering: *You haven't lived until you've died in the Land of Might and Magic.* Then beneath it, the phrase *Brought to you by Xperion* appeared.

They left the two boys and made their way toward the exit. When they were back in the main lobby, Parker motioned for Chi Chi to come closer.

Chi Chi leaned in. "Yes?"

"Those boys," he nodded back the way they came, "they seemed a little amped-up. You know what I mean?"

Chi Chi glanced at Jaden then shrugged. "Lot of the gamers think a little boost helps them perform better."

"Boost?"

"You know, honey. Speed. Most just take caffeine pills, but others," Chi Chi nodded in the direction Parker was staring, indicating the boys, "take stronger stuff."

Parker nodded and limped toward the exit.

Chapter 15
Leveling-Up

THE PATH HAD WOUND through a forest of white trees with papery bark and pointy green leaves that shimmered in the late morning sun. When they'd veered off the gate road in favor of the path through the forest, Falin had expected a long, gloomy march, but the unusual light hues gave the woods an ethereal quality that filled the dwarf with wonder. That is, until he reminded himself the shimmering trees were nothing but software objects, likely coded by college interns who worked for no more compensation than free snacks and the right to put LMM Developer on their resumes.

"What kind of trees do you think they modeled these after?" he called to Darshana who stood with her back to him a few dozen yards farther down the path. This is how it had been since they left the road. She, unable to moderate her long strides to accommodate his stubby legs, would get ahead of him and wait just long enough for him to catch up before continuing.

She turned toward him and tilted her head as if pondering his question. Her catlike yellow eyes took in the trees. "*Betula papyrifera*" she stated, then turned her back on him and continued down the path. Those had been the first words she'd spoken since they entered the forest.

"Is that a real-world name or more LMM gibberish?"

She stopped again. She was almost invisible among the trees. Her green skin and earthen-tone cloak and pack blended with her surroundings. One step off the path, and she would disappear entirely. Any would-be pursuer would pass her by, oblivious to her presence until they were red-screened by a bolt from her crossbow.

She was staring up into the sky when he caught up to her.

He peeled a piece of the white bark off the trunk of a nearby tree and held it up. "I have to admit, the friggin detail of this simulation is wicked amazing. This tree object alone is probably five thousand lines of code. What kind of tree is it again?"

She glanced down at him. "Paper birch. They are usually found in wetlands in the north. Should be plenty of them up your way."

He shrugged. "Never saw one before."

She tilted her head back toward the sky. Her black hair ran down her back in a long, braided tail. "See that kettle of vultures up there?"

He followed her gaze. Six or seven large black birds circled overhead. They appeared to be hovering over a point about a half mile from where he and Darshana stood.

"Yeah. So? And who the frig knows a flock of vultures is called a kettle?"

"Someone who reads," she quipped, not looking at him. "They are waiting."

"For what?"

"Carrion. Must be raiders up ahead. Probably a fight." She continued down the path toward the circling birds.

"Wait. You're just going to walk into the middle of it?"

"It's time to level up, Dwarf. Can't hunt the Gray Warrior as a level zero *càiniǎo*."

"Should I draw my axe?" he called as he jogged to keep up.

"Can't hurt."

They continued through the trees, her striding effortlessly as he ran behind her clutching his axe. Soon, the sounds of angry shouts and metal striking metal reached his ears. Overhead, the vultures circled. No longer distant black forms gliding through the sky, up close they were massive, terrifying birds with blood-red heads and twelve-foot wingspans. The trees thinned and through them Falin saw two men, one slightly larger than the other, both dressed in chain mail similar to his own. They were standing back-to-back and using their swords and shields to fend off attacks from what looked at first to be children.

As he drew closer to the clearing's edge, Falin saw, though childlike in size, the creatures attacking the men weren't children at all but resembled mythical figures that Falin recalled had something to do with a flute. They were no more than four feet tall, shorter than himself, slight of build and naked from the waist up. Their small bodies looked emaciated with every rib visible beneath milky skin the same color as the trees. They appeared to be wearing fur pants, but Falin soon realized they weren't wearing pants at all. Though appearing to be human from their hollow chests up, their lower halves resembled the hindquarters of goats. They had oversized, muscular thighs that tapered down to sticklike shins ending in hooves instead of feet. Their heads were crowned with the same thick brown fur that covered their legs, and sported long, spiky horns. In their hands, raised above their horned heads, they wielded gleaming swords with curved blades.

They circled the warriors like the vultures overhead, their hooves kicking up clouds of dust. Every now and then, one of the goat men let loose a shrieking war cry and broke from the others to charge the two beleaguered defenders. The charger would bring his curved blade down on the defender's sword and thrust his horns into the defender's shield, then retreat to the dusty circle. It was obvious the goat men where toying with the warriors, perhaps wearing them down in preparation for the entire herd to mount a full charge that would undoubtedly result in the warriors' dismembered bodies being left for the vultures.

Darshana turned and smiled. "Follow me, Boston. Time to dwarf up," she said, and laughed as she stepped into the clearing.

"Shit," Falin blurted as he tightened his grip on the axe handle and followed after her. What happened next had not been what he'd expected. Instead of attacking, the goat men took one look at Darshana and scattered into the trees. Not one of the mythical figures remained in the clearing. Falin lowered his axe. "How the fuck am I supposed to level up now that all the goat men have run away?"

"We're not fighting them," Darshana said as she drew her longsword from the sheath on her back.

Falin looked past her and saw the two warriors who moments before, were about to be slaughtered by the goat men, charging toward them. Darshana flashed a mean grin and raced to meet them. She moved so fast and with such precision Falin could have been watching a video on fast forward of a ballet dancer gone wild. Sparks flew as her sword met theirs. Her blows shattered the men's blades, leaving them with nothing but the hilts and jagged shards.

Darshana glanced over at Falin and shouted, "It's now or never, Boston."

Hefting his axe, Falin charged the men who appeared to be reconsidering the wisdom of attacking Darshana as they were inching backward toward the trees. Their eyes were fixed on the elvish ranger, and neither of them saw him coming until he planted his axe in the belly of the larger of the two. The man howled and toppled over, dead. When he hit the ground, a yellow light enveloped Falin and a woman's voice called down from the sky, "Level one achieved. Congratulations."

While Falin was distracted by the level up glow, the smaller warrior raised the remains of his sword and charged. The man was almost on him before Falin saw him coming. He braced for the strike that never came. The warrior fell face-first at Falin's feet, black feathers from one of Darshana's crossbow bolts protruding from the small of the dead man's back.

The exhilaration of the kills got the better of Falin. He raised his axe over his head and shouted "Goal," extending the "ohhhhl" for several seconds like excited fans do in soccer when their team's striker finds the net to score. When he was done with his celebration, he found Darshana standing cross-armed, staring down at him like a disapproving mother witnessing a child's poor behavior.

"You seem quite pleased with yourself."

"Fucking-ay. That was wicked awesome. Come on. Did you not see me plant my axe in that big fucker's belly?"

She scowled and said, "Would've been even more awesome if you had gotten them both. Then we wouldn't have to traipse around this wood for the next hour looking for another easy kill to get you to level two." Then she turned and strode toward the path.

As it turned out, it took them much longer than an hour, and Darshana had to rescue him twice from botched attempts before he reached the next level. The first time was when a small band of orcs swarmed from a cave and almost killed him. Darshana had directed him to wait at the cave's mouth with his axe ready while she went in and "shook things up." She had been inside the cave for less than a minute when the first beast came racing out from the darkness with a notched short sword in hand and red eyes fixed on Falin.

The orc was Falin's size—leaner, but with the same stubby legs. It had dark skin, the color of angry storm clouds, and huge yellow fangs that extended beyond its snarling black lips. A plain metal breastplate covered its chest, and an armored skirt or kilt made from leather woven through small iron rings protected its lower region. The rings clanked together as the beast ran toward him.

Falin dealt with the first orc easily enough. Though fearsome looking, the orc was surprisingly slow and easy to kill. It was the four that emerged behind it that gave Falin the trouble. They were on him before he could pull his axe from the dead orc's skull. Flashes of red filled his vision as the orcs hacked at him with their swords. A bar graph floated in the upper right corner of his view showing the percent of his lifeforce. The bar, which had glowed green and showed 100 percent when the attack started, was sliding toward zero and had turned red.

Just as the graph began to flash, indicating imminent character death, Darshana swooped in and cut down the orcs with no more apparent effort than if she had been mowing down weeds. Falin had managed to kill two in the melee but killing two simple cave orcs did not get him to level two.

He had been badly damaged in the fight. His lifeforce was so low that if he tripped and fell, he would red-screen. "How long will it take to recover?" he asked her.

"Too long," she said as she withdrew a magic orb from her pouch. She held the small gold ball up in front of him. It reminded him of a marble. "These cost a coin each. You owe me." She then whispered some words Falin did not understand and crushed the ball in her hand. She blew the resulting fine gold powder into his face, causing Falin to blink reflexively, and his lifeforce graph moved back to 100 percent and disappeared.

"Wow. I've got to get me some of those."

"Wouldn't do you any good; dwarfs can't use magic, remember? What you need to do, Boston, is get in a rig. You're too slow as a half-in." She pointed at the dead orcs. "These SIM creatures, the players in the clearing, they are nothing. We are in a tame zone near gates used by beginners. The rest of the Land is not so forgiving, and the Gray Warrior can go anywhere."

Their next encounter had gone slightly better, but she still had to rescue him. They had hiked for thirty minutes until the path emerged from the white woods onto the banks of a rushing river. The forest did not continue on the opposite bank. Instead, a great sea of tall, green grass extended to the horizon. A gleaming white bridge with towers on either end spanned the banks. The path resumed on its far side where it continued for a short distance until it intersected with a road that ran through the undulating green sea straight toward a white arch that stood on a hill like a fortress perched on an island.

"Finally," he exhaled, unable to conceal his relief at seeing the exit. He then added in a more downcast tone, "If that's the gate we are headed for, I guess I won't make level two today."

"We'll see," she said and stepped aside. "You cross the bridge first."

The mischievous grin should have tipped him off, but the truth was the trek had exhausted him. Moving about the Land, even if it was all virtual, was as taxing as it was exhilarating. The illusion of mobility was friggin awesome, but he was near his limits. Getting through the gate and resting was all he was thinking about when he stepped onto the simulated marble.

As soon as his boot touched the white roadbed, a pair of pale skeletal figures stepped out from a dark doorway in the nearest of the bridge towers. The figures held metal pikes with ends filed to deadly points which they aimed at his chest.

He'd glanced back at her. She'd, once again, assumed the posture of a disapproving parent. "What do I do now?"

"Got to get across that bridge."

"Do I attack them with my axe?"

"I wouldn't," she'd said while inspecting the nails on her right hand.

He'd taken that to mean he should use his sword. Which was a mistake. Before he could draw it from its sheath, the two figures lunged forward and struck him with their pikes. The lifeforce bar showed yellow this time and at 50 percent.

"Shield would be good," Darshana called.

Backpedaling away from their attack, he retrieved the shield from his back and used it to deflect their blows while he slashed at them with his sword. The slashing did no good. His sword strikes passed right through the frail-looking creatures and seemed to have no impact. At one point, they placed their pikes on his shield and forced him back off the bridge. He landed on his back looking up at them. His lifeforce was registering 25 percent. He assumed they would finish him, but they stopped their attack and stood like sickly statues with their pikes crossed, barring entrance to the bridge.

He remained down until he heard Darshana's laughter. Then he scrambled to his feet, but before he could launch into another futile attack, she pulled him back.

"It's not all fighting, Boston. The Land is full of riddles and puzzles. Not even I could force the bridge wraiths to let us pass."

"Then how do we get by them?"

"Ask them."

He turned back toward the wraiths, and she pulled him back again.

"Sheath your sword and put your shield away first."

He did as she'd said and approached the wraiths, not sure what words to use. "What do I say?"

"Ask if you can cross. Be polite."

He turned back to the ghostly figures who seemed indifferent to his presence. "Umm. Hi. Sorry about the fight. May I cross your bridge?"

The wraiths withdrew their pikes and turned to let him advance. When they did, he experienced the same yellow glow as when he'd killed the man in the clearing and the same voice said, "Level two achieved. Congratulations."

By the time they reached the gate, the real person behind Falin could barely keep his eyes open. He'd dozed off several times along the way, opening his eyes to find Darshana, annoyed, pulling on his arm and urging him to keep moving.

She waited at the gate's threshold for him to drag himself the last twenty feet.

"What's wrong?"

"Nothing. I'm okay," he managed as he reached her.

On the brink of unconsciousness, he became aware of a muffled voice calling to him. It was not coming from the speakers in his headgear.

"Can you hear me, baby?" the voice asked.

Oh shit, he thought. "Push me through, push me through," he shouted to Darshana as his cybermask was removed, and his mother's concerned face stared down at him.

Chapter 16
Falin's Mirror

DARSHANA LEANED AGAINST THE massive marble pier that supported the great arch of White Hall Gate. She was waiting for Falin to emerge, and she was growing impatient. The huge structure hummed and vibrated whenever someone or something passed through it, and she'd felt the stone at her back shudder three times since she'd settled against its surface. Each time she had expected the yellow-bearded dwarf to appear, and each time she'd been disappointed. The unknown players who had emerged, sometimes in pairs, shot her uneasy glances and quickly made their way down the hill toward the trading town of White Hall.

Two days ago, for reasons known only to him, she had shoved the dwarf, headfirst, through this gate. Since then, she had sent him several messages demanding to know what the hell was going on. The dwarf had not replied, and she'd begun to worry something had happened to him. Then, this afternoon, while she and Tony were servicing rigs at the Atlanta MetaSpot, Falin had sent a single-line message: *Meet me at the White Hall Gate at 7pm.*

No greeting. No explanation. She had contemplated responding with 'fuck off', but here she was, waiting. She had questions she wanted to ask him. For one thing, why did he need her to push him through the gate? That was very odd. Then there was his identity. She'd given the user ID she'd copied from his web page to Tony, and he'd passed it on to someone he knew who worked for Xperion. She'd received the ID's owner's information this morning. According to the Xperion employee, who Tony said was infallible, the ID was owned by a woman from Greenwood Lake, New York named Stacey Hanover. Stacey had social media accounts, and it turned out she was an avid bingo player and grandmother with six grandchildren. Darshana doubted very much Stacey was Falin, and she intended to find out if the dwarf ever showed up.

She checked the system time again, twenty past seven. She'd had to cancel a planned and paying trek to make the appointment, and she was growing angry. She had just about made up her mind to exit when the gate hummed, and Falin appeared.

The dwarf stepped through the threshold and stopped. He didn't seem to notice her. The sun was low in the western sky, and the gate's elongated shadow stretched toward the town. Falin stood illuminated in the shadow's arch with his back to her. His axe glowed in the flames of the virtual sunset. He glanced from side to side and then over his shoulder, shading his eyes against the fiery ball suspended between the piers.

Even a simulated sun burns, Darshana thought. She let him search for a few more moments, payment for making her wait, then stepped into the light. "It's about time," she complained as she strode toward him. "You said seven. I've been here for almost thirty minutes, and I was about to leave."

"Sorry. I had to make some last-minute adjustments."

"To what?"

"I'll show you."

He removed a silver object from his pack and held it out to her. Before she could take it, the gate began to hum again, and a group of midlevel warriors appeared beneath the arch. Falin shoved the object back in his pack.

The warriors marched past them. They nodded at Darshana and ignored Falin as they went by. When they had gone, Falin whispered, "Maybe we should move away from here."

She studied him for a moment. "Before we do, I want to know a few things."

Falin looked back at the arch. His headgear appeared to be working better this evening because she could detect the nervous expression on his face.

"Can we walk?" he asked.

She nodded and started down the hill at a slow pace that allowed the dwarf to stay at her side. "Why did you need me to push you through the gate?"

He shrugged. "I got interrupted, and I couldn't move. I was worried I'd lose all the points and have to start over again."

"Did one of your grandchildren interrupt you?"

Falin stopped short. "What are you talking about?"

"The social media profile attached to your user ID says you're a grandmother. It says your name is Stacey. I was just wondering if one of your grandchildren had distracted you."

Falin laughed. "Ain't that a pissah. Who's the hacker now?"

"What's your real name? 'Cause we both know it's not Stacey."

"Hey." He spread his arms in a what-gives gesture. "I thought we didn't talk about the Real-Real here in fantasy land."

"That went out the window when you learned my name, asshole."

"Asshole? What's with the hostility?"

"I don't like you having the advantage over me. You know who I am. You probably know where I live. I don't like it. So, tell me who you are," she scowled at him, "in the Real-Real or we're done."

He looked down. His ridiculous yellow beard hung just a few inches above the packed earth. "I can't."

"Why?"

He said nothing and continued to stare at the ground. She had the impression he was trying to think of some new lie to tell her.

"Don't bullshit me, Dwarf. Just tell me your real name."

"Look," he mumbled without looking at her. "You called it. I'm a hacker. I break into systems, and I live in the Dark Verse. No one knows who I really am."

"Except your mother," she shot back.

His head popped up, and the surprised look on his face confirmed what she'd thought she'd heard when he stood frozen beneath the arch.

"You said 'mom' at the gate just before I shoved you through."

"I did not. You misheard."

"No. You said, 'mom' or 'mommy.'"

"Fuck you," he shouted and pushed her, hard.

She couldn't believe it. The little fucker pushed her. Then he pushed her again, and with the speed that comes from years of practice, her character's level, and the special accelerated chipset she'd installed in her rig, she drew her sword and placed its edge on his neck. "Push me again, and you will start over on your own."

He raised his hands and withdrew.

She returned her sword to its place on her back. "One more time, who are you? Really."

He sighed and in a voice that was mixed with anger and sadness said. "I can't tell you."

She turned and began heading back up the hill. "Fuck you, then."

She was halfway to the gate when he shouted. "My name is Bobby, okay? I finished the tracker. Let me show it to you."

She turned. "Last name?"

He shook his head. His yellow beard whipped from side to side. "First name has to be enough for now."

"Sorry, Robert. Say hi to mom," she replied and continued toward the gate.

"Penn," he shouted. "My fucking name is Bobby Penn. Jeezus. Now you know. Now everyone will fucking know."

She stopped and turned back toward him. "Nice to meet you, Bobby Penn."

"Yeah, yeah." He held up the thing he'd concealed from the warriors. It caught the sun with a flash that almost blinded her. "Let me show you this."

She strode back down the hill, and he thrust the object toward her. It was a large, intricately tooled silver hand mirror like what one might find on a wealthy old woman's vanity. She took it from him and studied her reflection in its polished surface, then not sure what to make of it, she gave him a quizzical expression. "It's a mirror."

"Yeah. I know. I made it."

She examined it again, not sure if she believed him. "You made this?"

"Yes. Dwarfs can't fight, they can't use magic, but they are wicked good at making shit."

She laughed. "How did you know how to make this?"

"Like I said, there are things us dwarfs can do you badass rangers can't. I mean, why else would anyone want to be a dwarf? You think I like chasing after you on these silly short legs?"

"I know what dwarfs can do, but they need materials and

forges. You can barely find your way back to a gate, let alone to a mine and smithy shop."

He smiled at her. "You underestimate me and my ability to figure things out."

That was not true. Falin, or Bobby, had amply proved his information gathering and technical skills. She didn't doubt his abilities, she just thought he sucked at the game.

"Okay. So, you did arts and crafts with the other dwarfs. Good job. How will this help us track the Gray Warrior?"

He took the mirror back from her. "Arts and crafts, what a bitch."

She moved her hand to her crossbow. "Careful."

"Yeah, yeah. Watch and learn, oh-great-powerful-one," he snickered as he twisted the mirror's handle and turned it toward her. The mirror no longer showed her reflection. Instead, the polished surface turned black and filled with glowing green text, like what might display on a computer console.

"Wow. What is that?"

"It's the event data we looked at the other day, but this is in real time. These are all the events occurring with the Gray Warrior's unique, anonymous signature."

She took the mirror back from him and stared at the screen full of text. "This is happening now?"

"Yeah. He's in here." He motioned for her to lower the mirror so he could see. He slid one of his stubby fingers on the mirror's surface and the text moved. "It works like a touch screen in the Real-Real." Falin scrolled to the end of the text and tapped on the last line. A window opened showing more information. "These are the details of the last thing he did." He nodded at the window. "You can see where the event occurred."

"Blackwood. He's in Blackwood now?"

"That's what it says," he confirmed.

She looked back at the gate. "I could get there from here." She glanced back down at him. "But you've never been there, so the Blackwood gate won't be in your teleport list. I'd have to go alone."

"Not our deal," he said.

"But I can get him."

"He's in here often. We'll have other opportunities."

The mirror vibrated in her hand.

"It's shaking."

"It doesn't matter now anyway. The vibration means he ported out. It will shake again when he ports back in."

She scrolled through the event list. "Looks like he took out a few players this evening. This is really amazing." She handed him back the mirror. "How did you do it?"

He grinned. "I could tell you, but I'd have to kill you."

"Oh, yeah? You could try little man, but it would not end well for you."

He held up the mirror. "Just remember, if you kill me, you lose this."

She loomed over him. "I could take it."

"Fuckin-ay. Then I would just shut it down. You'd still have the mirror, but it would only be good for looking at your pretty green face."

She laughed and nodded toward the twinkling lights of White Hall. "The next gate is about three miles on the other side of town. It's called Miller's Gate because it stands near an old grist mill. We could make it there and add it to your list. Maybe pick up some more points along the way."

Falin followed her gaze then looked back up at her. "Can't tonight. I have other plans. I just wanted to show you the mirror." His eyes shined in the setting sun. "I might be able to grow my port list without us having to hike to every gate."

"That's cheating."

"Yeah, and it's smart."

She glared at him. "It took me almost two years to make it to every gate."

"Sucker."

She laughed. "Damn, Dwarf. How old are you in the Real-Real?"

"Old enough."

"I'm guessing you're just a kid. I think you're what? Fifteen? Sixteen?"

"No," he mumbled.

"Come on. Tell me."

He shrugged. "Seventeen, but I'll be eighteen soon."

"I knew it."

"You don't know shit."

"There's nothing wrong with being a kid. Especially a kid

who can do the things you can do. Imagine what you'll become."

He stomped past her and headed up the hill without answering.

She let him go, amused by his agitation. He disappeared over the crest of the hill, and she sprinted after him. Catching him at the gate's threshold, she grabbed his arm and spun him around.

"I'm sorry," she said. "No more about your age. I promise."

He looked up at her and gave her a sad smile. "Things are not what they seem, Shea." He backed through the gate and disappeared.

Chapter 17
Puzzled

PARKER LIVED LESS THAN seven miles from the FBI research center offices on the Marine base at Quantico, Virginia. Before he'd been shot, it had been an easy fifty-minute run. Now, his doctors worried about him making the ten-minute drive. After the Detroit incident, Becky had convinced Warner to sign off on a car service, but Parker refused to use it. His car drove itself. He wasn't a threat to anyone. When he reached the point that he couldn't get himself to work, he'd retire, perhaps using a bullet fired from his Glock to finish what the Devil's rounds hadn't.

A FedEx van was backing out of his driveway when he pulled up to the three-bedroom townhouse Carrie and he had purchased twelve years ago when he'd left his posting at the Newark, New Jersey field office to join the BAU. It was supposed to be temporary, something requiring little maintenance while they established themselves in their careers. The plan had been for Carrie to make partner at her law firm and Parker would become an assistant director. Then they'd trade up to something with a large backyard suitable for a big dog and maybe children. But careers are ravenous beasts that must be fed, and what they eat is time. And time is a funny thing. It seems endless until it's not.

Parker beeped his horn, and the van stopped. He left his car in the street and hobbled over to the FedEx driver's window. The driver was waiting with a thick envelope. Parker took the envelope back to his car and studied the return address. Detective Donna Baker, Nashville PD, Homicide. He'd spoken to Baker when he'd first received the Collector file from the Nashville field office. She had not been optimistic about finding Ms. Reddy's killer.

"He's a fucking magician," she'd said. "Got in without damaging the door. No one saw or heard anything, including the half dozen cameras that should have picked him up. No evidence. No witnesses. In, out, and gone. Poof, like magic."

He'd asked Baker for a copy of the case file. That had been almost two weeks ago. He'd expected her to send an email. *Guess I'm not the only luddite in law enforcement.* He considered the file's weight before dropping it on the passenger seat. No wonder she'd grumbled about the workload before agreeing to send it.

Inside his house, Parker tossed the envelope on the dining room table next to the partially completed jigsaw puzzle and put a kettle on the stove. His grandmother had been from London, and she'd taught him the proper way to brew and steep tea. She'd also left him the kettle and some fine china cups. Carrie had always been amused by the tea-brewing production, offering on many occasions to teach him how to boil water in the microwave.

He stood in the kitchen doorway waiting for the kettle's whistle and stared at the puzzle. It had sat there unfinished for three years. He'd added pieces here and there, blown off the dust that dulled the glossy finish of the completed sections, but other than that, hadn't paid much attention to it. The box containing the remaining pieces sat in the middle of the table. The box's top photo showed the sun rising over three pyramids with nothing but desert sand stretching to the horizon behind them. A camel with a saddle lay on its belly in the foreground, as if waiting for its rider. Carrie had longed to visit Egypt and take in that view for herself. She'd been so disappointed when they'd discovered the pyramids were actually surrounded by the sprawling cities of Cairo and Giza, and the puzzle's romantic view required precise camera positioning to avoid capturing high-rises and expressways.

The kettle whistle pulled him away from the memory. He dropped six tea bags into a pot and poured in the boiling water. Then he returned to the doorway to study the puzzle while the tea steeped. It struck him that his leg didn't ache. Every so often, the muscle seemed to tire of aching and just went numb. The absent throb wouldn't allow him to go run around the block or anything like that, but it would keep the painkillers in their vial.

A splash of milk, two spoons of sugar, and with a proper

cup of tea in hand, Parker returned to the dining room table. He slid out a chair and sat down. He couldn't remember the last time he'd done so. After a moment, he realized something wasn't right. He was sitting where Carrie had always sat. He moved to the other side of the table and emptied the box of pieces.

He picked through the pile, testing pieces, and joining the ones that fit. As he did, he inventoried what he knew about the Collector case. He started a new group of assembled pieces to represent the case facts, dubbing it the victim's group and saying their names to himself as he pressed the pieces together, *Abby Loveridge, Jyothi Reddy, and Charles Tate.* He added more pieces to indicate where the victims were killed, *Clearwater, Nashville, and Las Vegas—all in different cities.* Then he added more for their vocations, *Computer Programmer, Computer Programmer, Computer Component Engineer—all technology workers.* He assembled two more pieces for the traces of the Adderall found in Jyothi and Abby's blood and withheld a third he'd found to represent Charles's assumed stimulant usage. *Not a fact, yet. It would be another week before they had Tate's toxicology report.*

He stretched and rubbed his leg. Still no pain. He dug into the box, looking for pieces to denote the killer's methods. One bright yellow piece caught his eye, and he held it up. It was the center of the rising sun, and he chose it to represent the killer removing the victim's heads with a sword. He found another sun piece to mate with the first to indicate the taking of the victim's ears, and another for the ritualistic poses. He slid the completed sun next to the victim group and searched through the pile for a new group that he named selection.

"How does he choose his victims?" he asked out loud to Carrie's empty chair. *How does he know them?* Came the reply in his head. The ice cream and heat lecture on confounding variables came to mind again. Vocation was not the heat. *The game.*

A puzzle piece with the very tip of one pyramid caught his attention. He designated it the start of the selection group. Collecting and trying more pyramid pieces, he fit one to represent the game he'd watched with the over-stimulated boys. "What was it called?" he said to the chair. "Ah, yeah. The Land of Might and Magic." He fit two more pieces to represent the character killing he'd observed. *Swords and ears,* he said to himself. Then he tried several other pieces until he found another fit. Chi Chi had said gamers use stimulants for an edge. *Adderall.* He snapped it in place.

He pushed himself out of the chair with his cane and gazed down at the three groups of newly assembled pieces. The victim's group was forming the camel's body. Next to it sat the completed sun representing the killer's grisly methods, and next to that was growing a pyramid for the selection group, the *Land of Might and Magic.*

Now all we have to do is connect the camel with the sun and the pyramid. He sorted through the pieces until he found another camel part that belonged with the victims and their vocations. Chi Chi had said people who play the Land of Might and Magic were overwhelmingly technology workers. He snapped the new camel piece into place, then detached it and set it aside as he had done with the one connecting Tate to Adderall. He wasn't ready to make that connection until he had confirmation that the victims played the game. "How do we connect them, baby?" he said to Carrie's chair. Tate had Metaverse gear in his bag. Stands to reason he used it. He checked his watch. Still early in Vegas. He sipped some tea and called Jaden.

"Breaux, I've been doing some thinking."

"Don't hurt yourself, sir."

Parker smiled at the phone. "I need you to call Chavez and find out if Charles Tate played that Land of Might and Magic game we watched with Chi Chi."

Jaden understood right away where Parker was going and promised to call as soon as he connected with Chavez.

Two hours later, and after multiple bathroom trips, Parker had finished the entire pot of tea and assembled a large part of the puzzle when his phone buzzed with Jaden's call.

"Chavez spoke to Tate's wife," Jaden said. "She about jumped through the phone when he asked her about the Land of Might and Magic. Tate was addicted to the game."

"Addicted?"

"That's what Chavez said Tate's wife told him. It was destroying their marriage. Chavez got some more info and he's putting it in an email. I'll forward it when I get it."

"Good work, Breaux. Still think cyber's the way to go?"

"It looks like this case is all about cyber, sir."

Parker snapped the puzzle piece into place, connecting Tate to the Land of Might and Magic. It was only one piece. He wanted to connect two more for Jyothi and Abby, but it was too late to call Tennessee or Florida.

He reached across the table and retrieved the thick FedEx envelope and tore it open. It contained about 200 single-sided pages. A third of the pages were the M.E. report, which he'd already read. Another third were the crime scene investigators' findings, which also had been in the file he'd received from the Nashville field office. The last third were Baker's notes, including the results of Jyothi's criminal record search and transcriptions from the interviews Baker had done with Jyothi's neighbors and the apartment building manager. Like Abby and Charles, Jyothi had no criminal record of any kind.

Parker read through the transcripts. As Baker had said, no one had heard or seen anything, and nothing was captured by the security system. The building manager was adamant all the cameras and motion detectors on the property worked, and no one had tampered with the apartment locks. *Like magic.*

The last several pages contained notes from Baker's conversations with Jyothi's parents and siblings. None of them could think of anyone who would want to hurt Jyothi or any activities that would have brought her into contact with a murderer. Just like Abby Loveridge and Charles Tate, Jyothi Reddy was a low crime risk person.

The last few pages contained copies of photographs of Jyothi provided by her parents. They included those taken during her college graduation ceremony at Penn State, candid shots at family gatherings, and a picture of Jyothi holding a plastic sword and wearing a white T-shirt sporting a phrase stenciled in red Parker had seen floating on a monitor in a cold, smelly room in Las Vegas. He used his phone to snap a picture of the photo. Then he chose a puzzle piece from the shrinking pile that fit with the selection group containing the game pieces and snapped it into place. He slid the whole group over to the larger puzzle assembly and merged it in. The entire Khufu pyramid was complete.

"Look at that, baby," Parker said out loud. "We're almost done."

Chapter 18
The Hunters

THE GREAT BLACK HORSE stomped and snorted. Musuka looked over his shoulder at the beast. Fiery red eyes glowered back at him, and Musuka smiled. "B-b-b-beautiful," he whispered.

The brush behind the horse shuttered and a pair of game birds, pheasants, Musuka thought, shot out of the thicket like they'd been fired from a cannon. Akandu's helmet appeared over the brush, and a moment later the giant burst from the thickets, his gray skin impervious to the thorns that would rip Musuka's thin furry hide to shreds.

Akandu was dragging two men by their hair. The men were naked except for loin cloths and covered with blue tattoos. Neither of the men were resisting; not that it would have done them any good. As they neared, Musuka saw the bloody holes in the men's chests. The men weren't resigned to their fate, they were dead. Judging by the wounds, Akandu had shot the pair with his bow, and given the giant's immense strength, the arrows had passed through the men like hot knives through butter.

"Wh-wh-what are you doing?" Musuka asked.

Akandu raised his arms, lifting the bodies over his head. "Hunting."

"I ca-ca-can see that, but why? These two aren't wh-wh-worth the arrows."

"Then find me something better, Mouse," Akandu snarled. "I'm bored." He dropped his prey and sat down on a boulder. "And I'm sick of waiting."

Musuka turned his back on the giant and lifted his spyglass to his eye. He and Akandu had set up on the hill overlooking the road leading from the do-gooder wizard's town to the gate near the big lake. The road looped around a collection of low

115

rocky hills before it followed the lake's shore to the gate. A path ran through the hills, offering a more direct route to the gate. It cut almost four miles off the distance, but hills were full of the nasty tattooed creatures like those Akandu had shot. Only the skilled and foolish took the path. The elf they were hunting was no fool.

A popping sound made Musuka look behind him. Akandu was pulling the limbs off the dead men. *Bored.* Musuka resumed his scan. Four travelers came around a bend. Three were hooded. He worked the spy glass tubes to focus on the one that wasn't. A she-elf, but not the one they were looking for.

Musuka aimed the glass at the leader. Large; not Akandu large, but bigger than the other three. Musuka couldn't make out the leader's features through the cloak, but whatever it was, it was too bulky to be an elf. It was carrying a large shield and longsword. Most likely a warrior, he thought. It and a hundred like it would be no match for Akandu.

He moved the glass to the slight figure behind the warrior. This one wore no travel cloak over its plain brown robe. Spellcaster, probably a cleric or a mage; no match for the magic Musuka carried.

Finally, Musuka zoomed in on the figure bringing up the rear. This one was taller than the rest and strode confidently in high black boots, ranger boots. Musuka smiled. This was the one they'd take soon. Not today, though. It wasn't time. They weren't ready in his world. He wasn't ready. Besides, they had to visit a wizard first.

Musuka studied the tall traveler for a few more moments. "Soon," he said out loud. The "S" flowed off his tongue without a hint of a stutter.

"What did you say?" the sulking giant demanded.

"I-i-i-t's time to go," Musuka said as he shoved his spy glass into his pack.

Akandu sprang to his feet. The giant could move with frightening speed. "We go to the road?"

Musuka plucked a white teleportation orb from his spell pouch. "No. We go to Blackwood." *No stutter. Soon, he wouldn't need the giant.*

Chapter 19
An Important Call

DOZENS OF TINY BLUE and green hummingbirds zipped through the air. They darted between the yellow and red bell-shaped flowers that lined the path, stopping in mid-flight, hovering with their long beaks thrust into the sweet nectaries inside the yellow and red cups, then zipping away again. Their sudden movements were more insect-like than avian. Darshana smiled as she watched them. Until Falin had pointed it out, she had never appreciated the level of detail in the simulation or given much thought to how it was achieved. She wondered if the SIM programmers had studied real hummingbirds. Did they know the little creatures did not suck nectar through their needlelike beaks but actually drew it through tongues so long that when retracted, they coiled up like a fire hose inside their tiny skulls? Or that they could move at speeds up to forty-five miles per hour and were capable of gravity-defying aerobatics that would make a fighter pilot puke? The more she thought about it, the more she smiled.

"What are you smiling about?"

The question rousted her from her musings. She looked up to see the tall female elf she'd been following looking back at her with catlike yellow eyes that resembled Darshana's own. The oval-shaped pupils, so lifelike, expanded and contracted to slits as they focused. She searched her memory for the character's name. *Amy? No. Arlen? No, that wasn't it either. Arwen. That was it. Everyone wants to be a Tolkien character.*

"Just admiring the birds. Aren't they beautiful?"

Arwen nodded. "Yes. And they look so real. Everything looks and sounds so real." She stretched a slender bare arm out and grabbed one of the yellow flowers by its stalk, snapping it off in her hand. She touched it to her nose, then let it fall to the ground. "It's too bad we can't smell them."

Darshana watched it fall. "Maybe someday," she said, contemplating the consequences of the inevitable addition of smell and taste to the simulation. Junkers, like her, already spent too much time in these imaginary worlds. When the simulations covered all five senses and the Verse truly became indistinguishable from the Real-Real, why would they ever leave?

"Now you're frowning," the elf remarked.

"Sorry. My mind is wandering today."

"Well, don't let it wander too far. Wouldn't want to be ambushed because our high-priced guide was daydreaming."

Darshana felt Shea's face flush under the mask. She narrowed her eyes and wondered how the annoying elf princess would describe her expression now. It was the one she usually reserved for the target of her crossbow. She took a deep breath and swallowed the sharp rebuttal that had been poised on the tip of her tongue. The elf was right. They paid their coin. They deserved her full attention. "Don't worry, Arwen. You'll get what you paid for."

She quickened her pace and passed the haughty elf. They had set out from Staghead a little less than an hour ago. A party of four, including herself. The first segment on a three-gate training expedition, her usual course from Staghead to Jade Gate. The same one where, a little more than a week ago, she'd first encountered the Gray Warrior.

About a mile out of town, they had turned onto the path that cut through dense thickets and small scrub pines. Soon, Darshana knew, the path would lead them through a forest and past a large lake where it would intersect with the road that ran through their next gate. The brush was tall enough to conceal their movements from a distance, but up ahead rose a small, rocky hill, crowned by a ring of massive boulders that in a similar terrain in the Real-Real, might have been deposited by the recession of an ancient glacier. During the morning and afternoon when the sun was above the crown, the scrub provided no cover from spying eyes on the hill, but as the sun fell with the advent of evening, the approach was less conspicuous.

She came upon the party's cleric, trudging along in a brown monk's robe cinched tightly around their waist by a gold cord, with a mostly empty spell pouch dangling from it. The cleric's hood was drawn over their moonlike bald head and he or she—

Darshana was still not sure which—did not appear to notice her draw up beside them. *Oblivious.* This one was by far the most vulnerable of her charges. *Càiniǎo*-clerics couldn't fight. They didn't even carry weapons; not that they could use them if they did. At level zero, even their spells were mostly useless, aside from a healing incantation like the purchased spell she used to restore Falin's lifeforce, but since *càiniǎo*-clerics needed a 30 second recycle time between spell casts, they were no good during a fight.

That wouldn't always be the case. Someday, if this cleric made it to a mage level, they would wield more useful and lethal magic, and if they stuck with it, they'd level up to an enchanter which was the end of the line for most magic wielders. Very few went on to become sorcerers. It took a lot of rig time and risky battles to reach that level, and most enchanters didn't think it worth it. Instead, they avoided conflict and got rich making and selling spells like the ones Darshana carried in her pouch. Spell merchants made good money, easy money. No need to lead groups of *càiniǎo* through tedious basic training expeditions like this. She nodded as she passed the cleric and sprinted to catch up to the noob warrior at the head of the line, thinking maybe she should have gone the enchanter route. Then she saw the figure standing on the hill up ahead and thought, nah.

Darshana reached out and put her hand on the warrior's shoulder. The man jumped at her touch, telling her he wore one of the better cybersuits. Before he could turn to face her, she whispered "look" and pointed. She pulled him down to a crouching position and motioned for the others to do the same.

"Is that a man?" the warrior asked.

Darshana retrieved her spyglass from her pack and worked its barrels to focus. "Not a man," she said. She zoomed in on the creature's pale, muscular body, naked except for a loincloth. Its arms and chest were covered in blue spiral tattoos. A bow was in its hand and a quiver full of blue-feathered arrows was strapped to its back. It was scanning the horizon. She lowered her glass when it looked their way, mindful of the reflection off the telescope's lens and brass body. The creature's stare did not linger. The sun was at its back, and the party was concealed by the hills' shadow.

The warrior turned to look at her. "What is it?" he asked, a hint of excitement in his voice.

She smiled at him. "Wargarian, scout," she announced as she returned her glass to her pack. "Looks like a level eight or nine. No big deal, but it has special arrows in its quiver. Some are tipped with poison; others burn like a flare when they are shot."

"Flare?"

"Yeah. That's how it alerts its friends when it spots something."

"Like us," the warrior said.

She studied his chiseled face and nodded. She wondered if the player was as handsome as his character. He and the elf princess were a pair. Probably entitled rich kids in the Verse on Daddy's credit card. Tony would love them. The elf princess was annoying, but this guy wasn't so bad. He wanted to learn the SIM, and he listened. He even changed his character's name at her urging.

When they first met at Staghead Gate, he had come through as Aragon. You could name yourself after Tolkien characters, and many—like Falin and the princess—did, but choosing the name of the iconic Middle Earth ranger was begging for constant ridicule and beat downs. It would be like calling yourself Gandalf. Those who made that mistake were often FODed soon after emerging from their first gate. Now his name was Roman, which Darshana liked. It had a subtle classical ring about it.

"Yes. Like us, but this one won't get a chance." She retrieved her crossbow and crept around him.

Roman put out an arm to stop her. "Can I take him?" he asked, eager.

She liked that he asked. Most clients just nodded and let her do the fighting. "When I said it was no big deal. I meant for me," she said. "Stay here. You'll get a kill soon enough."

"What's going on?" Arwen's too loud voice came from behind.

Darshana looked back and put a finger to her lips. "Shhh."

Roman pointed to the scout and said in a hushed voice, "There's a creature up there. Darshana is going to go get him."

"Why can't we get him, Andrew?" she said, using Roman's Real-Real name in bad form. Then she folded her arms across her perfectly shaped breasts and gazed upward, looking spoiled and pouty. "This is so boring. We've done nothing but walk for forty-five minutes. Is this what we paid for? A hike?"

As with the warrior, Darshana wondered how closely the elf resembled her player. Men tended to emphasize their muscles when they created their characters, and women, even Shea, narrowed their waists and emphasized their breasts. In this case, though, Darshana had a feeling the real woman looked exactly like this elven barbie doll.

"If it signals its buddies, you're all going to die, and we will have to start over at the Staghead Gate. So let me deal with it," Darshana said. "Then we can sneak up on some lesser creatures further up." She knew there would be some—there always were. "And you can fight them for points." She glanced at the cleric whose name she still could not remember. "Except for you, of course."

The moon face in the hood nodded.

Darshana crept forward. Getting closer to the target wouldn't be necessary if she had a long-range weapon like the bow the scout was holding. Nothing in the Land was better for distant kills than a bow, but they got in the way. You had to carry them on your back which was where she preferred her sword. Besides, in her hands, the compact crossbow meant certain death to all but the most heavily armored within two hundred feet. What it lacked in range, the crossbow more than made up for in speed. Its pump-like cocking and loading mechanism allowed her to dispatch a half dozen armor-piercing bolts in the time it took an expert archer to notch, draw, and release a single arrow. It was the Land's equivalent of a semiautomatic rifle, but it required her to get closer.

She was just about in range when an alarm tone sounded in her ear and a small window opened off to her right and flashed the words "Message from Falin pending." Annoyed, she waved the window away like she was swatting at a bug and continued toward her prey. As she steadied the crossbow for a long shot, the tone and flashing alert message returned. *Give me a break, Dwarf. I'm busy.* She took a breath and squeezed the trigger.

The scout dropped, and she dismissed the alert window again only to have it pop back up. *Damn.* She swiped it away, then pumped a new bolt into her crossbow and climbed up to where the scout had been standing, checking as she went to make sure none of its friends were hiding in the brush. The creature had fallen down the opposite side of the hill. Its crumpled body lay among some boulders halfway down the slope.

She searched the terrain for other threats, and finding none, she paused for a moment to admire the familiar view. Spread out below her was the lake with its mirrorlike water turning pink in the twilight. Set in a forest of tall pines, its multiple coves gave it a bearlike shape. On its opposite shore, the gate road parted the trees and ran straight through a distant granite arch. Bear Lake Gate, the destination for today's trek. She signaled to the others to wait and descended to where the dead wargarian had landed. Staring down at the fallen creature, she wondered what to do about Falin's messages.

The SIM session wouldn't allow her to view them. She would have to exit to see what Falin wanted, though she already thought she knew. The Gray Warrior must be in the Land. It was time to continue the hunt. She gazed back up the hill. She could almost hear Arwen needling Roman. *Go see what's going on, Andrew. We didn't pay her to sit around.*

There were three ways she could leave the SIM to access the messages. She could exit through Bear Lake Gate. It was only three miles away, but it would take fifteen minutes to get there at a full run. She could bury Darshana's *Shēngmìnglì* and quit. This would allow her to leave and reenter the Land here instead of at a gate. Technically, this involved dying and respawning but with a full restore. Darshana would be the same, but a death would be registered. It was a shameful way to go, usually done to escape a fight. She taught all her trainees how to do it, but she hadn't done it herself in years. She shook the thought off, unable to bring herself to consider it, especially not in front of a paying party. Her reputation would be trashed. The last option was to suspend play and let Darshana sleep until she could resume. This was the quickest and riskiest alternative.

When a character slept in the Land, no matter its level, it was defenseless. A sleeping Darshana would be easy prey for a minor SIM creature like the wargarian scout or even a lowly *càiniǎo*, like the three crouching fifty yards below on the other side of the hill. She imagined Arwen plunging a sword into Darshana and instantly advancing multiple levels, getting her money's worth. No doubt the bitch would do it.

The message alert popped up again. What did Em say? *Gum on her shoe; more like shit.* She stepped off the path and selected a thorny blackberry bush for cover. Then she used the hand gestures to open the control panel and punched the suspend button. *Are you sure?* "No, I'm not fucking sure," she muttered to herself as she chose yes.

An instant later, Shea was back in the Sun Lobby standing in front of Darshana's empty case. "Hang in there, girl," she said as she brought up the messaging app and scrolled through Falin's texts. *Are you there? He just entered through the Blackwood Gate again. He just took out three players. Where are you? I'm going through the gate. Meet me. Hurry.*

Falin wouldn't last fifteen minutes in Blackwood without her.

She typed a response. *Don't enter Blackwood until I'm there to meet you. Be there in twenty.*

It felt like an eternity before she received a reply. *We're going to miss him.*

She said her response out loud as she typed. "Be there in twenty. No more messages."

She closed the app, said a prayer to one of her mother's old gods, and pushed the RESUME button on Darshana's panel.

Arwen asking, "What's wrong with her?" was the first thing Darshana heard when she woke.

Roman was kneeling next to her with Arwen, sword drawn, standing behind him. The cleric hovered over her, and the air was filled with a sparkling gold dust.

Darshana blinked. She looked at the cleric. "Did you cast a healing spell on me?"

The moon face beneath the hood smiled.

"Thank you. I guess," she said as she stood and brushed the gold dust out of her hair.

"What happened?" Roman asked.

She ignored him. "I have to go."

"What the hell does that mean?" Arwen said.

"Emergency."

The foolish elf princess pointed her sword at Darshana's chest. "We paid you. You have to—"

Darshana had no idea what the elf would have said had she allowed her to finish. It's doubtful Arwen was aware of the blade that passed through her before she received the red screen informing her that her character had died.

Roman grinned. "Shit. That was fast."

The cleric said nothing.

Darshana returned her sword to its sheath. "You'll get a refund," she said. Then she took off down the path at a full run toward Bear Lake Gate.

Chapter 20
Missed Opportunity

THE CANCER THAT HAD started in his blood had spread to his spinal cord where it had turned aggressive. That was his oncologist's word: aggressive. It had spared his brain so far. But he was losing the use of his lower body. It was difficult to stand and walk. Soon, he would not be able to go to the bathroom on his own. The only saving grace was he wouldn't have to endure the indignation for long. Four weeks—maybe more, probably less. Aggressive.

He stared at the array of computer monitors suspended in a semicircle above his bed. While the preponderance of the computing world had traded their large physical displays in for virtual reality headgear, he, like most old-school developers, preferred the physical configurations. Kind of ironic when one considered it was the old-schoolers who'd created the very virtual spaces they eschewed for their own work.

Several messaging windows filled the leftmost display. All idle at the moment. One in particular was frustratingly so. Even when he was well, the panes had been his primary access to the outside world. His occupation did not require or allow much personal interaction with his customers which suited him. Up close, people could be dangerous. Something he'd learned all too well growing up on the streets of Roxbury, back when its squares and streets were still named after colonials and slave-holders. It hadn't been the safest place for a nerdy half Asian, half Black kid unable to conceal his advanced IQ and prone to speaking his mind.

Books, computer games, and Dudley—a small dog his father had often accused his mother of eyeing for dinner—had been his entire world until a cousin from California had spent a summer with them. She had arrived early for her first semester at MIT and stayed until she moved to campus housing, a move he would make seven years later. She'd taught him to program, but more excitingly, how to follow and exploit the hidden links in the global network and explore the government and corporate systems that ran the world. She'd made him a hacker, and from that summer on, he'd lived in the dark cyberspace that existed beneath the web and the Verse.

The big display hanging directly in front of him beeped, and he studied a stream of white text scrolling through a black field. His contact had called it the Anomaly. This player character—he was no longer convinced that's what it was—had infiltrated their system and was defeating the rules of their world. The filter he had hooked to the simulation's main event loop had been a clever bit of programming, but not one beyond the company's developers. Sooner or later, they would do the same, and when they did, they would find his code. It wouldn't lead back to him, of course, but they'd know they were not the only ones searching.

The job, his last, kept his mind off the pain and the running out of his clock. Before she'd contacted him, it had been a long time since he'd entered the Verse, and then only for business. He hadn't played games since he left school, and he'd never been drawn to the fantasy worlds—not even hers. The whole thought of playing a role in a world simulation involving elves and dwarfs still made him chuckle. Though, he had to admit, it had its moments, and he did enjoy the interactions with the lovely Shea.

Little did Shea know, the dwarf she believed was a teenage boy named Bobby Penn was actually a middle-aged man whose nom de guerre, Mad Hat, was listed somewhere on the FBI's most wanted cybercriminal list, in a prominent position, he hoped. His true identity was known only to his mother, a small circle of doctors and final-care nurses, and a wealthy cousin trying to prevent another hacker from disrupting the IPO that would make her one of the richest women on the planet.

It had been two months since Jasmine had passed a note to him through his mother. *Got a job for you, Cuz. Take your mind off things. Things...*

She'd visited a few days later, her private jet waiting at Fort Lauderdale Executive Airport, FXE, while the two of them huddled there in the guest-room-turned-hospice of his mother's Palm Beach condo. She'd told him she needed a hacker to catch a hacker. It had to be kept secret, and she knew she could trust him. He'd done jobs for her before, and most had been on the up-and-up. Others had been less so; those had mostly involved planting trojan horse algorithms in competitor code-bases, some just providing information, others causing system crashes and instability.

As far as he could tell, this job was kosher: identify the hacker threatening her cash cow. She'd offered to pay him a million dollars. He'd laughed at her offer, and later, after she'd gone, cried. A million dollars wouldn't buy him more time, but it would cover medical bills that were eating away at what he'd set aside for his mother as quickly as the cancer was eating him. Besides, he wasn't doing anything else but dying, and as Cuz had said, it would take his mind off that, at least a little.

Two days after she'd left, one of Jasmine's employees, Angela, posted a coded message for him in the appropriate forum to initiate the project. They'd worked together before, but though he knew all about her, she knew him only as the consultant.

They'd discussed the details over the usual secure chat sessions. He was to determine how the hacker was exploiting the system, and if possible, identify him. As with all their en-gagements, he would have no direct contact with the Xperion team other than Angela. The Xperion developers would not know about him. It was essential the hacker's activities were not made public. If word got out Xperion's flagship simulation had been hacked, it would mean financial disaster for Cuz and her company.

The Anomaly, as Angela called the hacker's character, entered the simulation at random, seemed to target the most advanced players, and disappeared without leaving a logging trace. The Xperion team was spending all their time running test scenarios to figure out what bugs the hacker must have introduced into the system to enhance his character's capabil-ities and circumvent the logging and monitoring functions, but their efforts so far had proven fruitless.

It was the classic reproducibility dilemma. All program-mers knew the most difficult thing about fixing software bugs was recreating them. Once a bug could be reproduced and observed in a controlled environment, fixing it was almost always trivial. Shutting down this hacker would be no different. All he had to do was figure out a way to cause the Anomaly to strike a target while he was monitoring it. Then he could trace the system events and identify the changes the hacker had made. Once he had it, he'd turn over the trace data to Angela, and the Xperion team would use it to repair the affected code and plug the holes that allowed the hacker to make them in the first place. The problem was, as Angela had pointed out, there were millions of potential targets. He couldn't monitor them all, but Angela had come up with the answer. They would use bait.

"It's clear it's an ego thing," she'd written. "The hacker is going after the top levels. Let's dangle a few in front of him and see what he does."

She'd invented a whole new level she called Legend, then assigned the new status to a handful of longtime fifty-level characters who had made names for themselves for their excellent play. It took her less than a day to come up with four Legend level characters to use for the bait.

The four were notified of their new status and posts were crafted on various gaming boards praising their exploits and pumping them up even more. They were all wicked badasses that no normal player could take down. It had worked. The Anomaly killed the first one two days after the initial posts. The kill event had been trapped and analyzed. It took an agonizing two weeks for the next kill, a lot of time for a man with little left, but he'd learned much from it, enough to identify the killer's event data signature, though still not enough to link it to a user profile or identify the defects creating the security hole.

While monitoring the remaining characters, he'd stumbled on a post soliciting new players to join one of those characters on a pricey training trek. *Looking to Level up Fast? Come join our trekking party to be led by the Legend Darshana. One slot left. Thirty-coin. Contact Xu.* He, as his new Verse character, Falin, had contacted Xu.

The main monitor beeped again. The Anomaly had bulldozed through several more minor players. "What's the matter, big guy? No fifties around tonight? Just hang in there. I'm trying to bring you one."

According to the location data, the Anomaly was still near

the entry point called Blackwood Gate. Where was Shea? Damn, if they went in now, he was sure the gray fucker would bite. Then he'd capture about a gig worth of tracing data and have Cuz's problem solved by the morning.

It was doubtful Shea's character would survive the encounter. In order for the tracking program to collect the necessary event data to identify the modified code, she'd have to fight the Anomaly, and she couldn't win. The best he could hope for was she kept fighting long enough for him to trace the hacker's phony account and device address. Then it would be time for Cuz to pay up. Shea was growing on him, and he felt bad for deceiving her. He'd send her a big chunk of coin to make up for Darshana's loss. *Maybe even the half he'd promised.*

A message window chirped, and Shea's contact photo popped up on the screen. *Lovely.* About time. *Twenty minutes. No more messages.* After he read it, he stared at the ceiling and winced. The fire that had started in his tailbone was creeping up his back. The pain medication was wearing off. The time was nearing when the dosage required to blunt the pain would knock him out. He switched to the monitor containing his tracking code and banged away at the keys, forcing the pain to the back of his mind, enjoying the mechanical feel of the strikes on his fingertips. Another reason he didn't use a virtual setup. Even his ultra-expensive haptic gloves couldn't replicate this feel.

The door to the room opened, and his mother entered with a tray of what little food he was still able to consume along with a single syringe. Until a month ago, she'd come in with multiple syringes. She'd insert each one into the infusion port on his left breast and push the "Hail Mary" cancer therapeutics into his bloodstream, then sit with him to ensure he didn't vomit all over himself. Now, it was just one. Morphine. Soon that would be replaced by a continuous drip, and he would control the dose.

"Are you still working?" she asked with concern in her voice as she placed the tray on the tabletop next to his keyboard.

"A little longer." He glanced at the syringe. "I can't take that right now." He winced when he said it, and she glared at him.

"I can see you're in pain."

He laughed. "That doesn't take much vision."

She frowned, then nodded at Shea's picture. "She's pretty, but too young for you."

"What?" he replied. "You don't think I could get a babe like that?"

She smiled while she removed the lids from the food containers.

"Cream of wheat, toast, and raspberry jello. Mmm, mmm, mmm," he said.

"Try to eat it. You need your strength."

He studied her. She was only fifty-eight, but her once-raven hair was laced with gray, and deep creases had emerged around her eyes—eyes that were the same almond shape and color as his own. It was those eyes that had made him such a target in the old neighborhood. She'd been a looker back then, as pretty as Jasmine, and truth be known, just as smart. The gray hair, the creases, had all appeared over the last couple years. They'd been difficult years. First her husband, his father, had died suddenly of a heart attack, and now her only child was wasting away before her eyes.

"Would you like to go outside tomorrow? Maybe sit by the ocean for a little while?" she asked.

"Got things to do with this hot babe," he said nodding to Shea's picture.

She scowled. "Too young."

"Yeah, but we're givin' it a go in the Verse tonight." He wiggled his eyebrows.

"Don't overtax yourself like last time. I don't want to come in here later and have to pull that thing," she motioned to the cyber headgear on his rollover table, "off your head again."

"Go away, Mother. Let me die in peace."

As she turned to leave, the display monitoring the Gray Warrior beeped. He had left the SIM. Didn't go through a gate. The rules didn't apply to him. He just left.

"Looks like the date's off." He grimaced. "You can give me that shot. I want to be numb when I break my babe's heart."

Chapter 21
Killer in the Land

THE SMOOTH WALNUT OF his cane's derby handle formed a perfect cup for Parker's chin. He rested it there while he sat hunched over in a visitor chair across from Becky Fulbright's immaculate desk. His eyes were fixed on the polished surface devoid of all the things that cluttered his own workspace, including Becky herself, who had asked him to meet her this morning to review the Collector case. She'd stepped out to take a call the moment he'd arrived, leaving him to contemplate, like a Zen koan, the purpose for a desk if not to be a resting place for unopened mail, unread publications, and stacks of papers.

His meditative trance was broken when Becky returned and took her place behind the empty span of particle board and cherry veneer. She made a show of pocketing her phone. "Sorry about the wait. Had to take a call from Warner. It seems you made quite an impression in Vegas."

Rebecca Fulbright was a compact woman in her early forties who kept herself fit by cycling what Parker thought were absurd distances through the Virginia countryside. She had spiked auburn hair and big hazel eyes with white oval patches around them where the sun that tanned the rest of her face had been blocked by sunglasses. The masklike tan marks made her look like a raccoon and called attention to the fine lines visible at the corners of her eyes and between her eyebrows, evidence of a lifetime of both easy laughter and frequent worry.

Parker stared up at her without removing his chin from the cane. He was giving her his best bored, indifferent impression and believed he was nailing it. "Do you think the boss is still showing Divine his dinghy?" he asked, suppressing an urge to sing a verse from the old Beetles song, *Rocky Raccoon*.

"What?"

"I'm just wondering if Warner is still playing hide the torpedo with his old navy colleague."

She squinted at him the way she did when she was annoyed, further deepening the lines around her eyes. "Michael's married."

"And?"

"Stop. I didn't ask you here this morning to gossip about our boss." She leaned over her desk. "Besides, Michael looks out for you. He's a big reason why you're still on active duty."

Parker lifted his chin from his cane and gave her an apologetic look. "You're right. I should be more appreciative. Me, being a useless cripple and all."

She straightened. "Okay, enough bullshit. What do you have?"

"I think I've identified some common traits in the victims and the beginnings of a profile for our unsub."

"Our unsub? As in a single perpetrator?"

"Maybe."

"Then I was right," she said.

"There's always a first time, but don't let it go to your head."

"Whatever. Let's hear it."

"He," Parker began, "because it's almost always a man, has the means to travel or has a job involving travel."

She smirked and waved her hand dismissively. "Established."

"And he," Parker reemphasized the unsub's gender, "exhibits the following characteristics." Ticking them off on his fingers, he recited, "He's White, young, but not a kid. I'd say in his mid-twenties to early thirties. He doesn't have any close friends, and the people who do know him describe him as quiet, lacking confidence, and odd or quirky. He likely lives alone and possesses above average intelligence." Parker wiggled his eyebrows. "What do you think? Impressive right?"

"Well, I would be impressed," she said, "except you just described the prototypical serial killer." She pointed to a bookcase in the corner. "I think I may have read that exact description in one of your books."

He pushed himself out of the chair with his cane and hobbled over to where she was pointing. She had both his textbooks and the novel he'd written during the eighteen months he had spent on disability. He glanced over his shoulder at her. "My, my, I didn't realize you were such a fan."

"I am required to read what my employees publish," she quipped.

He selected the most recent of the texts, *Hunting the Hunters, A Guide to Forensic Behavioral Analysis, 2nd Edition* and flipped to a page in the first chapter. "Yes. Here it is." He turned toward her and read, "The common belief is the prototypical serial killer is an aloof White male, between the ages of twenty and forty, who is of high intelligence, and comes from an abusive household."

He looked over the book at her. "Is that what you are referring to?"

"Uh-huh."

"I guess you don't recall the next paragraph." Parker continued reading, "As forensic behavioral scientists, we must not rely on common beliefs, as they will bias our analysis, and they are often wrong. Statistics compiled from over one hundred years of homicide case data indicates serial killers, defined as those who kill two or more people with a period of inactivity between kills, come from all races and age groups proportional to their percentage of the overall population. Though, one common belief appears validated by the data, serial killers are overwhelmingly male." He closed the book. "There is no such thing as a prototypical serial killer."

She held out her hand and wiggled her fingers in a give-me gesture. He hobbled over to her and handed her the book.

"I remember that," she said as she flipped to another page. "But I also remember this: 'If the data does not support the prototypical serial killer profile, why does the public's perception persist? The simple answer appears to be serial murders perpetrated by the young, White male demographic get the most media attention. Again, as scientists, we must ask why? The easy explanation is killings by members of the privileged class gone bad are more newsworthy than killings by members of disadvantaged populations caught up in poverty-induced violence.'"

She raised a finger to ward off the triumphant sarcasm percolating in his throat. "But another possibility could be hidden in the numbers. Young, intelligent, White males may disproportionately commit more organized and complicated murders of random victims which makes those murders more terrifying to the public. Staying out of crime-ridden neighborhoods offered no protection from Ted Bundy."

"Man, can I write or what?" he said.

She tossed the book on her desk with a thud. "So, our killer is the prototypical, intelligent, aloof, young, White male with the means to travel. Great. That's probably what? Thirty million potential suspects. And only then if we limit it to US residents." She scowled at him. "A useless profile."

Parker gave her a diabolical grin. "Yes. Yes," he responded in his best Anthony Hopkins impersonation. "But as Hannibal Lecter might say, 'What does he covet, Clarice?'"

She made a face. "Ears."

"Exactly. He collects ears. Why would he do that?"

"He's sick. Maybe he has small ones or big ones and he's looking for something better."

Parker cocked his head. "Let me think about that for a moment." He tapped his finger on his chin and then wrinkled his nose as if the idea itself reeked. "No. I don't think so. He doesn't envy his victim's anatomy, if that's what you're suggesting," he said with mock seriousness. "You know what I think?"

"I'm dying to know."

"I think the ear collecting and the way he's killing with a sword are all part of some elaborate fantasy he's living." He studied her, impregnating the moment, "In the Metaverse."

She rocked forward in her chair. "What?"

"You say that word often."

"What?"

"See, you said it again." He pulled his phone from the breast pocket of his blazer and nodded at the television on her wall which was tuned to one of the cable news networks with the sound turned off. "Can I stream to that?"

Her big eyes got bigger. "First Metaverse and now streaming? What happened? Did you find technology religion in the desert?"

"Yeah. I've gone full-blown geek. I even visited one of those places everyone goes now. You know? To plug into the Verse, man." He made air quotes when he said Verse.

"You're kidding! Did you go in? To the Verse, I mean?"

"No, but I got enough of a look to make me curious."

He told her about how he'd stood with a pair of amphet-amine-fueled kids and watched a player kill another player and remove their ears. "The player took them for trophies. Like our unsub."

"Interesting. You think the killer is modeling behavior he sees in the Metaverse?"

"I think it could be where he's learned to do it, and where he selects his victims from."

Becky bit her lip. "Hmm. Seems like a bit of a stretch, but billions of people do this Verse thing."

"Do you?" he asked.

She shook her head. "I think it's weird. Though my cycling club has started organizing more virtual rides. No flat tires, no one gets hit by cars, and you can ride anywhere in the world. Who knows? Maybe I'll give it a try."

"Don't. It's weird." Although, he thought, if she did, she wouldn't get the raccoon-eye tan lines pedaling under a com-puter-generated sun. He pointed at the television again. "Make the screen do its thing so I can share this photo."

She pressed some buttons on the television remote, and he fiddled with his phone until the image of Jyothi Reddy's head-less body stretched out on a gurney appeared on the screen.

Becky jumped. "Jeezus, Parker. You could've warned me before putting that up."

"Sorry. Wrong picture." He grinned and selected anoth-er picture from his phone. The photo of a living Jyothi Reddy from Donna Baker's notes replaced the gruesome image of her decapitated body. "Honestly, I don't understand your reaction. You send me those kinds of photos all the time. I was beginning to think you had some kind of fetish for them."

Her eyes narrowed. "Fuck you. What are we looking at?"

"One Jyothi Reddy."

"The Nashville victim?"

"That's her."

"Pretty girl. Tragic. What's the point?"

"See what she's holding?"

"Yeah, a toy sword. So?"

"Look what it says on her T-shirt."

"'You haven't lived until you've died in the Land of Might

and Magic?'"

"That's the game where I saw the player take the trophies."

"Now that's very interesting."

"I spoke to the detective in charge of Jyothi's case. Nice lady. A bit of a downer, but nice. I got her to ask the woman's mother if the deceased played this game. It turns out she was obsessed with it. Jyothi's mother told the detective her daughter spent all her free time in the game playing a character called Danaka. The mother called it an addiction and said her daughter spent a fortune doing it."

"Hmm. What about the other victims? Did they play this game too?"

Parker rubbed his leg and reached for the pill vial in his pants pocket but reconsidered popping the pills in front of Becky. "Jaden spoke with LVMPD about Tate. Same story. Tate's wife said her husband was addicted to the game. It was destroying their marriage."

"What about the Clearwater girl, Loveridge? Did she play too?"

"Don't know yet. Turns out the detective working that case is out on a medical. Been out for a month. That's why it took so long for the ViCAP filing. Guy had a heart attack, massive."

"That sucks."

"Yeah. Especially for me, because the sergeant I spoke to said he had no one available to fill in on the case. He gave me Abby Loveridge's mother's information and told me to call her myself."

Becky made a hissing sound. "I seem to remember you teaching me we do research and analysis in BAU. We are not investigators."

"Becky, I need the information for the victimology, unless you are comfortable with the prototypical profile."

She sighed. "No. That isn't going to help anyone catch him. We need more."

"And we can't wait for this detective's heart to heal," Parker said. "Our unsub seems to be on a two-week kill schedule. If he stays with it, he's going to kill again in the next six days."

Chapter 22
Abby

ONCE, NOT TOO LONG ago, grief had been an academic topic for Parker. After all, his workday often began with a stranger's death. He was barely aware of the pain the victim's loved one's felt; to him, the victim's death was just the start to a puzzle to be solved.

Like everyone else, he had experienced personal loss, but back then it had all been remote with little lasting impact—grandparents and extended family members made strangers by time and distance—and colleagues he'd only miss when he needed something from them for a case. A few had been a surprise—car accidents and heart attacks—but most had come after long illnesses, the blow of their loss softened by the mercy of it. Parker had attended the funerals and offered his condolences. He had known exactly how to respond to the anguish; after all, he was an expert, trained in the psychology of grief by the FBI and George Mason University.

That was before he truly experienced it. Before Carrie's death, Parker had possessed only an abstract, analytical appreciation for how people process loss, and it had made him cold. *Aunt Margie will get over Uncle Bob's death once she gets through the acceptance stage.* All the books had taught him grief was overcome in a linear sequence, like steps in an instruction manual for reassembling a shattered life: Denial, Anger, Bargaining, Depression, then Acceptance. He'd believed it, too, until he held his dying wife in his blood-drenched arms.

Parker stared at the name and number on the page in his notebook and tightened his grip on the phone in his sweaty hand. He'd been sitting like that for several minutes, unable to punch the numbers into the phone's screen that would connect him to a mother's loss. The paralysis wasn't all out of empathy. Grief—intense grief, he'd learned, could be covered up, but it was always there. Acceptance, if there was such a thing, was nothing more than a layer of scar tissue over a wound that never healed. His scars were still thin and would be easily punctured by the shards of pain he knew would radiate from Abby Loveridge's mother like shrapnel from a bomb. He was afraid of what would happen when that barrier was penetrated. Would his emotional state hold? He took a deep breath and entered the numbers. It was time to find out.

"Hello," a woman's voice answered. The "oh" drawn out in an upper midwestern accent.

"May I speak to Sarah Loveridge, please?"

"Speaking. Who is this?"

"My name is Parker Reid, ma'am. I'm with the FBI."

The phone went silent for a moment. "Oh. Is this about Abby?"

"Yes. I'm sorry to trouble you, but I need to ask you a few questions."

"I still can't believe she's gone. You hear about these terrible things happening to other people, but you never expect them to happen to your family—to your child."

Denial.

"I'm sorry, ma'am. I truly am." And he meant it.

The high e and low o sounds that suggested a distant Swedish or Norwegian ancestry developed a harder edge. "When did the FBI get involved? We were dealing with a Detective Vargus from Clearwater City. He promised to keep us informed about the case, but we haven't heard from him in weeks."

Parker sighed. The last thing he wanted to do was to cause this woman any more pain. "I'm sorry, ma'am. Detective Vargus is out of the office for health reasons. Otherwise, I'm sure he would have called you."

"How do I know you are who you say you are?"

Parker had anticipated this question. Vargus or the Clearwater City PD's Victim Advocacy Office would have warned her to be wary of calls about her daughter from people claiming to be with other law enforcement agencies. Scammers and other lowlifes preyed on vulnerable people like Sarah Loveridge. "I can give you a number to call to validate my credentials." He paused to let her process what he offered. "Would you like the number, Mrs. Loveridge?"

"Yes."

He gave her the phone number and his FBI ID code and waited for her to call back. It took her almost thirty minutes.

"They called you Dr. Reid. Is that what I should call you?"

"No, ma'am. I go by Parker."

"Parker," she echoed, sounding uncomfortable with the familiarity of his first name, perhaps not willing to make a personal connection. "Okay, Parker," she said tentatively. "You can call me Sarah. What do you need to know?"

"I will make this quick, Sarah. Did Abby use the Metaverse?"

"The Metaverse?"

"Yes. Computer-simulated reality."

"I know what it is. I just don't understand what it has to do with Abby's murder."

Parker thought he heard her sniffle and guessed the long delay before she called him back may have been to give her time to get control of her emotions. "I know this is hard. The person who killed your daughter..."

"Person," she blurted. "Person," she said it again louder. "No *person* does such a thing. Only a monster would cut my baby's beautiful head off."

Anger.

"I'm sorry." He knew better than most how right she was. The man who killed this poor woman's daughter was indeed a monster. "He's done it to others, Sarah, and he will do it again unless we catch him."

"So, catch him," she snapped.

"That's what I'm trying to do, but I need your help."

The phone grew silent except for her sniffling, then she asked. "What can I do?"

"I am trying to determine how this monster knew your daughter." He said knew, but he meant selected. "Where he might have met her."

"So am I," she sobbed. "I think about it all the time. Abby hardly knew anyone down there. She had no time to make friends or," Sarah paused and sobbed, "enemies. She was always in such a rush. So eager to get started with her life after she'd finished her degree."

"What did she study?" Parker asked, but he already knew.

"Computers. She got a degree in computer science from Madison." The anger in her voice had gone and was replaced by something between pride and sadness. "Graduated with honors, don't you know. But then she had to run off to Florida of all places. The beach. It was always the beach. As if she ever took a break from working to see the sun. She spent all her time in that miserable little apartment. I should have never let her go. She'd still be with us if she'd stayed up here and went to work in the Cities. We told her there were plenty of good jobs here." She sobbed. "God, I would do anything to be able to go back and change her mind."

Bargaining.

"Sarah, I need to know if Abby played games in the Metaverse."

"Games?" She snorted. "No. my Abby didn't play games. She worked. All the time. Code, code, code is what she did."

It wasn't the answer he was hoping for. "Did she ever mention a Metaverse simulation called the Land of Might and Magic?"

The sniffling returned and there was a long pause as she considered the question.

"I don't remember her mentioning it, and we talked all the time," she sobbed. "Every night, about everything."

He sighed and rubbed his leg. "Do you know if she owned a cybersuit?"

"She has a mask and gloves, if that's what you mean. She had to, for work. It's how everything is done these days."

"So she did spend time in the Metaverse."

"Yes, of course she did. Like I said, she was a programmer. They all do, but she didn't play games. Not that I know of."

He looked over his notes and his eyes landed on a word he'd written in large block letters, ADDERAL. "Did Abby take any medications?"

"No," she answered immediately. Then she added, "Well, maybe Tylenol for headaches and cramps. Why?"

"Nothing for focus or attention deficit?"

"No," she scoffed. "My daughter had no issues with focus, Dr. Reid." The edge was back. "Again, why the question about medications?"

"Abby had traces of Adderal in her system, Sarah. Do you

know what that is?"

"I'm a nurse. Of course, I know what Adderal is. I don't know why she would have taken it. Maybe it was because of pressure from work. She was always under deadlines."

"What did Abby do exactly?"

"I already told you. She was a computer programmer, a coder." She pronounced it cohdar.

"Yes, but do you know what kind of programs she wrote?"

"She worked for a company that built security systems."

The hair on the back of Parker's neck tingled.

"What kind of systems? Do you know?"

"I believe she called them entrance way systems."

"Door locks?" Parker promted.

"I think that might have been part of it, but she worked on all kinds of things."

The tingle moved to the top of his head, and he had the feeling he'd found another hard-to-fit piece in the puzzle. "What is the name of the company she worked for?"

"ZCS. I believe it stands for Zhang Control Systems. Fucking slave drivers. Chinese, don't you know."

The obscenity and anti-Chinese sentiment startled him. "I see." He took down the company name. "Did she talk about her colleagues? Maybe mention anyone she may have been having problems with?"

"Detective Vargus asked about all this. I'll tell you the same thing I told him. She barely knew the people she worked with. Most of them were in Las Vegas. She only saw them on the computer."

Now Parker's hair was on fire. "Las Vegas?"

"Yes. That's where ZCS is based. Abby was a remote worker. She talked about moving out there, God forbid, but there's no ocean. Shit, there's no water, for that matter. She couldn't leave the beach she never visited."

"Would you happen to have Abby's manager's contact information?"

"Yes. Give me a minute to find it."

After a moment, she returned with the information, and he took it down. He scanned his notes, checking to make sure he hadn't forgotten anything. Satisfied, he said, "Thank you, Sarah. You have been very helpful. I'm sure Detective Vargus will be in touch soon."

"Wait," she said before he could disconnect. "I Googled you after I called the FBI number."

"Yes?"

"I read what happened to your wife."

He swallowed but didn't respond.

"Does it get any easier, Dr. Reid?"

A tear fell from his eye, scar tissue punctured, and he cleared his throat. "No, but you will get stronger, Sarah."

She sobbed. "Catch the fucking monster," she pleaded, and the line went dead.

Depression.

Chapter 23
A Dire Situation

A **LIGHT SNOW WAS** falling when Darshana emerged from the Wolfsburg Gate. The large flakes floated down from the gray sky unperturbed by even the hint of a breeze. They settled on the cobblestones of the gate road and promptly melted. It was still summer. Too early for snow, even there in the shadow of the northern face of the White Mountains. She guessed the flakes were refugees from the snowcap of the towering Zugspitze Massif, carried by the swirling winds of the storm perpetually raging on its summit. It was the tallest and most foreboding mountain in the range, and it loomed over the gate. On the rare clear day, when the clouds released their hold, its granite and ice peaks resembled the fangs of the fierce, dire wolves that roamed the boreal forest, crouching at its sheer face.

The gate road ran north into the wilderness and south to the Bavarian-style village of Wolfsburg. The collection of cream-colored *bauernhaus* buildings with brown, high-pitched roofs and wood trim looked like something out of a German travel blog. The snowglobe-like scene was made complete by an enormous fairytale fortress that rose above the town like a lesser bookend to the Zugspitze.

Darshana was admiring the view when Falin appeared. He trudged up beside her, stroked his ridiculous beard, and said, "Ah. Would you look at that? It's Neuschwanstein."

"What are you talking about?"

"The castle. It's the spitting image of the Neuschwanstein Castle in Germany. You know, the one Disney modeled Cinderella's castle after."

"How do you know that, Boston?"

"I've been there. In the Real-Real." He used a mocking tone when he said Real-Real.

143

She eyed him. "Go with your parents or was it something you did with your high school German class?"

He laughed and coughed. "Something like that."

"So, is he still in here or are you wasting my time again?"

Falin looked up at her and frowned. "You seem cranky today. What gives?"

"What gives? Nine thousand dollars. That's what gives. I had to give that party I left behind yesterday all their money back."

He looked down at his boots. "I told you I was sorry about that." He looked up and smiled. "Nine thousand is chicken feed compared to what we'll get when we get the fucker."

The mention of the bounty aggravated her even more. Only Em and this obnoxious dwarf seemed to know anything about it. She'd spent hours searching gaming sites and cheater blogs for any reference to it and found nothing. The whole thing was beginning to feel like a scam or maybe a stupid wizard test. She glared at Falin. "I haven't been able to find this bounty posting anywhere on the net or in the Verse."

He shrugged. "Well, well, imagine that. The legendary Darshana doesn't know everything."

"Kiss my ass, Boston. Tell me where I can find the posting, or I'm going home."

"Don't get your panties in a wad. I'll send you a link when we're done. Not that it'll matter, though. We're going to get him tonight, and then we'll be rich." He retrieved the mirror from his pack. "You'll see," Falin said while he studied the device. "He's still in here." He turned around and pointed through the arch to the forest. "Somewhere in there. Last event hit was twenty minutes ago in a location called Wolfwood."

"Wolfwood? You have any idea what that is?"

"A woods with wolves," he said with a grin.

"Yeah," she replied. "Big ones with big teeth."

"All the better to eat you with, Little Red Riding Hood," he chuckled.

"We shall see," she said, gesturing for him to take the lead. "After you."

He moved toward the gate, and she pulled him back.

"What?"

"These wolves are tough. They'll be a challenge even for

me. Are you ready for this?"

"Fucking-ay. Let's get bangin'."

He took off toward the forest again. This time, she stuck out her boot and tripped him. As he did in the Hunter's Horn, he toppled over like a felled tree and immediately returned to his feet looking confused and angry.

He pushed her. "Enough of that shit."

Darshana grabbed his beard. "You're not in a rig. You promised you'd find one."

He pulled his beard from her grasp and took a step back. "Yeah, well it's not that friggin easy for me."

She shook her head. "You can't fight as a half-in. Especially these wolves. I'm going to burn up lifeforce fighting your battles and then I'll have to face this monster."

"I'll try not to let that happen," he said. Then he began to cough. It took several seconds for his fit to subside.

"Are you okay?" she asked, genuinely concerned.

"Yes," he rasped. "Just a cough. Let's go."

The cobblestone road plunged into the forest. Unlike the Jade Gate road, no magic or community of wood cutters kept the trees from spreading their boughs over its span. It was like trekking through a tunnel. The sun was still up, hidden somewhere behind the thick clouds, but beneath the evergreen canopy, it was night. After more than thirty minutes spent inside the gloom, they stepped into a clearing. The snow had stopped, but the thick clouds were closer and darker than they were at the gate. Even so, the open sky seemed bright and cheery compared to the tunnel. The massif was right on top of them. They caught glimpses of its ominous presence in the shifting clouds.

Midway through the clearing, the road ran under a stone arch. This one was much smaller than any gate. It was no more than twenty feet tall and barely wider than the road itself. A carving of a snarling wolf's head looked down on them from its keystone. The wolf's eyes and mouth were painted red. The cobblestones came to an end beneath it and a dirt path continued out of the clearing into the trees beyond. A polished steel helmet rested on the ground directly below the wolf's stare.

"Is this a gate?" Falin asked.

Darshana shook her head. "It's a border marker."

"What does it mark?"

"The start of Wolfwood."

"The start? I thought we just walked through it."

She laughed and said, "No," then glanced at him and added, "you still have all your limbs." Darshana stepped under the arch and bent to pick up the helmet. As she did, she noticed the bodies and gear scattered about the field. She tossed the helmet aside and looked back at Falin. "He was here."

Falin took out his mirror and checked. Then he glanced nervously around the clearing. "Yep. Not too long ago either. How did you know?"

"Come look."

The dwarf came through the arch and stood gaping at the carnage. "Looks like what happened to us on Jade Mountain." He coughed again and gagged.

Darshana studied him. "You sure you're okay?"

"Yeah, but this is fucking gruesome; way too much photo realism for my taste."

"No one really died here," she said. "Right now, the players who owned these characters are exiting their rigs and heading for the bar. Probably mad as hell to have been red-screened."

She knelt near one of the bodies. It was clad in polished metal armor, still clutching a longsword. Its severed head, missing both ears, was laying a few feet away. "The owner of the helmet," she said. "His player must be really pissed. He was a high-level warrior—probably a forty. Lot of lost rig time." She eyed his torn pack, "Probably a lot of lost coin too." She ran a finger through the bloodstained grass and looked at it. *Still wet.*

Falin was examining another body. "I think this one was a warrior too. How long will the bodies stay here?"

"Until they rot or are eaten. Remember the vultures in the white woods. They clean up the Land."

"Those Xperion people are just fuckin' mad about the realism, aren't they?"

A loud "ayyyoooh" erupted from somewhere nearby, followed by a second, and then a third.

Darshana studied the trees. "It won't be vultures that get these," she said as she bent over the headless body of a midlevel magic user.

The mage lay in a large circular patch of burned grass. Similar circles were scattered throughout the field. Darshana flipped the mage over and located her spell pouch. It was empty except for a single, small golden orb. "Looks like they put up a good fight. She threw everything she had at him." Darshana picked the spell out of the pouch and stood.

"Is that one of those health spells?" Falin asked.

"Yeah. It will come in handy." She stared at the trees. "Soon."

As if to confirm what she said, another series of loud ayyyoooh sounds echoed off the hidden cliff face.

Darshana tucked the orb inside her own spell pouch. "These were no helpless *càiniǎo*. They were all mid- to high-level characters. This thing slaughtered them and took whatever coin and treasure they had. No way to be certain, but I doubt any of them got out by burying their *Shēngmìnglì*." She nodded toward the trees. "You still want to go in there after him?"

"Fuck, yeah. Like you said, no one really dies."

"Okay. Well, lead on, Dwarf. And get your axe ready."

They followed the path back into the forest. They hadn't gone more than two hundred yards when the first wolf attacked. It sprang out of the trees without warning and landed on Falin, snapping at his throat. It was as big as a grizzly bear with red eyes and fur the color of the clouds.

Darshana killed it with one strike from her longsword and pushed its carcass off the prostrate dwarf.

"Still want to keep going, little man?" she said.

"Yes. No one really dies," he repeated, this time as if reassuring himself.

The ground rose as they drew nearer to the massif's vertical face. The mountain's unimaginable size was no longer concealed by the clouds. Huge boulders peppered the landscape as if giants had hurled them down from the precipice above, and the trees that had been so dense, had thinned as they had increased in height and circumference.

"These would be redwoods in the Real-Real," Falin said.

"*Sequoiadendron giganteum*," she said.

"Show off."

About a mile from the clearing, the path made a sharp right turn and climbed onto the first tier of a two-tiered rock terrace that resembled enormous steps leading to the base of the massif. The path continued along the first step for several hundred yards, rising eight to ten feet above the forest floor. They had gone about a third of the way when an enormous black wolf appeared on the second tier above them. It let out a deafening aaaayooh.

The alpha, Darshana thought as she drew her crossbow, but before she could let loose a bolt, an equally large gray wolf fell from the sky and knocked her to the ground. For a moment, Darshana was pinned beneath it, but she'd managed to hold on to her crossbow, and just as snapping jaws closed in on her throat, she pressed it into the wolf's chest and fired. The beast went limp, and she pushed it off with enough force to send it careening over the ledge.

As Darshana got to her feet, more wolves, some black and some gray, all bear-sized, dropped from the second tier. Holstering her crossbow, she drew her sword, and cut and slashed through them with tornadic fury. Their fangs found her arms and legs, and though each individual bite inflicted little damage to her, they were adding up. Her lifeforce was falling as the dead wolves piled up around her.

Out of the corner of her eye, Darshana spotted Falin swatting at several wolves with his axe in the stunted jerky motions of a player using cyberglove controls instead of the full body motion system of a rig. It was like watching an arthritic fat man dance to fast music.

Damn half-in, she thought.

At some point, she lost sight of the dwarf when he fell beneath a roiling mass of gray and black fur. She hacked her way over to where she'd seen him fall and found him under two large wolves in the process of ripping him apart. Darshana barreled into the nearest one like a battering ram, driving it into the other. The three of them tumbled off the ledge and down into the trees, where they bounced along the forest floor until they came to rest against a building-sized sequoia. Darshana regained her footing before the wolves regained theirs and slashed at them with her sword until they were both dead. Then she sprang back up the hill and onto the ledge.

The wolves were gone, and the dwarf was on his back, covered in blood. She assumed he was dead, and they'd have to start over—something she was not certain she wanted to do—when he let out a loud cough.

"Whata fuck'n pissah. Spend all this time just to be killed

by a pack of dawgs."

"You're not dead yet, Boston," she said as she dug in her pouch for a healing spell.

"Yeah, well my lifeforce meter is flashing like a spastic stoplight, and when I try to move, the lady in my head says I've been critically damaged. If the bitch only knew."

Darshana held up a gold orb. "Told you this would come in handy." Then she said the elvish invocation words, crushed it in her hand, and blew its golden dust on Falin. A gold glow enveloped the dwarf, and a second later he popped up on his feet like an over-wound jack-in-the-box.

"That's two you owe me," she said as she counted her remaining health spells. Three left. Her own lifeforce was down to 70 percent. Nothing urgent, but she'd need to be 100 percent to face the monster that took out the party in the clearing. She retrieved another gold orb from her pouch and broke it over her head.

Fully restored, they resumed the trek along the ledge. They had made it another fifty yards when a vibration in Darshana's right temple alerted her to an incoming projectile. She twisted, but not in time to avoid the iron-tipped arrow that slammed into her right breast with a thud and a red flash. Her lifeforce meter registered an immediate 25 percent hit. One arrow had done as much damage as the pack of dire wolves.

It took her less than a second to spot the arrow's source. About a hundred yards away, at the point where the terrace disappeared around a bend, the Gray Warrior sat perched atop his demonic stallion with his great bow drawn for another shot. He let fly his arrow, but Darshana was faster this time, and it whistled past. She responded with three bolts from her crossbow, but even if the high trajectory she'd sent them on ended on target, the distance would rob them of the power needed to pierce the monster's armor or even its hide.

One of the bolts must have found the horse, because the animal let out a terrible scream that seemed as loud as the howls from the wolves. Despite its pain filled wail though, the bolt hadn't brought the animal down. On the contrary, it began to charge.

"Shit," she said. "Time to run, dwarf."

"No way," Falin said as he pulled out his mirror.

"What are you doing?" she said as she fired another volley of bolts at the rapidly approaching rider.

"Collecting data."

"Data?"

"Yeah. Even if he kills us, this is how we're going to get him."

A vibration at her temple told her another arrow was about to strike—on the left this time. Darshana turned, but once again, she was too late. This one punched through her breast plate and knocked her to the ground. Her lifeforce meter fell below 50 percent, and a voice in her ear said, "Serious damage sustained."

Fuck.

She sprang to her feet and pushed the dwarf back. "Run!"

They bolted back the way they'd come. The horse and rider had already halved the distance to them. One more arrow, and it would be red-screen for Darshana. Shea was not about to let that happen, no matter what data the fucking dwarf needed to collect. She dug in her spell pouch as she ran and drew out an iridescent red orb emblazoned with a fiery orange rune.

She checked her life meter. The spell would take its toll, but she should have enough. Darshana balled the orb in her fist and shouted, "Inectius Nuvium Su, Lovem." Then she closed her fist, spun, and thrust her open hand at the ledge above them. An instant later, the mountainside exploded in a flash of blue light and a deafening thunderclap that was followed by the roar of tumbling boulders and snapping trees. The avalanche buried the path under a fifty-foot mound of debris. The voice in her ear said, "Alert! life force below 10 percent."

"Holy fuck!" Falin exclaimed.

Darshana grabbed him by his pack and threw him off the ledge, then jumped down after him. At the bottom, she pulled him to his feet and dragged him farther down the slope.

They huddled behind one of the enormous trees. She dug out her remaining health spells while he fiddled with the mirror.

"God, I hope he didn't exit," he said.

"Are you kidding me?" she said as she crushed one of her two remaining gold orbs over her head. The arrows in her shoulder and chest disappeared in a golden flash. She put the remaining health spell in a pocket for quick retrieval and located the orb Em had given her at Staghead.

"I'm almost afraid to ask what that one does," Falin said.

"Hopefully calls Em."

He swatted at it with his hand. "Don't do that," he said.

"Why the hell not?" She motioned to the pile of debris above them. "You think that's going to stop that monster?"

"I'm hoping it won't," Falin said. "I almost have what I need, and I can't have the wizard learn about this." He held up the mirror.

"Need? What the hell does that mean?" she asked. Darshana grabbed his beard and pulled his face close to hers. "You and that wizard are up to something."

"If I was working with the wizard, I'd let you call him."

Darshana released her hold. "Maybe you're not working with him, but there's something going on and it has nothing to do with a bounty. What is it?"

Before the dwarf could answer, a vibration in her right temple told her to dodge left, and she did, just in time. An arrow grazed her right cheek. *Close.* She rolled to her feet and let loose six bolts in the direction of the arrow's flight. The horse let out another terrifying scream, and this time it was followed by the loud sound of it crashing down into the trees. She'd hit it. The arrow that slammed into her heart stopped her from celebrating.

Her view flashed red, and the voice in her ear declared, "Character death imminent."

Tossing aside Em's orb, she ripped the last health spell from her pocket and broke it over her head just as her life meter tipped to zero.

"He's coming," she heard the dwarf say as the imminent death alerts in her ear subsided.

Darshana grabbed the dwarf and rolled farther down the hill. They tumbled together until they slammed into a boulder. She pushed him behind it. A great roar came from somewhere above them, followed by the sound of something heavy running through the tangled scrub and pine straw.

"I can't believe I'm doing this," she muttered as she retrieved a shovel from her pack.

"What are you doing?" Falin asked.

"Burying my *Shēngmìnglì*. If you don't want to start back at zero, you better do the same."

The crashing grew louder.

"We'll never make it," he said as he pushed the mirror back into his pack and searched for his shovel.

Darshana reached into her spell pouch and pulled out a dark green orb with a silver rune.

"You going to blow up the hillside again?"

"No. Dig," she said. Then she closed her fist around the orb and said the invocation phrase followed by the elvish word for conceal.

The whole world turned a filmy green as if they were inside a bubble.

"What's going on?" Falin said.

"Concealment spell. We're hidden, but it will wear off quickly," she said as she continued to dig.

She was returning her shovel to her pack when the blurry form of the Gray Warrior approached.

"Can he see us?" Falin said over his shoulder as he dug.

"No. But he will soon." She stood and peered out at the monster. He came closer still, until they were almost face-to-face. "I'm going to make you pay for this, scumbag." She turned to Falin. "Are you ready?"

"Yeah, I think so."

She bent down and grabbed his beard again, drawing him close. "You and Em are playing some kind of game, and I'm done. This is humiliating. Don't contact me again."

She released him. Then she made the hand motions to open the game menu, and selected abort from the list. A glowing red ball emerged from her chest, her aura, and a voice in her head said, "You have ten seconds to bury your *Shēngmìnglì*." The voice counted down as she placed the glowing ball in the hole she'd dug and covered it with the loose dirt.

When the countdown reached zero, her visual field turned red, and a message window opened announcing, *YOUR CHARACTER HAS DIED!* A prompt appeared giving her three options, *QUIT, RESPAWN NEW, or RESTORE AT POINT OF DEATH.*

She fought back an angry tear and selected *QUIT.*

Chapter 24
Resurrection

SHEA REMOVED HER HEADGEAR and unbuckled the harness, but she did not step out of the rig. She sat in the quiet darkness of the bay, fuming. On the one hand, she was glad Darshana would be restored. On the other, she was upset the suicidal exit would mar her perfect profile, its stain forever visible on the stat card her customers used when deciding whether to go with her or another guide. The legendary Darshana had slipped a rung down on the top player ladder. No doubt about it.

Trinity meowed and leapt into her lap. Shea removed her gloves and stroked the cat's fur as she considered her losses since she'd met the dwarf. She'd refunded an entire party's money, burned through all her health spells, used her most expensive and powerful lightning spell—the Finger of Jove—and a concealment spell. That one wasn't cheap either. All the magic would have to be replaced. That would set her back quite a bit. Then, there was her reputation. She'd abandoned players she'd contracted to protect, killed one of them, and aborted a session to flee from a battle. She'd done all this while helping the dwarf cheat.

The cat emitted a loud meow.

"Right," she said. "I forgot about the loss of the party that started it all." She scratched behind the cat's ears, causing her to purr loudly. Could she really blame that on the dwarf, though? Ultimately, yes. The Gray Warrior attacking one of her expeditions that happened to have this bullshit-*càiniǎo* dwarf as a member who would show up later with a million-dollar bounty she could find no posting for was too much of a coincidence. Shea was certain she was being played, and she didn't like it. She took Trinity in her arms and went to her laptop.

The dwarf, identifying himself as Bobby, had sent a message with the subject line, "Talk?"

She cursed under her breath and deleted it. Another message caught her attention. It was from the Ranger Guild. The subject shouted READ IMMEDIATELY in bold red letters. Shea considered deleting it too. She was in no mood for spam. The guild, as they called themselves, was nothing more than a few socially inclined players who sent out a newsletter and moderated technique and strategy podcasts. It had been over a year since she'd paid any attention to them.

She waffled for an instant but found the commanding subject line impossible to ignore. The message contained an invitation to a ranger meeting at midnight. Shea had never received anything like it before. The message instructed her to port to a little-known gate where the meeting organizer promised, *We will discuss a matter urgent to your character's survival.* Shea had a feeling she knew what, or more accurately, who they would discuss.

"What do you think Trin? Does Darshana go?"

The cat said nothing.

"Probably a waste of time, and if I am going to make it by midnight, I'll have to risk resurrecting her while that monster may still be hunting in the Wolfwood."

The cat purred and pushed her head under Shea's chin.

"Yeah. You're right. I might learn more about what this Bobby Penn and Em are up to."

Meow.

"Okay. We're going."

Shea left the cat in the kitchen with a bowl of tuna and climbed back into the rig. A moment later, she was standing in the Sun Lobby staring at Darshana's empty case. She sighed and tapped on the case's touch screen. A message prompt asked her if she wanted to restore, and she punched the yes button.

Darshana woke, sitting with her back to the same boulder she and Falin had hidden behind when she'd died. She scrambled to her feet and brought her crossbow up.

The sun had set while she was out. The heavy clouds were gone, and a full moon was rising above the giant trees. In its silver light, she saw she was alone. A wolf howled in the distance, but none answered its call. Darshana checked the ground for the dwarf's body and found only a fresh mound of dirt indicating he'd made it out—not that she particularly cared. The moonlight glinted on an object near her feet. She bent down and found the wizard's spell she'd discarded during the attack. She returned it to her pouch and made her way back to the Wolfsburg Gate, glad to be alive again but still pissed off.

Chapter 25
Rangers

THE INVITE HAD SPECIFIED a time and a gate with no other details. Though she'd been through the obscure gate once or twice before, Shea had to look it up to refresh her memory. It was not a place anyone visited unless it was part of a quest or challenge. Located miles from the nearest town or village, she'd thought it pointless when she'd last visited it, but now she understood its purpose. What better place for a large group to assemble without drawing unwanted attention than the middle of nowhere?

She'd ported in with no idea how she'd find the meeting's exact location and discovered her concern unwarranted. The gate overlooked a barren field that had been cut into the surrounding forest. In the center of the field, halfway to the tree line, a large bonfire burned as a beacon to draw attendees.

Darshana followed other players to where several dozen cloaked figures formed a circle around the flames. Eyes from beneath drawn hoods tracked her as she took up a position in the shadows beyond the firelight, her hand never far from her crossbow. From a distance, the group might be confused for a gathering of monks or druids, but up close it was clear by their high boots, travel cloaks, and packs that they were rangers. More than that, their orange and red auras showed all of them were elite players.

She estimated their number at two hundred with more continuing to stream down from the gate on the hill. This many rangers in one place was unheard of. Rangers, after all, were solitary by nature and rare. Becoming one took a lot of rig time. Only players who had visited every gate and survived a long list of difficult quests known as the ordeal, were invited into the profession. She'd heard there were less than two thousand total, a tiny fraction of the Land's fifty million players.

At precisely midnight, a tall, dark-skinned ranger stepped into the circle and climbed up onto a large, flat rock that Shea guessed had been placed there as a speaker's platform. He raised both hands and stared down at the crowd. His yellow, elvish eyes shined in the firelight, and he spoke in a loud, clear voice that could be heard by everyone. Including those, like her, who'd positioned themselves outside the ring. "Well met, Rangers."

Like worshippers at a religious gathering, the circle responded as one, "Well met."

"For those of you who don't know me, my name is Samuel. I am the one who sends the newsletter that none of you read."

There were several laughs, but most of the group remained silent.

"Look around you."

Hooded heads turned from side to side.

"Assembled here are all the top-level rangers in the game. And because we are rangers, we are also the top players."

The hoods nodded.

"Just three months ago, there were two hundred and forty-three elite level and four legend level rangers."

Shea listened intently. Legend was the new level just added to the Land. Players at this level were the top of the top, those with the highest possible life scores. Darshana was legend level.

"As of this meeting, there are two hundred and thirty-six of us. Eleven have red-screened in the last thirty days." He paused and then added, "Two of them were legends."

The crowd let out a collective gasp, and Shea's heart thumped. *Two legends dead.* Elite level characters rarely red-screened. Though she reminded herself just how close she'd come twice now with the Gray Warrior. She surveyed the gathering until her eyes met those of a large male ranger. Bashal—he and she were the only legends left. That meant Danaka and Pharoah were gone. Thousands of hours and tens of thousands of dollars—they must be mad as hell and heartbroken. She would be. She nodded at Bashal and turned her attention back to Samuel, who was staring down at another ranger who had stepped into the light.

"It's got to be the wizards," the other ranger was saying. "They are the only ones who could take out legend levels, and they are always screwing with us."

Shouts of "Down with the wizards!" came from some.

Samuel raised his hands again. "Enough of that. It's not the wizards, and we don't need any of them showing up here FODing you for insulting them."

"How do you know it's not them?" the ranger inside the ring asked.

"I've spoken to several. They all assured me they have nothing to do with it."

Did they tell him about the bounty? Shea wondered.

"What do they think is killing us?" asked the querying ranger.

"They believe it's another player. A better one—law of the Land they said."

Shea suppressed an urge to join in the shouts of *Bullshit*. It was obvious to her what was happening. The dead rangers must've been hunting the Gray Warrior like she and Falin were, and he'd kicked their asses, just like he'd kicked hers. They must have known about the bounty. She waited for Samuel to say something about it, but he continued to engage in speculation with other rangers without mentioning the reward. It wasn't possible for him not to know. Up until a day ago, she'd been willing to believe she'd just missed the bounty posting. After all, she didn't pay much attention to the gamer blogs and podcasts, but not Samuel—he lived for that stuff. Even in the unlikely case he'd missed it, the wizards would have told him about it. Táma had set the bounty. Shea could understand not talking to her. She was terrifying, but Em knew. Surely, he would have been one of the wizards Samuel had spoken with.

"Which wizards did you ask?" she shouted.

Every head turned to face her, including Samuel's.

"I'm glad you came, Darshana," he said. "It's nice to see you taking a break from that kindergarten you run."

Many in the crowd laughed. Those nearest to her did not.

She pushed her way into the ring and stared up at Samuel, her hand returning to the stock of her crossbow. "I repeat, for the last time, who did you ask?"

He looked down at her, all traces of a smile gone. "It was just a joke. We're all friends here."

"I'm not concerned about your joke. I want to know what

wizards you spoke to. Did you talk to Em?"

"Of course. He's the easiest to reach."

"And the least likely to FOD you," someone in the crowd shouted, prompting some subdued laughter.

She studied Samuel and lowered her voice. "How about Táma?"

The crowd groaned at the sound of the red wizard's name.

"No, and let's not say her name again," he urged.

Darshana climbed up on the rock and stared out at the crowd. Four hundred eyes, most of them yellow like hers, stared back. "Are any of you hunting the Gray Warrior?"

The crowd's eyes turned on each other. No one said anything. Then four rangers pushed their way into the ring.

"Are you hunting him?" she asked.

One of them spoke up. "I'm not hunting him, but I think he's hunting us."

The other three nodded.

"What makes you say that?" Darshana asked.

"I've seen him. He rides a big, black horse, and he mows down players like they're nothing—no matter their level."

One of the other rangers joined in. "I just barely got away from him. I had to use a concealing spell and bury my *Shēngmìnglì*."

"Same here," the other two confirmed.

The entire crowd seemed to snicker. Someone shouted "pussies," and a roar of laughter erupted.

The four rangers drew their swords and the one who had done most of the talking shouted, "Fuck you. You would have done the same. And if any of you comes across this monster, you'd better run."

"We're rangers. We don't run," several shouted back.

"I did," Darshana said.

The crowd gasped and fell silent.

She jumped down from the rock and headed for the path that led to the arch. The crowd separated to allow her to pass. All of them stared.

"Wait. Wait," Samuel called after her.

She stopped and turned to meet their reproachful eyes.

"Where are you going?" Samuel asked. "We need a plan. We have to do something about this thing."

She pointed at the four rangers still standing inside the ring with their swords drawn. "Listen to them. Don't attack this gray warrior alone." Darshana stared up at Samuel. "If it took out Danaka and Pharaoh, it's going to take something more powerful than one of us to kill it."

"What are you going to do?" Samuel asked.

"Talk to a wizard," she said and resumed her march back to the gate.

Chapter 26
A Secure Connection

DISORIENTED, HE WAS VAGUELY aware of a female voice repeating, "Parker, can you hear me? Parker?" The voice, that had started out distant and strange, was growing clearer and more familiar.

A short burst of gentle slaps to his stubbled cheek shocked him to consciousness. He smacked his lips and opened his eyes to see Becky's worried expression inches from his face and her manicured fingers poised to strike him again.

Still groggy, he lifted his hand in a wobbly attempt to block her blow. "Stop hitting me."

"Are you okay?" she asked in a gentle, concerned voice. Before he could answer, she turned and said to someone behind her, "Call 9-1-1 and get an ambulance."

Parker bolted up in his chair. "Whoa, whoa, no ambulance. I'm fine."

"Do you know where you are?"

He blinked and looked around at the drab gray surroundings. "Yeah. I'm in my beautiful cubicle." He retrieved a tissue from a box and wiped drool from his mouth and neck, then looked into Becky's worried eyes. "I must have dozed off. I'm sorry."

"Should I still get the ambulance?" a man's voice said.

Parker swiveled around to see his coworkers peering over the cubicle walls at him. Recognizing the man, Parker put his hand on the pistol hanging from his shoulder harness and said, "Tom, if you call an ambulance, I will shoot you."

"Okay, that would be a 'no,'" Tom said. "Glad to see you're back to your normal asshole self," he added as he walked away.

"Wait," Becky barked. "I still want him to get checked out."

"Go away, Tom. It's not necessary," Parker said. "I was up late last night, and I must've fallen asleep. That's all."

161

Becky studied him for a moment, then turned to the others hovering nearby. "Let's give him some breathing room. You know what he's like when he thinks people care about him."

"Fuck you all," he said.

"See? Go back to work, everyone." She sat on his desk and stared down at him. "You didn't just fall asleep. Tom said he heard you talking on the phone and then he heard the handset hit the keyboard. He rushed over and found you staring at the ceiling and drooling all over yourself. You blacked out."

The handset was dangling from its cord. Parker lifted it to his ear and said, "Hello?" Silence. Whoever had been on the other end must have hung up. He placed the handset back in its cradle, and as he did, he noticed the web page from the National Institute of Health on his computer screen.

"Who were you talking to?"

Parker scratched his head and glanced at the screen again. The NIH web page contained a list of medical papers on genetic disorders. "Not really sure. Whoever it was will probably call me back."

She took his hand in hers. "How often is this happening?"

"What? Me napping at work?"

"No. You know damn well what I mean."

"It's rare, Becky," Parker said. "It is what it is. I'll be okay." Then he remembered who he'd been on the phone with. "I was talking to Jaden about some interesting facts I've learned about our Collector case."

The corners of Becky's eyes crinkled. "Maybe you should take a break from this."

He shook his head. "I'm fine." He really was feeling better. "I want to tell you what we learned."

She sighed. "Okay, tell me."

"If you give me my hand back."

Becky let go, looking a little embarrassed.

"LVMPD spoke some more to Charles Tate's wife about his Metaverse addiction."

"Uh-huh, and?"

"His wife said Tate had recently lost his character in the game." Parker pulled a sticky note from his computer monitor. He'd written the word Pharoah on it. "He called the character Pharoah."

"Like an Egyptian king?"

"I think they considered themselves gods," Parker said. "But, yeah. This Pharoah character was a big deal to Tate. Somebody killed it and Tate was out of his mind, like he'd lost a close friend."

"Huh."

"I know. Weird."

"Yeah," Becky said. "That's why I like your Metaverse theory. This Land of Might and Magic game is full of weirdos. Did you ask the Clearwater victim's mother if she played it?"

"She said her daughter didn't have time for such nonsense. Her words."

Becky frowned. "I still like the game angle even if the Clearwater vic doesn't fit."

Parker grinned. "Abby didn't play the game, but it turns out she had a very interesting job. She was a programmer for a firm called ZCS." He retrieved his tablet from the desk and opened his note-taking application. "Zhang Control Systems."

"Okay? Why is that interesting?"

"It's what they make and who owns them," he said. "ZCS manufactures security systems, and Abby worked on entryway access systems."

"Door locks," Becky said with a hint of excitement.

"You got it. She wrote the software for those systems."

"You think our unsub used that software to gain access to his victims while they were sleeping?"

"I do."

"Do you think she helped him? I mean before he killed her?"

"I don't know. But wait till you hear who owns the company."

Becky arched her eyebrows. Her raccoon mask seemed to glow. He motioned for her to draw nearer. When she'd bent close to him, he whispered. "You look like the Lone Ranger. You need to get some sun around those eyes."

She pushed back from him. "You're such a fucking jerk. Who owns ZCS?"

"Zhang Control Systems was founded by a Chinese immigrant named David Zhang."

"So? Who the hell is David Zhang and why do we care?"

"He's just another rich tech guy, but he has a daughter. A

very special and smart daughter named Jasmine, who, like her daddy, is a computer and engineering genius."

Becky motioned for him to get on with it.

"Jasmine and her husband, Marcus, founded their own company, a computer software firm called Xperion."

"This is going somewhere, right Parker?"

He grinned, relishing the build-up. "Patience, patience. Guess what Xperion does?"

"I have no idea." She glanced at her watch. "And since you are not dying, I have to head back upstairs for a meeting."

"Xperion creates Metaverse simulations, also known as games."

Her eyes widened. "No way," she said.

"Yep. They produce the Land of Might and Magic."

She slapped her hand on the desk and said, "Hot fuck," loud enough for everyone to hear. Then she covered her mouth.

"Language," a woman's voice said from over the cubicle wall.

"Oops."

Parker grinned. "Get a handle on yourself. It gets better. ZCS is based in Las Vegas."

"Wait," she said. "I thought this Abby was in Clearwater."

"Remote work. You might have heard of it."

She nodded. "Yeah, but if we had that, who would wake you up when you nod off?"

"True," he said. "Anyway, LVMPD is going to work the ZCS angle. I think that's what I was setting up with Jaden. I'm actually hurt he hasn't called back. What if I had blacked out?"

She ignored his joke. "Who's working Xperion?"

"Funny you should ask."

"No," Becky said before he could complete his thought.

"Come on. I want to go talk to these people."

"Parker, we're not investigators. Remember?"

"I know, I know, but I want to meet them. See what they do, who they are. You know, profile them."

She sighed. "Where are they based?"

"San Francisco. Palo Alto to be precise."

"You can't go alone."

He wiggled his eyebrows. "You want to come?"

She smiled and shook her head. "No."

"Okay. I'll take Jaden. He's cuter."

"He's not on the team. You can't just take him with you to San Francisco. He belongs to the Las Vegas field office."

"Belongs?"

"You know what I mean. I'll get San Francisco to assign someone."

Parker crossed his arms. "I've already bonded with Jaden."

"Bonded? You just met him."

"He's seen me in my underwear."

She raised her hands. "Not another word. I'll see what I can do, but I don't know if I can make it happen."

"Sure you can. The Lone Ranger can do anything."

Chapter 27
Stalking a Wizard

AKANDU AND MUSUKA CROUCHED behind a low wall across from the crystal door that led into the Evil Queen's fortress. Akandu was on his hands and knees, but the gleaming steel helm covering his massive head still poked above the wall. The giant was not good at concealment. Musuka had no trouble. Hiding came naturally to him; he'd spent his life doing it.

The predawn air was thick with warm, misty rain. It wet their faces and their cloaks, but was not unpleasant. They heard the click-clack of her boots on the stone walkway before they saw her. Obscured by the dark and the mist, it took them a moment to be certain the hooded figure moving toward them was the wizard.

"She's coming," Akandu said, and even though he spoke softly, the words boomed in Musuka's sensitive ears.

"I-I, s-s-see her," Musuka said, ashamed by the fear and weakness in his voice.

Akandu pushed his legs out from under him and rested his back against the wall. The giant's scuffling movements were loud and Musuka grimaced. "Shhh. Sh-sh-sh-she will hear you."

Akandu curled his lips and placed his hand on Musuka's head.

Musuka shook it off. "Stop," he said, this time with strength and confidence, his stutter gone.

"Don't be a mouse, and I won't crush you like one," Akandu growled.

"I am no longer a mouse."

The giant chuckled. "Perhaps not. Not quite a man yet, but less mousy. Maybe a dog now. We will have to get you a new name after we kill this wizard."

Musuka shook his head. "We can't take her in the dream

world. She's too powerful there."

Akandu grunted. "We need more magic."

"Too risky. We will take her in this world, and she will disappear in yours."

Akandu touched the necklace of ears Musuka wore around his neck, just six, unlike the hundreds that encircled his own. "You will get two more, but alas, I will not."

"Stop complaining. You have plenty."

Akandu fingered his own trophies. "No wizard ears, though."

"Too risky," Musuka repeated.

Akandu stood, his dark form towering over the wall like a newly sprouted tree. "I'm tired of this shameful hiding."

"Get back down here," Musuka said, and as he did, the hooded figure turned toward them. Damn, the witch must have heard them. He dropped below the wall. "She'll see you," he whispered.

"She can't see me. It's your cowardly whining that attracted her gaze."

"What is she doing?"

"Going inside."

Musuka took a long breath, then chanced a look. As Akandu had said, the hooded figure was no longer looking their way. She was at the fortress gate, working some magic with its lock. The crystal door opened, and she lingered on the threshold for a moment, as if listening. Then she glanced over her shoulder and disappeared inside.

"She's gone," Akandu said.

"Get back down here before someone sees you."

The giant begrudgingly eased down beside him.

"We will take her when she sleeps, like the others," Musuka said.

"No honor in such kills," Akandu said. "Only rodents and snakes raid the nests of their sleeping prey."

Musuka frowned at the rebuke. He had come so far, but Akandu was right. He still killed like the mouse he was.

Chapter 28
Jazz Session

ANGELA SAT IN WHAT she suspected was an intentionally uncomfortable visitor chair waiting for Jasmine Day to finish talking on her cell phone. The heart rate monitor on Angela's watch buzzed, signaling her resting pulse had risen above a healthy threshold. She didn't need the stupid device to know her heart was racing. She could feel it trying to pound its way straight through her chest.

Her anxiety was only partially due to the early ad-hoc meeting. She had other things on her mind today, and besides, morning sneak-attacks from her demanding and always intimating boss were not uncommon. Lately, though, they had become excruciating. The pressure on everyone to find and shut down the hacker threatening the IPO had increased to an unsustainable level. Even Jasmine, who Angela had always admired for her coolness under extreme pressure, had shown signs of cracking, but her boss had been in a bad mood for months, even before the Anomaly turned all their lives to shit.

Angela's peers on the senior staff believed the cracks in Jasmine's armor and her angry demeanor—bitchy is how most described it—had something to do with the Day's troubled marriage. Rumors were swirling about a pending divorce. Angela found the theory laughable. Not the part about the divorce, she didn't doubt that at all. Jasmine being rattled by it was the laughable part. Jasmine would treat such an event as a business transaction. She'd execute it flawlessly, like she'd done countless other deals, then move on. She wouldn't let it bother her, and even if it did, she'd never let others know she was bothered. Something was bothering her, though, no doubt about it, and whatever it was, it was making Angela's life miserable. All the same, that wasn't why Angela's heart was racing.

Angela uncrossed her legs and took a deep breath, trying

to will the anxiety away and slow the hammer in her chest. Jasmine-stress, even dialed-up to ten as it'd been, was normal. That being said, the twenty-four seven hunt for the Anomaly was wreaking havoc on LMM, not to mention the *unconventional* tactics they were using to stop it were taking their toll. Not only on Angela, but the entire team. Some of her people had taken to living in the office. Angela, herself, hadn't slept more than four hours in weeks, and she was eating nothing but junk. She could practically feel the fat cells multiplying. On top of all that, she now feared she was being stalked.

It started last evening when she arrived home and noticed the stranger.

She had been checking her mailbox when the hairs on the back of her neck had prickled, causing her to turn around, and there he was. It could have been a woman, but Angela was almost certain it was a small man. His face was concealed by the drawn hood of a dark sweatshirt, and he was peering at her from behind a shrub across the street. It was not unheard of for homeless people to find their way into the affluent neighborhood, but it creeped her out. She had run inside intent on calling the police, but the stranger wasn't there when she checked a few minutes later from the safety of her front porch.

Then this morning, as she was badging in, she had heard whispering behind the low wall that surrounded the parking lot across from the building's main entrance. It had been dark, as it always was when she arrived, and she couldn't be sure, but she thought she'd glimpsed the same hooded figure. As she studied Jasmine's silhouette framed in the floor-to-ceiling window, she thought maybe she should excuse herself and call the police. After all, she lived alone, and crime in the area had been on the rise. But, something in Jasmine's tense stance told her leaving before the meeting would not be a good career move. She'd wait. Give herself time to settle down, and besides, she should only be thinking about the designer clad psycho in front of her, and not the one who might be living in a shrub across from her house.

Jasmine, dressed in formfitting black slacks and a black three-quarter sleeve knit top that, despite its simplicity, Angela knew cost more than the average bay area family's monthly grocery bill, stood motionless with the phone pressed to her ear. She could have been confused for a mannequin in a Santana Row boutique if it wasn't for the occasional sharp "yes" or "no" barked at the person or persons on the other end of the call.

Angela's gaze wandered to the glass shelves mounted on the wall to her left. The top shelves were lined with plaques and awards. Some of the most prominent included a row of crystal pyramids with the words Technology Woman of the Year etched in their prismatic surfaces. Angela had seen them all before, and she had attended the ceremonies where many of them were presented.

It wasn't the awards that held her attention. On the shelves below them were many silver-framed photos. Most of these also celebrated Jasmine's accomplishments, including those taken at the finish lines of countless marathons and the summits of the world's tallest mountain peaks. There were a few of the Day family, and it was this section that drew her eyes. Among the precisely placed frames was a gap. It appeared one photo had been removed and another lay face down as if Jasmine could no longer bear looking at it.

The glass and steel office was a temple to discipline and meticulous order. The gap on the shelf was odd, and Angela found herself looking around the room for other evidence of a break in her boss's obsessive precision. She found one right in front of her. The missing picture frame was laying faceup on the desk's translucent surface. Jasmine must have been looking at it before Angela had arrived and not returned it to its proper place.

Curious, Angela leaned over the desk to see the photo, wondering if she'd find a picture of Jasmine's soon to be ex-husband. Nope. It appeared to be a picture of a very young Jasmine posing with a child. *Odd.* The Matterhorn rollercoaster rising behind them gave away the location. The child, who Angela first mistook for the Day's son, Lincoln, was wearing a huge green top hat like the Disney Mad Hatter character posing along with them. The idea of the razor-edged woman, who some Xperion employees referred to as the Evil Queen, posing with a Disney character almost made her laugh. She had never noticed the picture before, and after studying it, she realized the child could not be Lincoln, the boy's complexion was way too dark. The Day's son had inherited his father's stark white skin. Besides, the Jasmine in the photo was too young, no more than a teenager. Jasmine had been almost thirty when her son was born.

Angela looked up to find Jasmine, who had finished her call, watching her. "I'm sorry, Jazz. I noticed the photo and was drawn to it." She pointed to the boy. "Is this Lincoln?" she asked, already knowing the answer had to be no.

Jasmine snatched up the frame and studied it for a moment. "No, this was taken many years before Lincoln was born. It's my aunt's son." She returned the photo to the shelf and lingered for a moment before flipping the frame that had been laying facedown back upright.

This one did contain a photo of Lincoln. Unlike the other photos of the Day's only son peppered throughout the family section, Lincoln was not a child in this one. He was a young man standing in front of a sign for the Massachusetts Institute of Technology. Angela guessed it had been taken two years ago when Jasmine and Marcus had dropped him off for his freshmen year. They had had such high hopes, and why wouldn't they? The boy had inherited so much from them: Their intelligence—he was purported to be a genius, their computer programming abilities—he was definitely a gifted software developer, and their influence—both Jasmine and Marcus had graduated with honors from the prestigious institution. But he had inherited other characteristics too. Lincoln did not do well with other people, and something happened during his second semester that resulted in him being asked to leave the school.

For the first time, Angela noticed all the photos of the boy had something sad in common. No matter his age, Lincoln's expression was the same in all of them—eyes focused downward and mouth fixed in a frown. Lincoln Day was not a happy child, and he'd grown up to be an unhappy little man.

When Jasmine turned away from the shelf, her eyes were rimmed red as if she'd been crying. "You okay, Jazz?" The icy stare that followed made Angela regret the question. One didn't ask Jasmine Day how she felt.

"I asked you here for a progress report on the Anomaly, not so you could ogle my photos."

"Yes, ma'am, of course," Angela recovered. "As you know, we've been working with our consultant."

Jasmine slid into her seat, her red-rimmed eyes locked on Angela's. "You and the consultant have been working on this for two months." A tear formed at the corner of her eye. Its presence shocked Angela. "You are running out of time."

Angela thought Jasmine was referring to the IPO. "We are working around the clock."

"You have to. The consultant does not have much more time. He is very sick."

This was the first Angela had heard the consultant was sick. Jasmine never spoke of him other than in vague terms and always related to assignments.

"I'm sorry. I was not aware of that."

"Well, now you are. There is very little time."

Jasmine had introduced Angela to the consultant several years ago, though they'd never met in person. All their communication was through secure chat sessions and coded postings. They only ever referred to him as the consultant, but he had many aliases. Currently, he was going by Stacey Hancock. At least that was the name he used in his profile for his LMM character, Falin.

Over the years, Angela had seen him use many names: John Turner, Ed Black, and Sally Westbrook to name a few, but Angela knew he was known in the darker corners of the Verse by the hacker tag, Mad Hat. She thought about the boy in the photo dressed as the Mad Hatter and wondered if the consultant and he were one and the same. It would explain why Jasmine had been looking at the photo and, perhaps, given the news of his serious illness, her emotional state.

"I'm sorry," Angela said again.

Jasmine waved the apology away. "'Sorry' will not stop this hacker. Where are we?"

The cool indifference was an act. Jasmine was upset and on the brink of weeping. Angela found the prospect unnerving. This was not the Jasmine she knew.

"The consultant has gathered an enormous amount of trace data which he's turned over to us. My team is analyzing it now. I expect to know something soon."

"Soon?"

"We just received it. Give us time to perform our analysis."

Jasmine wiped her eye with the sleeve of her expensive

top. "Soon the consultant will be gone, and you will have to do this without him. I hope your soon comes before his."

Angela nodded and stood to leave.

Jasmine raised a hand. "Wait. I have something else I need your attention on."

Angela settled back down in her seat.

"I was just speaking with Marcus and Anand."

Anand was Xperion's in-house lawyer, another shark in the Day's school.

"The FBI is sending two agents here tomorrow to speak with us about a criminal matter."

"A criminal matter? Is it the Anomaly? How did word get out?"

"No. It has nothing to do with our hacker," Jasmine said and wiped her eyes again. "Either of them."

"What then?"

"They say they want to talk about a series of murders and what they believe may be a connection to our simulations."

Angela leaned forward in the uncomfortable chair. "Murders?"

"Yes."

Angela thought about the feeling she had about being watched. Her heart monitored buzzed and she covered it with her other hand.

"What simulation?"

Jasmine frowned. "Our current problem child, LMM."

"Are we in any danger?"

"From what?" Jasmine barked.

"A murderer?"

"Don't be ridiculous Angela," Jasmine snapped, her eyes narrowing. "Keep this quiet until we know more. We have enough problems getting our people to come to the office." She slid her tablet in front of her and tapped on its screen. "I need you to show these agents around tomorrow. I'm forwarding you the details. Give them the tour, then Marcus and I will meet them when you're done."

Angela considered mentioning her fear she was being stalked, but her already typically tightly wound boss seemed on the verge of unraveling—she'd probably fire Angela on the spot. She stood to leave, and this time Jasmine did not stop her.

Chapter 29
Summoned

AFTER TOO LITTLE SLEEP, Shea had gone to work still angry with Falin or Bobby or whatever his name was and had been a total jerk to Tony. She'd even fought with him, something she never did.

Now, sitting at her desk, staring at her rig, she felt terrible about mistreating her boss. It wasn't his fault she'd been duped by a hacker and a wizard. The whole situation was making her crazy. Who or what was the Gray Warrior and why had Falin and Em used a phony quest to mislead her into hunting him? The questions nagged at Shea, making her even more miserable. Maybe her mother was right. It was time to grow up, put the fantasy world behind her, and follow the family dharma.

Trinity raced past, chasing a mouse. Small gaps between the bay door and the floor made it impossible to keep them out. Rodents were just one more reason to move on.

Another unread message from the dwarf appeared in her inbox, begging for attention. The subject line screamed, *NO TIME, NEED YOUR HELP.* She didn't know what "NO TIME" meant, and she didn't want to know. She sent the unopened plea to the delete folder. He could find another sucker to lead him around the Land, maybe Samuel. She was ignoring the Ranger Guild leader's messages too—six of them since his emergency meeting two nights ago. Same plea: Help hunt down and kill the Gray Warrior. From what she'd seen, that was impossible. She needed to talk to the wizard behind the quest. It was time to use the summon spell.

She crossed the bay to her rig and strapped in. A moment later, she was in the Sun Lobby staring at Darshana's control panel, trying to decide which of the Land's gates would put her in the best place for a private conversation. Her careful search was more nervous procrastination than planning. Any place would do; she'd be with a wizard. But where intentionally summoning the most powerful, evil-aligned character in the Land had seemed like a good idea a moment before, it now seemed incredibly foolish and likely an act of character suicide. Most players, including herself, did everything they could to avoid the red wizard, and here she was about to use a magic spell to call her. Táma would likely FOD her on the spot for the temerity, but Shea needed answers.

She selected the gate labeled Land's End from the list. Few players, other than rangers, ever reached it. *Perfect*, she thought and punched the button. Her visual field faded to black. When it returned, she was standing under an alabaster gate, perched atop a massive promontory projecting into the azure blue of the great Southron Sea. Sounds of crashing waves and squawking gulls filled her headgear, and she could almost smell the ocean. It was one of her favorite views, and she'd often thought of trying to find out if it had been modeled after a place in the Real-Real that she might someday visit.

North from the gate, the road continued over a flat sand and scrub plain. South was the cliff's edge and then the sea. Darshana headed south, following a narrow walkway that led to a bench placed a few feet from the precipice. The bench was carved from the same translucent stone as the gate and glowed like white fire in the sun. She withdrew the spell orb from her pouch and sat. She'd never cast a summon spell before, and she wasn't quite sure what to expect.

She studied the orb, replaying Em's words in her mind and allowing herself more time to consider what Táma might do to her. When she was sure she remembered the casting instructions, and before she lost her nerve, Darshana crushed the silver ball in her fist and whispered the elvish invocation phrase. Then she blew the glittering silver dust toward the sea and shouted as loudly as she could, "Arcesse, Táma the Terrifying."

She held her breath and waited. Ten seconds, twenty, forty, a minute, gasp, nothing happened.

She shouted "Arcesse, Táma the Terrifying," again, and waited; another breathless minute passed and still nothing happened.

"Táma."

A gull landed beside her, but there was no sign of the

wizard.

Frustrated, she shouted "Fuck you, Táma!"

The gull squawked and flew away.

Still no wizard.

Darshana crossed her arms and stared at the waves below. After several minutes, she shouted, "Fuck you, Táma!" one last time before making her way back to the arch.

At the end of the walkway, she opened the gate menu and was about to select EXIT when her view filled with a gold light, so bright she had to close her eyes. When she opened them again, her surroundings had changed. The gleaming alabaster gate and blue sky had been replaced by gray stone walls illuminated by flickering torchlight. She had been teleported to a large round chamber with a high-domed ceiling, pear-shaped windows, and no visible door. Worked into the smooth stone floor tiles at her feet was the image of a red eyed Raven.

Raven's Perch. Shit.

She turned slowly and saw nothing but a darkening sky in every direction and surmised the room was atop a tall tower.

A hooded figure, draped in a red robe stood gazing out the east window with her back to Darshana. The figure laughed in a woman's voice and said, "Fuck you, Táma? Really?"

Oh shit.

"Umm. Sorry about that," Darshana said.

The wizard turned to face her. When she moved, waves of golden light rippled through the folds of her robe. She pulled back her hood, revealing long, silver hair that framed an angelic face with skin the same brilliant white as the gate at Land's End. Her eyes were closed, and when she opened them, they were not those of an angel. Red as her robe, they shown like two fiery rubies in the torchlight. *Terrifying.*

Darshana lowered to one knee and bowed her head. She'd come for answers, not to be FODed.

"No need for that," the red wizard said and motioned for her to stand.

Darshana stood. "I did not expect the spell to work this way."

"When you summon a wizard, you take a chance. A wizard gets to decide whether to accept the summons or not. I was indisposed when you called." Her red eyes flashed. "I hope this time works for you."

"Fine. I mean, it's good," Darshana stammered. Then she added, "Thank you," and readied herself for the Finger of Death.

The wizard studied her. "Where did you get the spell?"

"Em."

"Ah. I should've known. Something tells me he did not expect you to summon me with it."

"No, probably not."

"What does the legendary Darshana want from Táma the Terrifying?"

Darshana spread her arms. "I have questions."

Táma chuckled. "I bet you do." The wizard glared at her, and Shea trembled. She actually trembled. "Well, ask them."

Shea's nervous words tumbled out of Darshana's mouth. "I want to know about a quest notice I saw issued from you calling for the head of a character called the Gray Warrior."

The wizard glided toward her, and Shea glanced around again for an exit. "Is that what you call him? The Gray Warrior?"

Darshana nodded. "Yes. What do you call him?"

"The Anomaly."

"That's an unusual name."

"He's an unusual character. Don't you think?"

Just a little.

"Did you post the quest for his head? Is it real?"

Táma motioned with her hands and two heavy, wooden chairs inlaid with, *gasp*, elaborate carvings depicting scenes of torture and death slid noisily across the tiles and came to rest next to each of them. "Let's sit," she said and lowered herself into one.

Darshana sat.

"No. I did not post the quest."

"I fucking knew it," Shea blurted before she could check herself. "If the quest isn't real, what are Em and this dwarf up to, and what is this Anomaly?"

Táma folded her glowing hands in her lap. Her long, red fingernails resembled bloodied talons. "The quest is real."

"I don't understand. You just said it wasn't."

"I said I didn't post it. No need. It was created for a specific player and delivered directly to them."

She had to be joking. "For the dwarf? Seems like a lot to

expect from a *càiniǎo* half-in who can't fight and knows nothing about the Land."

Táma's red lips turned up in a slight grin. "The quest wasn't created for Falin." She touched Darshana's arm. "It was created for you."

"Me? I'm supposed to kill this gray monster? With the dwarf?" Shea laughed. "You need a fucking army. You should have every ranger and warrior in the Land hunting for him."

Táma's spooky eyes met hers. "You're assuming he can be killed."

"He can't?"

Táma shrugged. "Don't know yet."

"You don't know? What's the point of the quest then? And if it was meant for me, why give it to this noob Falin?"

Táma's evil grin grew. "I think we both know Falin is more than a noob, Shea. May I call you Shea?"

The sound of her real name coming from the wizard's mouth startled and annoyed Shea. "How does everyone in here seem to know my name? Is it posted somewhere?"

Táma shook her head. "Not that I know of. If it makes you feel better, my real name is Angela Harding. I work for Xperion."

Shea's annoyance had exceeded her fear of being FOD'd. "No. It doesn't make me feel better. Can just anyone who works at Xperion access my personal information?"

Táma shook her head. "Not just anyone. And those of us who can, sign stacks of legal documents that prevent us from disclosing it."

Shea thought about Tony's friend who had looked up Falin's user profile. Those stacks of documents hadn't stopped him. "Well, someone's disclosing it. Was it you who gave Falin my name?"

Angela laughed. "No. Falin wouldn't need to ask me for that. Nothing stored online is really safe from him."

"He's just a kid," Shea said, but as she said it, she was even less sure about the dwarf's identity. "Isn't he?"

"Hardly."

Shea thought of what the dwarf had said at White Hall Gate, *Nothing is what it seems.* "I take it his name isn't Bobby Penn?"

The wizard's grin broadened even more, like Shea had said something funny. Maybe she had.

"He told you his name is Bobby Penn?"

"Yes. Is it?"

"I doubt it. I don't know his real name." The wizard's red eyes bored through Darshana's into Shea's. "What else did he tell you about himself?"

The question made Shea suspicious. The wizard worked for Xperion. Was she trying to learn about Falin's hacking? "Not much," she said. "He's a half-in from Boston who almost got my character killed."

Angela laughed again. "No point in pretending, Shea. I know what he's doing. I know all about the thing he created to track the Gray Warrior."

Shea swallowed, worried now she'd be banned from the game. "You know about the mirror?"

"Yes."

"Then you know he's hacking your systems."

"Of course. That's what I hired him to do."

"You hired him? For what? And how could you not know his real name then?"

"He keeps his identity secret, and I don't care to know it, probably better I don't. He's a special kind of consultant. We use him for secret projects, mostly cyber security."

"But he's a hacker," Shea said.

The wizard gave her an amused look. "Sometimes you need a hacker to catch a hacker."

"Is that what the Gray Warrior is? A hacker?"

"Yes, a good one."

Shea remembered what Falin had told her about what it took to build simulation games like LMM. "If Xperion built all this," Shea spread Darshana's arms, "why do you need a special consultant? The company must have plenty of expert programmers."

"We do, and they'll find and stop the hacker, eventually." The wizard's eyes stared out one of the pear-shaped windows as if she'd seen something in the dark clouds. They lingered there for a moment then their laser-like gaze refocused on Darshana. "But Falin specializes in breaking into systems. He knows the techniques that hackers use. I hired him to speed things up."

"That's what this is all about? Finding and stopping a

hacker?"

"Yes."

"But why the phony quest?"

Angela sighed. "We needed a way to trick the hacker into revealing himself. He's very good at evading our monitoring systems."

"Em told me. He said you couldn't see the Gray Warrior—the Anomaly."

The wizard's eyes flashed. "Em talks too much, but it's true what he told you. Falin can see him, though. He created special programs to track him."

"The mirror," Shea said.

"The mirror is only the part you see here in the Land. Think of it as the user interface. It's really a system of sophisticated data collection and analysis programs."

Táma took Darshana's hand in hers. "The virtual reality we are in is created by thousands of programs working together. The programs communicate with each other using special messages. Players like you and I generate thousands of these messages with our movements. Me taking your hand just now created hundreds of them."

Shea nodded. "Falin calls that the event stream."

"That's right. When I took your hand, our characters interacted. The programs that told our headgear what to show and our gloves what to feel had to know about both of us. Your events have data identifying me, and my events have data identifying you. The hacker's character's events are somehow being erased, and he leaves no identifying data in the events belonging to the players he interacts with. Falin's programs look for the data gaps and uses them to recreate the Gray Warrior's event stream.

Shea remembered Falin explaining the gaps. "He calls them the Gray Warrior's shadow."

The wizard smiled. "Shadow. I like that."

"Do the shadows only occur when the Gray Warrior interacts with other players?"

"Mostly, but there are certain simulation functions where he leaves a shadow as well, like when he teleports from place to place."

"The gates," Shea said. "That's how Falin's mirror knows

when the Warrior enters and leaves the Land."

"Yes."

"So if you know all this, why haven't you caught him?"

Angela laughed. "You sound like someone I know. The problem is the amount of data. The simulation generates millions of events every second. Storing them all for Falin's programs to analyze would slow everything down."

"Not sure I understand."

"The game would come to a crawl, Shea. Players like you would stop playing. Falin's programs must analyze interactions between the Gray Warrior and other players as they occur, in real-time."

"That's why Falin wouldn't let me summon Em when we were attacked by The Gray Warrior in the Wolfwood. He was gathering data for analysis."

The wizard nodded. "Yes. His programs look for patterns in the data. We call them signatures. We can use the signatures to determine what security holes the hacker is exploiting to do what he is doing, and if we're lucky, the right signatures will lead us to information about the hacker himself."

Shea thought for a moment, remembering Falin's words. "He calls that his trap."

The wizard squeezed her hand again. "Yes. That's sounds right. Falin's trap will spring when the analytic functions find the right data signatures."

"What will the right signatures tell you?"

"We hope enough to put an end to this nightmare. We're analyzing what was captured during your fight in the Wolfwood now, and we believe it will tell us how to close the security holes. But what we really want is to catch the hacker."

"Falin's trap."

"Correct. The signatures we get from the trap will lead us to the hacker's account and the network addresses of the places where he enters the Land. Maybe even the unique addresses of his devices."

"His rig and headset's device addresses, their MACs," Shea said. "With that you can find out where he is in the real world."

Táma showed her pointed teeth when she smiled. *Creepy as fuck.* "If we're lucky. Then the police can arrest him, and we can all go back to normal. You can resume your guide business, and I may even get some sleep."

Shea had been angry, but now she found herself intrigued by the details of the behind-the-scenes hunt. "Did the Wolfwood battle provide enough data to find him? Did it spring the trap?"

The wizard's creepy smile disappeared. "Falin says no. His analytic programs need more events of the kind generated by intimate player-to-player physical interactions."

"Fuck that. There's no way I'm getting intimate with that thing."

Angela laughed. "I didn't mean that kind of intimacy. Though, it would work too. I meant fighting with strike weapons. Things that come into contact with the player and the Gray Warrior at the same time. You know, swords, clubs, axes."

"Not my crossbow."

"No."

"Why didn't you just ask? Why trick me into doing it?"

The wizard hesitated, like Angela was considering her answer. "The hacker is deep in our systems. We're trying to keep that secret until we catch him."

Shea laughed. "Hate to tell you, but the Gray Warrior is no longer a secret. He's killed way too many characters." Some of the anger at being deceived returned. "Seems like with all the characters he's slaughtering you'd have plenty of opportunities to collect data without using me."

"It's true," Angela said. "He's killed many characters—hundreds—but over fifty million exist in the Land. In order for the trap to work, Falin needs to know in advance what character the Gray Warrior will attack so he can configure his programs to analyze the character's event stream. We started by monitoring a small group of high-level players and waiting for the Gray Warrior to attack them. That worked to a point, but we were unable to collect the right data to spring the trap. We need to focus on a single player."

"Me."

The wizard's creepy smile returned. "Now you know the reason for the quest. Falin uses his mirror to set the trap when you and the Gray Warrior fight."

Something about the explanation troubled Shea. "You said you monitored a small group of high-level players before you selected me. How did you know which ones the hacker would go after?"

The wizard released Darshana's hand, "Most of his victims are just random characters in the wrong place at the wrong time. They're just the unlucky ones he encounters while going after the ones he really wants." She paused, again taking time to craft the right answer. "Once we figured out what he was after, we focused our monitoring on the characters he really wanted."

The characters he really wanted. "He's hunting elite players, isn't he?"

"Yes. Probably to show how invincible he is, but also to cause the most pain for our customers and the company. I don't have to tell you how much players invest in their characters to reach the elite levels."

Shea nodded. "But you couldn't monitor all the elite players."

"Still too many. We had to narrow it down. Get him to focus on just a few."

Legends. "That's why you created the new legend level. You used it to lure him. That's why he killed Danaka and Pharaoh." She gripped the arms of her chair and leaned toward the wizard. "That's why he attacked my party on Jade Mountain. He wasn't going for them; he was going for me."

The wizard nodded. "Danaka was the number one player in the Land before she was killed. You and Pharaoh were tied for number two. Bashal was number three. All four of your characters were already well known on the social platforms, and they became even more well known when we assigned them legend status. That generated quite a buzz in the messagesphere."

"Buzz." Shea snapped, growing angrier. "You and Falin hyped our characters on the social platforms to attract the hacker. You used our characters for bait."

"Yes, but you can't blame Falin for that. Using you as bait was my idea."

Maybe she really was evil.

Shea folded Darshana's arms. "Danaka and Pharaoh have not come back to the game since you sacrificed them. They probably never will."

Angela sighed. "It's hard to lose something you work so hard to build." Then the wizard's cold features seemed to soften. "But when they come back, I'm sure they'll pass through the

levels fast and get back to legend status before they know it."
She smiled. "Who knows? They might even have some help."

That pissed Shea off. "Fuck you."

Táma looked away. When she looked back, her eyes did not
meet Shea's. They landed on a point on the floor between them
and remained there. "I understand you're angry, but now we
should discuss what to do."

Shea scowled. "What if I don't want to be the bait anymore?"

"That's no longer an option, really. Unless you plan to stay
out of the simulation altogether."

She knew Angela was right. The Gray Warrior already had
Darshana in his sights, and after the battle in the Wolfwood, he
was probably even more eager to red-screen her. Shea sighed.
Another wizard had chosen the path for her. "Not much of a
choice," she said. "Give up the game or help you get rid of the
fucker."

Táma's eyes came up, and she shrugged. "We don't have
the data we need yet."

"You want me to go back in with the dwarf and get more?"

"I do, but..." the wizard's expression turned sad, "it may be
too late for Falin."

"What do you mean, too late?"

"The consultant is very sick." Táma stared out the window
again, perhaps trying to decide how much to share. "He's dying.
I'm told he may go any day."

"Dying?"

"Cancer."

NO TIME. Shea winced. "I didn't know."

"I'm sorry for the bad news, and for what it's worth, I'm
sorry for using you and the others." The wizard rose from the
chair and smiled down on Darshana. "I hope I answered all
your questions."

Darshana stood. "I would have helped if you'd asked. It
wasn't necessary to trick me."

The wizard nodded. "I'm glad we met. After this is all over,
perhaps I won't FOD you when I see you in the Land." Her evil
grin returned. "No promises though." She raised her arms in a
spellcaster pose.

Shea shut her eyes against the bright gold light that filled
her view. When she opened them, she was back at the Land's

End Gate, her anger at Falin now replaced with sadness. *NO TIME.*

Chapter 30
Through the Looking Glass

PARKER FOUND JADEN WAITING for him at the baggage carousel in the San Francisco airport. He was easy to spot as he was the only one at the carousel, and like Parker, he was dressed in a charcoal suit that screamed government agent. Jaden had already retrieved Parker's bag. He didn't appear to have one of his own.

"Morning, Breaux," Parker said as he hobbled up to the young agent. "I'm touched. You remembered what my bag looked like."

"It was easy to spot. All the other passengers have already been here and gone." He held up his phone. "You didn't answer my calls or messages. I was about to call Ms. Fulbright, and she would've had me badge my way through security to find you."

"Aw. You were worried about me. I'm really, really touched now," Parker said and bounced his cane on the floor. "Moved as fast as my three legs could carry me."

Jaden gave him an annoyed look and pointed toward the exit. "Car's this way."

"Where's your bag?" Parker asked.

"I had to come in last night. Apparently, you can fly all the way here from DC and arrive at 9:30 a.m., but there are no morning flights from Las Vegas."

"At least you got to sleep," Parker grunted. "You know how early I had to get up to make this flight?"

"I don't. Just like I'm not sure why I'm here. Was the San Francisco office out of agents to drive you around?"

"Ouch, Breaux. I thought we were friends. I told Becky we bonded."

"You told her I saw you naked."

"Did not. I specifically said I was in my underwear. Besides, we're partners on this, and I think I'm going to need your technical insights."

Jaden grunted. "Answer your phone next time." Then he grinned. "I am interested in seeing inside Xperion. Maybe a little more than interested."

Parker wiggled his eyebrows. "Cyber."

They wound their way through the parking garage until they reached a plain four-door sedan.

"Got a real special agent car today, I see," Parker said.

"Glad you like it, sir. No chauffer's hat though."

"Maybe next time."

Jaden put Parker's bag in the trunk. "My ass."

They climbed in and headed south on the 101 toward Xperion's headquarters in Palo Alto. Forty minutes later, they pulled into a visitor parking lot outside a large white brick and glass office building near the university.

"How's it feel to be back near the old alma mater?" Parker asked as they entered a high-ceilinged lobby bustling with a steady stream of incoming backpack-wearing men and women who, like Jaden, all looked to Parker to be too young to have graduated.

"I woke up in a cold sweat last night afraid I had overslept and missed an economics exam."

A uniformed security guard with a crew cut, fleshy pink cheeks, and a large midsection glared at them from behind the security desk in the lobby. Jaden showed him his credentials. "We're here to see Ms. Harding."

The guard tapped on a keyboard, then sorted through a collection of plastic badges hanging on a chrome tree. He picked out two and handed them to Jaden. "These have to be worn at all times," he said with the authority of an ex-cop and with an edge that suggested he didn't like something about their appearance or, maybe, who they worked for. "You two armed?"

Parker leaned in and said in a whisper. "I know it's hard to tell, but we're federal agents."

"You can't take your guns in. You'll need to lock them in your vehicle."

"Says who?" Parker asked, tone sharp.

"Company rules. California law allows businesses to require law enforcement to disarm before entering."

"Ain't going to happen," Jaden said. "We're required to carry at all times."

The guard frowned and pointed to a furnished waiting area across the room. "Wait over there. I'll let Ms. Harding know you're here," he scowled at Jaden, "and that you refused to leave your weapons in your vehicle."

Several minutes later, a woman with shoulder-length blonde hair, dressed in a blue cybersuit approached them. She was of average height, maybe five-foot-six, and had an average build. Her face was tanned, and her eyes were the same color as her suit. She appeared to be in her early thirties, attractive, but not overly so. With the suit, the hair, and the tan, she resembled a surfer on nearby Casa Gunz beach.

Jaden stood to greet her, and Parker pushed himself up on his cane to do the same, still annoyed by the firearm dispute at the desk. He was far from a gun nut, and he was not much for many of the FBI rules, but the requirement to carry at all times had saved his life.

"Good morning, gentlemen. I'm Angela Harding." She glanced at the visitor badge around Jaden's neck. "Nice to meet you, Mr. Breaux." She shook Jaden's hand and turned to Parker.

Before she could say anything, Parker said, "Special Agent Parker Reid, and Mr. Breaux is Special Agent Breaux, and we're not giving up our guns."

She glanced at the security guard. "Of course not." Her eyes landed on the visitor badge in Parker's hand. "But I must insist you wear the badge. We are very serious about security here." Angela motioned for them to follow her. "I was asked to give you a tour and answer any questions you might have about what we do. Then we can meet with the founders."

Parker hung the badge around his neck, and they followed Angela to a large room set up with Metaverse rigs. It looked like a smaller version of the MetaSpot Parker had visited in Las Vegas. None of the rigs were in use, and except for the steady hum from the air conditioning, the room was silent. She led them to a table where headgear and bundled cybersuits, like the one she was wearing, had been placed.

"I thought we'd start in here. This is our product demonstration and customer test lab." Angela handed them each one of the folded suits and pointed to a series of doors. "You can change in those rooms. Your things will be safe in there." She stared at Parker. "Even your guns."

Parker shook his head and pointed at a rig with his cane. "I can't get in one of those things."

"Sure you can," Angela said. "I'll help. It's the best way to understand what we do, and it will be fun. You'll see."

Jaden took his bundle and headed for a door. "Come on, sir. It's time you see what this is all about."

Parker thought about protesting, but he couldn't deny his own curiosity. He changed into the suit. It felt stiff and strange. It was interlaced with dozens of cords that formed webs around his limbs and torso. Its collar rode high on his neck like a sweater and a short wire with a plug hung from a spot on his right breast. As she'd instructed, he left everything besides his shoes and cane in the changing room and rejoined her and Jaden at the table.

Angela studied their feet and laughed. "Normally, you wouldn't do this in those fancy leather loafers." She was wearing athletic shoes that matched her suit.

"They don't seem to go," Parker agreed.

She handed them each a pair of gloves webbed with the same cording that crisscrossed the suits. The gloves had small plugs that inserted into receptacles at their suit cuffs. Next, she gave them headgear which looked like scuba masks with solid white lenses attached to padded helmets that resembled something a college wrestler would wear. Jaden plugged the cable that dangled from his chest into a receptacle on the helmet and Parker followed his lead.

"You've done this before," Angela said approvingly.

Jaden smiled. "I've spent some time in your SIMs—mostly sports. I've never been in the Land of Might and Magic, though."

"LMM is my baby. I'll show you why it's so popular."

They walked to three nearby rigs.

She pointed out one to Jaden. "Why don't you get strapped in since you already know what you're doing."

Angela helped Parker into a rig and ensured he was buckled in. She adjusted the harness to take the weight off his bad leg so he felt no pain when he stood and walked on the treadmill-like surface.

"How's that?" she asked.

"Not bad."

Then she had him put on the headgear and adjusted its fit. He was surprised when he discovered he could see through it as if its solid white lenses were transparent. He was also surprised by how light and comfortable it felt. It was nothing like he'd imagined. It sealed to his face like a scuba mask, but as it was intended to keep out light and not water, it didn't cover his nose and didn't squish his face like he remembered scuba masks doing.

Angela positioned a microphone boom a few inches from his lips, explaining it contained cameras that detected his mouth movements and facial expressions. "So, if you mouth something obscene to me, I *will* see it."

"I wouldn't do that."

"I think you might," she said, flashing a mischievous smile.

She plugged a cable from the harness assembly into another receptacle on his helmet and stepped back. "Okay," she said. "I hope you enjoy this."

"Take it easy on me."

"Remember, he's a cripple," Jaden called from the next rig over.

"Oh, Breaux, that's like a serious HR complaint."

"Sorry, sir. Couldn't resist."

Angela put on her headgear and climbed into her own rig. Parker could see her moving her hands around like she was working some invisible controls. Then he heard her voice in his ears.

"We set you up with sample characters. I didn't know what you'd like so you're both going to be what we call warriors."

"Will we have guns?" Parker asked.

"No, but you'll have swords if that makes you feel better."

"Sounds good," Jaden said eagerly. "Let's do this."

"You got it," she said. "Get ready, Agent Reid. We're going through the looking glass."

Chapter 31
Agents in the Land

PARKER STOOD BLINKING IN the brilliance of an unclouded midday sun. Above him was an enormous stone arch, larger than the famous Arc De Triomphe in Paris that he and Carrie had visited on their honeymoon. On his right stood a strange man with bluish skin and a black beard. The stranger was dressed like a soldier from a medieval army in a glittering steel chain mail shirt with a longsword and pack on his back. On his left was a beautiful woman with ivory skin and long silver hair. She wore knee-high black boots with tight green leggings tucked inside and a simple brown cloak that seemed to radiate an odd light when she moved.

"Look at you. You're walking without a cane," the bluish man said in Jaden's voice.

"Breaux? Is that you? You're blue."

"So are you," Jaden said.

Parker inspected his hands. *Blue.* He stood on his bad leg. No pain. The harness had removed enough weight for his diminished muscles to support him.

The blue man that was Jaden grinned. "You see? Chi Chi was right." Jaden drew the sword from his back and slashed at the air. "This is cool."

"Don't hurt yourself," Parker said as the woman stepped closer and squeezed his arm. When she did, the cords in the sleeve of his cybersuit constricted, and he imagined he could feel her fingers gripping his bicep.

"That's, uh, weird."

"Tactile sensation is key to making the Land feel real," the woman said in Angela's voice.

Parker gave her a sly grin. "Are those cords everywhere?"

She glared at him. "No. I knew you were going to be trouble."

"Maybe just a little," Parker said, flashing her the grin again.

They were standing on a cobblestone road at the top of a hill looking down on a small village of twenty or so huts and larger wooden structures. Parker turned and looked up at the arch. "This is something. What's it for?"

As he asked, two players walked past them and under the arch. They disappeared before making it through to the other side.

"It's called a teleportation gate, or gate for short," Angela said. "Everyone passes through one of these to enter and exit the Land."

"Where did those players go?" Jaden asked.

Angela shrugged. "Could have gone anywhere."

Not wanting to disappear himself, Parker moved out from under the arch, and Jaden and Angela followed. They stood admiring the view and watching other players come and go. Some passed through the arch and disappeared, while others appeared beneath it and continued down the hill.

After a long moment, Angela spread her arms and said, "This is the Land of Might and Magic. It's our most sophisticated simulation."

"It's spectacular," Jaden said. He motioned toward a group of characters. "Are all of these actual players?"

"Most are, but some are part of the simulation. It's hard to tell which is which unless you know what to look for."

"How many actual players?" Parker asked.

She shrugged. "There are close to sixty million account holders. About fifty million enter the Land regularly."

A large selection group, Parker thought. Too large to be useful. "How many in the U.S.?"

"About sixty percent. It's still our largest market. Only because of the restrictions the Chinese impose. Otherwise, we'd be more China focused like everyone else."

Thirty million was still a large group. *Too large.*

"Come on. Let's get a little deeper in," Angela motioned for them to follow, and she led them toward the village.

The road ran straight down the hill through a field of yellow and purple wildflowers. Some of the flowers grew in the ditches on either side of the road. Angela bent down and picked several.

"As with tactile sensation," she said with a glance at Parker, "we go to great lengths to make sure the visuals are as lifelike as possible." She handed them each a flower.

"The detail is amazing," Jaden said as he studied his. "There's a term for it right? Photo something."

Angela took his arm. "Photorealism. I'm impressed you know that."

"I'm a bit of a technophile," Jaden said.

"The word is geek," Parker said. He plucked the petals from his flower and watched as they fluttered to the ground, blown gently by a breeze he could not feel.

"The technology has come a long way in a short time," she said. "Our early simulations didn't render half this well. They were cartoonlike, not at all photorealistic," Angela said and smiled at Jaden. "Low-cost quantum chips changed everything. Before they became available, the processors were too slow to handle this level of detail, but as you can see, not anymore. Now, the central control processing units in the rigs and the image processors in the cybermasks double in power every year. Soon the Verse and the Real-Real will be indistinguishable."

They had walked several hundred feet, and Parker felt no pain in his leg. After three years of agony from the slightest movement, he was overcome with an urge to run and jump. "How closely do the rigs mimic motion?" he asked.

"Very. It can be intense. I suggest trying small things first."

Parker tested putting more weight on his leg, then hopped up and down. The rig rocked to simulate the movement. "That's something." He jumped higher. His leg registered little pain, nothing like what he'd experience if he executed a similar jump out of the harness. The feeling of having two fully functional legs, even if it was all virtual, was almost overwhelming.

"Careful," Angela said. "You are really moving, and if you fall, the rig will simulate it."

"What does that mean?"

"It will pull you down on your ass."

Parker jogged a few steps. He looked back at them and smiled. "I got to do this," he said. Then he sprinted down the hill until he reached the village. He knew it wasn't real, but it still felt good to use his leg. All he was missing was wind in his face. He turned, jumped up and down a few times, and sprinted back to them.

Jaden clapped and hooted.

Parker was breathing hard from the exertion. It had been years since he'd attempted anything that physical. A dull pain radiated through his leg with every accelerated heartbeat, but it wasn't unbearable—maybe a six. It was worth it. He kneaded his quadriceps and smiled.

Angela watched him. "Are you okay?"

He laughed. "Better than okay. This, ah, simulation is amazing."

"It can be very addictive," Angela said. "Some people get lost in here."

"Lost?" Parker said between breaths.

"They spend all their time and money in simulations like this. Their real-world lives fall apart. It's really no different from drug or alcohol addiction."

"I guess that makes you a drug dealer," Parker said.

"In a manner of speaking," she agreed.

When they reached the village, she led them to a small courtyard with benches and they sat on one. Other players wandered about them. Most looked inside the buildings that ringed the courtyard and departed. A few approached with weapons drawn. Angela stared at those that did, and her eyes flashed a spooky red which sent the players scurrying away. Even large, fearsome-looking ones ran when she gave them the look.

"That thing you do with your eyes is quite effective," Jaden said.

She nodded. "Just avoiding trouble. I don't want one of those players to get the wrong idea and try to score some easy points at our expense."

"They must see something in you that I am not noticing. You don't even have a sword," Jaden said.

"After you've played the game for a while, you learn how to gauge the threats from other players."

"We're threatening?" Parker asked.

She grinned. "Not you."

Parker stared at Angela's character. A barely perceptible gold glow enveloped her. Jaden's character had no glow. "It's the gold shimmer."

Her grin turned into a smile. "You don't miss much, Agent Reid." She appraised him with the spooky eyes. "I was told you came here today as part of a murder investigation. Is it true someone is killing our players?"

"Two that we know of," Parker said, staring into the eyes.

"Is an Xperion employee a suspect?"

"Not that we know of." Parker smiled. "Should we be looking at one?"

"I hope not, but if you don't suspect one of us, why did you come here?"

Parker's gaze shifted to the players in the courtyard. "To learn more about the kind of people who play this game."

She laughed. "All kinds of people come here."

"All killing each other for points," Parker observed.

"People like violence, no doubt about it," she said. "You must have seen our tag line. It's on a sign in the lobby in big red letters. 'You haven't lived until you've died in the Land of Might and Magic.'"

"I'm familiar with it," Parker said.

She shrugged. "Not everyone comes here to kill, though. There are treasure hunts and quests. Lots of puzzles to solve, and for some, just existing in a magical place like this is what draws them. But there's no getting around it; fighting and killing other characters is the primary way players earn points." Angela reached over and pulled the sword from the sheath on Parker's back. "That's why you carry one of these." She handed it to him.

He grabbed the sword's hilt in both hands. The cords in his suit and gloves tightened, making it feel like he was actually holding it. He raised the sword and brought it down in a chopping motion. "The two murdered players had their heads cutoff with one of these."

"With a sword?"

"Yes." Parker made the chopping motion again. "Bet that happens all the time in here."

She frowned. "Beheadings?"

"Sure. Don't you think?"

She shrugged and pointed at the sword. "It's a fantasyland where everyone has one of those. I'm sure it happens, but no extra points are awarded for it."

"If you wanted to do it, this would be a great place to learn how. Wouldn't you agree?"

"Do it?" she repeated, sounding confused. "You mean cut people's heads off?"

Parker nodded.

"I guess," she said and quickly added, "but we have other simulations where you can learn how to use a rocket launcher too. Don't hear about too many people using those in the Real-Real."

Jaden jumped in. "Rocket launchers are hard to get."

She studied them. "You two are joking right? You can't blame us for what crazy people do in the Real-Real."

"People get the ideas from somewhere," Jaden said. "No getting around the desensitizing impact of violent entertainment."

"And our killer is a very desensitized individual," Parker said.

"You two really think whoever killed those poor people did it because of our game?"

"Don't know, but both victims spent a great deal of time in here. Their families even used the same word you used. They called them addicts. What if they ran into someone so caught up in this fantasy," Parker said as he raised the sword again, "he got himself a real one of these and started acting out the simulated killings on the actual people behind the characters."

"You said it yourself," Jaden offered, "some players get lost in here. Lose the ability to separate the fantasy from the real."

"What do you want us to do? Shut our simulation down because some nut kills some of our customers with a sword? Fire everyone?"

"No," Parker said. "Help us catch him."

"How?"

"We are trying to determine where the killer met his victims. How he selected them."

"And you believe he met them in here."

"Let's assume he did."

She looked at Jaden and back at him. "Okay. Possible. I guess. What do you want from us?"

"A list of all the players the victims came in contact with before they were murdered."

She blinked at him. "I don't know if we store that kind of information."

"You don't keep log files that would show that?" Jaden

asked in a doubtful tone.

Her face split into a wide grin. "My, my, Agent Breaux. You keep impressing me with your system knowledge."

Parker winked at Jaden. "He is quite impressive."

She shrugged. "I guess we might have something in our log files, but if we do, we don't keep it for long. Too much data."

"Then we should get what you have immediately," Jaden said.

"I can't just give you our log data. I'll need authorization from the founders, and it will take time to pull together."

Parker stood. "Then let's go ask them, so you can get started." He attempted to slide his sword back in its sheath. The blade missed the opening and fell to the ground with a loud clang. The sound startled him. "Even the noises are realistic."

Angela's character seemed to beam. "Like I said, we go to great lengths to give our customers a real experience."

Jaden bent down and retrieved the sword. He slipped it in Parker's sheath. "Maybe too real for some," he said.

"I don't want to believe that," Angela said then led them back up the path toward the arch.

As they walked, Parker said, "I saw a player cut the ears off another player in Las Vegas. What happens to them?"

Angela stopped and turned to face him. "What do you mean, what happens to them?"

"What happens to the ears?"

"That's an unusual question." She eyed him. "One I haven't heard before."

"It's kind of my thing," Parker said, wiggling his eyebrows and wondering if his blue character's eyebrows were moving.

"I bet it is. If you store or wear them, they are yours. Players keep parts of monsters they kill all the time... dragon teeth, wolf hides, things like that."

Parker made a face. "Kind of gross. Don't you think? Why do they do it?"

She shrugged. "Some parts are valuable. Warriors who kill a dragon can sell the teeth and scales to magic users who need them for spells and potions. Players wear animal and monster hides to brag about their deeds. You know—look at me, I killed a wolf."

"What would they do with another player's ears?"

"Same thing. Take them as trophies. Like scalps." She flashed her red eyes at him. "It's just part of what goes on in the Land, Agent Reid."

"You haven't lived until you've died," Parker echoed.

Chapter 32
Day Time

ANGELA UNSTRAPPED HERSELF FROM her rig and helped Parker out of his. Jaden didn't require her assistance. They deposited their headgear on the table and changed out of the cybersuits. Angela led the agents to a conference room and showed them a stocked refrigerator and how to work the coffee machine.

"Help yourselves," she said. "I'll go round up the founders."

She left them and hurried to Maxwell Morris's office where Maxwell, the Days, and Xperion's lawyer, Anand Patel, were waiting. Angela stopped at the office door and steadied herself. Meeting with the Days one at a time was challenging enough. Talking with them together could be excruciating. She took a deep breath and opened the door.

The room was quiet and dim. The only light came from the partially opened blinds. They'd been waiting for her, and she got the impression they had done so in silence. Everyone, including herself, was dressed in black. It looked and felt like they were attending a funeral. Maybe they were. Maybe it was their dreams of wealth that had died. If the security threat posed by the Anomaly didn't frighten investors away, a serial killer targeting Xperion's customers surely would. The beats per minute on her watch's heart rate monitor were in the red as she closed the door behind her.

Her eyes first found Jasmine's but moved to Marcus's and stayed there. Those who did not know the Days might have concluded at first meeting them that they were polar opposites. She'd heard them described as fire and ice. Their appearances certainly suggested it. Jasmine was Asian, muscular, richly tanned, and had an intensity about her that made everyone in her presence fear she might explode at any moment. Marcus was none of those things. He was Caucasian, frighteningly thin, and white all over, skin, hair, even his eyes were such a light gray they looked bleached. Where Jasmine radiated energy, he seemed to absorb it. No matter the circumstance, when Marcus Day entered a room, his ghostly presence seemed to draw all the life out of it. But once you got past the stark, external contrasts, you discovered Jasmine and Marcus were the same. Driven, brilliant, conquest-oriented, and intolerant of anything short of perfection. People who marveled at the details of Xperion's simulations only did so because they did not know the Days.

"There you are," Marcus said in his soft, controlled voice. He pointed to one of three empty chairs. "Please, sit and tell us about our guests. Did they enjoy the tour of our little world?"

She lowered herself into the chair, taking care to smooth any wrinkles that had formed on her slacks and blouse. Wrinkles would attract Marcus's attention. She'd seen him stare at uninitiated subordinates until, by the sheer weight of his discomfort, they'd realized their infraction and removed the intolerable imperfections.

"Yes, I believe they were impressed." She chanced a smile. "Two more customers."

Maxwell and Anand laughed, but not the Days.

"Good. And what did they have to say?"

Angela took a breath and responded in the staccato, bulleted style she knew Marcus preferred. No narrative beyond what was necessary to provide context. Facts and analysis without opinion. "The agents suspect a serial killer is targeting our customers. Two have been killed so far."

Marcus waved his hand. "We already know this."

She hastily continued. "Both customers had been killed with a sword." Angela paused, waiting for a response. Marcus gestured for her to continue. "The agents believe the killer met his victims in LMM, and they want the identities of all the players the victims' characters had come into contact with."

"That's absurd," Jasmine barked.

"What do you think, Anand?" Marcus asked the lawyer.

Anand shrugged. "We could insist on a subpoena. They'll get one. I did some research on them. Agent Breaux is a kid, but Parker Reid has some serious clout. If he feels he's onto something, he'll get what he needs to pursue it."

"PR risks on both sides of this," Maxwell said.

Marcus peered at him. "Explain."

"If we don't cooperate, we're putting customers at risk. That will get out, and if there's anything the media likes better than serial killers, it's serial killers protected by Big Tech."

Marcus nodded. "And, if we cooperate?"

"We risk violating the privacy agreements we have with our customers guaranteeing their real identities will never be disclosed."

"Our terms and conditions clearly stipulate those guarantees do not extend to lawful government inquiries," Anand said.

"We'll still get roasted on social media. Some of our simulations cater to demos that believe the security state is out to get them."

"That's because they are," Anand said.

Marcus gave the lawyer a cool stare, and the banter ceased.

"It's only two players," Angela offered.

"Not so fast, Angela," Jasmine said. "Have you looked at the names?"

Angela had come prepared with the names. Entering the room without them would be unthinkable. She glanced down at her tablet. "Jyothi Reddy and Charles Tate."

Jasmine gave her the high dimpled predatory smile, making Angela wonder what she'd overlooked. "What about their LMM IDs?"

Shit. How did she forget to get their LMM IDs? "No. I don't have those."

"I do," Jasmine said. "Jyothi Reddy's unique ID was REDDYELF@4242 and Charles Tate's ID was OLDDOG $$52."

The IDs rang a bell in Angela's head, but she was not sure why. Jasmine clearly expected her to recognize them. "I'm sorry, Jazz. I don't follow."

Jasmine looked at Marcus. "I think you should leave now. Angela and I have been working with the special external entity you prefer to know nothing about."

Angela's heartbeat monitor moved into the red zone again, and her head swam. Those IDs had something to do with the Anomaly. Now she recognized them. They were the two characters the consultant had used for bait before Darshana. REDDYELF@4242 was the character Danaka, and OLDDOG$$52 had been Pharoah. They'd been killed in the game and murdered in the real world. This was no longer about quietly catching a hacker.

Marcus speared Jasmine with a freezing stare. "I thought we agreed to stop those methods."

She dismissed him with a wave. "I do what I must."

"Take unnecessary risks," he shot back. The tension between them filled the room with the same charged feeling that precedes a thunderstorm. Talk of the Day's marital difficulties would fly like birds ahead of the storm.

"Stay if you must," she spat. The air seemed to crackle as if lightning had arced between them. "But if you do, you won't be able to claim ignorance of my methods, as you have in the past."

Marcus shifted his arctic stare to Anand.

The lawyer nodded. "It's best to compartmentalize these kinds of things."

"Fine. I will leave our FBI guests to you," Marcus said to Jasmine. "Try not to get us arrested," he added as he floated out the door.

After he'd gone, Jasmine turned back to Angela. "Do I need to spell out the connection to you?"

"No, ma'am. I recognize the players now." She was still processing the meaning. *The hacker was the murderer.*

"Good girl," Jasmine said as if she were praising a pet that completed a trick. "Needless to say, we must be careful not to give the FBI anything that could lead them to the consultant."

They had used the consultant often over the years. All the engagements had been off the books. Some of them involved questionable, more than questionable—illegal—activities. If the FBI connected the consultant to Xperion, the stock price would be the least of their concerns.

Angela took two deep breaths to tamp down her growing panic. She had been the only Xperion employee to work directly with the consultant. She was as guilty of the things he'd done for them as he was. But people were dying, and she'd unknowingly made them targets.

"Jazz, this hacker is killing people. We need to do whatever we can to help stop him."

Jasmine's stare bored through her. "I understand the situation, Angela. Do you?"

The agitated cofounder continued without giving her a

chance to reply. "I don't know what other players these two may have interacted with, but I do know one for sure."

"The consultant."

"Correct. What good would it do to have the FBI focus on him?"

Angela sighed. "None."

"We need to learn how the hacker is doing what he is doing and put a stop to it. Then we can tell the agents what we know. Has your team shut down the hack—Angela?"

In her nervousness, Angela lost control and blurted, "You know we haven't."

Jasmine smirked. "Then, what would we tell the FBI?" Again, she continued before Angela could answer. "Nothing. We have nothing to tell them. They will just ask questions we cannot answer. When your team determines how the hacker is getting through our security and we plug that hole, then we will go to them. Perhaps we'll be able to tell them who, or at least where, he is. Until then, we remain focused on shutting this hacker down. Do you understand, Angela?"

Her palms were sweating. She was moments away from a full-blown panic attack. She took another deep breath, let it out, and said, "Yes, ma'am."

Jasmine turned to Maxwell. "How far back do our detailed logs go?"

"We keep a year in the archives."

"What about online?" she asked with a knowing smile.

"One week," Maxwell said.

"That's unfortunate. I believe both those players have been off-SIM for longer than that."

"Angela, would you please fetch our guests?"

Chapter 33
Linkage

PARKER LEFT THE CONFERENCE room with an urgent need to empty a bladder straining to contain the six cups of tea he'd consumed during the flight. He tested a few doors along the hallway. All of them were locked. Some had badge readers. He tried his visitor's badge at those without success. Eventually, he found a restroom, and after he'd relieved himself, Parker continued to explore until he came upon a group of employees queued up at a door. Each was dutifully waving their badge at a reader before entering, but they were holding the door open for each other. *My, my, wouldn't Angela be alarmed if she knew how unserious these employees were about security.* He joined the queue and when it was his turn to wave his badge, no one seemed to notice the red light indicating he did not have access. He stepped through the door, making sure to hold it for the person behind him.

The door led to a large dimly lit space, illuminated only by a few overhead lights, and the glow from computer monitors. The group that Parker had followed into the room broke up. Individuals fanned out and made their way to clusters of open-walled workspaces. Parker hobbled unchallenged about the room, smiling at the occasional curious glance, and pausing now and then to look over shoulders at screens filled with endless lines of squiggly brackets and unintelligible words he guessed were computer programs.

He wandered into a sparsely populated cluster and sat down at an unoccupied workstation surrounded by a ring of dark monitors. An empty coffee mug and half a candy bar sat next to a keyboard, and a collection of toy figures lined a small shelf. One of the larger toys caught his eye, an over-muscled creature holding a sword in a striking stance. Its plastic skin had been inexpertly painted gray, green showed through where the painter had missed spots. A label was stuck to its chest with FUCKING ANOMALY scrawled in black marker. He reached for the character and a familiar woman's voice froze him.

"Agent Reid, what are you doing in here?"

He turned to find Angela glowering at him. Jaden stood behind her, grinning.

"I had to go to the bathroom."

"Not in here, I hope."

He levered himself out of the chair, reminded by the pain in his leg that he would pay dearly for the day's activity and tempted by the pills in his pocket. They would stay in their vial for now. He suspected he would need every one of them tonight.

"How did you get in here?" she demanded.

He held up his badge. "I used this."

Her gaze turned suspicious. "I'll have to look into the access we grant visitors," she said.

"I would if I were you."

They made their way back through the large space.

"Why is it so dark in here?" he asked as he followed her out.

"The official reason is the overhead lights cause glare on the monitors, but programmers are eccentric, especially the good ones. I think they just like the cave atmosphere."

She led them into an elevator and from there to a large office where two men and an intense-looking woman were waiting. They sat in the available seats and did introductions.

The man who'd introduced himself as the company's lawyer spoke first.

"Gentlemen, we are eager to provide any information that will help stop a murderer, but if I detect any attempt at incrimination, I will put an end to this meeting."

Parker rested his chin on his cane and made eye contact with the lawyer and then the woman who'd introduced herself as Jasmine Day, though he'd recognized the company's cofounder as soon as he'd spotted her. He'd Googled her before they arrived. Even if he hadn't, he would have known her. Her face was all over the investment news media lately. He smiled despite his throbbing thigh. "We'll try not to coerce any confessions."

"Is that humor, Agent Reid?" Anand asked.

Parker lifted his head. "Just trying to break the ice. As we told Miss Harding, we're here on a purely speculative basis. We see a potential connection between the killer and your games. We're hoping you can help us explore that connection."

The man behind the desk who'd introduced himself as Maxwell Morris cleared his throat. "Angela told us about the log data you asked for."

"Specifically," Parker said, "we would like a list of players who interacted with the victims."

"Yes," Maxwell said. "We understand the request, and we are happy to provide that data, but the timeframe is the problem."

"How's that?" Jaden asked.

"Our online systems only keep detailed logs for one week. Will that still help?"

Parker studied Maxwell's movie-star-handsome face, sensing there was something too precise in his response. He glanced at Jaden, and Jaden did not look convinced.

"What about your offline files? Your archives?" Jaden asked.

Maxwell glanced at Jasmine and Parker knew by his expression Jaden had tripped him up.

"You must be a horrible card player, Max," Parker said.

Jasmine jumped in before the busted executive could respond. "We will, of course, look into our archives," Jasmine said.

"It will take some time," Maxwell added.

"Don't take too long, Max. Another one of your customers might lose their head soon."

"That was uncalled for, Agent Reid," Anand said.

Parker glared at the lawyer. "Advise your employers what happens to people who lie to the FBI." He stared at Jasmine. "Even the wealthy ones."

Jasmine gave Parker a Cheshire-cat grin. "We will get you the data."

"When you produce a subpoena," Anand added.

"Preserve what you have. You will be served," Parker said.

"What else do we need to discuss here?" Anand asked.

"There was a third victim."

"Another one of our customers?" Angela asked, her eyes wide, showing surprise.

"Don't know. We'll want you to check." Parker looked at Anand. "The request will be in the court order." Then he looked at Jasmine. She stared back at him, her dark eyes giving no ground. He returned his gaze to Anand, letting her win the staring contest. "The other victim was a twenty-three-year-old woman named Abby Loveridge." He glanced at Angela. "She was a computer programmer."

Angela nodded.

"She worked at Zhang Control Systems," he said and saw Jasmine twitch. He turned his attention back to her. Her eyes met his, but there was no contest in the stare. This time she broke it off and turned to Anand.

"My father's company," she said.

"Yes," Anand said. "I'm sure the agents know that. I'm also sure Agent Reid intended to surprise us with that information as it was not provided in advance."

Parker placed his chin back on his cane and gave the lawyer his best puppy dog eyes. "No surprise was intended. We didn't understand ZCS's connection to your company until after we made the appointment."

"That's because there is no connection," Maxwell blurted. "ZCS creates commercial automated controls for things like lighting and HVAC systems. They have nothing to do with our simulations."

"The agent means the connection to me," Jasmine said.

Parker nodded.

"Ms. Loveridge was killed in Las Vegas, then?" Jasmine asked.

"No. Clearwater, Florida," Parker replied.

"Clearwater? ZCS has no offices in Clearwater."

Parker shrugged. "Remote worker."

"I will have to look into this," Jasmine replied. "When was she killed?"

Parker gave her the date.

"Five weeks ago. In Clearwater Florida," Jasmine uttered almost under her breath. She seemed preoccupied by the fact. The intensity she displayed when they first entered the room was noticeably blunted. She looked Parker in the eye again. This time, Parker thought he detected worry or maybe even fear. "Have you spoken to my father's people at ZCS?"

"Las Vegas PD is heading there tomorrow."

She nodded. "I'm sure my father's people will be eager to

provide any information they can to help find this killer, as are we." Jasmine glanced at her tablet and abruptly stood. "I have another appointment that requires my attention. Angela and Maxwell are our top people. They will continue the conversation." She glanced at the lawyer. "And Anand."

"Someone has to make sure the agents behave themselves," Anand said.

They continued without her for several more minutes. Parker and Jaden reiterated the need to preserve the log data and asked Maxwell and Angela to search their customer support records to see if anyone reported peculiar or unhinged calls recently.

Maxwell laughed. "We must get over a thousand peculiar and unhinged calls a week."

"I'd like to see them," Parker said. He glanced at Anand. "We'll put that in the court order too." He returned his attention to Maxwell. "You need to take such calls extra seriously until we catch this," Sarah Loveridge's voice exploded in Parker's head, "monster."

After they'd run out of topics, Angela escorted them back to the lobby where she collected their badges.

Parker winked at her when he handed over his. "Remember to check the access," he said.

"You can bet I will."

She walked them to the door.

Parker stopped and turned to her. "I did some research on Jasmine Day before we came."

"Is that so?"

"Quite a resume. The search results were endless."

"She's very accomplished."

"Everything I read suggested she was tough as nails."

Angela laughed. "Only if those nails are made of something indestructible and very sharp, like diamonds."

"Unflappable," he said.

"That's an understatement."

Parker nodded. "Yes, I could see that, at least at the start of the meeting, but she seemed a little off her game at the end, after I told her about the victim from ZCS."

"That was a big surprise to us all."

"Seemed to hit her hard," Jaden added.

Angela looked at him and then leveled her eyes on Parker. "The Days have a son."

"Yes, I read that. Couldn't find much information about him. Seems he's not been able to get out from under his parent's shadow," Parker said.

Angela made a hissing sound. "I'm sure he tries to be as far away from that shadow as he can." A mix of sadness and disgust was woven in her tone.

He pressed her. "Doesn't get along with his parents?"

"Lincoln's a sweet boy," she replied in a way that suggested she had more to say but was reluctant.

"But?" Parker said.

She looked back at the security guard and motioned for them to continue the conversation outside. They followed her through the door and out to the walkway that led to the parking lot.

"Lincoln is a bit odd. He doesn't do well with people."

"Aggressive, like his mother?"

She gave a quick laugh. "Just the opposite. Lincoln is very shy. Very quiet. He has a speech impediment."

"What kind of speech impediment?"

"He stutters, which infuriates his mother. He talks, she criticizes him, he stops talking. The guy had a really tough childhood."

Jaden nodded. "I know a little about being the only child of hard-driving parents. It can be tough."

Angela frowned at him. "The Days are much more than hard-driving." She turned back to Parker. "Everything you may have read about them is true and then some. They are the toughest, most uncompromising people you will ever meet." Angela looked around as if checking to make sure no one other than them could hear what she was about to say. "Jazz and Marcus were brutal with Lincoln, especially Jazz."

"Abuse?" Parker asked.

"Nothing physical. I don't think she ever struck him, and he certainly never wanted for anything, but..." she hesitated, and glanced at Jaden before continuing, "he had to be the best at *everything* he did. Top grades, top chess player, top swimmer. Everything."

"Sounds like they had high expectations for him," Parker

remarked.

"High expectations," Angela coughed out the words and laughed. "They demand perfection. From everyone, but especially their son. That's why he doesn't work here anymore."

"What did he do when he did?" Parker asked.

"He was our top programmer, of course. A natural, like his parents. But the pressure was just too much."

"Couldn't cut it?" Jaden asked.

"Jeezus, no," she answered. "No one could. Jasmine is relentless. She would tear him to pieces for the most inconsequential things, and she would do it in public meetings. Any defect, any deliverable below her standards, and she would light into him."

"Sounds like the Days were asshole parents," Parker said. "But what does that have to do with why the ZCS murder rattled Jasmine?"

"Jasmine's father is back in China where he has many other businesses. I'm sure he doesn't even know one of his employees was murdered. But Lincoln works at ZCS. He must know, and apparently, he never told Jasmine. She's probably online with him now, tearing him apart.

"Is that so?" Parker said, knowing he'd discovered another important piece to the puzzle. "Anything else unusual about the Day's son?"

Angela shrugged. "I assume you've seen pictures of him."

Parker had found photos of the boy on the internet. "Yes. Very light skinned, like his father."

"Well, that wasn't easy on him either," she said, then turned and went back into the building.

Parker watched her go. He turned to Jaden. "Good catch in there with the archive files, Breaux."

"Yeah, they are trying to hide something."

Parker nodded. "Yes, I got that feeling too. What do you make of their son working at the same firm as the Clearwater victim?"

"As Higgs would say, dat fricken stinks."

Parker laughed. The impression was spot on. "We need to be at that ZCS meeting tomorrow. Looks like I'm flying back to Vegas with you tonight."

"Great, sir," Jaden said in a decidedly insincere tone.

Chapter 34
Modules

ANGELA WAS STILL REELING from the revelation that the players they used for bait had been murdered. She was no lawyer, but she knew Jasmine directing them to withhold that connection from the FBI was a crime. "Accessory after the fact" was what Anand had called it when she'd raced to his office after the agents left. He said he had advised Jasmine to reconsider her decision, but Angela knew there was no chance of that. Jasmine had already made it clear she had no intention of revealing anything until they had a lock on the hacker. Once Jasmine decided on a direction, the course was set until the object was either achieved or a new discovery altered the plan.

It turned out, a new discovery had been made that afternoon. Angela was in Anand's office when she received Rituraj's messages. She almost cried out with relief when she got the first one. *We found something. Meet in fifteen minutes.* Then, five seconds later, she received the second and felt like a balloon after all the air had been let out. *You're not going to like it.* Anand must have seen the waves of changing emotions wash over her face as he'd asked her repeatedly if everything was all right. "Probably not," she told him as she rushed from his office to her own to await Rituraj's report.

Twenty agonizing minutes later, a disheveled Rituraj showed up at her door. He slumped into one of her visitor chairs and opened his laptop without making eye contact. The pungent scent of his body odor made her nose wrinkle.

"You look like shit, Rituraj."

"I feel like shit. We all feel like shit. I haven't been home in three days."

That explained the body odor.

"I'm having a really bad day too," she said. "Your drama

211

message didn't make it any better."

"No dramas, just mysteries," he said. Then he looked up, searched her desk, and snatched the remote for the large monitor that hung on her wall. He turned it on and streamed the display from his laptop. On the screen was a list of six file names she recognized as program source code files.

"The tracking data we received led us to something."

"Thank God."

"Yes. Your consultant is very good."

"You don't know about him," she reminded Rituraj with an edge in her voice.

He shrugged. "Whatever. The event trace data included request and response pairs."

Angela knew by request and response pairs Rituraj was referring to the messages the LMM simulation's programs used when communicating to one another.

"When we tried to execute the captured requests in the clone world, the response programs crashed—brought the whole clone system down."

"That's not right," she said. "If the programs in the clone world are the same as the live world, why would the requests cause the clone world to crash?"

"Because some of the programs in the live world are different."

His words shocked and infuriated her. The clone world was a small-scale replica of the simulation systems customers used. The software in the clone world was supposed to be kept identical to that used by customers in the live world at all times.

"That's never supposed to happen."

"We were as surprised as you. We've been over it a hundred times. My guys haven't slept since we received the trace files. There's a code mismatch."

"Someone is going to lose their job for that Rituraj," she fumed. "The clone has to match live. That's the whole point. We keep the clone world in synch with the live world so we can debug online problems."

Rituraj's eyes met hers for the first time since he'd sat down. They were bloodshot, and looked both angry and wounded by her statement. "Don't you think I know that? We all know that. No one screwed up. The synchronizing routines work perfectly.

Someone replaced the files in the live world after they were last synched with the clone, and there's no record of it."

"What do you mean replaced?"

"*Replaced*," he almost shouted. "Copied new programs over the old ones."

"Why did it take so fucking long to figure that out? Didn't we look for modified files when all this started?"

"Of course we did. All the program files on the clone system are the same size and have the same date and timestamps as the live system."

"I don't understand," she said. "You just said some of the live files were replaced."

"The files look the same on the outside, but they're not the same on the inside."

"That's impossible."

Rituraj shook his head. "Difficult, but not impossible. We did a byte-by-byte comparison of all the files on the clone and live systems. All twenty thousand of them." He nodded toward the screen. "These six program files were modified."

Angela put her head in her hands. "How did someone do this from the outside?"

Rituraj gazed down at his laptop as if he were searching the keys for the answer.

"Rituraj?"

He looked up. "I don't believe it was done from the outside. The person who did this had full administrative access to the live world servers and knew how to deploy code to them without causing an outage or triggering alerts."

"Someone on the operations team?" she asked in an almost leading manner—hoping it wasn't a developer, though not wanting it to be one of Em's people either.

Rituraj violently shook his head. "No way. There's no one on that team who could pull this off." His eyes dropped back to the keyboard. "Whoever did it, changed the player-character management system. That's sophisticated stuff. Only a SIM programmer could do it, and it couldn't have been just any programmer. These modules are really old. Some of them go back to the original world versions."

"Then it is someone on our team."

Rituraj laughed. "I don't think so. I'm the best you got, and

I couldn't do it."

He tapped on his laptop and the screen filled with program source code. The first line read: /* Author: *Marcus Day.* */

Angela stared at the code. "Marcus?"

"Yes. All six modules were originally developed by him. The stuff is uber-complex. No one on the team understands the code." He emphasized, "No one."

"Someone obviously understands it," she replied.

He shook his head. "None of us. These files are part of the core artificial intelligence engine that controls the simulated characters. You see who wrote it. We're all scared to touch it."

Angela stood and walked over to the monitor as if a closer look at the cryptic code would reveal something worthwhile. "Whoever changed the modules couldn't have rewritten them from scratch. They had to make changes to the existing source code. Can't we see who downloaded the source code files?"

"We checked that, and that's something else you're not going to like."

Her patience was gone. "Who accessed them?" she snapped.

"No one has looked at these files in almost a year."

"Come on, Rituraj, enough with the fucking suspense. Who was the last to access them?"

Rituraj pressed a key on his keyboard and a single user ID appeared next to each file.

Angela felt the room spin when she recognized it. "No fucking way," she hissed.

Rituraj nodded. "She's the last person to download these files."

"Jasmine? She hasn't worked on a program in years."

"It's her ID."

Angela stared into the monitor. Jasmine couldn't be behind the Anomaly. She knew that at her core. Someone had to have stolen her ID. She turned back around. Rituraj's eyes were closed. She clapped her hands and his eyes popped open. "Can we put the correct files back on the live world servers and shut down the Anomaly?"

"It's not that simple," he said. "I talked to the security team. They said there could be a booby trap that brings the whole system offline if it detects a restoration attempt. This is what they feared most. This hacker owns our world. If we try to fix it, God knows what he will do."

"What did they suggest?"

"Resigning."

She scowled at him.

"We need to build a new live world environment from the ground up. It's thousands of servers."

"Shit," she muttered. "Have you started?"

"Not yet. It's going to take weeks."

"I know, but you got it easy."

"How is that easy?" Rituraj asked, incredulous.

"You're not the one who has to explain it to the Days."

Angela walked to the door and motioned for Rituraj to leave. "Get started on those servers."

He stood and headed for the office door.

"The hacker is not Jasmine," she said as he passed.

"Probably not."

"And Rituraj."

He turned.

"Everything about this is top secret, especially what you just told me."

He punched his chest in a gladiator salute and strode off.

Angela took five deep, slow breaths and headed for Jasmine's office.

Chapter 35
Nearing the End

THE LAST MORPHINE DOSE was wearing off, and he was drifting toward consciousness. A buzzing in his ears, a milky light, and pain heralded its arrival. Then there was the cold. He was always cold now. Reduced to only skin and bone, his body no longer retained the little heat it generated. This is what it felt like to become a ghost, he thought. The sound of a turning page reached him through the buzzing. He tilted his head and focused. His mother was sitting in the same chair she'd been in when he'd fallen asleep. The final vigil had begun, all but one milestone behind him now.

"What are you reading?" he croaked.

The sound of his voice startled her. She stood and smiled down at him the special smile she reserved for her only child. The same loving smile she'd graced him with through years of hope, months of worry, weeks of sadness, and now days of grim acceptance. She ran her hand across his forehead brushing bangs no longer there from his eyes. "One of your father's old mystery books. You remember how much he enjoyed those."

"I do," he said.

She placed the straw from a water bottle between his cracked lips. He could feel the cool liquid moving through his entire body, as if all his nerves knew the end was near, and every sensation was precious. Or maybe it was just because there was so little of him left to feel. When she took back the bottle, he noticed the tabletop that usually held his keyboard and cyber headgear had been rolled away. "Where's my table?"

She nodded at the computer monitors suspended above him. "I thought you might want to give that a break. You've seemed so upset by it lately."

He felt anger flow through him like the water, but like heat, he could no longer retain it, especially not directed at this woman whom he owed so much. He returned her smile. "Just want to check my messages."

She retrieved the table from a corner and positioned it over his chest, then helped him adjust the bed so he could reach the keyboard. Pain shot through his spine and radiated around his hips and into his back. He winced, and she protested, but he waved her off. "Just a little while," he said. The sadness in her eyes confirmed she understood the double meaning of his words.

He tapped on the keys, enjoying their feel. An odd thing to love, the feeling of keys at your fingertips. He'd shut down most of his secure message connections weeks ago. All that remained active were the ones he used for Jasmine, Angela, and Shea.

Jasmine's session contained a short and direct message befitting her nature. *Goodbye, Cuz. Hope we meet again. Trust you to scrub all links to me before you go.* He shrugged away her coldness. Everything had already been erased. Once this connection was deleted, nothing would remain to suggest they were anything other than distant cousins who hadn't spoken for twenty years.

He turned his attention to Angela's session. She had sent him three messages. The first expressed sadness for his condition. It went on to thank him for the trace data he'd been able to collect during his and Shea's encounter with the Anomaly and assured him payment would be wired to the offshore account already controlled by his mother.

The second message shocked away the remanence of morphine slumber. *Met with FBI today. I think our hacker is murdering people in the real. FBI may learn of Falin.*

"Oh my," his mother said.

He glanced at her. "I'm sure she's being overly dramatic," he said, but inside he thought: *What the fuck? Murder?*

He always suspected the hacker was crazy, but until now he had believed his lunacy was confined to the Verse. He wondered if the FBI had any suspects. Based on the sophistication of the hacks, he had his own short list of possible culprits. It had to be someone with expert knowledge of the simulation which meant only a handful of candidates. Out of those, there were only two he thought were genuinely disturbed.

As for the FBI learning about Falin, that was a dry hole.

218 | RED SCREEN

Falin would lead them to a grandmother in a small town in New York. Poor Stacey Hanover and her grandchildren would get a nasty surprise when a dozen agents wearing blue windbreakers swarmed her home and dragged her out for questioning. It was heartless, but he still grinned at the thought.

Angela's last message suggested she was panicking which might've concerned him if he wasn't at death's door. *Can we talk? Need to tell the FBI about your trace data. They can use it to catch the killer.* He doubted that was true. Even if they extracted the hacker's device address, chances were good it would lead them nowhere. MAC addresses were too easy to spoof. He left the message window open and moved to Shea's session.

His heart skipped a beat when he saw she had finally sent him a message. *Spoke with Táma, aka Angela. Know you are sick. I'm very sorry. Meet?* The pain in his back subsided some. He looked over at his mother again. She was still watching the screens. "Told you I could still get the babes."

She shook her head and gave him more water. "Never had a doubt."

He wondered what else the panicked Angela may have told Shea. It didn't matter. He was glad he'd get a chance to explain. He spoke the words as he typed his response. "Greetings from a dwarf. Would very much like to talk. Where and when? Got to be soon, though."

He heard his mother choke back a sob.

Shea's reply came back right away. "Glad to hear you made it back from Wolfsburg. Not easy."

He'd cheated. He knew that wouldn't surprise her. Táma had teleported him out of the Wolfswood after he'd restored Falin. "Have to confess, I had help," he said as he typed.

She replied, *It pays to have friends in tall towers.*

He laughed, but it came out more like a cough. "Indeed."

Meet at Land's End in fifteen?

"I will be there," he said as he typed.

He looked over at his mother. "Look at that. Got a wicked hot date tonight."

She wiped a tear from her eye and shook her head.

He brought up Angela's session and typed, *Falin will be in the Land tonight. A wizard should be able to find him.* Then he allowed his mother to help him put on the headgear and gloves.

Chapter 36
A Beautiful Sunset

A **FIERY ORANGE SUN** floated above the waves when Darshana emerged from the Land's End Gate. The dwarf had arrived before her. He was sitting at the bench watching the sunset, his yellow beard glowing in the fading light. He didn't seem to notice her as she settled in beside him.

"Beautiful, isn't it?" she said.

He didn't turn to face her. "Oh. Hi there. Yes, it is. Amazing what these quantum processors can do. So, what did Angela tell you?"

"That you are very sick, and you don't have much time left."

"Yeah. It's a bummer."

She took his hand. "Can you feel me?"

He turned to face her and smiled. "Sure, I can. I might be a half-in, but I have great gloves. Best money can buy."

She laughed.

"What else did she tell you?"

"I know about being the bait, and I know you're not a teen-age boy."

He chuckled. "That was only a partial lie; I was one once."

"How long ago?"

Gulls squawked overhead as he seemed to consider her question. "It's been over twenty years since I was seventeen. I guess that makes me too old for you, huh?"

She squeezed his hand.

"I'm sorry I lied to you, Shea."

"Apology accepted. I told Angela I want to keep hunting for the Gray Warrior."

"You can't beat him," Falin said. "No player can. He needs to be stopped on the outside."

"We can spring your trap, and Angela's people will shut him down."

He shook his head. "You'll lose Darshana."

"Darshana has more tricks in her pouch than you give her credit for."

He reached in his pack and retrieved the mirror.

"Is he in here now?"

Falin studied it for a moment. "No, but he was in earlier. Got himself another level-fifty."

"Ranger?" she asked.

He showed her the mirror.

"Bashal," she hissed. "He fucking killed Bashal. That makes me the last legend level."

Falin handed her the mirror. "Take this. The programs behind it will keep running after I'm gone. It will help you avoid him."

"Avoid him? I don't want to avoid him. I want to hunt him. I want you to help me."

He smiled. "I wish I could, Shea. I really do, but this is game over for Falin."

She held up the mirror. "Can I spring your trap with this?"

"Yes."

"Show me."

"You sure you want to risk your character?"

"He's going to get me, anyway." She stared into the dwarf's simulated blue eyes and grinned. "Show me."

He shrugged. "There's nothing to it. I've set it up to notify you whenever he enters the Land. All you have to do when you find him is push and hold this button." He pointed to a red ruby on the mirror's handle.

"That's it?"

"Well, then you have to fight him and stay alive long enough for the event capture program to hook his event stream and collect the trace data."

"How will I know when that happens?"

"The ruby will turn green."

"Then what?"

"Angela's team will use the data to find the program behind him and shut it down."

"The program? Don't you mean the player?"

He grinned mischievously. "Maybe."

"How do I get the data to Angela?

"The trace program is configured to upload its data to the Xperion cloud. You don't have to do anything. Her people know where to look."

He grew quiet. They sat watching the sun sink below the waves. When the sky's blue faded to purple, she squeezed his hand. He didn't squeeze back. "Falin," she said, a little worried.

"Sorry. Just dozing. I'm going to sit here for a while. I like the sound of the crashing waves. Soothing."

She stood. "Message me later?"

"You bet," he whispered.

She left him on the bench and made her way back through the arch, sensing it would be the last time she'd see him in the Land.

Chapter 37
On the Edge

THE NIGHT DROVE THE dusk below the waves, and Falin sat alone on the bench staring up at a million simulated stars, wondering if there was any place in the real where they were still this beautiful. He stood and took a step toward the cliff's edge. Somewhere in the darkness below, the sea crashed into the rocky shore. Peering down, he caught glimpses of starlit foam.

"Don't jump," a woman's voice said, startling him and almost sending him into the abyss.

"If your intent was to stop me from going over, sneaking up behind me was probably not the best plan." He backed away from the edge and turned to face the voice.

Táma stood on the walkway behind the bench. Her ghostly face glowed in the starlight like the sea foam and her red robe seemed to burn with a golden flame.

"Forgive me if I don't kneel," Falin said. "I just don't have it in me."

"How are you feeling?"

"Not a lot of time for dumb questions, Angela."

She took a seat on the bench. "I saw you talking to Darshana."

"Yeah. Patched things up. Thank you for helping with that."

"I'm glad it worked out."

"I gave her the mirror. She wants to keep hunting."

"Good," Angela said. "If she gets the data, we'll have his device address."

He smirked inside his headgear and wondered if his doubtful expression was rendered on the dwarf's face. "Lot of good that will do you."

"Maybe we'll get lucky."

He shrugged. "Falin's headset address wouldn't lead you

to me. This guy we're chasing is smart—real smart. He'll know how to spoof the device addresses so even if you discovered them, they won't lead to his location. I can almost guarantee it, but... I guess you have to try. Who knows? Maybe I'm wrong. Maybe he's some nut who hacked your game for the fun of it, and you'll find him in his parent's basement. I'm sure you can picture him, he'll be wearing nothing but his underwear and be surrounded by empty energy drink cans."

"Is that how we'd find you?"

He looked at her and smiled. "Close. Now tell me what's going on. Why do you think the hacker is killing people and how did the FBI figure it out?"

"They haven't yet, but it's him."

"How do you know?"

"The players behind the characters Danaka and Pharoah were murdered. Their names were Jyothi Reddy and Charles Tate."

The character names made him rock forward in his bed sending waves of pain crashing into his body like the waves hitting the rocks on the beach below. "Fuck," he gasped. "When?"

"Danaka's player, Jyothi, was killed about four weeks ago. Pharoah's player, Charles, a little under two."

"About the time their characters were killed by the Anomaly," he said.

"Exactly and get this. The lead agent, Parker Reid, told me they were both killed with a sword just like it's done in here."

"Killed with a sword. Ain't that a pissah? This guy is a real psycho." The pain was making it difficult to think. It took him a moment to complete the connection between Danaka, Pharoah, and Darshana. "Christ, Angela. We got to warn Shea. We need to tell the FBI she's in danger."

"We can't."

"Why the frig not?" he shouted. "This is no longer about stopping a hacker from screwing up your IPO."

She stared at him. Her mask's facial movement cameras did a superb job capturing her wide-eyed shock at his hostility. "Why are you yelling?" she said.

"I don't have any patience left, Angela. I have no time for it. Why can't you tell the agents about Shea?"

"Because I didn't tell them about the Anomaly. Jasmine

wouldn't allow it. Now, how am I supposed to tell them about Shea?"

"You spoke with them only a few hours ago. Tell them you just put it together. They won't think that unreasonable."

"I need to talk to Jasmine first," she said.

The pain radiating through his back and abdomen made it difficult for him to concentrate on her words. "Jasmine will have to get over it," he said through gritted teeth.

"It's not just about defying her. I need to tell her what we found in the trace analysis, and I can't reach her. She's gone."

"Gone?"

"Left right after the meeting with the agents, and she hasn't returned any of my messages. I hate to say it, but we found something that makes me worried she might have something to do with this."

"With the murders?" he struggled to get the words out. "That's ridiculous."

"The trace data you sent pinpointed where the hacks were made to create the Anomaly."

He brushed her words aside with his hand. He knew what modules the hacker had modified. "The character is AI."

"You knew before we analyzed the trace."

"Only way the Anomaly could do what it does."

"Jasmine was the last person to access the source code."

"That's bullshit." The pain was almost unbearable now.

"I think so too, but it's her ID in the access logs."

He laughed. "Yeah, and Falin is a grandmother named Stacey Hancock."

"I know it can't be her," she said. "But why did she leave so abruptly, and why isn't she returning my messages?"

He shrugged. "I don't know, but you can bet it has something to do with her controlling the situation. Jasmine does things her way."

"The fucking Day way," Angela said bitterly.

"Jasmine was intense and controlling long before her last name was Day." His voice trembled as he pushed the words out past the agony. He needed the relief in the syringe he knew was waiting in his mother's hand.

"How do you know so much about her?" Angela asked.

"We go way back." He sighed. "Way back."

"I saw a photo in her office of a boy in a Mad Hatter top hat. Was that you?"

Falin managed a smile.

"That reminds me," she said. "I didn't tell you about the third murder. A programmer at her father's company was killed with a sword too. The FBI agents think by the same killer."

The news forced him to focus again. He grunted and gritted his teeth against the pain. "Her father's company?" he said, almost to himself. David Zhang owned several companies. Most of them in China. "ZCS?" he hissed through his clenched jaw.

"Yes."

He took another agonizing breath. "Isn't that where Jasmine banished her son?"

"It is," Angela said. Then she grew quiet and stared out into the void. After a moment, she turned back to him. "Do you think Lincoln could be the hacker?"

He shifted in his bed. *Fuck. It hurt.* Lincoln was high on his list. He knew the AI modules, and he knew how to deploy changes to the system without being discovered. Yeah, Cuz's son was wicked smart. He was a genius like his father. Unfortunately, he was like him in other ways, too. "Lincoln could do it."

"What about the other thing? Could he, you know, kill people?"

He coughed. "I don't want to think he could, but it's not out of the question. I'll tell you this, though: If Lincoln's the killer, you can bet Jasmine knows."

"Why do you say that? Lincoln hates his mother. I don't think they ever talk."

He forced another smile. "How much do you really know about Lincoln?"

Angela shrugged. "I've worked at Xperion for ten years. I've seen the way Marcus and Jasmine treat him."

He choked out a laugh. "That's not what I asked. What do you know about him?"

She shrugged. "Only the rumors. That he has issues."

"Issues." He laughed again. "Do you know what happened at MIT?"

Angela shook her head.

"He did things to his roommate. While he was sleeping."

"Things?"

"Let's just say it was disturbing. So much so, they had to send him away."

"What do you mean away?"

"Do I really have to spell it out for you? Lincoln's been in and out of several special hospitals. Jasmine keeps very close tabs on him." He coughed, and the pain was like what he imagined being kicked by a horse must feel like. "Very close."

"I had no idea it was that bad. Does she have someone watching him?

"Not someone," he took a few shallow breaths. "Some things."

Cuz had her son under constant electronic surveillance. He hadn't been involved in setting it up, but, through his mother, he had made suggestions how she could do it.

"His phone?" Angela asked.

"I'm sure, and every other connected device he uses."

"I see," she said. "I need to find Jasmine. I need to tell her before I tell the FBI."

"Fuck Jasmine, Angela. Contact this Parker Reid as soon as you exit. Tell him about Shea. If you don't, I will."

"What do I tell him if he learns about you?"

He looked up at the stars for a moment, then back down at her. "The truth." Then he stepped off the cliff's edge and his view turned red.

Chapter 38
Real Terror

AFTER THE CONSULTANT HAD leapt from the cliff, Angela had exited the Land and returned to her office. Parker Reid's business card was waiting where she had placed it on her desk. She snatched it up and took out her phone. The consultant was right; this was no longer about protecting the company's image or herself. She keyed in Parker's number and waited for the call to go through, practicing in her mind what she would say. She was poised to race through the script she'd settled on when she got his voice mail. She hung up and paced around her office. Then she hit redial and got his voice mail again. This time she left a message.

"Agent Reid. This is Angela Harding. I've discovered something that might help with your investigation. Please call me back."

As soon as the message left her lips, she felt better, like a great weight had been removed from her shoulders. She would soon no longer be an accessory after the fact. Though, at the same time, she knew telling the truth, as the consultant had urged her to do before he'd disappeared over the cliff's edge, would likely lead to the FBI learning about their other dealings. Did they put people in prison for corporate espionage? Angela mulled that over as she gathered up her bag and keys and headed out her office door.

She poked her head into several cubicles as she made her way through the aisles. All the monitors were dark and the chairs empty. It looked as though everyone had left, probably hours ago. Good. The team needed a break. Then she saw the lights on in the corner conference room that Rituraj had commandeered for the hacker hunt war room and sighed. She would have to order Rituraj and his team to take a break soon or they were going to hit burnout.

Angela felt a pang of guilt for not checking on them as she badged out and headed into the night. Outside, she dug into her bag and retrieved the can of pepper spray she'd purchased to ward off stalkers. Just a few short days ago, she would have felt silly walking to her car holding the spray, but that was before she'd been stalked by whispering homeless men and learned the hacker behind the Anomaly was killing people. Worse, she probably knew the hacker. It might even be Jasmine or Lincoln. *Please God, no*, she thought.

Before the Anomaly had turned things upside down, Angela almost always left the building to find the parking lot empty. Ordinarily, only the Days' sleek black sedan and her small white convertible would still be in the lot at this hour. But since the Anomaly, things had been anything but ordinary, and a half dozen cars belonging to Rituraj and his team had become permanent fixtures in the lot. She'd find them parked in the same spots when she arrived in the morning and when she left at night. Angela sighed again. *The team really was going to hit burnout.* She should know.

As odd as it still seemed to walk out and see the lot occupied, it was even stranger to see the Days' car missing. The co-founders had left uncharacteristically early today. No one was quite sure why because no one dared ask.

She was staring at the Days' empty space as she headed for her car, when the high beams on one of the new fixtures came on and blinded her. She stopped walking and shielded her eyes with the hand holding the pepper spray. She'd been startled by the light, but now she was annoyed that the driver either didn't notice her discomfort or didn't care enough to switch to their low beams.

She was about to march over to the car and ask the driver if they knew they were blinding their boss's boss, when the car lurched forward. She froze like the proverbial deer in the headlights as the car raced toward her. Just as she was certain the driver intended to mow her down, the car glided to a stop next to her. The driver's window slid down. A young male developer, whose name she did not recall beamed up at her. His white smile shown with all the intensity of his car's headlights.

"Hi, Angela. Sorry if I startled you. I guess I was just focused on getting home. Too many late nights. You know?"

She managed to smile, despite wanting to kill, or at least fire, the man. Her stupid heart monitor was buzzing again. "No worries," she said as she tried unsuccessfully to read the name on the employee badge hanging from the man's neck. "Please be careful driving home."

"Will do," he said and sped off.

After he'd gone, she stood in the dark for a moment before power-walking to her car. She dropped into the driver's seat and took five deep breaths to steady her nerves as her yoga instructor had taught her. She was still clutching the pepper spray. Feeling silly, she tossed it into the passenger seat and emitted a relieved and somewhat embarrassed laugh. Then she let the car drive itself the short distance to the small home she shared only with a three-year-old French bulldog named Louie.

She waited in the car for the garage door to close, keeping her eyes on her rearview mirror to ensure no hooded homeless men ducked in under it. Now that she was home safe, all Angela could think about, as she plugged the charger into the car, was who would take care of her dog if she went to prison.

It couldn't be her parents. They were too busy traveling the world or playing golf or both. Would the FBI really send her to prison? She had an MBA from Harvard, for God's sake. It was all benign white-collar stuff. Maybe if she did go to prison, she'd go to one of those low security places like where they sent actors and politicians. Who knows, after years of hundred-hour workweeks, a few months in a place like that might do her some good. Maybe they'd let her take her dog.

"Louie," she called as she stepped through the door and braced herself for the mad scamper and excited sniffling and pawing that would follow. It didn't come. Louie was not in the house. He must be in the backyard. She'd had a doggie door installed when the demands at work had made it difficult for her to make it home to walk him. Nothing worse than returning from a long exhausting day at the office to find a home full of dog shit. She opened the backdoor and called, "Louie! Louie!"

She peered into the dark corners of the backyard, looking for the dog. "Louie," she called again, but Louie did not come. He must have dug under the fence and escaped, or maybe someone had taken him. Angela had heard French Bulldogs were one of the most frequently stolen breeds. She was about to retrieve a flashlight to go search for him when she felt a presence behind her and froze.

"I'm afraid Louie will not be coming home tonight," a soft voice said.

Angela screamed and something struck her in the head, and everything went dark.

When she came to, it took her a moment to realize she was lying face down on her kitchen table. Her hands and feet were tightly bound, and tape had been wound around her head, covering her mouth. A piece of the tape covered one of her nostrils, making it difficult to breathe. Her heart pounded against the wooden tabletop. Thump-thump, thump-thump, thump-thump. The heart monitor on her watch must be redlined. She tried to twist her body but found she had been tied or taped to the table. Terrified, she rotated her head from side to side looking for her attacker.

"Behold the great Táma the Terrifying," the soft voice said.

"We must take her before she uses her magic," a deep voice boomed.

"She has no magic in this world," the soft voice said. "Only in yours."

The swish of a long metal blade drawn from a leather sheath came from close behind her. The sound was familiar. Angela had worked with the audio team for weeks to get it just right. She rocked her head back and forth trying to dislodge the tape from her mouth. Maybe she could reason with them.

"Stop moving," the soft voice said. Then the cold tip of a sword's blade touched the exposed base of her neck. Angela held her breath as the tip was dragged down her back with enough pressure to cut through her shirt and scratch her skin. *Undressing me. Rape? Oh my God, they're going to rape me.*

Hot, sour-smelling breath fanned the back of her neck, and the soft voice hissed, "So powerful and evil in the dream world and yet, so fragile in this one. Soon, you will kneel before me."

Her muscles locked with panic, and the same thought repeated in her head with every beat of her thumping heart. *They're going to kill me.*

"Not so terrifying now," the soft voice laughed. "No, in this world, Akandu and I are the real terror." The voice laughed again.

Angela thought she recognized the soft voice. Tears welled up in her eyes, and she knew there was no reasoning with its owner.

"Enough talking. Take her now or I will, mouse," the deep voice said.

The deep voice belonged to a stranger, though like the drawn sword's swish, it had a familiar, simulated quality about it. Like it belonged to a character in her land.

The sword's blade that had come to a rest at the base of her spine withdrew.

"Don't call me a mouse again," the soft voice said, this time not so softly.

She heard a loud clang as if the sword had been knocked to the ground, followed by the thump of a body being thrown against a wall. *They were fighting each other.*

The deep voice laughed and boomed, "You are far from ready to challenge me, little mouse."

"Take your hands off me," the soft voice yelled.

Their anger had made them loud. Maybe one of her neighbors would hear and the police would come. She worked at the tape with her teeth again. If she could just get it below her mouth, she could scream and maybe scare them away. She heard the blade slide across the kitchen floor as one of them picked it up.

"Take her, or I will," the booming voice said.

Rocking her head, she managed to get the tape below her mouth. She took a deep breath and shouted, "Please no, Marcus."

"N-N-not Marcus. I-I-I am Musuka," came the reply.

"Take her now."

Chapter 39
Missing Link

PARKER WAS WEDGED INTO the passenger seat of Jaden's roadster with his phone pressed against his ear.

"Still no answer?" Jaden asked.

Parker nodded as he twisted in the tiny seat, struggling to fit the phone back in his pocket. This was his fifth attempt at returning Angela Harding's call since he'd received her message last night. "Voice mail again. I don't get it. She leaves an urgent message saying she's discovered information important to the case and then doesn't answer her phone." He winced as he tried again to find a comfortable position for his leg. "I hate this car."

They had flown from San Francisco to Las Vegas last evening to join Higgs and Chavez at an 8:00 a.m. meeting with ZCS's head of operations. They'd arrived early and were parked in the aging office building's visitor lot, watching employees stream through the entrance and taking turns guessing which of the better-dressed ones they would be meeting with. Parker had his money on a tall, silver-haired White guy in a cream-colored suit. Jaden dismissed the guess and pointed out their appointment was with a man named Vincent Wan.

"That guy doesn't look like a Wan to me."

"That's because you're a racist," Parker said.

Jaden gave him the finger.

"Whoa, Breaux. That marks a significant change in our relationship."

After they debated a few other possible candidates, they lost interest in the game just as Higgs and Chavez pulled up next to them, looking comfortable in their roomy, department-issued vehicle.

"Why can't the field office issue you a car like that?" Parker said.

"Look at it. Besides being boring, it screams law enforcement. They might as well have flashing lights on the roof. This car lets us blend in."

They climbed out into the already oppressive Vegas heat and headed for the entrance. Higgs, his usual pleasant self, quipped, "Wasn't it nice, Chavy, for dese guys to come help us with our case? Make sure we ask da right questions?"

"Very nice," Chavez said.

"You're welcome," Parker said.

"I didn't mean it, Mind Hunter."

"Neither did I."

Inside, they were met by the tall, silver-haired man who introduced himself as Chuck Baker, head of public affairs. Parker wiggled his eyebrows at Jaden, and Jaden pretended to rub his nose with his middle finger. Chuck led them to a conference room where they were joined by a middle-aged Asian man dressed in a light polo shirt and golf pants. It looked like his next appointment would involve a set of clubs.

After the obligatory introductions, Parker jumped right into his questioning. "What does Lincoln Day do for your company?"

Wan, looking surprised, glanced at Chuck, and the silver-haired man cleared his throat. "I thought you were here to ask about Abby Loveridge?"

"Yes. I want to learn more about what Ms. Loveridge did for your company as well, but right now, I'm interested in Lincoln Day."

"*We* are interested in Lincoln Day," Higgs corrected.

Parker grinned. "Right. We."

Wan stood and fetched bottled water from a small refrigerator. He held the bottle out toward them. "Anyone else want one?"

No one accepted his offer. He removed the cap and took a long drink. When he was done, he turned back to Parker. "Lincoln Day is one of our top programmers."

"The best," Chuck said in an overly enthusiastic way. Parker searched his brain for the psychological term for the PR man's toady-like behavior and settled on ass-kisser.

"Will he be in the office today?" Parker asked.

"I don't know," Wan said as he returned to his seat. "He

doesn't really have a formal schedule."

"What does dat mean?" Higgs asked.

"He does special projects, and he often works from home. He," Wan seemed to struggle for the right words and settled on, "has a condition."

"He's sick?" Higgs asked.

"No, but he does have health issues that make it uncomfortable for him to come to the office."

"Uncomfortable how?" Higgs asked.

Before Wan could answer, Parker said, "I'd like to talk to him." He glanced at Higgs. "We'd like to talk to him. Can you find out if he will be in?"

Wan shook his head. "No real way to know. Like I said, he doesn't have a fixed schedule."

"Call him." Higgs said.

Wan squirmed. "We can try. He's not good about answering phones either."

Parker grinned. "Prima donnas can be so difficult." He shot a glance at Jaden. "Maybe we'll visit him at home. Could we get his address?"

"The house belongs to his parents," Wan said, and frowned.

"We still want the address," Higgs snapped.

Wan glanced at Chuck.

"I'll get it for you," Chuck said.

Parker picked up a worried vibe from the men. Sharing Jasmine Day's Vegas address and answering questions about her son before clearing it with her first was probably career suicide. Maybe a little investigating by the non-investigator was in order. "Can we see where Lincoln works when he's here?"

"You mean his desk?" Wan said.

"Yes."

Wan squirmed again. "What do you think, Chuck? Will that be okay?"

"We could come back with a warrant if dat would help," Higgs said. "Might not be as cordial dat way, though."

Chuck nodded. "Yes. Of course. I can take you to Lincoln's desk."

Wan stood and said he would see them on their way out, and Chuck led them up two floors to a room full of gray cubicles not unlike the ones in Parker's office. They followed him to a dark corner where four large cubicles sat beneath a bank of overhead light fixtures that had had their bulbs removed. Only one of the cubicles was occupied. A young Indian woman turned from her monitor and offered a friendly smile as Chuck led them to the cubicle next to hers.

"This is Lincoln's."

"It's so dark," Higgs said. "What's up with dat?"

"Lincoln's condition," Parker said.

Chuck nodded in confirmation.

"What does dat mean?"

"Doesn't like light," Parker said.

"What's he a friggin vampire?"

"No," Parker said, "albino."

The woman in the next cubicle poked her head over the wall. "Visitors?" she said to Chuck.

"Yes, Kavitha. We'll try not to bother you."

"No bother. Just curious. Lincoln hasn't been here for weeks, and he gets the visitors. No one visits me, and I'm here every day."

Chuck laughed a nervous laugh. "We'll be out of your hair soon."

Parker had the impression Chuck would have preferred if Kavitha remained silent and returned to work, but she didn't seem to be picking up on his cues. This kind of unscripted, random encounter was exactly what Parker had hoped for.

Lincoln's workspace resembled those Parker had seen at Xperion. Dry erase boards covered in precisely drawn block and arrow diagrams hung on the walls, and three large, curved monitors formed a semicircle around Lincoln's empty chair, giving the small space the feel of an aircraft cockpit. Parker used his cane to lower himself into the seat. He looked up and smiled at Kavitha who was still hanging over the short wall that divided her workspace from Lincoln's.

"This is comfortable," Parker said.

"His chair is the best. The rest of us don't get $3,000 chairs."

"Come on, Kavitha," Chuck said. "You know Lincoln bought his own chair."

"Right. The rest of us aren't rich enough to buy $3,000 chairs."

"Do you and Lincoln work together?" Parker asked.

She wobbled her head in a yes-no fashion. "Sometimes. But not recently. He's been working on some special project. I think that's why his mother was here yesterday."

"Jasmine Day was here yesterday?" Chuck said, apparently as surprised by the revelation as Parker was.

"Yes. Last evening. I think I was the only one up here when she came in. Startled me. She didn't stay long. She just strolled up like she'd expected to see Lincoln here and stormed off when he wasn't. I don't know why she was surprised. He's never here."

Chuck's mouth twitched and Parker could almost feel him willing Kavitha to sit back down and return to her work.

Parker did the travel time math. The Xperion cofounder must have taken a flight right after their meeting yesterday. He wondered if the trip had been planned before Jasmine had learned of Abby's murder. "Does she come here often?"

"Occasionally," Chuck answered. "It's her father's company. It will be hers one day." He stared at the woman hanging over the wall, his expression saying go away, and asked, "Do you have any more questions for Kavitha?"

"I do," Parker said. "Kavitha, did you know Abby Loveridge?"

Kavitha's gaze dropped. "Poor Abby. It's awful what happened to her. She was part of our team."

Parker made a circular motion with his hand to indicate the four cubicles. "This team?"

"Yes, but," Kavitha mimicked Parker's hand motion, "not here. She was based in Florida."

"Did Lincoln work with her?"

Kavitha wobbled her head again. "Some." She dipped below the cube wall for a moment, then returned holding what looked like a deadbolt locking mechanism for a door. She handed it to Parker. "They worked together on the controls for these." She tapped on her keyboard and the locking mechanism in Parker's hand engaged. *Magic.*

Higgs said, "Let me see dat."

Parker handed it to him, and they exchanged knowing glances.

"Who do you market these to?" Jaden asked Chuck.

"We install these as part of our site security package. Mostly to customers who need to control a large number of entryways."

"Hotels?" Higgs and Chavez said at the same time.

"Sure. Several right here in Vegas, but our customers are everywhere."

"Apartment complexes?" Jaden asked.

"Yes, sir. We're the biggest in that market."

"What do the site security packages control?" Jaden asked.

Chuck spread his hands. "That depends. Our suite is highly customizable. We sell modules for all aspects of security and building automation."

"Cameras?"

"Oh, sure."

Jaden inched closer to Kavitha. "Your systems must be very secure to prevent unauthorized access," he said in a conspiratorial tone, one techie to another.

"Very secure. We've never had a breach," Chuck answered.

Kavitha wobbled her head.

Parker picked up on her non-committal response. He stared at her. "Very secure?"

"Can't be hacked?" Jaden added.

"Be very hard," she said.

"But not impossible?"

She again wobbled her head.

"Could you hack it?" Jaden asked.

Kavitha smiled. "I would never do such a thing."

"But could you?"

"No. She couldn't," Chuck stressed, giving Kavitha another sit-down-and-shut-up stare.

Kavitha shrugged him off. "I could think of some ways it might be done."

"Kavitha," Chuck pleaded. "Careful in your speculation."

"And that's all it is," she said, "speculation."

"Okay," Jaden said. "How would you do it?"

"You'd have to be one of us." She made the circling gesture with her hands to indicate the team. "'Have access to the code. Then you could put in a backdoor.'"

"What's a backdoor?" Higgs asked.

"A secret way to get into the system that gets around the security," Jaden answered.

Kavitha wobbled her head some more.

"There are no backdoors," Chuck snapped.

"We're just speculating," Kavitha confirmed, then glanced at Parker in a way that suggested this 'backdoor' might already exist.

Parker levered himself out of the chair with his cane. As he did, his eyes landed on a shelf hidden behind the half-ring of monitors. Placed on it looked to be twenty or more fantasy figures like the ones he saw at Xperion. Someone, he guessed Lincoln, had taken great care to arrange them in what appeared to be deliberate poses with characters poised to strike each other with a variety of weapons. He spotted a gap in the formation where one appeared to be missing.

"What is it with these toys and programmers? I saw some of the same figures on the desks at Xperion."

He reached for one, and Kavitha stopped him. "Please don't touch those. It took me forever to get them right."

Parker pulled his hand back and looked at her. "I thought they were Lincoln's."

"Yes, and he is crazy about them. He can tell instantly if anyone has tampered with them. One time, last year, a cleaning person knocked some of them over, and he went berserk. He was literally in tears. It took him all morning to get them back where he had them."

"Does he obsess about other things?" Parker asked.

"Not really," she said, and after a moment added, "besides his work. Especially his code. No one can touch his code."

"Anything else?" Parker asked, intrigued.

"His food. No one can touch his food; not even the containers. That's it, though." Then she looked down at Parker and sighed. "His chair. He's going to be upset if he learns you sat in his chair. It will take him an hour to get comfortable in it again."

"I'd put dat down as he obsesses about everything, Mind Hunter," Higgs snickered.

"Hmm," Parker turned back to the figures. "It looks like one is missing. Does he know?"

"No, and he is going to freak. I found them all knocked over this morning, and when I put them back in place, the big gray one was missing."

"If they were all knocked over, how did you know where to place them?" Jayden asked.

Kavitha looked at him and shrugged. "I see them every day, but after what happened with the cleaning person, I took pictures so I could arrange them exactly to avoid another meltdown."

"Really?" Parker said. "Can I see your pictures?"

She picked up a tablet and poked at its screen for a moment. Then she handed it to him.

Parker held it up to the characters for comparison. "Looks like you did a great job." As soon as he saw the missing figure, he knew he'd seen it before. "I saw a toy like the big gray one at Xperion. It had a label on it calling it the Fucking Anomaly."

Kavitha giggled as if the profanity tickled her. "That's not its name."

"They have names?" Parker said.

"Oh yes."

"What's the gray one's name?"

"Akandu," she said. "He's paired with that little one there." She pointed at a small, furry figure that appeared in the picture to be groveling at Akandu's feet. "That one is Musuka. Those are Sanskrit words. Akandu means destroyer and Musuka means mouse.

Parker felt as though he had just picked up an important piece to the jigsaw puzzle he was assembling in his head, but he wasn't quite sure where it fit. He handed Kavitha her tablet. "Can I get a copy of those pictures?"

"Email okay?"

He dug out a business card from his credential case and handed it to her.

"I'll send them right now," she said.

They left Kavitha. Parker thought it was much to Chuck's relief, and they returned to the conference room. Wan met them there, and Parker asked about Jasmine Day's visit the day before. Like Chuck, Wan denied any knowledge of it.

"She comes and goes as she pleases," Wan said, checking his watch. Probably late for a tee-time.

"We met with her at noon yesterday in Palo Alto," Parker said. "She must've already had the trip planned to be here at the time Kavitha said she'd seen her."

Wan shook his head. "Not necessarily. The Days have their own jet and crew. Two, maybe two and a half hours door-to-door from Xperion to here."

They spoke for another fifteen minutes. Parker probed them about Abby's employment history and her relationships with other employees, including Lincoln. Abby was an excellent employee and neither man could comment on Abby's relationships. They confirmed what her mother had told Parker, Abby had only been to the Vegas office once for new employee orientation, and all her subsequent dealings with her team and her managers had been through web conferences and phone calls.

On the way out, Parker reminded Chuck they needed Lincoln's home address, and they all stood around in the lobby while he disappeared to retrieve it.

"I want a copy of dat too," Higgs called to Chuck as he left. Then after he'd gone, he turned to Parker. "Dis was very fricken enlightening."

Parker grinned. "You're welcome."

"Yeah. Thank you. Dis time I mean it."

"What do you say? Next stop Lincoln Day's residence?"

"Abso-fricken-lutely."

Chapter 40
The Trainee

THE VAN SMELLED OF coffee and cardboard. The coffee smell came from Tony's monster-sized mug sitting in the cup holder between their seats. The cardboard scent was from the dozens of cartons containing OmniRig components she and Tony had just finished loading. They'd left the warehouse and were about to head to their first appointment when Tony had received the call summoning him back to the office.

Shea checked the time on the van's dashboard display. Tony had been gone for ten minutes. His coffee would be cold when he returned. She assumed changes were being made to their route, which meant they would be unloading some of the heavy cartons and replacing them with new ones. That, and the cold coffee, were bound to send her boss into a long rant when they finally got on the road.

After fifteen minutes, she was about to go inside and see what was going on when Tony and a young man she did not recognize emerged from the office and headed toward the van. The stranger was small and looked like a boy next to her large boss, but lots of people looked small next to Tony. The stranger was ghostly pale and had jet-black hair. Dark sunglasses covered his eyes. Tony was saying something to him as they approached, probably complaining about the delayed start. The stranger trailed two steps behind him with his head down.

Tony led the stranger around to her side of the van and pulled open the sliding door. "Hey, kid," he called. "Meet Ethan. He's a new trainee. He's going to ride with us for a few days."

Shea turned around in her seat and poked her head out the door. "I'm Shea. Welcome aboard." She stuck her hand out, and he stared at it for a long moment as if he wasn't sure what to do before finally shaking it. His hand was smaller than hers and so white. Around his wrist was an expensive smartwatch.

"Nice watch," she said.

He withdrew his hand and covered the watch with his other hand as if ashamed she'd noticed it. "Th-th-thank you," he said. "P-P-Present from m-m-my parents."

Gosh. The poor guy looked and sounded terrified.

Tony climbed into the back, rolled his eyes at her, and flipped down the jump seat that was mounted on the driver's side wall. Then he backed out and pointed the nervous looking trainee toward it. "Up in there, young man. You get to ride in the bitch seat." Tony called the jump seat the bitch seat because it was where InVerse management sat when they rode along and bitched about every little procedural infraction they noticed.

Shea watched as the trainee climbed in. He caught her looking at him and gave her a shy smile as he fastened his seat belt. Tony took his place behind the wheel and tasted his coffee. Shea braced for the outburst, but Tony, perhaps not wanting to startle the nervous trainee on his first day, just made a face and steered the van out of the lot and into Atlanta's morning traffic.

She twisted in her seat. Ethan had removed his sunglasses. His eyes were a light gray, almost colorless, and they were almond shaped suggesting he was Asian. They conflicted with his snow-white complexion. She smiled. "You are the whitest Asian guy I've ever seen."

Tony snorted and spat a mouthful of coffee all over the dash. "Jeezus kid, you almost made me drown myself."

"Look at him," Shea said. "I'm half-Indian and half-White, and I don't have pale skin like that. I hope you're wearing sunscreen."

Ethan frowned for an instant then laughed. "Y-Y-Yeah. This is what happens when you cross an albino with a chink."

"A chink?" she said. "Now that's highly inappropriate."

He looked down at the floorboard, but not before giving her another shy smile. He was cute in an impish way.

They had three rig installations on the schedule. A big day. It turned out Ethan knew his way around the tech. After getting over his initial nervousness, he performed installation tasks that had taken Shea weeks to learn.

"You've done this before," Tony observed after their first stop.

"I-I w-w-worked at a MetaSpot for a few years. W-W-We did a lot of our own repairs."

Shea was impressed by his skill and had to admit she found his unusual appearance, little stutter, and shy demeanor interesting. He reminded her of an elf from the Land.

"You play that Mighty Magic game?" Tony said.

"Might and Magic," Shea corrected him.

"L-L-Live in it," he said. "I mean, when I can afford the rig time."

Tony punched Shea on the shoulder. "He's one of you." Then he glanced back at Ethan. "Bet you didn't know it, but you're riding with the mightiest, most magical girl in the Land."

"Shut up, boss," she said, feeling her face flush.

"He could be your soulmate," he glanced back at Ethan again. "Shea's got her own rig. You two should hook up."

"Boss!" Shea yelled. "Stop." She looked back at Ethan. The shy trainee avoided her eyes, and his white face seemed to have gone a little pink.

Staring at the floorboard, he said "Y-Y-You g-g-got your own rig?"

She nodded. "I do. It's the only way to go."

"Th-Th-That must be great."

"Maybe she'll show it to you sometime," Tony prodded.

"Boss. My God," she growled through gritted teeth.

With Ethan's help, they breezed through the installations, and despite Tony's attempts to fill the extra time by reorganizing the van between stops and even making two unscheduled visits at MetaSpots to do what he called customer relationship building, something Shea had never seen him do before, they still returned to the shop over an hour early.

Tony was on salary and got paid the same whether they worked their full shift or not, but Shea and Ethan were paid by the hour. "Sorry, kids," he told them. "I tried to fill the day so you wouldn't be short."

Shea didn't mind. They always had too much work. She'd make it up with overtime later in the week. After they finished unloading the van, Tony said he'd see them in the morning and headed into the office, leaving her and Ethan alone for the first time.

"It was good working with you today, Ethan. You really

know your stuff."

Ethan gave her that cute impish smile. "M-m-maybe we could meet in the Land sometime."

"I'd like that. What level is your character?"

He kicked at the concrete with his shoe. "Not too high. In the th-th-thirties."

"That's not bad. Sounds like you can hold your own in the wild."

"H-H-How about yours?" he asked.

"Fifty-nine," she said trying not to sound too boastful but couldn't help herself and added, "as high as you can go."

His head snapped up, and he leveled his dark glasses on her. "No way."

"Yes. I've been playing since the game launched."

"Y-Y-You must like your character," he said.

"I love her," Shea beamed. "She's a big part of me."

He frowned. "I don't like mine." Then he brightened. "B-B-But I'm working on a new one."

"On a new character?"

"Yes. One with the right attributes to be successful."

She gave him a mischievous grin. "The right attributes are very important."

He followed her to her bike like a lost puppy.

"I-I-I would never be able to r-r-ride one of these," he said.

"Nothing to it," she said as she strapped on her helmet.

"I-I-I'd be too afraid."

"Get yourself a helmet, and I'll give you a ride. Maybe you'll get over that fear." She winked at him and started the engine. "See you tomorrow," she said over the rumble and twisted the throttle. The bike roared and darted toward the lot's exit. In her rearview mirror she saw dark glasses following her. She couldn't be sure, but as she watched his reflection shrink, it seemed as if his shy smile had turned into a confident grin.

Chapter 41
I Can Do

LINCOLN DAY'S ADDRESS LED Parker and Jaden to a gated community north and west of the Las Vegas strip. Higgs had called ahead and an LVMPD patrol unit met them at the gate and escorted them past the sleepy-eyed security guard. Parker had Googled and learned nothing in the neighborhood sold for under two million. Despite the obscene property values, he did not find the architecture or the scenery appealing. All the homes looked the same to him, sprawling tan and brown stucco Spanish-style ranches with red solar tiled roofs. None of them had lawns or anything green growing in their yards, even the ultra-rich were bound by the area's water restrictions. Instead, the homes were all surrounded by crushed stone, cactus, and sickly date palms. The color schemes and landscaping appeared purposefully crafted to blend in with the sun-blasted Mojave that stretched for miles in every direction.

"Welcome to where the rich and famous live," Jaden announced.

"Everything is brown and dead. Makes me want to run home to Virginia," Parker said.

"It is an acquired taste."

The Day's house was perched on a hill in a cul-de-sac overlooking Red Rock Canyon. Even Parker had to admit the view was spectacular. A shirtless elderly man with a wide-brimmed hat and khaki shorts stood by a mailbox smoking a cigar. His watchful dark eyes crowned by bushy white brows tracked them as they passed. The patrol car parked in the street near him. The two uniformed officers showed no signs of leaving their air-conditioned ride. Higgs and Chavez pulled into the empty driveway and Jaden slid the roadster alongside.

"What do you think?" Jaden said. "Is he here?"

"No," Parker said. He wiggled his eyebrows. "Who knows,

though? Maybe Jasmine's in there."

"You think?"

"No."

Higgs and Chavez climbed out of their car and stared at them from behind dark sunglasses.

Taking his cue from the uniforms, Parker said, "I'm staying here."

Jaden looked at him. "You hate the car."

"I like the air conditioning. Besides, as Higgs said, it's their case."

Jaden opened his mouth but climbed out without speaking. All the cool air in the little car exited with him, much to Parker's dismay. Higgs said something that made Jaden laugh and the three of them went to the front door, where Higgs and Chavez took turns pressing the bell. After a minute or so, Chavez moved between the windows reachable from the porch and cupped his hands on the glass as if he was trying to see in. Parker could tell from where he sat the windows were covered by shades. Jaden glanced back at him and shook his head.

Parker lowered his window as the three of them returned to the cars. "You got a judge that will approve a warrant, Higgs?"

Higgs shrugged. "We don't got much in the probable cause department."

"The Day kid murdered Abby Loveridge to hide his backdoor," Jaden said.

"You don't think I know dat," Higgs snapped. "We'll talk to da boss lady and see what she says. You feebs have the juice. Magistrate's office is fifteen minutes away, why don't you pay dem a visit?"

"We're just consultants on this, Higgs," Parker said. "But we'll see what we can do."

"Consultants, what da fuck does that mean?"

Parker slid his sunglasses down his nose and looked over the frames so Higgs could see his eyes. "We are from the government and we're here to help."

"Fuck you."

"Work on Divine, Higgs, and I'll work my side."

"Yeah, yeah," Higgs groused and waved at the patrol unit. A moment later, the interceptor flashed its lights and crept out of the cul-de-sac.

Jaden dropped into his seat. "What now?"

"Let's go talk to the old guy across the street."

They backed out of the driveway and stopped in front of the man as Chavez and Higgs disappeared down the hill.

"Kind of hot to be standing out here in the sun," Parker said.

The old man blew a puff of smoke into the open window. "Old lady won't let me smoke in the house. You guys cops?"

"FBI," Parker said.

"Democrats," the old man said flatly—a statement, not a question.

Parker nodded. "I am." He hooked his thumb toward Jaden. "But he's a right-winger."

The old man glanced at Jaden. "You're fucking with me."

Parker grinned. "A little. We are from the FBI, though." He retrieved his credential case and presented it to the man. "We need to talk to your neighbor. Have you seen him around?"

The old man blew another puff of smoke. "Nah. There's been no one up there for weeks. Weird guy though."

"How's that?"

"Whitest person you ever seen."

"Our kind of people," Jaden said.

The old man's face flattened like a plate, then he smiled. "That's good," he said. "Got Chinese eyes, though. Weird."

"Huh," Parker grunted. "Anything else weird about him? You ever seen him with a long knife or a sword?"

The old man coughed, smoke bursting from his nose like a dragon. "Sword? Not that I ever saw. Wait. Does this have something to do with the beheading that was all over the news last week?"

Parker didn't respond.

"Ah, you're barking up the wrong tree. The guy's weird, but he's harmless. Small." He held his hand level with his chin. "He can't be much more than this tall and no more than a hundred and forty pounds soaking wet. I thought he was a child when I first saw him."

"You ever talk to him?" Parker asked.

"Some. He comes down and gets his mail. Always after dark. Like I said, weird. But I'm always out here." He looked back at his house. "She won't let me smoke in the house I bought."

"What's he like?"

"Soft talker. Might be gay."

"Those gays are all soft," Jaden said.

The man frowned. "Now, I didn't say that. All I meant was he talks really soft, and he never has women over there. A young guy, rich enough to own a house in this neighborhood. You'd think he'd have a harem."

"Does he have male visitors?" Jaden asked.

The man shrugged. "Workmen mostly. Can't say that I've seen him have any guests." He blew some more smoke and grinned. "A young Latin pool guy is over there every week." Then he cast a thoughtful look across the cul-de-sac at the Day's house. "Now that I think about it, there was this one guy. He was only over there once that I know of. I never actually saw him, but I remember him because I heard them fighting one evening, and I did think maybe it was, you know, a lover's quarrel."

"Fighting?" Parker said.

"Not physically, I don't think. Like I said, I doubt Day could fight his way out of a wet paper bag. They were shouting at each other. It got heated. They must've been out back by the pool because I could hear them clear as I can hear you."

"When was this?"

"Let me think. I was sitting right over there watching the sunset." He pointed to a pair of pink Adirondack chairs beneath some palm trees. "I was drinking a beer." He looked back up his driveway again. "Old woman only lets me have those on Saturdays. Guess it would've had to have been three weeks ago. That was probably the last time he was home."

"Since you could hear them so clearly," Parker said, giving the man sheepish eyes, "do you remember what they were arguing about?"

"I wasn't listening *that* close," the man said, sounding put off by Parker's implication. "But I remember there seemed to be some foreign words. Probably Chinese, given those eyes of his. Even when he yelled, Day's voice was soft, but the other guy's voice was loud and deep. I remember thinking he must be huge, and I was worried Day might've bitten off more than he could chew. Thought I might have to call the police."

"But you didn't?"

"No. Things settled down."

"And you don't remember anything they were saying? Maybe a name of the big guy?"

The man stared at the Day's driveway for a moment and shrugged. "Like I said, I think he was speaking in Chinese. It sounded like he was shouting something like, 'I can do', over and over."

"I can do?" Parker repeated for confirmation.

The man nodded.

Parker glanced at Jaden and the young agent gave him the raised eyebrow. "Could it have been Akandu?"

"Maybe," the man said. He puffed on his cigar. "Yeah. I think that's right. Day was yelling Ay Kan Doo over and over. Is that Chinese?"

Parker ignored the question. "Then what happened?"

"Nothing. Like I said, they settled down. Frankly, I thought the big guy killed him, but then I saw Day drive off in his sports car."

"With the big guy?"

The man's eyes tilted skyward as if he was trying to recall an image. "I don't remember seeing him. I assume so, though."

Parker fished a card out of his credential case and held it out the window. "You've been a great help, sir. If you see your neighbor, do you mind giving me a call at this number?"

The man tentatively took the card like he was afraid it might bite him. "Ah. I guess. Don't much like your politics, though."

"Get over it," Parker said as he raised the window.

They left the man puffing on his cigar and headed back toward the city. After they passed through the security gate, Jaden pulled the roadster over.

"Where to?" he asked.

Parker stared out the window at the Vegas skyline shimmering like a mirage in the distance. He had been thinking about their next move all morning. "I want to go back to Xperion and shake up the Days. Get them to tell us how to find their son."

"Assuming he's still alive," Jaden said. He turned in his seat and looked back into the neighborhood. "Maybe the big guy killed him and left him in the house up there."

Parker shrugged. "The thought crossed my mind."

"Should we get a warrant and go back?"

"Call Chavez. Tell him what we learned. That should be enough for them to go inside."

"What about us?"

"We're going back to San Francisco."

Jaden grimaced. "Long ride."

"I'll call Becky and get travel arrangements made. We're going tonight. I want to be sitting with the Days first thing in the morning. We'll personally shove the subpoena up their lawyer's ass."

Chapter 42
A Dwarf's Warning

THE MICROWAVE BEEPED LETTING Shea know the package, dubiously labeled "Healthy Meal," that she'd chiseled from her freezer's permafrost was ready. No telling how long it had been trapped in the ice. She'd intentionally avoided looking at the expiration date. She burned her fingers pouring the molten mix of vegetables and pasta into a bowl. The colors looked a little washed out, but it smelled okay.

Trinity followed her to her desk, sniffed the steaming bowl, and darted into the bay. Not a good sign, Shea thought as she tried a tentative forkful. It tasted like chicken. She wolfed it down, without regard to whether or not it actually was chicken. She'd spent the evening sweating away calories in her cybersuit as she ran what were known as the loops, a series of interconnected trails and roads that circled the most visited gates, and now hunger overruled caution.

She had gone into the Land to hunt, or more accurately bait, the Gray Warrior, but Falin's mirror never vibrated. The monster was a no-show, and the only action she'd seen was from the occasional roaming band of simulated characters whose programming didn't know better than to attack the game's last legend-level ranger. She hadn't realized until tonight's solo trek how much she had enjoyed trekking with Falin. As disastrous as those journeys had almost been, it had been nice to have someone to share the adventures with. Maybe tomorrow she'd invite the cute new trainee to join her, assuming he could get the rig time.

As she ate, she brought up her email and selected Darshana's inbox. She scanned the requests for guide gigs. Shea could use the money. Her job at InVerse covered her rent, the bike, food, as long as it came in a frozen box, and little else. Without the guide income, Versing would drain her bank account in no time, and she'd join the panhandlers around the EV charging stations before she'd ask her parents for money. She sighed as she turned each request down. Taking a guide job while the Gray Warrior was still in the Land was out of the question. Her reputation wouldn't sustain another abandoned or annihilated party.

She moved on to her personal mail. Her mother's weekly request for a med school admissions status had shown up on schedule. She skimmed it to make sure it contained no mention of any looming family crisis or tragedy. Her grandparents in India had both been sick recently, and there was some talk of Shea joining her parents on a trip to Mumbai to check on them. Though she enjoyed those trips, the food, the culture, and most of all, seeing her extended family, she didn't relish the air travel, even if it would be first class. Tony's head would explode if he learned what her parents shelled out for those tickets.

She skipped over a message from the former classmate who seemed to be in league with her mother on the med school campaign and scrolled down to one from Falin. When she read the subject line, her heart ached as though someone had reached into her chest and squeezed it. *Final goodbye and urgent warning.*

She clicked on the heading and read.

Dear Shea, this will be my last message. Don't be sad. I am ready to go. I do regret we never met in the real. I know if we had, you would have fallen madly in love with me. How could you not? I'm pretty hot for a dwarf. She rubbed her eyes and laughed, then read on. *Now, you need to take the rest of this seriously. The hacker behind the Gray Warrior is murdering people in the real. You are in danger. Below are links to two news stories about the murders. You knew the victims as Danaka and Pharoah.* She gasped. *Don't hunt him, Shea.*

Be safe and farewell, Falin the Dwarf, also known as Mad Hat, Bobby Penn, a dozen other aliases, but always, Mùyáng "Mikey" Jackson (from South Boston.)

She smiled through the tears. Not being familiar with the Chinese name, she didn't know if Mùyáng fit Falin's personality, but she could picture him as a Mikey.

The sadness of the message had temporarily overshadowed the shock of Danaka and Pharaoh's deaths and the surreal nature of Falin's warning. But now, the horror and fear were cutting through the grief. Danaka and Pharaoh were murdered, and she was in danger. The first news article was from a Nashville TV station and described the grisly beheading of a young woman named Jyothi Reddi. Shea assumed Jyothi had been the ranger she'd known as Danaka. The second link led to a similar article published by a Las Vegas station detailing the beheading of a fifty-six-year-old man named Charles Tate who she assumed was Pharaoh. Both articles said the killer had used a sword. The Vegas station's article had led her to other stories. One claimed the killer had taken body parts but did not elaborate.

Shea shivered as her mind drifted back to her first encounter with the Gray Warrior. She'd watched him cut Darian's head off with a sword and take Ava's ears. Since then, she'd seen several of his kills. Always the same. Heads and ears removed. *Body parts.* The Vegas articles creeped her out. She was about to see if she could find any mention of missing ears on the internet when the hairs on her neck stood up like she was caught in some electrical field. The source of the sensation wasn't electricity, though, it was the feeling she was being watched. She spun around in her chair to find Trinity's yellow eyes staring down at her from the ventilation duct high up near the ceiling. The cat's tail swished back and forth. She looked like a panther in a tree preparing to pounce.

"Damn. You gave me the heebie-jeebies, Trin," Shea said as she walked under the cat's perch. "How did you get way up there?"

Trinity meowed then padded along the duct into the darkness, her paws making a soft tin, tin sound as she went. Shea was about to return to the desk when another sound caught her attention. Tap, tap, tap. Something was tapping on the small, four-paned window in the people door next to the bay. It had to be close to midnight. Who could be tapping at her door? She retrieved her phone in case she had to call 9-1-1 and made her way toward the sound.

Tap, tap, tap. "Who the fuck is there?" she whispered as she approached the door. Just as she reached the window, a large insect slammed against the glass. Tap. Then another one. Tap. She let out a long sigh that turned into a nervous giggle. Then she noticed she'd failed to lock the deadbolt. She locked it and looked at the outline of her rig illuminated only by its power and status LEDs. The thought of Danaka and Pharaoh's murders made her consider how vulnerable she was living alone on this empty stretch of road halfway between Atlanta and the Alabama line. She would never hear anyone come through the door while she was in the rig. She checked the lock again and looked out the window. Nothing but suicidal insects, tap, tap, and a dark road.

Chapter 43
Tip

PARKER AND JADEN HAD made it to their hotel in Palo Alto in time for a late dinner at a Mexican restaurant that, after much explanation in Spanish by Jaden, agreed to accommodate Parker's culinary restrictions. No spice, no sauce, no cheese, just plain white rice and a chicken breast. As uninteresting as the dish had been, its passage through the remnants of Parker's intestines kept him up all night. He was showered, dressed, and pacing his hotel room when Becky called at 6:30 a.m.

He answered with, "Did you do anything about the eyes, or do you still look like a raccoon?"

"Fuck you, Parker. I was going to apologize for waking you, but now I'm not sorry."

"Well, you didn't wake me. I've been up for hours, so there. Why are you calling this early? You have another headless body?"

"No, thank God. The Xperion subpoena should be in your inbox by noon my time."

Parker did the time zone math. "That should work. I want to present it to their lawyer first thing. Is that why you called?"

"No. An online tip form came in early this morning, and it specifically mentions you."

"So what?" Parker scoffed. "I get about a dozen a month. Fame is an awful cross to bear."

She sighed heavily. "A person identifying themself only as Shea, I assume that's a woman's name but not sure, claims she has information about the victims she needs to share with a Dr. Reid. That would be you. She provided an email address. I'm sending it now."

Parker's phone vibrated. He looked at the address. "Probably a crank. You know that, right?"

"Yeah, but you should still follow up."

"Sounds like something my flunky should do."

"If you mean me, I'm not doing it."

"I was thinking Breaux, but you can be my flunky too."

"Fuck you again, and Jaden isn't your flunky."

"Anything else?" he said.

"Yeah, that thing you asked me to have the research team look into."

"The security systems used at the scenes."

"Yeah," she said. "All the same."

Parker smiled. He could almost see the puzzle pieces completing the Khafre pyramid.

"And Parker?"

"Yeah?"

"Remember these Xperion people are rich and well connected. Don't be too heavy-handed."

"I'll take that under advisement," he said and ended the call.

He stared at the tipster's email address for a few moments. Chances were high this Shea was either a wannabe detective with some useless theory or a sicko looking to share in the killer's mayhem. He loathed to encourage her. Once she had his email address, he'd never get rid of her. He had a special folder filled with hundreds of messages from others like her he'd indulged in the past. No doubt he'd be adding her messages to it.

He eased down on the sofa next to the bed and typed into his phone's email app. *Received your message. What do you know?* That done, he turned the TV on and tuned it to a cable news channel. He spent twenty minutes watching impeccably groomed anchors spout the usual apocalyptic news stories, then stretched out and dozed.

Loud pounding on the room door woke him. "I'm coming, I'm coming. For God's sake, don't break it down." He threw open the door as Jaden was about to deliver another volley.

"You're dressed," Jaden said.

"Disappointed?"

"No."

They went down to the hotel's restaurant, where Parker drank tea and watched Jaden eat something called a vegan scramble. It smelled awful.

"What's in that?"

"Seasoned vegetables, fried tofu, and non-meat chorizo."

Parker put his finger in his mouth and made a gagging sound. He took out his phone and checked his email. The tipster had replied. He cringed as he opened the message and promptly almost spit out his tea when he read: *I think Jyothi and Charles were killed because they played a Verse simulation game called the Land of Might and Magic. This is going to sound weird, but were their ears missing?*

"Holy shit," he said.

Jaden looked up from his fake sausage. "Everything okay?"

Parker ignored him and typed, *Can we talk?* He hit send and placed his phone on the table. Jaden was still staring at him. "I think we got something."

"Was the subpoena signed?"

"I don't think we're going to need it," he said as his phone buzzed.

The tipster replied: *At work. Can't talk. DM me.*

Parker clicked on the message connection and typed. *How do you know about the game?*

She responded instantly. *There's a player in LMM who is killing the advanced characters. He cuts their heads off with a sword. Sound familiar? He takes their ears. Jyothi and Charles were trying to stop him.*

Parker's hands were shaking from the adrenaline rush, and it took him three tries to type, *How are you involved?*

I am working with a woman from the company that owns the game to find and stop the player. I don't think she knows he's really killing people.

"Fuck," Parker murmured.

"Come on. Tell me what's going on," Jaden said.

Parker typed, *Who in Xperion are you working with?*

Angela Harding.

He furiously thumbed his reply, *I've been trying to get in touch with her. She doesn't return my messages.*

Mine neither.

Parker looked up at Jaden. "Those fuckers at Xperion have been lying to us." He showed his confused partner the message thread.

"Holy shit. Who is that?"

"I'll explain on the way," he said as he typed. *It's important we talk. Where are you?*

Atlanta. I'll be home by seven. Message me then.

Parker checked the time. Eight-thirty, eleven-thirty in Atlanta. He typed, *Can't you talk at lunch?*

No fixed lunch time and no privacy. Seven works best.

Okay, he replied, then he thought about Lincoln's missing action figure and typed. *One more thing. Is the character you're trying to stop named Akandu?*

Never heard that name. I only know him as the Gray Warrior. Three dots indicated she was typing something else. *Angela called him the Anomaly.*

"The Fucking Anomaly," Parker said as he used his cane to push himself out of his seat.

Chapter 44
Figures of Interest

THE SECURITY GUARD WITH the military hair and pancake-house build glanced indifferently at Parker's credentials. He was the same officious man who had tried to make Jaden and him leave their firearms in the car during their last visit.

"I'm sorry, but Ms. Harding is not in today," the guard said.

"Then we would like to speak to Mr. and Mrs. Day,"

"No one sees the Days without an appointment."

Parker leaned on his cane and glared. "Call them and tell them federal agents, with guns, are demanding to see them."

The guard scowled and typed on a keyboard. He nodded toward the waiting area. "Someone will be with you shortly."

Twenty long minutes later, Anand Patel emerged from the elevator. He steamed toward them with his eyebrows pinched in anger. "Did you really threaten to shoot your way past security?"

"Don't be silly," Parker said. He looked over at the guard then nodded toward Jaden. "We wouldn't need to use our guns."

"Your behavior is very unprofessional. You can't just show up here demanding to see the Days."

"Actually," Parker said, "we can. They are persons of interest in the murders of Jyothi Reddy, Abby Loveridge, and Charles Tate."

"That's absurd," the lawyer scoffed. He thrust an accusatory finger at Parker. "Are you two behind the search of the Day's Las Vegas residence this morning?"

Higgs and Chavez must've gotten the warrant. *Good for them*, Parker thought, and wondered if they'd found Lincoln Day's rotting corpse inside. He glanced at Jaden. "You know anything about a search?"

Jaden shook his head. He almost convinced Parker.

"Bullshit," Anand erupted. "I've already been in touch with both our senators' offices. I hope you enjoy your retirement."

Parker hobbled to within a foot of the lawyer, who was several inches shorter than him, and grinned his nastiest grin. "I'd wish you the same, counselor, but a federal supermax will make an awful retirement home."

Anand glowered up at him. "Idle threats are beneath a man with your reputation."

"I know about the player Angela calls the Anomaly," Parker said. "I know she has been working with a woman in Atlanta to find him, and I know she believes he's the killer. I have reason to suspect Angela isn't the only Xperion employee who knows, and I'm ready to charge you, Angela, Jasmine Day, and Maxwell Morris with lying to federal agents to obstruct an interstate murder investigation. That's a felony—good for a couple years at least. I want to talk to the Days now, or we will be back with half the San Francisco field office to arrest every one of you."

Anand studied him and appeared to be gauging whether he was bluffing. Parker wasn't.

"Give me a minute," Anand finally said and took out his phone. He placed a call and moved away from Parker and Jaden so they couldn't hear the animated conversation that followed. After the call ended, he slunk back to them, looking defeated. "Against my advice, the Days have agreed to see you."

"Good," Parker said, "But I need to get something first." He pushed off with his cane and took off down the hallway behind the security station.

Anand and Jaden followed, while Anand muttered repeatedly, "This is private property," and "You can't do this." Parker ignored him and led them to the badge-secured door he'd snuck through during their last visit.

"Open it," he said to Anand.

"You have no right to go in there without a warrant."

"Open it or we'll arrest you for obstruction."

Anand sighed and waved his badge in front of the reader. As soon as the lock released, Parker pushed the door open and led them to the workstation where he'd seen the same large gray action figure as he'd seen in Kavitha's photo. A young Indian man with a three-day beard and overwhelming body odor was seated at the workstation. Without saying a word to the man,

Parker hobbled up and snatched the gray figure.

"Hey, you can't take that," the man shouted as Parker hobbled away.

They left the man looking confused by the theft and made their way back to the lobby. Anand led them to an elevator. Inside he turned to Parker. "Why did you take that toy?"

"It's a figure of interest."

"Very funny," Anand said. "Did I mention the governor frequently uses the Day's cabin in Lake Tahoe for his ski vacations?"

"That's nice. Perhaps he'll stop and visit you at Atwater when he passes the prison on his way to the cabin."

The elevator door slid open, and Anand marched them into a large conference room that was as dimly lit as the room where Parker had snatched the action figure. Jasmine Day and Maxwell Morris were seated at the end of a long rectangular table. Next to Jasmine sat an extraordinarily pale man who Parker recognized from his research as Xperion's cofounder and Jasmine's husband. Parker had read the man suffered from a rare form of albinism and was prepared for his unusual appearance. Jaden, on the other hand, seemed stricken by the cofounder's hypopigmentation and was openly staring at the man.

The ghostly cofounder rose and floated in their direction. He stopped several feet before reaching them. Without offering his hand, he said, "Welcome back agents. My name is Marcus Day." Appearing to notice Jaden's stare, he turned to him and added, "It's called oculocutaneous albinism, or OCA for short."

Jaden gave an embarrassed smile. "I'm sorry for being rude."

Marcus waved his hand. "Nothing to be sorry about. You are by no means the first to stare."

Parker leaned on his cane and, unconcerned about being rude himself, said, "I read your condition is very unique."

Marcus's colorless eyes met Parker's. "Yes. It's known as OCA type-9A, and it's quite unique. Today there are less than two hundred known cases in the world and almost all of those are in India." He gestured at chairs near the head of the table. "Please have a seat," he said and continued as he floated back to Jasmine's side, "An interesting family tidbit about type-9A, my grandfather was the first with the variant to be studied by western doctors."

"Is that so?" Parker said as he lowered himself into a chair.

"Yes," Marcus said. "It turned out to be quite fortunate for me and my family. If my grandfather had not taken part in the study, he would not have immigrated from India, and I may have never existed."

"I wouldn't have guessed your family originated in India," Parker said.

Marcus's translucent lips curled. "My father had normal pigmentation levels. You would have had no trouble believing he was Indian."

"I'm sure," Parker said. "But that's not what I meant. The name Day does not sound like an Indian name."

"Ah. You're right. It's not. My grandfather's name was Dayal. He shortened it to Day when he applied for citizenship." Marcus's translucent grin spread. "An English name fits the complexion better. Don't you think?"

"Marcus doesn't sound particularly Indian either," Jaden offered.

The cofounder directed his gaze at the young agent. "Right. I'm named after Dr. Marcus Becker. He's the geneticist who studied my grandfather and sequenced OCA-9A. He inspired my father to go into medicine, and he's also the scientist who linked OCA-9A to TBS."

"What is TBS?" Jaden asked.

"Tanner-Barr Syndrome," Parker said adopting his instructor tone. "It's a genetic disorder affecting the endocrine system in males. It mostly affects growth rates and longevity. Men who have the condition tend to be small and rarely live into their sixties. They are also likely to develop mood and behavioral disorders related to a disruption in the production of serotonin. Not everyone who has TBS has OCA-9A, but all 9A-albinos have TBS."

Marcus emitted a short laugh. "You've certainly done your homework, Agent Reid. I don't know if I should be impressed or concerned."

"Concerned," Anand barked.

"Nothing to be concerned about," Parker said. "Research is what the FBI pays me to do." He studied Marcus. "It must be difficult for you." Then he added, "And your son."

Marcus shrugged. "It's not as bad as it sounds. If you are going to be an oculocutaneous albino, type 9A may be the best kind to be, despite the TBS."

"Why is that?" Jaden asked.

"Most OC's have severe vision problems. Type-9As do not—that is, except for a little light sensitivity." Marcus grinned again. "We may be short and moody, but both my son and I have perfect vision. Now, agents, what questions do you have for us?"

Parker placed the gray action figure on the table. Jasmine glanced at it, then trained her eyes on him. She looked different. It took Parker a moment to pinpoint why. Her eyes, which had burned with such focused energy last time, were now tired and distant. "Thank you for seeing us on such short notice."

She dipped her head. "Of course. How was your visit to ZCS?"

"Very informative."

Her eyes focused on the action figure. "Why do you have that toy?"

"You like it?" Parker said. He picked it up. "I took it from one of your employees."

"Rituraj," Anand said.

Jasmine made a face like she'd just tasted something bad.

Parker turned the toy toward her so she could read the sticker on its chest.

She read it out loud, "Fucking Anomaly." Her slender fingers drummed on the table. "Rituraj never ceases to impress. What am I supposed to make of this?"

"I believe this toy represents a player in your game that is linked to the deaths of Jyothi Reddy and Charles Tate. I also believe Angela Harding and other Xperion employees knew about the linkage when we met earlier. Failing to disclose that connection was a crime."

"This conversation is over," Anand blurted and stood. "The Days should have legal counsel present."

"I thought you were their lawyer," Parker said.

"Contract and corporate law. If you're implicating the Days in a crime, they need different representation."

Jasmine exchanged a look with Marcus. "Sit down, Anand," she said in a tone that left no doubt who was in charge. "Let the agent ask his questions."

"I want to hear about the Fucking Anomaly," Parker said.

"Anomaly," she said the word like it caused her pain "is just a term we use to describe behaviors in our systems that we can't explain."

Jaden perked up. "Does that happen often?"

She shrugged. "Our simulations are extremely complex. They require thousands of program modules to work flawlessly together. Unfortunately, programmers, even the best, make mistakes." Her eyes shifted to her husband in what Parker interpreted as an accusatory glance. "Every complex system has bugs. We find and fix the ones we know about, but some go unnoticed for years. Every so often these hidden bugs create unexplainable system behaviors. Those are what we call anomalies."

"I don't understand." Parker tapped the toy. "You're saying this character is a bug in your system?"

"If only it was that simple." She turned to Maxwell. "Explain the situation to the agents."

Maxwell held his hand out for the action figure and Parker gave it to him.

"A little over two months ago," Maxwell began, "we discovered a player in the Land of Might and Magic had somehow created an unbeatable character." He held up the figure. "At first, we thought the player had discovered a hole in the system, *an anomaly*, and was using it to cheat. We didn't take it very seriously. After all, it's only a game." He cast a nervous glance at the Days as if worried by referring to the simulation as only a game he'd offended them. "But when we tried to remove the character and block the player, we discovered we couldn't. That's when we realized we had a significant security breach."

"Why couldn't you block the player?" Jaden asked.

"It's kind of embarrassing actually," he said, casting another glance at the Days. "Both the character and the player are somehow evading our monitoring systems. We only learned of their existence through customer complaints." He studied the action figure in his hand. "Eventually, we determined the player wasn't exploiting an existing anomaly but had hacked the system and introduced their own. That's when the team began referring to the character itself as the Anomaly... or as Rituraj so crudely put it, the Fucking Anomaly."

"Curious how you didn't mention this when we met last," Parker said. "Why is that?"

"Because their stock is about to go public, and they didn't want Wall Street to know how seriously they'd been hacked," Jaden said.

Marcus spread his bony, white hands in concession. "It was a foolish mistake," he said and stared at Jasmine. "We over-managed the communication."

Parker took the action figure back from Maxwell. "Is this what the character looks like in the game?"

Maxwell shrugged. "More or less. We provide 3D printer instructions for all our character types. Customers download the plans and modify them to create action figures of their characters. Rituraj used descriptions of the Anomaly provided by players, usually just before it red-screened them, to create the instructions to make this."

Parker looked to Jaden for help with the unfamiliar phrase. "Red-screened?"

"Character death. Game over."

Parker's focus returned to the Days. "Your son had an almost identical toy at his desk at ZCS. He called his Akandu." He held up his phone and showed them Kavitha's picture of Lincoln's collection. He pointed at the gray figure. "After we left ZCS, we stopped at your home in Las Vegas. While we were there, we spoke to one of your neighbors. He told us about an argument he'd overheard between your son and a man he heard him call Akandu. Does Lincoln have a friend that goes by that name?"

Marcus frowned and shook his head. "Akandu isn't a person. He's a character from a simulation game Lincoln and I developed. We worked on it together for years, a kind of father and son bonding thing. It's how Lincoln learned to program."

"You're sure? There's no real person with that name? Maybe a nickname?"

"Lincoln has no friends he would give a nickname like that," Marcus said, all while shooting Jasmine a confirmation-seeking stare.

She nodded and said solemnly, "Our son has no such friends."

Marcus continued, "Lincoln chose that name for the character in our game from an ancient Indian children's story I would tell him when he was a child."

"I'm not familiar with the story," Parker said. He glanced at Jaden and Jaden shook his head.

"It's not very well known. It's similar to the *Lion and the Mouse*. Do you know that one?"

Jaden answered, "It's an Aesop fable. The lion spares a mouse, and later the mouse rescues the lion from a hunter's net."

"That's correct," Marcus said. "*The Tale of Akandu and Musuka* is a similar story about the weak gaining power over the strong."

Jaden raised an eyebrow. "I didn't realize that was the point of the Aesop fable. I thought it was about gratitude."

Marcus's translucent lips curled into a tight smile. "The stories are similar, but not the same. In the ancient Indian version, a timid peasant named Musuka, comes across a mighty warrior, Akandu, who has fallen into a deep pit and cannot escape."

"Like the lion in the net," Parker said.

Marcus nodded. "Musuka agrees to rescue Akandu if the warrior promises to train him to be just as powerful as he. Akandu agrees, and Musuka frees him."

"Let me guess," Parker said. "Akandu trains Musuka, and Musuka becomes a great warrior, and they all live happily ever after."

"Not exactly. In the process of training Musuka, Akandu transfers all his power to him, and after Musuka no longer needs Akandu, he kills him and takes his place."

"Not quite the ending I was expecting," Parker admitted.

Marcus shrugged. "Both fables are about repaying a debt of gratitude, but *Akandu and Musuka* is also about preparation."

"For what?" Jaden asked.

Parker smiled. "Succession."

"Perceptive, Agent Reid," Marcus said. "Musuka labors in Akandu's shadow until he acquires enough knowledge and power to fulfill his dharma and surpass him."

"So, Lincoln is Musuka, and you're Akandu?"

"No. Not me," Marcus said and speared his wife with a quick, icy stare.

Jasmine turned away from his gaze. Her eyes looked teary,

as if something about Marcus's story or accusation had wounded her.

Parker tapped the gray figure again. "Could your son be behind this," he glanced at Jasmine, "anomaly?"

The lawyer grew agitated again and before Marcus could answer said, "I've heard just about enough of this. If you've come here to accuse the Day's son of murder based on this toy, you're going to regret it."

Parker tilted his head toward him. "Careful, counselor. Threatening a federal agent is even worse than lying to one. We did not come here simply because Lincoln has the same toy as this one." He looked into Jasmine's moistening eyes. "Your son worked closely with Abby Loveridge, the Florida victim. They worked on entrance way security."

Jasmine swallowed, seeming to anticipate where Parker was going.

"All three victims were killed in their sleep by someone who was able to evade security cameras and unlock their doors." Parker looked at Marcus then back to Jasmine. "Care to guess the manufacture of the locks and cameras used at all the crime scenes?"

"My father's company," she said without returning his stare.

"That's not a coincidence, Mrs. Day. Someone used..." Parker trailed off, and looked to Jaden for help with another unfamiliar phrase.

"A back door," Jaden said.

"A back door in the ZCS systems to gain access to the victims," Parker said, watching her. "We have reason to believe your son is that person."

"That's not possible," Marcus almost shouted. His outburst appeared to startle Anand and Maxwell. He stared at the action figure in Parker's hand. "It's true. Lincoln could be the hacker. I have to admit the thought has occurred to us. He's one of few programmers who knows enough about our SIMs to make the necessary software changes, but he's no killer."

"Marcus, please be careful," Anand cautioned. "Everything you say to these men can be used to make their case against your son."

Marcus ignored him. "Agent Reid, my son could make the

software changes, but he could not have killed these people."

"How can you be so sure?" Jaden asked.

"Because he is Musuka, not Akandu. Like we told you, Lincoln has an almost debilitating timidness about him. He couldn't harm an insect, much less kill a person."

"Where's your son now, Mr. Day?" Parker asked. "He hasn't been at work or at your Las Vegas home for weeks. The phone number we have for him goes to voice mail, and he doesn't reply to email."

Marcus and Jasmine shook their heads. "We don't know where he is. He doesn't answer our calls or respond to our messages."

"You have no idea where he might've gone?"

"He could be anywhere," Marcus said. "He has plenty of resources."

"Such as?"

Marcus gave a little, superior smile. "My son has ample funds."

"Does he have access to your private jet?"

"We have two jets, Agent Reid. Jasmine and I often need to be at different places at the same time."

"Okay. Does your son have access to your jets?"

"No, but he wouldn't need them. As I said, he has ample funds. He is more than capable of arranging for his own."

"Ah. And you're sure he doesn't have a male friend that might play the role of Akandu? A lover, maybe?"

Both Days shook their heads. "Like we told you, Lincoln doesn't have friends or lovers, male or female," Marcus said.

"He must have some social life. Where does he spend his time when he's not working?"

"The Verse," they said together.

"Does he play the Land of Might and Magic?"

Both Days shook their heads. Marcus said, "Not in a long time. It bored him."

"Then what does he do? In the Verse?"

"He builds simulations. One day he might be a competitor."

Parker looked at Anand. "We want to know the last time Lincoln played the game."

"When can I expect the subpoena?" Anand said.

"You should have an electronic copy in your email. If that

won't work for you, I'll make a call and have a Marshall deliver one now."

Anand waved his hand. "We will consider it served."

Parker placed the toy back on the table. "A federal request to apprehend and detain your son will be posted to all law enforcement agencies by this evening. We will find him." He looked at Anand. "But it would be better if he came to us."

Anand nodded.

Parker stood and rubbed his leg. He looked down at the toy. It occurred to him he'd never heard back from Angela. "What happened to Ms. Harding?" he asked the room.

"What do you mean?" Anand said.

"She hasn't returned my calls, and she's not here. Given the circumstances, it doesn't seem likely she'd be on vacation. Where is she?"

Maxwell shifted in his chair. He was looking at Jasmine like he was waiting for permission to speak.

"You have something to say, Max?" Parker said.

Maxwell's eyes lowered. "No one has seen or heard from her in two days."

"Let's not be too dramatic," Marcus said. "She's been under a great deal of stress. She's probably home in bed."

Maxwell shook his head. "She hasn't called in, and she doesn't answer her phone. It's not like her."

Parker pulled the pill vial from his pocket and shook two pills into his palm. He put them in his mouth and swallowed them dry. "Has anyone contacted her family to see if she had an emergency?" he asked.

"Angela lives alone, and no one is sure how to reach her parents. They travel. I don't even think she knows where they are at times," Maxwell said. "The police told me she had to be missing for a minimum of seventy-two hours before they can open an investigation."

"You called the police?" Marcus asked.

Maxwell avoided his stare. "Yes. I'm worried about her."

Parker stood and looked at Jaden. "We need to pay Ms. Harden a visit."

"She lives less than two miles from here. I could take you there now," Maxwell said.

Parker snatched up the figure. "Let's go."

Chapter 45
Dispo Conspiracy

TONY GLANCED OVER AT her. It felt like the tenth time she'd caught him staring at her since they'd left the shop.

"What?" she snapped.

"There's something wrong with you again today."

"No, there's not."

"Ethan," Tony bellowed. "Is there something wrong with Shea?"

"Sh-Sh-She s-s-seems a little cranky," the trainee stammered from the back.

"I'm not cranky. I'm just tired." She hadn't been able to sleep after Falin's email, and she'd spent the night scouring the internet for more articles on Jyothi's and Charles's murders. Most of what she'd turned up had been a rehash of the articles Falin had sent her, but a Las Vegas news site called the *Las Vegas Daily*, the same one that had reported the victims were missing body parts, claimed to have connected the killings to a single serial killer, and they'd identified a third victim in Florida. Falin hadn't mentioned that one, and she wondered if the dead Florida woman had been a ranger, too.

The *Las Vegas Daily* reported they had no official confirmation the killings were connected, but all three victims' heads had been cut off, and a famous FBI profiler, Dr. Parker Reid, had been photographed at the scene of Charles's murder. Despite the obvious involvement of the FBI's serial killer expert, the agency was not commenting. The article included a picture of a tall thin man leaning on a cane in a hotel lobby who they identified as Dr. Reid. A Google search had turned up dozens of hits on the agent including stories about his own wife's murder and how he'd almost lost his leg.

Her phone vibrated in her hand, and she checked the incoming message. It was from her landlord letting her know she had mail. It wasn't the message she'd been waiting for. She had been exchanging texts with the FBI agent from the news article. She tapped out a reply telling her landlord she'd pick up the mail, probably all junk, this evening. The message from Agent Reid came in as soon as she hit send: *Will contact you at 7 pm.* Relieved, she tucked her phone back in her pocket.

"You keep messing with that phone," Tony groused. "Is everything okay?"

"Everything's fine, boss. Just got weird Verse stuff going on." She looked to Ethan, junker to junker, for support, and he gave an empathetic nod.

The office had sent them out with a packed route schedule, three new rig installs, several tune-ups, and a repair call. Tony must've told them Ethan didn't need much, or any, training. It was twice their usual load. She welcomed the work, though. The jam-packed day kept her mind off the gruesome murders and the possibility the killer might come after her. She'd decided to keep the situation to herself until she spoke with the FBI agent. He might not want her to talk about it. Besides, telling Tony would just cause him to freak out and send him into full-fledged Papa Bear mode. He'd insist she stay with him and Marci. Leaving her rig, even for a couple days, was not something she was willing to do. At least, not yet.

Their last service call involved swapping out a harness assembly. The old unit was in good shape—better than Shea's. The rig's owner, a very large man, had wanted it replaced because he found it too uncomfortable. Ethan had whispered to her the man would be better off laying off the pizzas than wasting his money on a new harness. She expected a comment like that from Tony, but not the shy trainee. It made her laugh. He'd said a few other funny things during the day in his cute little stutter. She'd begun to suspect he was hitting on her.

After they finished the swap, Ethan carried the customer's old harness to the van. "Wh-wh-what d-d-do we do with this? It's still per-per-perfectly good."

"It's the customer's part," Tony said. "We either leave it here or take it back to the shop for dispo."

"D-D-Dispo?"

"Disposal."

272 | RED SCREEN

"Tra-Tra-Trash?"

Tony shrugged and looked at Shea out of the corner of his eye. "Unless the scavenger wants it."

Given how little they knew about Ethan—it was only his second day with them—she thought Tony should be a little more circumspect. Ethan could be a manager spy, maybe even some executive's kid. "The boss knows we're not allowed to keep customer parts. We'll throw it in the dumpster at the shop."

"Then the scavenger will take it out and bolt it to her hot rod rig," Tony said and winked at her.

So much for caution. She examined the harness. "It sure is in great shape, but it's too big for me to take on the bike. I have no way to get it home." She looked at Ethan and batted her lashes, "I mean, if I could do such a thing without violating company policy."

Ethan gave her the impish smile. "H-H-Hate to see g-g-good tech wasted. I-I-I could follow you home with it." His smile turned conspiratorial. "We-We-We'd be partners in cr-cr-crime, and I could see your hot rod rig."

"Sounds like the perfect plan," Tony said.

She gave her boss bug eyes.

Back at the shop, after Tony had left them to complete the day's paperwork, Shea carried the harness to the dispo dumpster while Ethan went to get his car. She was surprised when he rolled up in a gleaming black electric roadster. *Manager spy, for sure.*

"Jeezus," she said. "Whatever you do, don't let Tony see you in this car. That MetaSpot you worked for must've paid well."

He popped the car's frunk and climbed out. "N-N-No, it paid shit. This is a r-r-rental."

"Rental?"

"M-m-mine's in the sh-sh-shop."

He took the harness from her and dropped it in the sports car's frunk.

She climbed on her bike, and the little black car stuck to her tail like glue as she weaved in and out of traffic. Ethan could drive. When they left the interstate for the twisty back roads that led to the onetime tractor repair shop/onetime church she called home, she let the bike fly and Ethan stayed right with her.

The shy trainee was not shy behind the wheel.

She made the turn onto the unlined blacktop road that led to her place and glided to a stop in the driveway of her landlord's large house. Ethan pulled in behind her. Still wearing her helmet, she walked back to meet him.

He slid down his window and peered at her from behind his dark glasses. "N-N-Nice house. D-D-Does Tony know?"

She laughed. "This isn't mine. It belongs to the people I rent from." She pointed up the road. "My place is another quarter mile that way. It doesn't have its own address, so this is where I get my mail."

Her landlord emerged from the house and gave her a small bundle of envelopes and flyers. "This is a few days' worth," he said. "We're going to be out of town, and I wanted to make sure you got it in case there was something important."

She shrugged. "Sorry I haven't had time to stop by. I'm sure it's all junk."

She introduced Ethan, and they made small talk for a few minutes. Ethan remained in his car, and she kept her helmet on. Then she climbed back on her bike and roared off with the little black car close behind.

The bay door rose as she pulled into her gravel lot, and she guided the bike inside. The little black car did not follow but parked outside in the space once used by tractor mechanics and parishioners.

Ethan walked through the open door carrying the harness. "This is amazing," he said without a stutter. He handed her the harness and stepped deeper inside. "Tony wasn't kidding. This is some setup." He took off his glasses and scanned the bay.

She pressed a button on her phone and the door rattled down. She tapped another one to turn on the overhead lights. He squinted and she turned them off again. "Sorry."

He grinned and circled her rig while she put the harness on a shelf with her other spare parts.

"Can I take a closer look?"

"Sure." She joined him at the rig's control panel and watched as he navigated through the settings.

"I like how you have it configured, but there's a f-f-few parameters I could suggest some tweaks to."

"Really?" she said. "Which are those?"

"I'd start with the outer ring axis control motor limits. They are too low. If you bump them up, you'll get more lateral spin in the Verse."

"Yeah, and I'll be thrown around like a rag doll."

He grinned. "No more than the way you throw yourself around on that b-bike."

She studied him. "Is it me, or are you stuttering less?"

He gazed straight into her eyes with those strange light-colored ones of his. "I could stutter more if y-y-you like."

She smiled back. Ethan's shyness was disappearing as fast as his stutter. The contrast of his glossy black hair and eyebrows against his whiter than white skin and silver-gray eyes caught her attention. She had not thought about how unusual the combination was until this moment. It went against everything she'd learned in her genetics classes about albinism. "Can I ask you a personal question?" she asked.

"You can ask." His unusual eyes sparkled. "I d-d-don't guarantee I will answer it."

"Fair enough. Your hair. It's so black. Don't people with albinism usually have light hair too?"

He touched his hair and frowned. "I-I-I dye it. My eyebrows t-t-too. Does it l-l-look bad?"

She shook her head. "No. It looks nice. I was just curious."

His smile returned, and he drew a few inches closer.

Trinity dropped from a nearby shelf and trotted over, rescuing Shea from the awkward moment.

Ethan jumped. "Y-y-you have an a-a-animal," he almost shrieked.

Shea bent down and scooped her up. "She's not an animal. She's a cat. Her name is Trinity." She held her out to him. "Do you want to pet her?"

Ethan raised his hands and backed away. "N-N-No." He sneezed. "I-I-I'm allergic to cats."

"Oh. That's too bad. Let me put her in another room."

She brought Trinity to the kitchen, and after scooping food into her dish, she looked for something for her and Ethan. Her refrigerator contained little to offer a guest. A single can of beer was hidden behind a couple of old Chinese food containers. God knows how long it had been in there. Did beer go bad? Guess they'd find out. She grabbed two glasses—the only matched pair she had—and returned to the bay.

Ethan's hands were busy on the rig's control panel.

"Hey," she said. "You're not changing anything, are you?"

He shrugged. "M-M-Maybe a few small things."

She cringed. This guy sure knew his way around a rig, but she had it configured the way she liked. Besides, touching her settings was almost like touching her, and she wasn't ready for that.

"You're making me nervous," she said and raised the can. "Let's sit over here and have a drink."

Ethan tapped a few times on the control panel before joining her on the thrift store sofa. She poured half the can in each of their glasses and took a sip. It tasted okay.

Ethan sniffed at his.

"What's the matter?" she asked.

"It's b-b-beer."

"Yes. Do you want something else?"

He sipped and squeezed his eyes shut as if he was terrified to taste it. He swallowed and opened his eyes. "That's not bad."

She laughed. "Is this the first time you've had beer?"

"M-M-Maybe."

Wow, she thought. *I can't wait to unravel this mystery.* She was about to ask what else he'd never tried—the thought intrigued and frightened her—when her phone buzzed with an incoming message. She'd almost forgotten the FBI agent. She read the message and her heart fluttered in her chest. Ethan's mysteries would have to wait.

He must've noticed the shocked expression on her face.

"I-I-Is everything okay?"

"I'm sorry, Ethan. I don't mean to be rude, but I need to ask you to leave."

Chapter 46
A Dead Wizard's Plan

PARKER LEANED ON THE hood of the rental car in Angela Harding's driveway, watching white-suited officials from the Santa Clara County Coroner's Office load her body into a van. The menthol smell of the vapor rub he'd dabbed under his nose filled his nostrils. He'd left Jaden inside the house with the crime scene investigators and Palo Alto detectives and came outside for some air. According to the coroner's estimate, Angela and her small dog had been decomposing for two days, and no amount of vapor rub could completely mask the smell.

They'd found her taped down on her kitchen table with her head left on the floor where it had fallen after being removed with, what Parker knew the medical examiner would rule a sword. Her dog had been discovered in a laundry room. It had been cut nearly in two, no doubt by the same sword. Though the weapon and manner of death were consistent with the Collector's other murders, Angela's body had not been posed and her ears had not been removed. The killers, Parker now believed there were two—Musuka and Akandu—had subdued her, taped her down, and cut her head off. They had not surprised her while she slept as they'd done their other victims. Evidence of violence was everywhere: busted furniture, damaged wallboard, and a mutilated dog. The M.O. had changed. It had become much less controlled, almost chaotic.

Maxwell Morris sat slumped over the steering wheel of his car. Parker limped over and tapped on the driver's side window, careful to avoid the vomit puddle. The three of them had been the ones to find her. After knocking on her door and receiving no answer, Jaden had jumped the backyard fence. He'd come back moments later, saying he could see a woman's legs hanging off the kitchen table through the back window. Both doors had been locked, but the front door's electronic dead bolt offered little resistance to Jaden's shoulder. The smell had hit them immediately, but they had not been able to catch Maxwell before he'd raced into the kitchen. Parker was no stranger to horrific crime scenes. Jaden had at least seen training videos, but Maxwell had never encountered anything like it outside of a Hollywood movie.

The car window slid down, and Maxwell stared up at him through bloodshot eyes. "I can't get the image out of my mind," he said.

"It'll pass," Parker said, but he knew the sight would change the despondent technology executive forever.

"No way. I'll never forget it. Who would do such a thing to her? She was so beautiful and brilliant."

"Could it have been the Day's son?" Parker asked.

Maxwell shook his head. "I don't think so. Not like that. Certainly, not by himself. You heard what his parents said. Lincoln is afraid of his own shadow, and he could never over-power Angela. Jesus, he's... he's..."

"Musuka, the mouse," Parker offered.

"Exactly."

"Then who's Akandu? Could it be one of his parents?"

Maxwell gagged, pushed open the door, and added to the vomit puddle. Parker was relieved he hadn't wiped away the vapor rub.

"Not Marcus," Maxwell said, and spat some more into the puddle. "He could never do a thing like that. Couldn't handle the mess. All that blood and gore. He'd hyperventilate and pass out."

Pass out? Parker raised his eyebrows.

"Marcus has a thing about neatness. It's probably some kind of OCD. Everything around him must be clean and ordered. He can be very...." Maxwell's voice trailed off.

"Very what?"

"Odd. I've seen him refuse to enter cluttered rooms, and God help you if you met him with wrinkled clothes."

"Wrinkled clothes?"

Maxwell took several strained breaths, almost panting. "Yeah."

Parker had found dozens of articles on the internet describing Marcus's legendary attention to detail and compulsive behaviors. Many of the articles had been unflattering accounts by fearful anonymous employees who'd signed strict nondisclosures threatening them with financial ruin if they discussed the company or its founders. None of them suggested the extreme obsessive-compulsive disorder Maxwell was describing, but OCD was common among men with TBS.

"Does Marcus have any other extreme behavioral traits? Anything that would have you question his mental well-being?" Parker asked.

Maxwell closed his eyes, perhaps contemplating the nondisclosure. When he opened them, he said, "We all think Marcus is a little out-there, but he's not crazy enough to have done that to Angela."

Parker remembered the way Marcus had looked at Jasmine when he'd denied being Akandu. It sure seemed to him the Xperion head had implicated his wife, but the Vegas neighbor said Akandu was a man. Voices could be faked, though. "I got the impression from Marcus that Lincoln might think of Jasmine as Akandu."

Maxwell spit. "When?"

"When we were talking earlier. The way he looked at her when I asked if he was Akandu."

"I wouldn't read too much into how those two look at each other, at least anymore. They are both lawyering up for a divorce battle."

"Hmm. What do you think though? Could Jasmine be Akandu?"

Maxwell gulped more air, and Parker stepped back out of vomit range. "She's certainly strong enough. She could've overpowered Angela easily."

Parker pictured Jasmine's slender, almost sleek, build. "She seemed small to me," he said. "Angela probably had fifteen pounds on her."

Maxwell chuckled. "Jasmine is a world-class triathlete. She's climbed Mount Everest, swam the San Francisco Bay, and ran about a hundred marathons. Angela wouldn't have stood a chance against her. But unlike Marcus, Jazz is not crazy, and she would never do anything to jeopardize Xperion. The company's her life, her real baby. Lincoln was just a distraction. Besides, if

Lincoln is killing people, his mother wouldn't be helping him, she would be number one on his list."

"That bad?"

"You have no idea."

Angela had alluded to the same dysfunction between mother and son. Parker glanced back at the house. A crime scene tech was fingerprinting the front door. If the killers had left any prints, they'd likely been obliterated by his and Jaden's when they'd forced their way in.

"What was Angela doing to stop the Anomaly?"

Maxwell burped and an acidic hint of vomit made it past the vapor rub.

"She was working with a security consultant. They had a plan to trap the hacker and close the holes he exploits."

Parker thought about the tipster from Atlanta. "Is the consultant a woman?"

"I don't think so. As far as I know, the consultant is a man. He's some kind of secret hacker. No one is supposed to know his true identity."

Parker leaned on his cane to take some of the weight off his throbbing leg. "I need to talk to this consultant."

Maxwell shook his head. "I have no idea how to get in touch with him. Only Angela did. Besides, he's very sick. I think he may even be dead."

"How was the consultant going to trap the hacker?"

Maxwell rubbed his eyes. "It's all about getting what we call event trace data. The consultant tricked the hacker into performing actions he could trace. Then he collected the event data and sent it to Angela's team so they could use it to find and close the security holes. They've been doing it for weeks."

Parker didn't know what any of that meant. He looked around for Jaden. This techie stuff was much more up his alley.

The crime scene investigators finished with the door, and Jaden stepped out onto the porch. Parker waived him over, but Jaden held up his phone to show he was on a call.

"If Angela's team has that data, why is it taking them so long to shut down the hacker or identify him?" Parker asked.

"Now you sound like Jasmine. So far, Angela's team hasn't collected the right data to identify the player controlling the Anomaly. That's what the consultant's trap is supposed to do, but it has to be sprung while the Anomaly is fighting a player we are monitoring. Not easy when you have over fifty million players. The consultant's trace programs can't monitor them all."

"What was the plan?"

"Angela and the consultant have been luring the hacker to certain players."

"Bait for the trap," Parker said.

Maxwell nodded.

"Were Jyothi and Charles bait?"

"Yes," Maxwell said, then hastily added a qualifier: "But we didn't know the hacker was going to actually kill them."

Jaden walked over, and Parker pointed out the puddle. "Watch your step."

The young agent drew close and whispered, "Need a moment."

"We'll be right back," Parker said to Maxwell and the two of them stepped away from the car window.

"Chavez called," Jaden said.

"Let me guess, no dead Lincoln."

"Right. No Lincoln and no big guy. Chavez said the house was vacant and sterile."

"Sterile?"

"That's the word he used—sterile. No dust, no fingerprints, no sign anyone actually lives there."

"No furniture in the house?"

"Plenty of furniture, just looks like a showroom."

"Like father, like son."

Jaden looked perplexed.

"Marcus is obsessive about cleanliness."

"Interesting. Chavez used that word too. He said everything in the house is obsessively ordered. Clothing meticulously folded, cabinet contents precisely arranged. Nothing random." Jaden worked the screen on his phone. "Except in one room. I have a picture."

Parker waited, expecting Jaden to show him a room full of victims' ears.

Jaden held up his phone. It showed pieces of a torn-up poster-sized photo of what appeared to be Jasmine Day strewn across a neatly made bed.

Parker took the phone and studied the image. The photo looked as if it had been taken at a costume party or promotional event. Jasmine, dressed in a black robe and wearing a golden crown was sitting on a throne that Parker thought he recognized from an old movie or television program. He handed the phone back to Jaden. "That's not what I expected."

Jaden grunted. "Yeah. What do you make of it?"

"I think Lincoln doesn't like his mother very much." Parker glanced back at Maxwell. "Apparently, Mrs. Day never aspired to be mother of the year."

Jaden put his phone away and looked at the house. "This killing seems different from the others."

"Very different," Parker agreed.

"Time frame is off too," Jaden said.

Parker scratched his beard. "Yes. Been a little less than two weeks since Tate. Not much, though."

"Could it be a copycat?"

Parker shook his head. "The Xperion connection makes that unlikely. Angela wasn't selected randomly. Her murder is connected to the others." He rubbed his leg. "The evidence of struggle bothers me, though."

"Angela was awake," Jaden said. "She resisted."

"I don't think the struggle was between Angela and her killers."

Jaden raised his eyebrow. "You think there were multiple killers this time?"

Parker leaned heavily on his cane. "Remember that fable Marcus told us?"

"How could I forget?"

"I think maybe Musuka joined Akandu as part of his training."

Jaden's eyebrow climbed nearer to his hairline. "And by Musuka, you mean the Day's son?"

Parker nodded. "Yes. I came away from the meeting today believing Lincoln Day was doing the hacking and Akandu was doing the killing, but I think they did this one together, and it didn't go well."

"You think Lincoln and Akandu got into it while they were killing her like they did back in Vegas?"

Parker shrugged. "Don't know, but something different

happened in there."

"Where does that leave us?"

"Same place we started this morning, looking for Musuka and Akandu."

Parker studied the younger man. "How are you handling this?"

"This, sir?"

Parker nodded toward the house. "Angela. The way we found her."

Jaden shrugged. "I'm okay. I guess. It was pretty awful in there, though."

Parker put his hand on the young agent's shoulder. "That's about as bad as it gets. You may have trouble sleeping."

Jaden grinned. Bravado. "Then you'll have to give me some of those pills of yours."

Parker studied him some more. Despite the joking and claim of being okay, Parker suspected the young man would feel differently after the adrenaline and shock wore off. "I find mixing them with scotch works best."

The young man's grin evaporated. "I hope it doesn't come to that."

They returned to Maxwell's car window. Maxwell's eyes were still rimmed red, but the color of his face looked better, less green.

"Let's begin again," Parker said. "You were explaining Angela's and the consultant's plan for trapping the hacker."

"Not really much to it," Maxwell said. "The consultant was supposed to bring the bait player to the Anomaly. While the Anomaly and the bait player fought, the consultant would use a special program to collect the data containing the hacked account and the hacker's MAC address."

"MAC address?" Parker asked.

"Media Access Control Address," Maxwell said. "All devices that access the net have them. They're supposed to be unique and permanent."

Parker didn't like the way Maxwell said *supposed to*. He glanced at Jaden. Jaden shrugged then asked what a bait player was and while Maxwell explained it to him, Parker thought about the woman in Atlanta. She had to be the player Maxwell was talking about. He checked the time on his phone. Almost seven back east. He sent her a message asking if she was available and stared at the screen. After several seconds without a reply, he added, *Angela Harding has been murdered. Must talk now.*

He was still staring at the screen when he heard Jaden's voice.

"Everything okay?"

A rivulet of drool had run from Parker's mouth, and he had the feeling Jaden had asked the question multiple times. He wiped his mouth with his sleeve. "Yeah," he said.

"You sure?"

Parker gave the concerned agent a reassuring smile. "Sure." But he wasn't sure. Instead, Parker offered some bravado of his own and wiggled his eyebrows. "Nothing to alarm Ms. Fulbright about."

Jaden nodded slowly.

Parker turned his attention back to Maxwell. "Who else at Xperion knew about Angela and the consultant's plan?"

Maxwell shrugged. "Rituraj, but he's fried. He's been practically living in the office throughout this whole ordeal."

"Call him. Make sure he doesn't leave. We're on our way back to talk to him now."

Chapter 47
Bait

A TELEVISION NEWS CREW had set up outside of Angela's house, and another one was waiting for them in the Xperion parking lot. The reporter recognized Parker and shouted questions to him as he hobbled past.

"Agent Reid, did the Vegas Headhunter kill Angela Harding?"

Parker winced. The story broken by the *Las Vegas Daily* connecting the murders was national now. Unfortunately, someone, Higgs had speculated from the Clark County M.E.'s office, had leaked to the *Daily* the killer had taken trophies. The news site had contacted LVMPD before releasing the gruesome fact, and Divine had convinced them not to identify what particular body part. The *Daily* knew the killer was collecting ears, but they hadn't learned about the Collector nickname, leaving them to come up with their own: The Vegas Headhunter. Soon the Palo Alto police would reveal more than one killer was involved in Angela's murder, and Parker guessed the press would change that to the Vegas Headhunters, which sounded like the name of a sports team.

He stopped and faced the reporter. "Have the decency to keep the victim's name quiet until the family is notified."

The reporter shrugged. "Too late. It's all over social media."

"Jeezus," Parker said and hobbled into the building.

Marcus met them in the lobby looking unfazed. His clothes and frost-white hair were as perfect as when they'd left him several hours ago. "Everyone knows," he said. "Jasmine is a wreck. I've never seen her like this. She's gone home."

"What is she most upset by? The IPO or Angela's murder?" Maxwell snapped.

Marcus shot him an icy stare. "Given the circumstances, I'll ignore that."

Maxwell's face darkened. The angry redness in his cheeks stood in stark contrast to Marcus's deathlike pallor. "I'm taking them to meet with Rituraj,"

"Yes, of course. Give them anything they need to find Angela's killer."

Parker drew close to the cofounder. "Palo Alto police will want to interview you and some of your employees, especially those who worked with Angela. They will offer to have patrol cars check on those who want it. I suggest anyone who was working to stop the Anomaly take them up on the offer. That would include you and your wife."

"I will ensure the staff knows."

Parker turned to follow Maxwell, and Marcus grabbed his arm. "My son didn't do this."

Parker stared into the man's unsettling, colorless eyes. "If you want to help your son," he said as he pulled free of Marcus's grasp, "find him and have him turn himself in."

Maxwell led them to a conference room where they found the scruffy Indian man Parker had taken the toy from sitting with his head down on the table. He appeared to be sleeping.

Maxwell nudged the sleeping man's shoulder. "Rituraj, Rituraj, wake up."

The man raised his head. "Is it true? Is Angela dead?" he said groggily.

"Yes," Maxwell said. "These are FBI agents. They want to talk to you about the Anomaly. They know about the hacker." Maxwell waved his hand in front of his nose. "You need a shower."

Rituraj pushed himself upright. "And you need a breath mint. Which hacker?"

"Both," Maxwell said. He turned to Parker. "The second hacker is the consultant."

"We haven't received any new tracking data from the Anomaly in days," Rituraj said as he ran his fingers through his unkempt hair.

"Does that mean the Anomaly hasn't been in the game?" Jaden asked.

Rituraj shrugged. "Don't know. The consultant's gone, and no one is hunting him."

"What about the other bait player, Shea?" Parker said.

Rituraj blinked. "Who is Shea?"

"I think she is Darshana," Maxwell said.

"Of course," Rituraj said, more alert. He slid a tablet in front of him and tapped on its screen. "Give me a moment." He tapped some more. "Found her." Rituraj looked up. "Shea Britton. Lives in Lithia Springs, Georgia." He shrugged. "No good to us now without the consultant."

Parker didn't like the cool way the exhausted looking man said Shea was no good to them. "You realize you people put this young woman in a great deal of danger?"

"Wasn't my idea," Rituraj said and laid his head down.

Parker rapped his cane on the table and Rituraj popped back up.

"What now?" Rituraj grumbled.

"I was messaging with her on the way here. She told me she has something called Falin's mirror."

Rituraj's eyes widened. "Then she can spring the trap."

"Only if she's willing to be the bait," Maxwell said.

Parker took out his phone and fired off the question.

A one word response came back instantly. *Yes.*

"She's willing, and she's ready to meet with us," Parker said.

"Are you connected to her now?" Rituraj asked.

Parker nodded.

Rituraj tapped on his tablet and the large monitor on the wall flashed to life with a split screen view. Half the screen showed the four of them gathered around the table and the other half displayed: Waiting for Participant.

"Tell her she has a web conference invite in her email."

Parker sent the message. After several minutes, a young woman's face filled the screen. She was leaning close to the camera, and Parker was struck by the contrasts of her blue green, almost turquoise eyes and her dark Indian complexion. The combination gave her an exotic look like the Land of Might and Magic characters he'd seen when Angela had given him and Jaden the tour.

"Hi," she said with the cheerfulness of someone distant from the grim reality of the afternoon. "I'll be right back. I have to say goodbye to a guest."

The camera followed her. Its view widened as she receded,

revealing what looked like the inside of a garage. She disappeared for several moments before coming back and sliding into a chair facing them.

They introduced themselves. When it was Maxwell's turn, he gave her his name then added, "You know me as the wizard Em the Magnificent."

Parker mouthed "The Magnificent" at Jaden and rolled his eyes.

"I knew it," Shea said. "You work for Xperion like Angela." Then her expression turned sad. "We were all so afraid of her in the game, and it turned out she wasn't terrifying at all. I'm so sorry."

"No. She wasn't," Maxwell agreed.

Parker let them go on for a minute before he snapped them back to the urgency of the moment. "What happened to Angela was terrible, but we need to talk about her killers. You're a target, just like she was." He looked at Maxwell and Rituraj. "None of you are safe until we catch them."

"I'm thousands of miles away from there," she said.

Marcus's words came back to Parker. *Lincoln has plenty of resources.* "Distance doesn't mean anything to these monsters."

They spent the next hour hashing out the plan to spring Falin's trap. Shea would enter the Land after work like she did almost every night. Once in, she would remain close to a gate and wait for Falin's mirror to notify her when the Gray Warrior, as she called the Anomaly, appeared. Then she would teleport to the gate nearest to the Gray Warrior's location and engage him.

Rituraj's team would know as soon as Darshana entered the Land, and they would monitor her. Maxwell, as Em, would teleport to Darshana's location and help her stay alive for as long as he could while Rituraj's team used the data from the mirror to gather the hacker's account details and MAC address. Em would not FOD the Gray Warrior until the team had what they needed. They had to explain all the teleporting and wizard stuff to Parker who found it all to be a bunch of "Geek Babble."

Jaden would work with the FBI's cybercrime division to gain access to the Internet Service Provider database which contained the physical locations of all device addresses that passed through their networks. Parker would have an FBI hotline established to coordinate the analysis and response activities. Rituraj's team would call a number to initiate the hotline when Shea and the hacker were in the SIM. The team would announce the hacker's device address as soon as they pulled it from the data. The agents monitoring the hotline would look the device address up and retrieve the hacker's physical location. Once the hacker's location was determined, FBI agents and local law enforcement would be dispatched to arrest him.

When they were done discussing the plan, Parker returned to the topic of Shea's safety. He wanted an FBI agent or police officer to guard her night and day. Shea wouldn't agree. She argued no one knew how long this would go on for, and she wasn't going to be a prisoner. After some debate, she conceded to Parker arranging for the police to check in on her regularly.

"Keep your doors locked," he told her. Then remembering how the killers had gained access to the other victims, he'd asked. "What kind of locks do you have?"

"I don't understand the question," Shea said.

"Are they electronic or manual?"

The camera moved to show a view of a closed overhead door. "This is my door. It has an electronic opener."

"You live in a garage?" Jaden asked.

Her face reappeared. "Better than a barn." She turned the camera again, and they could see an OmniRig glowing in the distance. "These don't fit in your typical apartment." The camera returned to her face. She squinted. "Aren't you a bit young to be an FBI agent?"

Parker laughed. "Can you physically secure that door from the inside?"

She nodded.

"Make sure you do." He eyed Rituraj and Maxwell. "That goes for you too. Don't trust your electronic locks."

After the meeting, Maxwell escorted Parker and Jaden out. His voice cracked when he spoke. "I can still see Angela's body taped to that table."

"It's a terrible memory that will be tough to forget," Parker said. He touched the executive's arm. "Get some rest. Do you have someone you can talk to?"

Maxwell nodded, grim.

Parker squeezed his shoulder. "Do so."

He and Jaden left Maxwell standing there, looking pale and sick just like he'd looked at the scene.

More news crews were waiting for them in the parking lot. Reporters and camera operators buzzed around them like angry bees. Parker and Jaden kept their heads down and plowed past without commenting. "I've never seen anything like this," Jaden said.

"It's a circus," Parker agreed as he hobbled toward the car. "It will only last for a few days. They'll lose interest." He looked back at the swarm. "Until there's another victim."

"Do you think the killers will go after Ms. Britton?"

"She's the bait," Parker answered, maybe too matter-of-factly.

Jaden grabbed his arm and pulled him to a stop. Parker almost fell over. First the Xperion ghost and now his young partner was tugging at him. He studied Jaden's face and saw distress and maybe sadness. Parker glanced at the fingers digging into his arm. "What's on your mind, Breaux?"

Jaden released his grip. "She's not just baiting a character in a game," he said fiercely. "She's in real danger."

The parking lot lights reflected off the young agent's glistening eyes. The shock and adrenaline were wearing off. A first murder scene could be rough. "You still okay?" Parker asked. Concerned.

"I don't know. I'm not ready for scotch and pills yet, but we spent time with Ms. Harding, and now we're getting to know Shea—I mean Ms. Britton."

"We're going to catch these fuckers," Parker said. "We know Lincoln Day is Musuka. Every law enforcement agency in the country is looking for him. We'll get him. Then we'll learn who this Akandu is and get him."

Jaden rubbed something from his eye. "I know, but it's like what you told Ms. Britton: The Day kid could be anywhere. He could be watching her right now."

"Hey." Parker put a hand on the young agent's shoulder. "We're the FBI. We're everywhere."

Jaden smiled and surprised Parker with another outstanding impersonation of Higgs. "Blow me." Before Parker could react, the young agent's expression turned serious again. "What if they get to her before we get them?"

Parker cocked his head and smiled. "Ms. Britton made quite an impression on you. Didn't she?"

Jaden shrugged. "I just don't want her to end up butchered like Ms. Harding."

"We're not going to let that happen. We'll get them."

"Do you think we have two weeks?"

Parker thought about how violent Angela's murder had been compared to the other three. Something had changed. The lack of control and the apparent fight between Lincoln and Akandu bothered him. "I don't know if we can count on the same pattern," he said and resumed his hobble toward the car.

"Wait," Jaden called.

Parker stopped.

"Why was there a pattern in the first place?"

"I don't know for sure," Parker said, "but I have a theory. Lincoln is a type-9A albino like his father. That means he has TBS."

"What does that have to do with the pattern?"

"TBS affects the endocrine system which, among other things, is the body's clock. It controls everything from the pace of growth to sleep cycles. You ever hear of biorhythms?"

"Timed cycles in the body. Like a woman's menstrual period."

Parker nodded. "Yes. That's one example. A good one actually. It's a hormonal cycle controlled by the endocrine system. Do you know what serotonin is?"

Jaden shrugged. "Brain chemical of some type."

"Outstanding, Breaux. It's what's known as a neurotransmitter. It's how nerve cells send messages to each other. The amount of serotonin in the brain affects everything from mood to judgement. Insufficient serotonin can also cause obsessive-compulsive traits."

"Like extreme neatness?"

"Among other things."

"So, you are saying Lincoln's TBS affects a biorhythm that turns him into a monster every two weeks?"

"In a manner of speaking. Yes. What is likely happening is he experiences high and low emotional states due to alternating hormone levels related to his TBS, and these level oscillations occur on a regular cadence. It's probably like a wave that builds then crests. When the wave is low, Lincoln is a planner. When it's high, he's an actor."

"Every two weeks?"

"Just a theory."

"Why is the pattern changing?"

Parker rubbed his leg. "No way to know for sure. Maybe Lincoln's TBS is changing. Or, maybe the fantasy he is living with Akandu is impacting his emotions more than the disease. Maybe it's like in the story. Musuka is becoming stronger and doesn't require the wave of serotonin to build before he acts."

Jaden frowned. "He's becoming Akandu."

Parker nodded and headed for the car.

Chapter 48
Flight

IT WAS AFTER MIDNIGHT. Parker was sitting in the hotel bar sipping a scotch on the rocks that had turned into scotch-flavored ice water. The memory of Angela's headless body splayed out on her kitchen table had made sleep impossible. Now, as he'd confided to his young partner, he was carefully blending alcohol and painkillers to ward off the nightmares. If he was having a tough time driving the image out of his head, he could not imagine what Em *the Magnificent* must be going through. He'd considered calling to check on him but thought all he'd be able to offer was cold textbook advice on dealing with trauma and loss. It wasn't as if his own recovery from the catastrophe that had become his personal life was going swimmingly. And Maxwell would need a friend, not a psychologist. Though, Parker had no doubt the executive would need therapy soon and likely for a long time.

Parker, Jaden, and Becky had spent the evening making the preparations for the plan they'd outlined at Xperion. Jaden and Becky had met with the cybercrimes division to enlist their help with the MAC address search while Parker had spent forty-five excruciating minutes on the phone with a supervisor at the FBI operations desk, the same people who ran the tip system that led Shea to him, to set up a case hotline. He'd chased that call with a thirty-minute conversation with the Palo Alto detectives working Angela's murder.

The call had started poorly, with accusations by a surly commander that the FBI had kept them in the dark about the potential existence of a serial killer in their city and ended with Parker promising the Bureau would do better. The accusations were unfounded, but Parker played along to avoid conflict that would land him in hot water with Warner, and because he hadn't wanted to extend the call one second longer than necessary.

In the morning he'd follow up with the Atlanta field office about keeping an eye on Shea. Rituraj had sent him her address, and he'd already passed it on to the Atlanta assistant special agent in charge. The ASAC had messaged him agreeing to do what she could, but he knew her busy agents would farm it out to the local authorities.

A quick Google search of the Georgia town where Shea lived told him its tiny police force likely lacked resources to devote to protecting a potential victim. Like Jaden, he couldn't bear the thought of the confident young woman with the green eyes being taped down to a table and beheaded. Parker would ask Becky to apply her mix of charm and pressure to get the resources assigned. *We won't let that happen.*

He downed the remains of the scotch-water and motioned for the bartender to close out his tab. His phone buzzed as he stood to head back to his room. An unknown number with a San Francisco area code. He took the call and settled back down on the stool.

"Agent Reid," Marcus Day's soft voice said.

Parker didn't know what to make of a call this late from the enigmatic Xperion head. All that was certain was he wasn't calling to say goodnight. "Kind of late, Mr. Day. Is everything okay?"

"I'm sorry, but no. Everything is not okay. Jasmine is out of her mind. She stormed out of our home twenty minutes ago after calling to arrange for her jet to be prepped."

Parker's skin tingled. "Where is she going?"

"I don't know. I think she's going to find Lincoln."

"She knows where he is?"

"I don't know that either, Agent Reid. All I know is she's heading to the airport now, and she's not herself."

"Is she on her way back to Vegas?"

"Possibly. I'm not sure."

"You did the right thing by calling, Marcus, but now I need to know where she's heading."

"I'll make a call."

Marcus hung up.

Parker motioned for the bartender to bring him another scotch. He'd taken his first sip when his phone buzzed again. This time it was a message from Marcus with Jasmine's destination. "Shit," Parker murmured.

294 | RED SCREEN

He checked the time. It was almost one in the morning, four in Virginia. He tapped a message to Becky. *Jasmine Day is taking her private jet to meet her son. Jaden and I are following her.*

He used his phone to book Jaden and his flights. First class, because of the leg. The future email battle with accounting over his expense account would be epic.

Becky's reply came in as the bartender closed out his second tab.

You are not a field agent anymore. You're an analyst. I will get agents assigned.

He tapped. *Good. Have them meet Jaden and me at the airport.* He thought about Jaden's cramped little roadster. *Make sure they have a real car. Sending you our flight info.*

Her reply made him laugh. *Fucking First Class!!!*

He pocketed his phone and went to bang on Jaden's door for a change. They had a flight and an Xperion cofounder to catch.

Chapter 49
Gone Hunting

IT **WAS WELL PAST** seven in the evening when Tony and Shea finished unloading the van. They'd skipped lunch and busted their asses, but they still couldn't make it to all their appointments. The scheduler had planned their route assuming a three-person crew, but Ethan had not shown up that morning. It wasn't until midday when they'd learned he'd quit. No notice, no reason, he would not be back. Shea was disappointed. She'd been looking forward to getting to know him.

The day had been so busy, she'd barely thought about the Gray Warrior and the hunt. She would have forgotten about them altogether if the good looking, young FBI agent named Jaden hadn't messaged three times to check on her. The first two were friendly queries asking how her day was going, like a girl might receive from a boy interested in her, but the last one kind of creeped her out. *Hi, Jaden again*, as if she hadn't added him to her contacts and couldn't see his name, *keep your eyes open for strangers who might be watching you. Go straight to the police if you suspect anyone is. Call me if you are not sure.*

She'd rolled out of the InVerse lot after the evening rush had depopulated the city. Traffic was light. The setting sun burned through her visor as she sped home. Crouched over the tank, she kept her eyes low, watching the white dashes of the center line race toward her windscreen.

The bike whined as she downshifted and leaned hard to make the turn onto her road. As she did, she glimpsed a police cruiser lurking behind some brush across from her landlord's driveway. She'd taken the turn too fast, and she watched the cruiser recede in her mirrors expecting a flash of blue lights and a siren's wail. She got neither. They were there to keep an eye on her, not give her a ticket. She doubted this was what Jaden meant by stalking strangers, but maybe she'd give him a call, just to check. She smiled to herself as she coasted into the gravel drive. *The agent was awfully good looking.*

Trinity was waiting as she climbed off the bike. She scooped her up, and they stood together watching the sun set from the open bay. After the sun had dipped below the trees, she lowered the door and, as Agent Reid had urged, engaged the manual lock to prevent someone from opening it with a hacked transmitter. At first, she'd thought the precaution silly. The door made a heck of a racket. She'd hear it rattling up no matter what she was doing. But then what? The aluminum baseball bat by her bed wouldn't stop a lunatic with a sword. So, she slid the lock bar in place.

She ate the aging contents of a Chinese food container, fed Trinity, showered, and put on her cybersuit. Then she messaged the hot agent. *Strangers in a police car are watching me. Does that count?* His response was disappointingly terse. *No.* Oh well, she thought. So much for flirting. Another message popped up. *Keep those pretty green eyes peeled, though.* Hmm. Maybe flirting wasn't out after all. She sat down at her laptop and scanned her emails. A message was waiting in her personal inbox from a sender she did not recognize. The subject hinted ominously at its contents. *Falin has Red Screened.*

I regret to inform you, Mikey Jackson, aka Falin, went permanent red screen this morning. He passed peacefully in his sleep. He wanted you to know he enjoyed hunting with you very much. The message was signed, Yan Jackson, Mikey's mother.

She blinked away the tears and focused on the next message. It was from her bank. A deposit had been made for $500,000. Her mouth fell open. This had to be a mistake or a joke. A note read: *Your share of the bounty.* More tears filled her eyes. For a moment, she wondered how he had learned her bank account information, but she remembered Angela telling her nothing online could be hidden from him.

Trinity rubbed against her leg, purring. Shea took her up into her arms and buried her face in her fur. "Got to spring the trap, Trin." She placed the cat on the desk. Then, Shea wiped away the tears and tapped out a message on her phone to Jaden: *Going hunting.*

Shea put on her gloves and carried her headgear to the rig. As she strapped in, she considered the fading light streaming in through the skylights and the small window in the people door. The bay would be dark soon. All the killer talk made her want to turn the overhead lights on, but the app that controlled them was on her phone which was sitting in its charger next to her laptop. Screw it. She pulled on her headgear and became Darshana, who wasn't afraid of the dark or killers that may hide in it.

Chapter 50
Red Screen

A **SIMILAR TWILIGHT GLOW** filled her view when Darshana stepped through the Staghead Gate. Lights from the small town twinkled beneath the deep blue sky as she made her way down the hill and through the orchard, oblivious to the other players who traveled the road with her. She thought of Falin as she leaned against a tree outside the Hunter's Horn, remembering how he'd presented the false quest to her in the busy inn. The deception had been wrong, but she wished she hadn't treated him so badly after the attack in the Wolfswood. Even though they'd only known each other for a few weeks, she'd still miss him and was sad she'd never get to know the man behind the dwarf.

A golden flash interrupted her thoughts. Em, dressed in his dirty robes, appeared beside her, leaning on the rough stick he used as a staff. "Any sign of the Anomaly?" he asked.

She removed Falin's mirror from her pack and studied it. "According to this, he hasn't been in for two days. Do you think he's figured out how to hide from Falin's programs?"

Em shrugged. "I hope not. I'm want nothing more than to spring the trap and give the police what they need to find him. The fucking monster needs to be locked up forever for what he did to Angela and the others."

Shea told Em about Falin's passing, and he shared with her what little he knew about him. Then they talked about Angela and the terrible way she'd been killed. Maxwell had been interviewed by the police that afternoon and had to relive the horror of finding her. He didn't think he'd ever sleep again. They sat on a rock wall opposite the inn watching players come and go until the virtual sky had filled with virtual stars.

She stood and stretched. "Looks like he's a no-show. Maybe better luck tomorrow."

Em rose with her, and they walked together up the hill toward the gate. They had almost reached it when the mirror vibrated in her pack.

Shea stopped. "He's in," she said as she retrieved the mirror. She scrolled through the text displayed in the window open on its polished surface, wishing she'd paid more attention to Falin's instructions on how to interpret it. After a moment, she turned to Em. "Raven Perch, I think." She scrolled through some more text. "Táma's castle."

Em smiled. "Can't think of a better place to take the fucker out. You ready?"

Shea handed him the mirror and pointed to the red ruby button. "Push this when the fight begins." Then she drew the sword from her back. "FOD the fucker if he kills me."

"I plan to FOD him either way."

"Not before the ruby turns green. That's how we'll know the trap was sprung."

Em raised his staff. "Here we go."

Her view was filled with a bright gold light and then she was standing before the lowered draw bridge of a vast fortress. No moon or star light penetrated the thick clouds that swirled around its spires. The outline of its walls and towers were barely perceptible against the black sky. Across the bridge a single torch flickered beside a raised portcullis. Nothing stirred. The gate and the battlements were unguarded. The castle looked deserted.

"This place should be crawling with guards. Where are they?"

Em shook his head. "Don't know. Maybe the Anomaly ran them off."

"Nice of him to make it easy for us," she said. Then Shea grinned and charged across the bridge and through the open portcullis with her sword held high.

Inside the passage was wide enough to accommodate a dozen men walking abreast. Torches illuminated her way, revealing dark side tunnels cut into the left and right walls. She ran past them heedless of concealed attackers. The wizard had her back and would incinerate any character, player or simulated, that emerged to challenge her. She'd been here before and knew the wide passage led to the great hall in the castle's heart where the mirror had showed the Gray Warrior was waiting.

The passage ended at a massive wooden door with iron hinges and a black knob shaped like a raven's head. She turned the knob and pushed. The hinges squealed as the heavy door swung inward, revealing a huge open space resembling the nave of a medieval cathedral. Enormous iron chandeliers ringed with hundreds of burning candles hung from the vaulted ceiling, bathing the stonework in a orange glow.

Shea studied the cavernous hall. Like the rest of the castle, it was deserted. "Where is everyone?" she whispered as she eased into the room.

She hadn't taken two steps before her right temple tingled with a warning vibration from her headgear. She veered to the left as an arrow whistled past and struck the wall inches from her head. Em raced up from behind with his staff raised high above his head. He shouted an invocation phrase and a golden bubble formed around them.

Deep laughter echoed off the stone walls. The Gray Warrior stepped out from behind a column. He drew back his great bow and released another arrow. The missile had been aimed at Darshana's heart, but it bounced off the bubble and skipped across the stone floor.

The warrior let loose a terrible scream and tossed aside his bow. Then he drew his longsword and bounded toward them. Darshana met him at the bubble's edge. He hewed at her with his sword, but the spell held back his blade. The monster screamed again. This time the high-pitched wail was almost unbearable. He struck over and over at Darshana's sword. Each time Em's spell prevented his blade from reaching hers, but with each tremendous blow Shea could feel the simulation tighten the cords in her arms. The monster was breaking through.

He let go another ear-piecing scream, then raised his sword high over his head and brought it down on hers. This time, their blades met with a blinding flash of red light and a loud ring that reverberated in her headgear speakers. The shield spell had been broken, and Em was knocked to the ground by the force of its breaking.

"Push the ruby, push the ruby!" she shouted as she parried another blow. The monster was strong, but she was Darshana. She drove him back and chanced a look at the fallen wizard.

Em sat up and blinked. He looked dazed and surprised, like he didn't know what had happened to him. His staff lay in pieces on the floor, but the mirror was still in his hand. The confusion seemed to pass, and he scrambled to his feet. He pointed a gnarled white finger at the warrior. *The finger of death.* Was the ruby green? She couldn't tell. Em shouted the FOD incantation, and a lightning bolt leapt from his fingertip and struck the warrior in his chest with a deafening thunderclap.

The monster paused, and Shea held her breath, wondering if the wizard had struck too soon. But nothing happened. The Gray Warrior didn't disintegrate as he should have. Instead, he seemed to glow for a moment, then the lightning bolt reemerged from his sword and arced back into the wizard's finger. Em pirouetted like a dancer, dropped the mirror, and collapsed into a smoldering pile of dirty robes.

"Holy shit." *Wizards were not supposed to die.* The mirror lay several feet away. Its ruby glowed red. Em had set the trap, but the fight hadn't generated the right events to spring it. She thought about grabbing the mirror and running. She'd outrun this monster before, but she'd had a head start then. There would be none this time. She wouldn't make it out of the hall. Her only option was to survive for as long as she could and hope it was enough to trigger the necessary events.

Her resolve renewed, she lifted her sword and shouted, "This is for Táma," as she brought it down on the monster's electrified blade. The warrior deflected her blow like he was swatting away an insect and laughed. The ruby still showed red. She spun and parried his counter blow, thankful for Tony's gift of the faster CCP. Darshana swung again. "This is for Danaka." Again, her strike bounced harmlessly off his blade. The ruby remained red, and she shouted, "This is for Pharaoh." Her blade rode down the edge of his creating a shower of sparks. The tip of her sword caught the monster's chest in its downward arc and sliced open his hide. Maybe he wasn't invincible after all.

The Gray Warrior took a step back. He studied her with lifeless black eyes. One of his sausage-sized fingers ran over the slash on his chest, then moved to his mouth, as if tasting his own blood. Blue-gray lips curled, exposing yellow fangs, then he roared and lunged forward. As he did, she screamed, "This is for Falin," and brought her sword down with all her strength.

But once again, his blade was there to meet hers. When their weapons collided, it both felt and sounded like an explosion. Shea's rig simulated the impact by rocking her back and pulling her to the ground with enough force to knock the wind out of her. When she stood to resume the fight, she discovered her sword had shattered, and all she was holding was a useless shard. *Game over.*

"I am Akandu," the warrior roared. "Now, I will have you."

He plunged his sword into her chest and lifted her over his head. Her rig responded by rotating her. She stared down into his hideous upturned face as Darshana's blood ran down his blade and covered his arm and chest. The speakers in her headset punished her ears with his laughter. The mirror lay smashed on the ground beside him. She could just make out the green glow from its ruby as her visual field turned red, and the heartbreaking message appeared.

YOUR CHARACTER HAS DIED! – RESPAWN NEW OR QUIT?

Chapter 51
Invalid Address

SPECIAL **A**GENT **S**ANDRA **J**OHNSON had met Parker and Jaden at the airport and informed them Jasmine Day had arrived several hours earlier. The agent had been waiting when Jasmine had touched down and had observed her get into a black sports car at the offices of Travis Air, the Fixed-Base Operator that managed the Day's Gulfstreams. She had followed Jasmine to the Ritz-Carlton hotel and used her credentials to gain access to the valet garage where she'd located the sports car and affixed a magnetic tracking device to its undercarriage.

"Nice," Parker had said, impressed. "Bet you wouldn't have known to do that," he'd poked Jaden.

Jaden had responded by giving him the finger.

The three of them had checked into separate rooms at the Hyatt across the street from the Ritz. They'd opted not to stay in the same hotel as Jasmine; not out of frugality, but to avoid running into her. They had spent the afternoon in Parker's room, watching TV and playing cards. Jasmine had not left the hotel all day, at least not in the sports car.

They had just ordered dinner from room service, salads for Jaden and Sandra, boiled eggs and tea for Parker, when Jaden received a message from Shea saying she was going hunting. Twenty minutes later, the FBI operations desk called Parker. Rituraj had activated the hotline, and the desk had set up a web conference to coordinate the monitoring activities. The Xperion team was on the call. Parker brought up the conference on his tablet and placed it on the table where they could all see the screen.

Rituraj, looking showered and more alert, appeared in the meeting's main window. Several men and women that Parker did not recognize occupied smaller windows. They all looked bored. No one was talking. The only sound came from the periodic tapping of keys.

"What's happening?" Parker asked.

Rituraj shook his head. "Nothing yet. Both Em and Darshana are in the simulation. We're not receiving any tracking data."

"What does that mean?"

"It means we're not receiving any tracking data," Rituraj said.

Parker was tired and cranky. He'd been up all night. Their flight had been delayed. They'd spent hours in airports, on an airplane, and before checking into the hotel, in a cramped car with an air conditioner that was no match for the blistering heat. On top of that, he'd run out of painkillers and his leg was at full-blown ten pain level. "Then fucking ask Em what's going on."

The impassive faces in the windows snapped to attention.

Rituraj smirked and shook his head. "Once they're in the SIM, there's no direct way to communicate with them. We can send them a message, but they must suspend their session to read it and respond."

Jaden arched his eyebrow and peered into the tablet. "There's no back channel for Xperion employees?"

"No. It's dumb, I know. But Marcus wouldn't allow it. He said if we permitted any intra or extra simulation messaging, it would lead to mass coordination between players and ruin the game. It's called the Tower of Babel scenario," Rituraj said. "You know, after the story of how a god made humans talk different languages to keep us from working together to build a tower to reach him."

"Does that make Marcus God?" Parker asked.

"He is to us."

Parker turned to Jaden. "Let's get Higgs and Chavez ready to move in case we get lucky with the device address."

Several minutes later, Higgs' thick Chicago accent came through the tablet's tiny speakers. "Las Vegas PD has joined da call. We have a SWAT unit standing by."

They sat there, staring into the tablet with no one saying anything for almost an hour when Sandra's phone buzzed. She mouthed "Mute that," and pointed to the tablet.

Parker muted them.

"Jasmine's on the move."

Parker unmuted the tablet. "We're changing locations. We'll monitor in transit."

"What's going on, Mind Hunter?"

"We'll fill you in later. Get ready to move."

They rushed down to Sandra's car, and she placed her phone where she could follow Jasmine's GPS trail.

"She's heading west. Out of the city," Sandra said as she accelerated down an expressway entrance ramp.

They'd been on the road for fifteen minutes when Rituraj shouted, "We got tracking data. We got tracking data. Darshana is fighting the Anomaly! We're getting great character-to-character interaction events!" His excited shouts were replaced by the sound of frantic tapping on a half dozen keyboards.

Jaden leaned between the front seats and studied the map on Sandra's phone. He took out his own phone and tapped on his screen. A second later, he said, "I know where she's going."

Parker looked back, and Jaden showed him the address displayed on his screen. Parker nodded. He took Jaden's phone and showed it to Sandra. "She's on her way here. Can we beat her?"

Sandra smiled. "Hold on." The car lurched forward like it was hit from behind. Its silent electric motors had provided no audible warning that her foot had smashed the accelerator pedal to the floor.

The tablet buzzed with the simultaneous shouts of a dozen excited voices: "Holy shit", "No fucking way", "That's not possible."

"What happened?" Parker yelled.

"Em's been destroyed," Rituraj said over his team's excited chortling.

Sandra drove like she was on a NASCAR track. She rode inches from the rear bumpers of cars whose drivers lacked the sense to move out of her way, high beams flooding their interiors, illuminating the terrified backward glances of passengers. They rocketed down an exit ramp and sped along a dark two-lane road that was thankfully devoid of other travelers.

"We got a MAC," a woman's voice called.

An authoritative voice that Parker recognized as the operations desk supervisor said, "Shout it out."

The woman did. The supervisor read it back to confirm, then the tablet went silent.

A few seconds later, Rituraj announced, "Darshana's dead."

The supervisor's voice boomed over him. "The MAC belongs to a computer in Las Vegas."

"Address?" Higgs shouted.

"It's at a company called XCloud," the supervisor shouted back. Then he followed up with the street address.

"We're on it," Higgs yelled.

Everyone went quiet again. Then Rituraj asked, "What was that company's name?"

"XCloud."

The tablet's speaker erupted with excited technical chatter between the Xperion team. Parker couldn't make any of it out.

Sandra made a hard right turn, and Parker dropped the tablet as he clung to the handhold above the passenger door to avoid being launched into Sandra's lap. The car's high beams lit up a police cruiser parked in the grass across from a large home. Douglas County Sheriff's Department was emblazoned on its door, and a woman's surprised face stared out from the driver's side window. The house was dark and lifeless. Sandra pulled into the empty driveway.

Jaden had the rear door open and was out and running toward the house before the car stopped. Sandra turned and grinned at Parker. "Beat her." Then she dove out her door and chased after Jaden. Parker climbed out and looked back at the sheriff's car which was flashing like a Vegas slot machine.

A tall, thin woman wearing a wide-brimmed campaign hat exited the cruiser and shined a flashlight as powerful as the sun into Parkers' eyes. "That was some reckless driving. Do y'all live here?" she said.

"No. We're FBI agents," Parker said, shielding his eyes. He moved his hand to retrieve his credential case from his breast pocket, and the deputy's hand went to her firearm. "Whoa," he said. "I'm just getting my ID."

She nodded, and he withdrew the case and faced it toward the blinding light.

The deputy lowered the flashlight and crossed the street. As she came, Higgs' voice exploded from the tablet on the car's floorboard. "SWAT's at the address. It's a data center. They had to bust through the gate." Higgs was silent for several seconds. "They are going inside now. Standby."

Parker nodded toward the house. "Anyone inside?"

The deputy's campaign hat swayed when she shook her head. "Don't think so. Haven't seen anyone since we set up out here yesterday."

The house wasn't right, Parker thought. *Something was missing.*

Higgs' voice, softer now, floated up from the car's floor. "Security guard says the center is unmanned. It's what they call a dark site. No one's there."

"Is he sure?" Parker said.

"He's sure."

"Ah. Excuse me," Rituraj interjected, sounding nervous. "The device address is one of ours."

"What do you mean one of yours?" Parker said.

"XCloud is owned by Xperion. It's where we host our simulations. The MAC belongs to one of our servers."

"Dat's fricken great," Higgs snarled. "SWAT's fricken inside already."

Just then, Jasmine Day's black sports car turned onto the street and raced past Parker and the deputy.

"Ah, shit," Parker said and shouted toward the house, "Breaux! Get back to the car." He pointed at Jasmine's taillights and asked the deputy, "Where does this road go?"

"Nowhere. It's a dead end. The only thing down there is an old industrial shed."

Jaden trotted up to the car with Sandra close behind. "What's going on?"

"Jasmine Day just drove past."

"She has to be going for Shea," Jaden said. He turned back to the house. "But this is Shea's address."

Parker pointed his cane toward the house as he dropped into the passenger seat. "Look at it. Where's that big bay door she showed us? We got the wrong place."

Sandra backed the car out of the drive, and they raced after Jasmine with the deputy's flashing car trailing behind them. *The final puzzle pieces were coming together, literally.*

Chapter 52
Killer in the Real

DARSHANA WAS DEAD. SHEA'S heart pounded. She could feel it thumping in her chest and in her ears. Hot tears of anger and sadness filled her eyes and dripped into the lens cups of her cybermask. She'd selected quit from the red screen options and waited for the rig to rotate her back to an upright position. She'd expected her visual field to fill with the image of the Sun Lobby, and the unbearable sight of Darshana's missing case, but something had gone wrong. She was still suspended at the top of the rig's outer ring and instead of the ornate golden hall, her visual field showed only blackness.

Total system crash. Fuck.

Disoriented, it took her a few moments to disconnect and remove her headgear. The air, though warm, felt good on her face. The bay was dark, but not totally. Pale squares of moonlight checkered the floor from the skylights above and the small rectangular window in the people door shown with the same milky glow. Little points of green, red, and yellow glowed from the electronic devices scattered throughout the building. Around her, the rig's LEDs all flashed red indicating a significant system fault. *No shit.*

In all the years riding rigs, she had never been in this situation and only ever heard of it happening to one other individual—the rich bitch—and Shea hadn't believed her. The safety system should have released the rings and returned her to the ground. But here she was, dangling facedown, eight feet above the concrete floor. The harness straps dug into her shoulders and the inside of her thighs, and the large X-shaped center buckle pressed against her solar plexus, making it difficult to breathe.

She held her headgear in her left hand and touched the

harness release button with her right. If she pressed the button, she would fall face-first. Not a good option. She twisted her right arm behind her and felt for the support arm that connected the harness to the rig. It was attached near the small of her back. She could touch it, but there was no way she'd be able to get a strong enough grip on it to hold her weight when the buckle released. She was stuck.

Trinity hissed from somewhere near the bay door. The sound startled Shea. Trinity never hissed. "Hey, Trin. What's the matter, girl?"

Trinity hissed again, and then a loud sneeze erupted from the darkness. *Much too loud to have come from the agitated cat.*

Shea froze. She searched the gloom, and her eyes landed on the four small windowpanes that ran across the top of the people door. She never cleaned them. Three of the four were filthy. The moonlight that passed through their smudged glass was faint, but nothing impeded the light streaming in through the one over the deadbolt latch. It was crystal clear. She squinted at it. Not clear. Missing.

"Who's there?" she said.

"Here kitty, kitty," a deep voice growled.

Trinity spit and hissed. Something heavy hit the floor with a sharp metallic clang and Trinity's claws scraped the concrete. Shea caught a glimpse of the frightened cat in the moonlight as she darted into the living area.

Shea forced herself not to panic. In the most controlled voice she could manage, she said, "Whoever you are, you're trespassing." She thought of the police cruiser parked across from her landlord's house. "The police are right up the road. They'll come." Though, she knew they wouldn't. What was the point of having police guard her if they were going to sit a quarter-mile away?

The deep voice laughed, and a shadow moved toward her. A small, hooded figure dressed all in black stepped into a moonlit square. He was wearing cyber headgear and gloves. Something was draped around his neck, a cord with several half-dollar sized objects hanging from it. Shea looked around for the larger owner of the deep voice.

"We took her ears," the deep male voice said.

It seemed impossible, but the big voice came from the

small figure. She swallowed. "Who's ears?"

"Darshana. We took her ears. After we took her head." The booming voice had to be coming from external speakers on his headset. The man fingered one of the objects around his neck. She couldn't make out what it was, but she knew. She'd stared down at a similar string of objects hung around the Gray Warrior's huge neck and drenched in Darshana's blood.

Holy shit. It was him. It was the fucking monster. How? "The police are right outside!" she screamed.

The man pulled a large sword from his back. Its polished blade gleamed in the moonlight. A soft, vaguely familiar, voice said, "Now, we're coming for yours."

Just then the people door opened, and a wedge of milky light spread across the floor. Oh thank God. "Help!" Shea yelled.

A woman stood in the open doorway. She had long black hair and was wearing formfitting clothes that revealed a lean muscular build. Even from the distance, Shea could make out her Asian features.

"Watch out," Shea called. "There's someone in here with a sword. He's trying to kill me."

The woman put her finger to her lips, signaling Shea to be quiet.

Shea wondered if the woman was with the FBI. Maybe Parker had sent her. *Draw your gun lady.*

"Lincoln?" the woman said in a hushed voice. "Are you in here?" She stepped into the bay, still in the wedge of light.

The man with the sword had stepped out of the moonlight and disappeared. From the darkness, he said in a soft stuttering voice, "G-G-Go away. Lincoln's dead."

Shea knew the voice. *Ethan.*

The man, holding the sword, stepped into the wedge of light. "H-H-How did you find me?"

The woman stared at his wrist.

The man's cybermask followed her gaze. "M-M-My watch. You fucking tr-tr-tracked me by m-m-my watch." He jerked the watch from his wrist and flung it against the wall. There was an audible tinkle of the glass face breaking.

"What sorcery is this?" the deep voice boomed from the speakers on the man's headgear.

The woman stepped closer to the man.

"Lincoln, I'm sorry," she said. "I have not been the best mother. Let me help you now."

"N-N-Now you wa-wa-want t-t-to help me?"

"Quiet, mouse!" the deep voice roared. "We don't need the Evil Queen's help."

"Let me take you home. We'll go see a doctor. Get you help."

"P-P-Put me away again. Put me away again," Ethan's unsure voice grew stronger. "We won't let you," the voice deepened. "Lincoln's dead. Musuka's dead." The voice was deep now. "I am Akandu!" the voice roared, and the man lunged at the woman and drove the sword through her just like the Gray Warrior had driven his sword through Darshana.

Shea gasped and then screamed as she frantically twisted to find a handhold on the rig.

The woman stood, impaled on the sword, gaping at the man. She raised a bloodied hand and touched it to his pale face. Then she fell to her knees as the man withdrew the blade. She stared up at him. He cocked the sword over his shoulder like a baseball slugger preparing to hit a home run, and Shea looked away, expecting him to cut her head off. But, when Shea looked back, the man had stepped out of the light, and the woman was curled on her side, clutching her wound, with her head still attached.

Shea twisted around, searching for where the man went.

"Behind you, little elf," the deep voice said. Then the man stepped into the rig's flashing red light. He removed his headgear and let it drop to the floor. His impish, pale face flashed red from the LEDs. More demon now than elf, she thought.

"Ethan," she gasped. Struggling to catch her breath from the panic. "Please don't kill me."

He ignored her plea and drew a phone from his pocket. "Y-Y-You should n-n-not let strangers play with your settings. They can d-d-disable the s-s-safeties and," he held up the phone, "t-t-take control."

Then speaking to no one but himself, he said in the deep voice, "Stop talking, mouse."

He shook his head as if trying to clear his vision and showed her his phone's screen. "I-I-I'm going to release the harness and you're going to fall. Don't worry, you'll only be in pain for a little while. Then w-w-we'll take you."

She hurled her headgear at him. It struck him hard in the forearm and knocked the phone out of his hand. He yelped then growled, "Fucking elf-bitch. You'll pay for that."

He bent down to pick up the phone, and Trinity shot in out of nowhere with her back arched and fur bristling. She hissed and raked her razor-sharp claws across his face. Then she bit his cheek and darted back into the shadows, taking a hunk of his face with her.

"That's my girl," Shea shouted. "Hope she took one of your fucking eyes out."

Ethan let out a high-pitched shriek and rubbed his sleeve over the bloody hole in his face. "We're going to kill that fucking cat as soon as we're done with you," he shouted and thrust his sword up at her. Shea twisted in the harness to avoid his strikes as best she could, but the straps held her tight. The tip of the sword punctured her right side just below her ribs, and she wailed in pain. She thrashed and kicked, but it was no use, the blade tore her cybersuit and cut into her abdomen. *This is how she was going to die. A thousand cuts from a lunatic's sword.* She began to panic and flail from side to side. Then the blade found her. It sank deep into her shoulder just above her left breast. Close to her heart.

"Help!" she screamed, though she knew no one could hear. The sword cut her again. She twisted just in time to avoid the blade sinking into her chest, and as she turned, she saw standing in the moonlight a tall man dressed in a suit with his arms outstretched in a shooter's stance.

BOOM. BOOM. BOOM.

Like the thunderclaps from the Finger of Death, the shots echoed through the bay. Ethan's chest exploded. Flesh, blood, and pieces of his clothing sprayed against the rig. He staggered forward, looking down at his ruined chest. The sword fell from his hand, and he tilted his head back. Shea stared down into his snow-white face, now scratched and disfigured by Trinity's attack, and bearing his mother's bloody handprint. His mouth moved, but no words came out. Then he slumped to the floor and lay on his back staring wide-eyed up at her as blood from her wounds trickled down on him.

Jaden ran up with his gun in his hand and kicked away the sword. "Where is the other one?" he asked.

She shook her head. "I don't think there is another one."

"What about the big guy? Akandu?"

"I don't think he exists." Shea looked at Ethan. "I think he was only in his head."

Jaden followed her eyes down to Ethan's crumpled form. He holstered his gun and tried to push over the outer ring.

"Both of them down?" Parker called from the bay.

Jaden glanced at Ethan again. "Yes," he shouted. Then added, "I need help to get Ms. Britton out of this rig."

"Shea," she corrected, wincing from the pain.

He smiled at her and grunted as he strained to flip the ring. A woman who Shea didn't recognize joined him and began to push.

"You won't be able to move it," Shea said. "It's locked. Get the ladder."

"Where?" Jaden said.

Shea pointed to the darkness behind the rig.

He disappeared and returned a moment later with the ladder.

They freed her from the harness, and Jaden took her in his arms. She looked up at him as he carried her, strangely numb. She could hear her mother's voice in her head as if she were addressing residents during rounds. *Of course you're numb, you're in shock.* Shea gazed at Jaden's face, and all she could think was how he was most definitely hot. Jaden set her down near Ethan's mother and began checking her wounds.

"Most of these look superficial," he said. "But the one below your shoulder is a bleeder. Probably hit an artery."

She tried to think of a witty reply but all she came up with was, "Ouch." Her mother's voice in her head said, *Ooh. Arterial bleed. We'll need pressure on that immediately.*

He removed his coat and pressed it against her shoulder, sending a jolt of pain through her.

"Fuck," she gasped. "Real sword wounds hurt."

He gave her a concerned smile. "Sorry."

Parker Reid was kneeling on the floor beside her, busily tending to Ethan's mother. Like Jaden, he had sacrificed his suit jacket to plug a wound. A female police officer in a Smokey the Bear hat stepped over to them. "EMS is on the way. Five minutes."

Shea raised her head and looked at the flashing rig. Ethan was still lying beneath it. The woman who'd helped free her was kneeling over him. It looked as though she was performing CPR. The people door opened, and Shea turned toward it expecting to see more police, but a small, frail-looking, very white man with white hair stepped through it. His eyes met Shea's. They were the same light gray, almost white, as Ethan's. *The albino.* She looked over at Ethan's mother. *And the chink.*

The albino paused and conveying no emotion, seemed to take in the scene. His white head turned like a turret aiming those pale eyes, first toward Ethan's mother, then to Ethan and back to Ethan's mother. None of the agents appeared to notice him. They were too busy plugging holes in people. His eyes remained fixed, trancelike, on Ethan's mother.

Several seconds passed before Parker glanced up at him. "What are you doing here, Marcus?"

Parker's words seemed to break the trance. The albino glanced at the agent but didn't respond. Ethan's mother tried to speak, but her words sounded like croaking. The albino stepped over her and went to stand beside the woman performing CPR on Ethan. He stood looking down at his dying son, and Shea noticed how he made sure not to get any blood on his shoes.

Chapter 53
Real Time

SHEA WINCED AS SHE reached up to hand Tony the wrench. The doctors, with much unsolicited input from her father, had repaired the damage Lincoln's sword had done to her shoulder and the muscles in her abdominal wall, but certain movements still hurt like hell.

"Take it easy, kid," Tony said. "You might pop a stitch."

"It's been over a month, boss. Stitches are all gone. Just sore from rehab exercises." What she told him was partially true—rehab was a killer—but the damage to her shoulder had been significant, and it probably would never be the same. Technically, she was still supposed to be wearing a sling.

Tony removed the bolts that fastened the harness to the support arm and detached the unit that resembled a large toddler's bucket swing wrapped in heavy straps. He inspected it closely. "Still some blood on it."

"Where?"

He showed her, and she used a spray bottle cleaner and paper towels to remove it.

They'd been disassembling her rig all morning. The harness system was the last piece they could remove without help. Taking apart the ring sections required two people, and Tony would not allow her to do it. She'd argued with him, reminding him they had built and taken apart hundreds of them over the three years they'd been together, but he would not relent. He knew the doctors had told her no heavy lifting, and the ring sections were heavy.

They gathered up the harness system and cartons containing the other small parts and carried them to the van. After they stowed them, she and Tony sat with their legs dangling out the back door, staring into the bay. Trinity relaxed in a patch of sun on the bare concrete floor. Other than the reclining feline, a pair of ladders for finishing the disassembly, and the remains of the rig itself, the bay was empty. Shea had sold her bike a week ago. It had been almost as hard to part with as the rig. A buyer who Tony vouched for carted off all her spare parts yesterday. All the rest of her things were boxed up and ready to load into a rental van for the long ride up to her new apartment near Washington DC.

She'd given the rig to Tony; not to use, of course. He had no use for a rig. The very thought of her no-nonsense former boss role playing in the Verse made her smile. She'd given it to him to sell. He'd protested. The rig was worth at least fifty, maybe sixty thousand dollars. She'd insisted to the point of threatening to call Marci, telling him, "You helped scavenge most of the parts and helped me build it. It's as much yours as it is mine, and I no longer need it." She was giving the Verse a break. Truth was, she would have no time for it.

Both Parker and Jaden had come to visit her in the hospital. Parker advised her that doctors could not be trusted, and they had a good laugh when she told him she came from a family of doctors who all expected her to become one.

"What do you want to do?" he'd asked.

"I thought about going back to school for computers," she'd told him.

"Boring," he'd said.

She'd told him she kinda felt the same way. That's when he asked if she ever considered joining the FBI. "I could use someone like you. Someone who knows their way around this meta stuff."

"What would I have to do?" she'd ask.

"Learn the law," he'd said. Then he grinned in a devilish way and said, "And learn to hunt real killers."

That had piqued her interest.

"And probably carry my bags through airports and get me tea," he added.

She'd ignored that part.

A few weeks later, he'd pulled some strings to get her into law school for the fall semester and arranged for her to work for him at Quantico. Just an internship, but it was a start. It wasn't exactly her family dharma, but surprisingly, her parents had approved. Her father thought it might be useful to have an attorney in the family, and he was even more pleased when he learned she would be covering the tuition herself. Though, Shea hadn't told them what she planned to do with the law degree.

She turned and studied her former boss's face. "I'm sorry, Tony."

He looked perplexed. "For what?"

"All the lying. I hid that my parents had money, and that I'd finished college. I shouldn't have lied to you, but I was ashamed by the privilege."

He put his arm around her. "Kid, I'm thrilled you finished your studies, and I don't begrudge you growing up well."

"But you hate rich people."

He laughed. "No. I just think some of them don't see the rest of us."

She hugged him despite her shoulder's complaint.

"Did you figure out what happened with the rig? Why it crashed?" He asked.

"Yeah. Ethan—I mean Lincoln—put the rig in diagnostic mode when his character killed mine."

"You can't do that while the rig is in operation," he said.

"Right. The CCP went into safe mode. Brought the whole system down, even the headgear. He must've known that's what would happen."

"Little bastard knew his shit," Tony said.

"Uh-huh. Jaden told me he was a real-life computer genius."

Tony nodded toward the bay. "How did he fight you if he was in there waiting for you to get stuck in the rig?"

"He had headgear and gloves. He must have connected to my network and guided his character from inside while I was in my rig."

Tony grinned. "He beat you as a half-in?"

She punched him in the shoulder. "No. His Gray Warrior character, Akandu, wasn't your typical character. It was both an NPC and a PC."

"Speak English, kid."

"NPC, non-player character." She smiled and explained, "Simulated players. The really good ones seem so real it's hard to know they're programs. Lincoln's character was very advanced. Falin had suspected the Gray Warrior was more AI than player, and he was right."

"Artificial Intelligence. Wow," Tony said. "Like some kind of evil Metaverse robot."

Shea laughed. "That's right. The Gray Warrior moved and fought on its own. It was a program running on a server at Xperion, but it was also a player character. Lincoln guided it, but he didn't really become it; not like I became Darshana." Her heart ached when she thought about the red-screened avatar. Losing her had been like losing a friend. No, more like losing a piece of herself.

"How did he get on your network?"

She smiled at him sheepishly. "I may have given him my Wi-Fi password when he visited."

"Ah."

The sound of tires on gravel interrupted their conversation. A sleek new electric van with the words "U-MOVE-IT" and "1000 Mile Range" stenciled in big orange letters on its lime-green body pulled up next to them.

Tony stared at the rental van and grinned. "Looks like Prince Charming is here."

She punched him in the shoulder again. "More a warrior than a prince."

Jaden climbed out of the van and walked over. He shook Tony's hand, and Shea stood on her toes and gave him a kiss on his cheek. The two men went into the bay and disassembled the ring sections while Shea watched and offered advice to Jaden. "Be careful, don't grab it there. Watch out for that fiber optic lead." After a while, they shooed her away, and she worked on loading the boxes of her things into the rental van.

Her phone buzzed with an incoming message. It was from Maxwell Morris, Em. She sat on the ragged sofa that was destined for the county dump and read.

Hi, Shea. Hope you are healing well. Heard about your career change. Wish you would reconsider my offer to come work for us here. Would make you a wizard.

She looked up and watched Jaden sliding a ring section into Tony's van. The muscles along his back and arms rippled with the weight of the section. He caught her admiring him and smiled.

She looked back at her phone and tapped. *Thanks, Em, but going to give the Real a try for a while.*

Three dots indicated Em was responding.

Keep in touch. By the way, I restored Darshana. She'll be waiting for you...

Epilogue

BECKY STOOD WITH HER back to him staring out her window. She had one of the better views of the red-and-white checkered water tower that rose above the academy's training grounds. "I received the transfer request," she said.

Parker rested his chin on his cane and stared at her back. "And?"

She turned around. "Is that what he wants?"

"We make a great team."

"That's not what I asked."

He lifted his head and smiled. "I got bait."

She raised her eyebrows. "I guess you do. How is she doing?"

"Terrific. Started her internship today. She's going to make an excellent flunky." He inspected his cane nonchalantly. "She's downstairs right now. Want to meet her?"

"Some other time." Becky bent over the desk and tapped on her tablet. "Where did things end up with the Days?"

He shifted his stare before she caught him studying her face, no trace of the racoon mask remained. "Kid died at the scene, but you knew that. Jasmine's recovering. She's one tough woman. Not many people could survive being run through with a longsword."

"Will she walk again?"

"Doctors aren't sure, but I wouldn't count her out."

"What about the husband?"

"Not sure he's thrilled she survived. Going to be a hell of a divorce. The company's stock is worth billions."

Becky tapped some more on her tablet. "Seems like we should be pursuing charges."

Parker shrugged. "Jasmine knew where her son was. Which means she must have suspected him of the killings. We might make conspiracy and accessory charges stick. What do I know, though? I'm just an analyst."

She chuckled. "Company's really worth billions?"

"That's what CNBC says."

"Too bad the Days weren't as good at parenting as they were at building a company."

Parker nodded. "They raised a psycho. That's for sure."

"Yeah," she agreed. "But I guess you can't entirely blame them for what he did."

"Maybe not the mother," Parker said.

She studied him. The tan lines around her eyes were gone, but the worry lines had grown deeper. "What does that mean?"

"I did a little research into the story Marcus used to tell his kid."

"That Akandu and Musuka story?"

"Yeah. Interesting bedtime tale for a child. Real *Game of Thrones* stuff. Musuka, it turns out, was the son of a frail king who was dominated by his evil queen. When Musuka came of age to assume his frail father's throne, the queen had him banished from the castle, forcing him to live as a beggar." Parker leaned in toward her. "Until he became Akandu and killed her, rescuing his father." He grinned. "Sound familiar?"

She looked thoughtful, then frowned. "You're joking. You really think Marcus turned his son into a monster to rid their kingdom of the queen?"

"Don't know, but I learned Marcus had given his son a programming assignment to create a new class of simulated characters to challenge the game's lead players. Seems the God of Might and Magic thought the Darshanas and Danakas were too powerful." Parker reached down by his feet and picked up the Akandu action figure that had been missing from Lincoln's collection and placed it on her desk.

"Where did you get that?"

"Jasmine sent it to me. Seems her husband had given it to Lincoln for inspiration." He pushed himself out of the chair and scooped up the character. "Dinner tonight?" he said as he limped toward the door.

"Only if you're buying this time."

He stopped. "It would be a date then."

"Get out of here, Parker."

About the Author

Daniel Burke lives outside Atlanta, Georgia where he devotes time to writing, travel, and grandchildren. When not pecking away on a writing project, his favorite place to be is on the back of his Triumph motorcycle winding through the north Georgia mountains. He has had a lifelong addiction to great fiction and hopes his stories touch others with the same need.